10566644

WHEN SOULS MATE

_____

_____

_____

www.stmartins.com

Design by Kathryn Parise

LIBRARY OF CONGRESS CATALOGING-IN-PUBLICATION DATA

Jossel, Joylynn M.
    When souls mate / Joylynn Jossel.—1st St. Martin's Griffin ed.
      p. cm.
    Sequel to: The root of all evil.
    ISBN 0-312-32862-1
    EAN 978-0-312-32862-7
    1. African Americans—Fiction. 2. Female friendship—Fiction.
3. Single mothers—Fiction. I. Title.

PS3610.O68W47 2006
813'.6—dc22

                          2005031372

First Edition: March 2006

10 9 8 7 6 5 4 3 2 1

Also by Joylynn M. Jossel

Please Tell Me If the Grass Is Greener

World on My Shoulders

The Root of All Evil

Anthologies

An All Night Man

Twilight Moods

Joylynn
Jossel

WHEN

SOULS

MATE

St. Martin's Griffin
New York

Heavenly Father, a thank you isn't merely enough. You have been my umbrella in the rain and my plow through the deepest snow. Thank you for this phenomenal gift to tell a tale and tell it well.

As always, this book is dedicated to my family and friends, especially my children (Ran-Ran, Henney-Bop, and Li'l Joy). You all are more than just the wind beneath my wings . . . you are my wings. Without you I cannot fly.

Nancey Flowers and Marlon Green, there are no words to define our struggle and hustle in this literary game. I am so extraordinarily blessed to have been granted the privilege to cross your paths and work with you to get our written words out there. In my book and in my heart, we'll always be the literary Three Musketeers. Peace and Love.

And without my middlewoman, my agent Vickie Stringer, as well as the woman who fills in all of the potholes in my manuscripts, my editor, Monique Patterson, I would not be able to share my gift of written word on such a large scale. Thank you both.

Earth Jallow with Down to Earth Public Relations: You have been everything to me when it comes to this literary game. You were there when I was selling books out of the trunk of my car. Hell, you were selling them from your trunk, too. There is no verbal or written acknowledgment that would do your efforts justice. You have been everything from my PR to my PA. You were my entire corner when I fought the fight to knock down the door of the literary industry. But most importantly, you have been my friend. My genuine friend, and I thank you.

Thank you to my road dawgz all over the map; Dallas, Texas, especially (the Franklins, of course); B-more, MD; Milwaukee, WI (what up, Chris?); Detroit, MI; The NYC; Jersey; Philly; Chi-Town; Indy; and all of the other people I have met who show me helluv love when I come through your town.

Queen Turner, I'm glad we were both wise enough to use the bridge that was placed between us in order to divide us, to instead walk across it and unite.

Last, but definitely not least, my girls in Ohio: Without all of you, hell, I wouldn't have a damn thing to write about ;-) Thanks for your love and support of my work—and some of those book signings would not have been half as exciting without y'all rollin' with me (Jawan, Angie, Ayanna, Stephanie, Michele, Jheri, Angie M., Daria, and Gwen).

ACKNOWLEDGMENTS

Without my reading fans, this novel absolutely would not have been possible. The feedback you provided me was astounding. You let me know exactly what you wanted to read in this novel, which made it just that more interesting and fun to write. I made every attempt to give you what you asked for in your letters and e-mails to me. A few fans wrote me and told me how much my first novel, *The Root of All Evil*, moved them. Others gave me the ideas for some of the huge twists and turns that take place in this novel. So I would like to give an extra special thanks to: Nicka, Racquel Collins, Kristienne, Shenique, Lena Moore, LaFayetta Hodges, Chini Baldwin, Karleka, Tiffany, Sophia, Geneva Dickerson, Chan Howard, Lesha Lashley, James Porter, Keeish, Lakita Johnson, Sherene Davis, Gracey M. Watson, Ashley Haynes, Beverly Crist,

Crystal Freeman, LaShawn Hawkins, Irstone, Marcell Upshaw, Natalie Stigger, Kimberly Crawford, Tammy Roberson, Henrietta Ellis, Tonya Johnson, SaQuida Greene, Alicia Jackson, Yvette Schuler, Carolyn Archer, Spc Anderson, Kamisha, Kitty, Mark Stokes, Raquel Ojeda, Stacy Wilson, Anita Hubbard, SNRITA, FJAMOS**, Truee Black Mann, Gail Tate, Shanika G, Angel Bulluck, Gina M. Martinez, Cheryl Williams, Holana McDougale, Jessenia Lockward, MsTrice, Dana Jackson, Renee Taylor in New Orleans, Mina Malikouzakis, Karen (Ka2dunbar), Anglique (Jeeky05), Tiffany Dyane, Lisa a.k.a. Whipcream, Rema Gibson, dearyvette, Allison Williams, Stephanie Wilkerson-Hester, Angel Sawyer, Kandi Chitman, Rolanda, Monisa Barnes, Nancy a.k.a. Caramelhips, Gina "G," Keisha-klbj, Jacqueline Brown, Toya Anderson, Shana Wheelr, Donna (Lohocalt), Precious Blocker, Tracey Jeffries, Tajuana, LC, ShaNee Boisseau, Sheilamypooda, Beverly Jordan, Mike Hawkins, Marissa C. Joseph, Valentin, Quan, Aquarianchild, Undersan**, Sharon Williams, Winnell, Jewelann, Kendell a.k.a. whale8**, Mona McRae, Victoria, Cynlu, Dale (dmbook), Precious (libraladi), Lydia Phillips, Mitziken, Chenelle, HvnleeBlis, Lisa from Boston, Shante from B. Dalton Jersey City, Wendy Smith, Rella LaFear, Roslymm Grimmal, Nicohola, Ilka a.k.a. Panaamasilk, Katrina King, Syrette Green, Janet Price, Shanique Brown, Plystra, Gloria Williamsroberson, Lysette, Ebon, Ashley Bussell, Tysha, Lynne (luv.apooh), Coretta Jones, Dee a.k.a. Dnlhrtnt, Lakeisha Messam, Ms. Gypsyfied, Sheena, Geneva Dickerson, Tenez Quarles, Shenell Thomas, Vicky Davis, Mynika Alexander, ALLMINE90, Dana Bethea, Nicka a.k.a Mrs. Main Event, Tone Blaine, Alicia, Tawanna S., Wendy Mosley, Vicki Mitchell-Boyd, Christa Graddick, Kimberley Duff, SexyBlk, BlaqueGirl12**, Shanequa Berry, Mary Liddie, Patricia Robinson, Akeilah Campbell, Prettyni99, Michelle O'Brien, Jennifer Valentin, Donna Goodman,

Quasha, Deborah Sykes-Aziz, Jacqueline Dover, Tenia Grant, LaToya Dantzler, Toni Mckelvin, Susan a.k.a. Swinterlove, Bria Brooks, Cheryl Williams, Ramona Grant, Linda a.k.a Durandthelady, Sholley, Tiesha Whatley, Lakeshia, Shay, Cail Fuller, Brenda Willis, Kae, Tiana James, Shill01, Kelly Lawrence, MarQuette, Shirley High, Nicole Johnson, Tonicia Tate, Shawn Moss, Rayomi Huntspon, Silkeestee, Stephanie Sanon, Erin, Jeralean Reynolds, Nikki119****, Ria Pierre, Sheanee, Sharon Fields, Tya Moore, American Born, Franklin Santiago, Tami Jones, Jacqueline Dover, Akeilah Campbell, Vanessa Reyes, DLADYDK, Angela a.k.a. bonitaapplebum, Erica Butler, Susan Quashie, Edith Brown, Charlette Pusey, Donnisha, Danielle Brown, Deborah Vaughn, Mujibur Rehman, Sheikh, Shanna, Couzue Karbbar, Lawanda Thornton, Khadija Hubbard, Shelia5462, qlluvsdc (Danielle), Pearlie Jones, NikkiRashan1, Felice Kelly, ladiva, Tamara Jacobs, Yolanda Hawkins, Tanya, Buttons32***, Shaundra Johnson, Margery T. Gogins, Yvette Cobbs, Karen Benschop, Asante, Lynn Perry, Ella Saunders, Reeta, Cutiepie24K, Laronda Hardy, Babyphat2smart4u, Joanne Williams, Erica Garcia, Bonnie Edwards, Shaunay Nellon, Joann (miarah), Gina Pierre-Paul, Stephanie Nixon, Tammy (MistressDesire), TinaMarie2002, Elaine McChard, Crystal Gray, LaSheena Williams, India, Angela Jones, Shirl, Elsa, Tameka, Janis Harris, Renee Spencer, janet_larry, Bianca Smith, Tangela Thompson, Sephia, Margie Adams, Fred Middleton, Traci Carreker, Vickie Smith, Jenell, Sean, Candice, CCe, Antoinette Payton, Trena, Tammi Friley, libraladie, Drezeys, TopazJewels, SvTeddiebear, Bonnie C. McRae and the many many other fans who wrote me in support of my work.

And I can't forget the reading fans who hit me up from lockdown: C. Forster (Dakim), Christopher Lamb, Nano (Harlem World), Curtis Faulk, Marvin Murray, Derrick Fontaine, Nina

Ingram, Terry Raynor, Greg Brooks, Kenneth Hamilton, Joseph Booker, Harold Sattan, Oscar McLain, and Danielle Casseus.

> *Like Tupac said, Keep ya head up and Smile*
> *I'm going to keep penning it down for y'all*

WHEN SOULS MATE

1

THE BAD SEED

Vaughn sat in her trigonometry class, frustrated, as she struggled with the last section of her final exam. Being a senior in high school was hard enough without all of these tests. Her young life had already been full of enough damn tests as it was. Besides that, Sister Beasley, who taught the class, was a stone-cold bitch. She was the nun from hell.

Her black habit suited her dark demeanor. Just seeing her in the hallway always froze Vaughn. She swore that underneath her nun attire, Sister Beasley was a shriveled-up old white woman with a little stone pebble for a heart.

Vaughn's stomach churned every time she entered Sister Beasley's classroom. The teacher had a way of making Vaughn feel like a demon child who had to be exorcised and that she was the only one who could save Vaughn's soul. Sister Beasley purposely intimidated all of the students, but she paid extra attention to Vaughn.

The couple of students who pretended to like Sister Beasley did so out of fear. Every student dreaded the day that they would be one of Sister Beasley's pupils.

Vaughn and a couple of biracial kids were the only students of color in the mostly all-white Challahan Boarding School. The minority students were all treated just as fairly as the white students by the faculty. But Sister Beasley especially detested Vaughn, treating her awfully, and it had nothing to do with the color of her skin. She found delight in trying to embarrass Vaughn in front of the entire class. Vaughn wasn't easily embarrassed, though. She was as tough as nails, and besides, she didn't give a damn what other people thought about her. They could all kiss her ass and die as far as she was concerned. Even as a child the only people she did back flips to please were her father and mother. So Vaughn didn't waste an ounce of energy persuading any of the trust-fund brats who attended the school to be her friend. Befriending them wasn't anywhere on her list of priorities.

Because of Vaughn's nonchalant attitude, Sister Beasley's attempts to humiliate her were usually in vain. This, of course, didn't stop Sister Beasley's efforts. If Vaughn just happened to be reading, writing, or passing a love note to Syrin, her puppy-love boyfriend, while Sister Beasley was going over a formula, then Sister Beasley would deliberately call on Vaughn to come to the chalkboard and solve the formula. Becky-Sue and Barbara-Ann always passed notes to one another in class and Vaughn was sure Sister Beasley had witnessed them. Not once, though, had she ever called either one of them to the chalkboard.

Vaughn was smart, one of the smartest students in the school, and she was never stumped by anything Sister Beasley presented her with. Vaughn would work out the formula as if she were auditioning for the motion picture *A Beautiful Mind*. After solving it, she would look Sister Beasley up and down in contempt. She would then roll her eyes and walk away while switching her ass so that the skirt to her green, red, and plaid school uniform twitched from left to right. The little white boys loved watching her strut her stuff. It was that rare opportunity that allowed them the pleasure of seeing a real booty in action.

Vaughn's actions only angered Sister Beasley even more. But pouring salt into an open wound was Vaughn's specialty. Walking back to her desk, she would wink at a student or two with a wicked grin, then plop down at her school desk, swinging her two shoulder-length bouncy ponytails so that each would strike her on the cheeks. Knowing that Sister Beasley's eyes were burning a hole through her with that evil stare, Vaughn would act as though she wasn't fazed, whipping out a tube of lip gloss to feather her lips with. Vaughn would then quickly look up to capture Sister Beasley's stare. Batting her large brown eyes, Vaughn would look at Sister Beasley as if to say, "Will there be anything else, . . . *bitch?*" In a sick sort of way, Vaughn liked the attention, even if it was negative. As far as she was concerned, negative attention was better than no attention at all.

Eventually, instead of calling Vaughn to the chalkboard, Sister Beasley found another way to humiliate her. Whatever love note Vaughn just might have happened to have in her hand, Sister Beasley would snatch it up and read it out loud to the entire classroom. This evil tactic was how Vaughn's father found out that she wasn't a virgin anymore. She had even described the pain of the rug burn on her knees when she allowed Syrin to have sex with her doggy style on the carpeted floor in the back aisle of the school library. Deep down inside, Vaughn wanted Sister Beasley to make her read that note. She actually wrote it in hopes of it. She knew for certain that it would mean a call home to her father. From the day he enrolled her into Challahan he made excuses why he couldn't come visit her. It was like he was ashamed of her. But Vaughn knew that a summons from the school would force him to make a visit.

Vaughn's father had been furious. He wouldn't even look at Vaughn during the conference. She watched as he sat there with his jaws locked and his hands trembling with rage. Vaughn felt as though he would have torn her a new hide if he didn't fear child abuse charges. Instead, he gave the dean permission to punish Vaughn however he deemed fit and left without even saying two words to her.

Vaughn had been so hurt. She had only given her body to Syrin because she wanted a man—even a boy—to love her. She thought that this might be the eye opener for her father, that he would see that this was nothing but a cry for help and perhaps it would bring them closer. But instead, it only distanced her father even more.

All of Vaughn's privileges were stripped for two months and she had to go to counseling twice a week for an entire semester. But what bothered her most was the way her father had looked at her ever since. It's not as if he loved her to death before that incident, but this, to Vaughn, gave him even more reason to disown her. He now had a legitimate reason not to love her. For this, Vaughn would never forgive Sister Beasley.

It was at that point when Vaughn decided to fight fire with fire. Whatever dismay Sister Beasley shot her way, Vaughn would shoot it back to her to the tenth power. Vaughn's rebellion didn't make Sister Beasley back down any either. She didn't consider it a good day if she didn't send Vaughn to her dorm on the verge of tears. Little did Sister Beasley know that Vaughn's tears weren't tears of pain or hurt. They were tears of anger. Vaughn wanted nothing more than to take Sister Beasley's oversized face and ram it into the chalkboard. It took every ounce of self-control to keep

Vaughn from doing so. There was only one week left of school before Vaughn would return to her hometown of Toledo, Ohio, where
after only a couple of weeks she would then be shipped away to
Boston to attend college. In the meantime, hopefully, Sister Beasley
wouldn't do anything to push Vaughn over the edge.

After about fifteen minutes of struggling with the last formula
on the trigonometry final exam, Sister Beasley announced that
time was up and proceeded to collect all papers. Vaughn had never
been stumped by a formula, so she hadn't studied at all for the
exam. But Sister Beasley had decided to throw in something tricky.
Vaughn wondered if every other student had the same test or if
Sister Beasley had created one specifically for her.

"Pencils down, Miss Bradshaw," Sister Beasley said to Vaughn
rigidly.

"Yes, Sister," Vaughn said, slamming her pencil down without
completing the last formula.

Sister Beasley picked up Vaughn's exam and flipped through it.
She hadn't done this with any of the other students' papers she
had already collected.

"I hope you make your father proud with this one," Sister
Beasley said. "Your mother, too, not that it really matters to her."

Vaughn knew that Sister Beasley was only trying to get a rise
out of her. Vaughn's mother was in prison for life. She had been
charged with the murder of her third husband's baby from a previ-
ous relationship. Because of this black cloud that hung over
Vaughn's head, Sister Beasley felt that Vaughn had no place at the
boarding school. She loved to make little snide remarks about
Vaughn's incarcerated mother as often as she deemed fit. It was
Sister Beasley's personal crusade to punish Vaughn for her father's
decision to enroll her in that school. Vaughn's preference, not that
anyone asked her, would have been to trade places with her mother
instead of attending that school. After all, in Vaughn's eyes, the

boarding school was only one step from being in jail anyway. The students were told when they could do things as well as where they could do it. They were told what they couldn't do and punished severely if they did it anyway. They were told when to go to bed, when to wake, and when to eat. They even had set visiting periods as well as limited phone usage, not to mention the unfashionable uniforms. These ridiculous rules were said to give the students character and teach them discipline.

Challahan Boarding School was founded to house and educate those from privileged and well-to-do families. Vaughn's attendance cast a negative shadow over the reputation of the school, especially when she had first enrolled. The media had a frenzy with reporting every move made by the family members of her mother. When it was broadcast to the world that the Toledo baby murderer's daughter was attending the prestigious boarding school, some parents threatened to remove their children and cease individual grants and funding. A couple saw their threats through. Sister Beasley was one of the individuals who protested Vaughn's acceptance into the school. But in spite of all failed attempts, Vaughn was admitted into the school by the board. Supporters and Black Rights activists put up so much of a fuss—not to mention the handsome donations—that the board didn't dare reject Vaughn's admission application. Pretty soon all of the attention died down and everyone moved on—everyone except for Sister Beasley, that is.

Vaughn didn't want to be at the school any more than Sister Beasley wanted her there, but she didn't have a choice in the matter. Her father had promised her mother that he would send her away to get her mind off of things. He didn't want her to have to deal with the whispering around town about what had happened.

But sending her away hadn't helped. Vaughn cried at night knowing that her mother was in a cold, lonely place and that her freedom had been ripped away. Vaughn loved her mother dearly. She had always been such a good mother—irreplaceable—and now the world saw her as an animal and a murderer.

"Why couldn't it be me locked away behind bars?" Vaughn whispered against her pillow at night. "It should be me."

"So how'd you do, kiddo?" Vaughn's father, Harris, asked.

"Pretty good, I think," Vaughn said, switching the phone to her other ear. "I bombed out on the last problem of my trig exam."

"What about the rest of the test?"

"Pretty good," Vaughn said, twisting her left ponytail around her middle finger. The students waiting in line to use the phone sighed. By now even they knew that Vaughn's calls home were useless, a waste of time. She was taking up valuable phone use that they could have been utilizing phoning their parents who really did want to talk to them.

There was brief silence on the phone. Vaughn and her father never could carry on a decent conversation. Neither ever knew what to say to the other these days. They both feared that if they said anything, it would be the wrong thing and neither wanted to take that chance. So most of the time they just didn't say anything at all.

Vaughn had only seen her father two or three times since she started attending Challahan four years ago. Even when classes were on recess during holidays, Harris never invited Vaughn back home. He always saw to it that the school kept her busy with some extracurricular activity or made up excuses of his own why she shouldn't come home. After so long, Vaughn was onto him and just got used to the fact that her father didn't want to be bothered with her. After packing to go home the very first Easter, Thanksgiving, and Christmas that passed while Vaughn was in Challahan, she never packed to go home again. On each of those holidays her father told her that he would pick her up and take her home to spend the holidays with him; her little brother, HJ; and her little sister, Sissy. On each occasion Vaughn stared at her luggage for hours while waiting impatiently for her father's car to drive up the school entrance path. It would be hours before the dorm mother would get the phone call from Harris relaying that he would not be picking Vaughn up for the holidays after all.

"You coming for graduation next week?" Vaughn continued the phone conversation with her father.

"Your brother has some father-and-son camp out at his school. I'll have to check the dates and get back to you."

"But, Daddy, I'm graduating!" Vaughn said in disbelief. If he never came through for her at all, he could still have the decency to show up at her graduation.

"Sweetie, come on," Harris said, trying to convince his daughter. "You're the older one. You know HJ would be torn apart if I wasn't there for him. He's your little brother. Don't be so selfish."

"Sure, Daddy," Vaughn said sadly. "Is he around?"

"Uh, no. Well, uh, yeah," Harris stuttered. "But he's doing homework. He's studying for his exams."

"Which is it, Daddy?" Vaughn asked in a dry tone. "Is he there? Is he not there? Is he doing homework? Is he studying?"

"Yeah, sweetie," Harris answered. "Well, I gotta go. Call me next week."

Harris hung up the phone in Vaughn's ear.

"Okay, Daddy." Vaughn pretended to talk to her father as the kids in the phone line glared at her. "I'll see you next week. I love you, too. Good-bye!"

Vaughn hung up the phone, gave a fake smile, and then proceeded to her dorm room where she pulled out her hope chest. In her chest were tons of letters from HJ, her mother, and her mother's best friends, Breezy and Jeva, who had promised her mother that they would keep in touch with her. The majority of the letters were from HJ. Writing letters to their mother was part of the counseling their father had put him in to deal with having an incarcerated parent. HJ felt that since Vaughn had been taken away from him, too, in a sense, it would make sense to write to her as well.

Over the past few years the two had grown closer than ever. They had always been close, but they had grown closer ever since their mother had been sent to jail and she had been shipped off to boarding school. It seemed as though being apart brought them even closer.

Vaughn laughed out loud as she reread HJ's last letter. She felt like she could hear him, as if he were right there in the room talking to her.

HJ would send Vaughn what the two referred to as "prayer letters" and she would send him some in return. The letter was a prayer that each had especially written for the other. They would designate a date and time and each would kneel down on their knees at bedtime and recite the prayer. During the prayer Vaughn always felt as though HJ was right there beside her. This was always so uplifting for Vaughn. During this prayer ceremony Vaughn always felt as though her and HJ's souls were mating. HJ felt that the prayer letters helped keep away the nightmares that haunted his sleep.

"Congratulations, class," Sister Beasley said as she passed out the corrected final exam papers. "I'm pleased to announce that each of you passed with flying colors."

When Sister Beasley got to Vaughn she cleared her throat and handed Vaughn her exam. "Some of you with colors that weren't actually flying but just took a little hop," Sister Beasley snickered.

"Thank you, Sister Beasley," Vaughn said as she politely took the exam. She was so glad to soon be rid of that woman. Sister Beasley made her skin crawl.

When Sister Beasley dismissed the class she asked Vaughn to stay behind so she could have a few words with her. Once the other students had collected their belongings from the cloakroom, they each filed out, leaving Sister Beasley and Vaughn to talk.

"So you made it through all four years?" Sister Beasley said.

"Looks like I did, Sister Beasley," Vaughn said. "I did so even in spite of all of the evil people that tried to stand in my way."—Vaughn leaned in, aiming her words directly at Sister Beasley—"And they can rot in hell."

Sister Beasley turned turnip red and grabbed Vaughn's arm.

"Listen here, you daughter of Satan," Sister Beasley scolded. "You have soiled the name of our fine school with your presence and your Jezebel ways. But what more could one expect out of the seed of a killer?"

Vaughn felt herself beginning to lose control. She had feared that one day she would reach her breaking point and this woman would be the one to push her there. Vaughn wanted to spit right in Sister Beasley's face. She hated this woman so much.

"No, you listen, you witch," Vaughn snapped. "My mother is no killer. She would never harm a fly so you take it back. You take back everything you've ever said about her over the years. You take it back or else."

"I will not. I will do nothing but pray for you, child. I'll pray that you won't have to pay for the sins of your mother."

"Stop it!" Vaughn began to cry as she covered her ears with her hands.

"I know the truth hurts, child," Sister Beasley said while still clinching Vaughn's arm. "It's not your fault that you are the product of evil. Your mother couldn't control herself. The root of all evil controlled her. The love of money possessed her soul. She's a bad woman, a murderer. She was a selfish woman who committed a selfish act, but you mustn't feel sorry for her. You must pray for her wicked, wicked ways."

Sister Beasley closed her eyes and began to pray.

"Dear Father, Mother, God. Please forgive this child for her sins and the sins she has inherited. She must be forgiven, Lord, for she knows not what she does." Sister Beasley prayed with her hands folded. "Please do not punish her for being birthed by evil. She can't be punished for the crime of her mother. Have mercy on this poor child's soul. Her mother can no longer be saved for she chose to walk with the devil, but, Lord, this child can still be saved."

The sound of Sister Beasley's voice was beginning to sound like nails down a chalkboard.

"Oh, Father, Mother, God," Sister Beasley continued. "She is still your child. Do not allow Satan's blood to taint her. She did not ask to be born to evil."

"No! Stop it! My mother didn't do it. She didn't kill that baby. Shut up," Vaughn ordered Sister Beasley, to no avail. Vaughn knew that she was about to say something that she shouldn't. She had already said too much. But to hell with "the plan" of hiding the real truth. It was eating her up inside. The weight was too strong for her to bear any longer. "What if I were to tell you I did it? I bet that would change your opinion of my mother, wouldn't it? What would you think about that? I did it. Okay? How's that? My mother had nothing to do with it."

Vaughn had finally said it. For years Sister Beasley and the rest of the world had thought bad things about her mother. Well, once and for all, Vaughn was putting it all to rest and it felt good.

"My mother is not a bad person," Vaughn continued. "She did this for me. She confessed to a murder that she didn't commit because she believed she was protecting me. She's behind bars for me. So you take it back. You take it back!"

"I know what you're doing," Sister Beasley said. "You don't have to do this, child. You don't have to cover for her."

Vaughn couldn't believe her ears. Here she had finally told the truth, that her mother hadn't murdered the baby, and leave it to Sister Beasley to try to take the glory out of it.

"She's poisoned you, child," Sister Beasley said. "She's evil."

Sister Beasley continued to verbally bash Vaughn's mother as she had repeatedly done over the years. Only now her words seemed so much harsher. She was saying things that she hadn't dared say before. Every put-down she stated began to burn Vaughn from the inside out.

"Shut up!" Vaughn pleaded, but Sister Beasley continued lashing out and praying until Vaughn was on the razor's edge.

Vaughn grabbed her by the shoulders, shaking her uncontrollably. Sister Beasley couldn't speak. She couldn't breathe. She stood grasping for air at Vaughn's clutch.

"Now take it back, I said. Take it back, you horrible bitch!" Vaughn continued in an almost subconscious rage. "My mother went to jail so that I wouldn't have to. When I told her that I killed that baby she took the blame and I let her. I'm the one who's selfish. That baby was going to ruin our lives anyway. I could just see it."

By this time Sister Beasley was turning blue. Vaughn released her and backed away. Sister Beasley reached out for Vaughn with one hand while she clutched her heart with the other. Before Vaughn knew it, Sister Beasley fell to the floor. Her body jerked twice, then lay frozen. Vaughn stood still, breathing heavily. She walked over to Sister Beasley and on sight knew she was dead.

Fearful of any consequences one might try to pin on her for the death of Sister Beasley, Vaughn scrambled for her belongings and ran out of the classroom. Sister Beasley lay dead with her eyes wide open, looking as if she had seen the devil himself.

A few moments went by before the sound of footsteps came from the cloakroom. The footsteps made their way closer to Sister Beasley's body. Trembling with every step was one of Vaughn's female classmates, Barbara-Ann. She had been in the cloakroom the entire time and had heard every word of Vaughn and Sister Beasley's argument.

The frightened pale girl, looking like a reject from the movie *Carrie*, stood shivering over the corpse. Upon seeing Sister Beasley's body lying dead on the floor, she dropped her belongings and ran down the hall.

2

FEELS SO GOOD

Meka stood in her huge master bedroom twirling around in the full-length mirror. She held a little lingerie number up against her body. It was a little risqué for Meka, but tonight she was going to model it for her man.

Meka couldn't wait to jump his bones once he walked through the door. She had almost forgotten how good it felt to make love to her husband. Being the wife of a national bestselling author who was constantly out of town on book tours was difficult and often lonely. Meka found herself alone quite often. If it wasn't for their two children, Junior, who was almost four years old, and one-year-old Kimiya, Lord only knew what she would do to keep busy and keep her mind off of missing her husband.

Married only nine months, they were still considered newly-weds. Meka could count on one hand how many times they had made love during the past nine months. It wasn't that Meka didn't enjoy having intercourse with him, he was just never in town long enough for her to get his dick hard. And when they did make love, it was always quick, in and out. On top of that, he was easily satisfied, which meant he rarely wanted seconds.

Since reciting their nuptials, his book tour schedule seemed to have almost doubled. If he wasn't in New Orleans he was in New York. If he wasn't in New York he was in Atlanta. Meka thought she was going to lose her mind worrying about him running off to various cities to meet and greet a bookstore full of women. She had nothing but trust in her man. It was those gold-diggin' bitches out trying to snatch up a man, anybody's man, whom she didn't trust.

Meka also tried not to be jealous of her husband's success, but more supportive instead. She herself could have indulged in a career that she loved if she had wanted to. She had gone to medical school while practicing as a dental hygienist. She had initially hoped to have her own practice one day. But when marriage and raising a family came along, Meka quickly swept her career goals under the rug and made a run to the altar.

It would have been nice to be an independent woman, but Meka saw herself as a priceless jewel, a woman who deserved to be taken care of and treated like royalty. Why should she get her hands dirty if she didn't have to? Meka's philosophy was that a person should only work hard to earn lots of money if they had to, but it was always better if they could get someone else to do the hard work instead. Work hard at getting more and work little at giving even less was her motto.

Her husband's bank account was a big plus, but she felt that she truly loved him. She would even kill for him. Meka saw herself as a born winner. She'd rather cut her wrists than lose anything, especially her man.

Meka did not get married for the single purpose of a life of the rich and famous. She had a nice little nest egg of her own put aside that she could have easily lived off of for the rest of her life. But no amount of money was worth more than being the bride of the one and only, national bestselling author Reo Laroque. Not to mention that he was her high school sweetheart. As long as the money was flowing right she couldn't see any other man being her husband. Even if she did have to share him with his fans.

Meka got up every day before sunrise to work out. She was determined to keep her body in shape. She wasn't about to give her man a reason to stray. She then prepared breakfast and got the kids ready for school. Once she dropped them off at their private preschool she headed back home. She would grab the mail from the mailbox, sort out the bills, and pay them. There were always bills, but the business of maintaining the home was part of her stay-at-home duties. The rest of the day she spent shopping, watching stories, or reading a book.

She had joined a local book club, Black Women Advocating Reading, to take up some of her leisure time. It was also her way of showing her husband that she had a literary interest. On those rare occasions she and her husband had pillow talk, it allowed her to have something to talk about that they both could relate to.

The book club meeting was only the third Sunday of each month, but the reading list kept her busy. Meka always read the book of the month as well as the alternate readings. The members of the club were never surprised when Meka was able to talk about any book on the current reading list. Meka always felt a little special because of this, a step ahead of the other members, more intellectual, even. But to the other members, it was a dead giveaway that Meka was spending long hours into the night with a good book instead of a good dick.

Meka was too in love with herself to be too bothered by it. She couldn't walk by a mirror without giving herself props. At five foot four inches, she had a dainty Jada Pinkett build. She had "I got Indian in my family" jet-black wavy hair. It flowed to the middle of her back, but she always kept it tucked into a tight bun. She had flawless light complected skin and was convinced that her fair-colored skin had a lot to do with getting what she wanted in life. As a teen, Meka would often include in her prayers a *thank you* to God for not letting her be born with dark skin.

"Do you think I would have gotten where I am today if I had dark skin and kinky hair?" Meka would often say to anyone who would listen.

Reo was probably the only other person outside of Meka's family members who could tolerate her and that was because they had grown up together. They had been a couple since their freshmen year in high school. Of course, they had the typical on-again-off-again drama that most couples go through. Reo was simply used to Meka and her controlling ways. On the outside looking in, it appeared that Reo might have been too passive when it came to Meka. But she had always been the dominating figure in their relationship and he had learned to only pay her half a mind half of the time. The other times, anything she said or did was moot.

But Meka's powerful personality was one of the things that had attracted him to her in the first place. She wasn't just a pretty face, she was also strong, powerful, and could hold her own. He was comfortable with that. Some men just don't mind allowing a woman to believe she wears the pants. It keeps turmoil down. Reo was one of those men. He was content with what was familiar to him. He loved her and was accepting of her set-in ways, and Meka was more set in her ways than an eighty-year-old heiress was, especially when it came to sex.

Meka was satisfied with the handful of sexual encounters she and Reo had engaged in. And as long as she was satisfied, that's all that truly mattered. She wanted sex when she wanted sex, other than that she could take it or leave it. Besides, sex had never been a major factor in her and Reo's relationship. Even as high school sweethearts and college lovers, Meka enjoyed cuddling more than anything. As far as Meka was concerned, sex was more like a chore, something that eventually had to be done in order to keep the house intact. She could only allow the chore to go undone for so long before someone else came along to do it. That's why every now and then she had to pull out her bag of tricks and get nasty for her man.

If you asked Reo, it was only more like a chore because Meka had to be in control of how they had sex. She gave directions and sometimes instructions. But this is how their sex life had always been. Every now and then Meka would pull out her bag of tricks and try it on him. It would definitely be enough to tide him over.

Reo didn't really hound Meka for sex either. It was too extra when it came to all the particulars. Sometime having sex with Meka was a task as far as he was concerned. Now, he wasn't one to turn pussy away, but he never got his hopes up about it either. That was probably why when he did do the deed, it was never anything to write home about. By now, Reo was just simply trying to get his rocks off. He figured if he hurried up and came, then the sexual act itself would be less of a challenge.

Being the woman, Meka was pretty much in control of what went down in the bedroom. Meka loved authority during lovemaking. She had even taken the liberty of writing down a list of *do*s and *don't*s, what she liked and what she didn't like. Needless to say, Reo had the list memorized, which made lovemaking like putting a bike together. It was hard to enjoy the ride after strenuously trying to recall where every nut and bolt went.

Strangely enough, Meka and Reo didn't even make love on their wedding night. Imagine being the bride of the famous and sexy Reo Laroque, record-breaking author in book sales, and not raping his body every chance that was available. Most women would have died to be in Meka's shoes. But Reo had been too tired. Too tired for sex.

He had gone out of town two days before their wedding date. He was scheduled for an NBC morning show appearance. His publicist had booked him in the place of another one of her clients who had canceled at the last minute due to a death in the family. Although the actual taping was scheduled on the day before Meka and Reo's wedding, it was a once in a lifetime opportunity for Reo. His latest novel, *Friend or Foe,* was due to be released that following month, and Carla advised him that an appearance on the morning show was sure to increase his pre-order sales and get him on the bestseller's list out of the gate. Carla was absolutely right. His novel debuted at number one the first month of its release and stayed there for seven months after that.

The taping of the TV show was in L.A., which was about a four-hour flight from the Columbus, Ohio, airport, not to mention the three-hour time difference. Between that and last-minute wedding preparations, Reo was exhausted. After the taping of the show, he caught a red-eye back to Columbus, which put him in town only eight hours before his wedding ceremony. Needless to say, Reo could hardly keep his eyes open. He barely had enough strength to last through the brief ceremony that the pastor of their home church, Reverend Sandy, conducted, let alone a night of passionate lovemaking. Meka understood and wasn't offended when Reo dozed off while she was on top of him in an attempt to get herself off. She rode his limp dick, pressing her clit against it, until she came. She would never forget that night.

Since their wedding day, Reo had kept so busy with his book tour and the writing of his new book, and Meka's time had been so filled with the children, that neither of them seemed to have the time or energy for lovemaking.

Tonight was going to be different, though. While Reo had been away, Meka thought a great deal about their marriage. She wanted more than part-time bliss. She wanted longevity. She and Reo had been through so much together. But not only that, Meka had received word that Reo's ex-wife might resurface in their lives to try and stir things up. Meka was going to be ready for her ass though. By the time she finished with Reo, he would be blind to any other woman.

Meka had taken the children to Reo's parents for the evening. She had that sexy new piece of lingerie and some lickable massage oil. Meka had planned on giving herself to her husband any way he wanted, no rules this time. Lord only knows how long it would take.

Meka was going all out on this premeditated sexcapade, which meant she had also gone out and purchased a bottle of Hennessy. No way could she do to her man the things she planned on doing to him without being inebriated.

Reo's flight from Philly, where he was finishing up his four-day East Coast tour, was expected to land in less than four hours, and Meka hadn't even taken the ground beef for the meat loaf out of the freezer to thaw. She laid the lingerie down on the bed and ran downstairs to the oversized chef's kitchen to take the meat out of the freezer.

Reo loved Meka's meat loaf. He really didn't have a choice but to love it. It was the only main dish she had ever learned to make. Ironically, the chef's kitchen was of no benefit to Meka. Reo had offered to hire a cooking maid for Meka as a wedding gift, but she insisted on maintaining the womanly duties around the home herself. There'd be no Latino heifer with clammy skin glistening on a permanent suntan running around her house playing the faithful servant. Therefore, after returning home from an exhausting book tour, instead of coming home to a table covered with exotic foods, Reo always expected to be greeted by Meka with a warm kiss, a dozen roses, and a meat loaf.

While the ground beef thawed in the microwave, Meka opened a can of deliciously seasoned Glory greens and put them in a pot on the stove. She pulled out a pack of sweet potato patties from the fridge that she had picked up from Krogers grocery store. She had never tried them before, but one of the women in the book club swore by them. A box of four-cheese Deluxe Kraft Mac'n'Cheese was a must. Mac'n'Cheese from scratch was unheard of in their home. That involved more work than Meka was willing to do.

"The candles," Meka said to herself as she stood in the kitchen trying to figure out all of the things she had yet to put in place. Meka untied the yellow apron she was wearing from around her waist and headed to the living room closet. She opened the door and pulled out a Pier One Imports bag that was loaded with a variety of fragrant candles.

Meka strategically placed the candles throughout the living room. The living room—not the bedroom—was what she planned on turning into her sex den. Meka had also purchased some scrap sheer material from Joann's Fabric and tied it around lamps and the table legs. It gave the living room a canopied look. The huge wicker fan she had purchased from the flea market a few months earlier would finally come in handy. She planned on fanning her man down with it after making him so hot. The fan would go perfectly with her toga-like lingerie outfit.

She planned on taking down her bun and wearing her hair in a long ponytail. She anticipated Reo grabbing hold of it as he fucked her from behind. Maybe he would even use it as a control device to guide her as she gave him the blowjob of a lifetime. Meka was indeed ready to handle her business with her man. The question was, was he ready to handle her?

Time had gotten away from Meka. As she lit the seventh of a dozen candles, she heard Reo's taxi pull up.

"Damn it!" Meka shouted as the match burnt down to her fingertips. She blew it out, struck another match, and proceeded to light the remainder of the candles. The time it took her to light them was the time it took for Reo to acquire his luggage from the trunk of the taxi.

Meka took one final look around the living room and at the dining table. Everything looked splendid. The room screamed romance and sex appeal.

"Hey, Meka," Reo shouted as he came through the front door, dropping his set of Ralph Lauren luggage at his feet. "I'm home, love."

"And so am I," Meka said seductively as she stood there in her lingerie holding two glasses of champagne. Reo's mouth dropped open. He had never seen Meka looking so delicious. And now he wanted to eat her right up. He was speechless.

Meka smiled as she strutted over to him with her bare feet, toenails freshly French manicured. She sipped champagne from her glass, not taking her eyes off of Reo. She admired her five feet, eleven inch, well-sculptured spouse. His ebony complexion was as smooth as a pimp's vocabulary. His natural low-cut curly locks and neatly trimmed goatee were so becoming.

When she reached Reo she planted a hard French kiss on his butter-soft lips. He could taste the champagne on her tongue as she slipped it in his mouth.

"Well, damn," Reo said, pulling back from the kiss. "So this is why you couldn't pick me up from the airport? Knowing you're at home waiting on me looking like that, hell, I would have walked home."

Reo always knew what to say to make Meka blush. This time was no different.

"Um-hm," Meka said, placing Reo's glass of champagne in his hand. She took another sip of her own. "Welcome home, baby."

Meka kissed Reo again then walked over to the desk that sat by the doorway. She picked up the dozen red roses that were wrapped in red tissue paper and tied with a long red satin bow. She handed them to Reo.

"These are for you," she said with a wink.

"Thank you," Reo said, smelling them. "You went all out, didn't you? You got the new ling-a-ri, candles, champagne, roses. It's not our anniversary already, is it?"

"I just felt like doing something special," Meka said, finishing off her champagne. "For my special man."

Reo then took a couple of swallows of his champagne. He licked his lips seductively while staring at Meka.

"Where are the kids?" Reo asked as he walked over to the couch and sat down. He laid the roses on the table and proceeded to finish off his glass of champagne.

"Gone," Meka said as she walked into the kitchen. She grabbed a couple of pot holders and began moving the food from the oven and stovetop to the dining room table.

"For the night?" Reo asked as Meka set down the dish of greens.

"Yep. They're at your mom and dad's for the entire night. They're going to take care of the kids while I take care of you . . . and Simmy," Meka said, referring to the nickname Reo had given his penis. "But first, I figured you'd be starving so I prepared you a meal."

"Meat loaf again?" Reo asked as Meka made her way back into the kitchen.

"Yes, meat loaf, *again*." Meka mocked Reo as she walked over and picked up the roses and began placing them in the vase she had carried out of the kitchen.

"I didn't mean it like that," Reo said, lightly smacking Meka on her butt. "You know I love your meat loaf."

"Um-hm," Meka said, rolling her eyes. "If you know what's good for you, you better clean that shit up."

Reo pulled Meka onto his lap and began kissing her. He ran his hands across her breasts then down between her legs. He fondled his way in between Meka's pussy lips. He rubbed her clit then attempted to go deep with his fingers as he continued kissing her. Reo knew that putting his fingers inside of her was on the *don't* part of the list. But she had told herself that tonight anything would go. It was all about pleasing her man. She felt so good to Reo. She was so beautiful. This was the sexy playful girl that he new existed inside of Meka.

Meka pushed herself away from Reo. "The rolls!" she said, quickly removing herself from Reo's lap. "I forgot the rolls."

Meka raced into the kitchen and leaned up against the refrigerator. She put her head back and sighed. She had to get rid of the feeling of Reo's fingers being inside of her. She didn't want to ruin the mood by reminding him how much she hated that, so instead she used the rolls as an excuse.

Meka walked over to the cupboard and pulled out the bottle of Hennessy. She cracked it open and poured herself a shot. She grabbed a few ice cubes and placed them in the glass. She swiveled the ice around a few times then she downed the drink. The Hennessy going down took Meka's breath away. It was hot, but it was just what she needed in order to make her man hot. So she didn't hesitate drinking one more shot for reassurance.

"Chow time," Meka said as she hurried out of the kitchen without rolls in hand. "Silly me," she began to explain to Reo, not looking at him because she didn't want to look dead in his face while lying to him. "I forgot to even buy the rolls while I was at the grocery store. We'll just have to do without them."

Meka pulled out her chair and sat down. "Do you want to say grace or shall—"

Meka's words came to a complete halt as she looked up and saw Reo standing at the opposite end of the table butt-ass naked. She had never paid much attention to the make and model of Simmy. But hell, her husband was nicely hung. Still and yet, the Henney hadn't kicked in so Meka wasn't quite prepared to be his love slave.

"Come on, baby," Meka whined. "That's dessert. I spent all of this time on dinner. I want you to eat it while it's hot. You're messing up my game plan."

Reo sighed. "Okay, okay." Reo put his boxers and pants back on then took his place at the table. Meka blushed at the sight of her husband's beautiful bare chest.

Reo wasn't mad about eating first. He had fallen asleep on the plane when the meal was being served, so he hadn't eaten. He barely said two words to Meka at dinner because he was so busy stuffing the food down his throat. Meka watched him put away the last bite of his fourth slice of meat loaf.

"I see you weren't that hungry," she said jokingly.

"Oh, baby that was delicious," Reo said as he sat back in his chair and yawned.

"Why don't you go sit down on the couch, have another glass of champagne, and I'll join you in a minute?" Meka stood up and began clearing the table as Reo followed her orders. "And pour me a glass, too," she added.

It was about five minutes before Meka joined Reo. He had already drunk his glass of champagne and had laid down on the couch. Meka picked up her glass of champagne and began to drink it. She was feeling nice. She was liquored up well.

Meka began to feed Reo some of her champagne. She took a long look into his eyes then threw the glass down. She climbed on top of him and began to straddle him. She then clutched Simmy through his pants and began squeezing.

"Simmy said he likes that," Reo smiled.

"Um, I can tell," Meka said as Simmy grew rock hard. Meka proceeded to kiss Reo's neck while stroking Simmy at the same time.

"I sure do hope you left room for dessert," Meka said as she unzipped Reo's pants and pulled out Simmy. She began to lick him, but not suck. She didn't ordinarily suck dick. She was one of those snobbish pretty girls, always wearing her hair in a tight bun to match her tight ass. Meka was far too pretty to suck dick. Reo never expected Meka to pleasure him with oral sex. He knew the most he was going to get out of her was a few kisses, two or three licks, five and one half strokes and two tongue swirls around the tip.

Meka had a surprise in store for him tonight, though. Hennessy gave a motherfucker nerve. Meka had mentally prepared herself to suck Reo's dick for real, until he came. But by the time she got to the fourth stroke Reo let out a loud yawn, and totally fucked up the mood.

"Oh, I'm sorry," Reo apologized, realizing that he had committed the ultimate act of rudeness.

"I can't fuckin' believe you just did that," Meka said as she stood up from the couch, tipsy, almost falling over. "Am I that fucking boring to you? I'm sitting here sucking your dick and you don't say, 'Ooh, baby that feels good.' What do you do? You yawn."

The entire scene was starting to fuck up Meka's buzz.

"Baby, I said I was sorry," Reo said as he remained laid across the couch with Simmy hanging out. "It's just that I'm—"

"I know, I know," Meka said, cutting Reo off. "You're tired. You just had a long weekend and a long flight and you're tired. Well you know what Reo? So the fuck am I! I'm tired of you."

"Whoa, hold up," Reo said, followed by a small laugh.

"Oh, now you think it's funny?" Meka yelled.

"Baby, calm down," Reo said. "I'm just weighed down a little bit. You see all of that food I just ate. You know black folks can't eat a big meal then keep their eyes open."

"You sound like a little bitch," Meka said with spit spraying.

"Look, you're drunk," Reo said. He knew Meka would never have spoken to him like that otherwise. Reo walked over to hold Meka, but she pushed him off of her.

"No," she said, on the verge of drunken tears. "I did all of this for you and you don't even appreciate it."

"Baby, I do. I do," Reo said as he began to kiss Meka, which calmed her down. Eventually she began to kiss Reo back. He was worthy of a second chance. The alcohol did have him slightly horny, but he was conceivably tired.

Meka, once again, clutched Simmy and began stroking him, only this time he didn't get rock hard. No matter how hard Meka kissed Reo or how hard she jerked his dick, Simmy just wouldn't get hard for her. How dare a dick, a piece of meat, make her feel less than a woman? Meka pulled herself away from Reo.

"I'm sorry, baby," Reo said, looking down at an unexcited Simmy. "I don't know what's wrong with him."

By now, Meka had tears forming in her eyes. "Who do I have to be, Reo?" she asked in a soft, sincere tone.

"What are you talking about?" Reo replied.

"Who do I have to be to make you love me, to make you want me?"

Reo sat in silence.

"Who, Reo?" Meka demanded to know.

"Meka, baby . . ."

"Just forget it." Meka walked over to the porcelain halogen lamp on the desk by the doorway and turned it on. She then blew out any candle that was still burning. Meka stared down at Reo with disgust. Reo was sitting on the couch, with his head tilted back, looking up at the ceiling. Simmy was still hanging free.

"I'm going to bed in the guest room," Meka said before storming off. "And for God's sake, put that thing away. It's not like you're going to put it to any use."

"Pawn queen four," Reo said as he made his move. He and his best buddy, Nate, were playing their usual game of chess.

Reo had arrived at Nate's Victorian-style home a half hour ago with a bottle of J. Roget in hand. The two sat in the den area at the oak table that was actually a chessboard with large chess pieces. The two matching chairs were hand-carved high backs with gold silk padding on the seats. The two had eagerly sat down to enjoy their game and bottle of champagne.

It was unspoken that the host provided the chessboard and snacks and the guest brought the bubbly. Nate was a pro at chess. He had learned to play during a two-year bid for attempted robbery thirteen years ago when he was twenty-three. He taught Reo how to play seven years ago when the two first became friends after meeting on an online group for writers.

At first, when the two started playing, the guest would try to outdo the other by bringing Moet or Dom. Nate even brought a bottle of Cristal one time, which was a gift from his agent for making the *New York Times* bestseller's list. Then finally one spoke up and the other agreed that the poor man's champagne had the best taste, for they each preferred sweet bubbly.

Nate took a sip of his champagne as he contemplated his next

move. Reo sighed. Nate looked up at him, then went back to studying the board. Reo sighed again. Nate continued studying the board,
then once again Reo sighed.

"Are you going to tell me what the hell is wrong with you,
man?" Nate said, bothered by Reo's unusual silence, not to mention all that damn sighing.

"Everything is good," Reo said, staring at the chessboard. "Just
make your move."

Nate took a sip of his champagne, then went back to studying
the chessboard. Reo sighed.

"Okay, that's it!" Nate said, fed up as he moved all of the chess
pieces to the right side of the board. He got up and walked over to
the glass-and-mirror bar that hugged the corner of the den. He
grabbed two shot glasses and a bottle of Grand Marnier. He
poured two shots then walked back over to the table.

"With all that sighing it must be serious," Nate said, setting
Reo's shot down on the chess table. Nate sat down with his own
shot in hand and looked at Reo, waiting for him to speak what was
on his mind.

"I told you already, there's nothing wrong," Reo said, putting
his hands up and smiling a fake smile.

"Man, we been friends how long?" Nate said, sipping his
drink. "Ahhh. More than six years at least. I know when something's wrong. Speak now or forever hold your piece."

"Maybe I shouldn't have passed up that opportunity ten months
ago when Reverend Sandy asked that same question," Reo said.

"Trouble in paradise?" Nate asked.

"No, not really. I mean, well." Reo fumbled around with his
words. He wasn't one to bad-mouth his wife to anybody. He didn't
get down like that so he was careful of his words.

"Just spit it out. What is it this time, Meka won't let you cum in
her because she doesn't like lying in a puddle afterward? Oh, let

me guess, you still can't get her to suck your dick instead of just kissing it?" Nate said, laughing.

Reo had just taken a sip of his drink. "That's why I don't like telling you nothing. You always got jokes." Reo put his glass down and walked over to the French-style glass doors that overlooked Nate's half-acre backyard.

"Aw, man, you know I'm just fuckin' wit cha. You my boy. On the serious tip, you know you can talk to me." Nate paused, then continued. "It's expected that you and Meka are going to run into some problems. All marriages do. But you two have had to deal with some shit that most dudes would have choked a bitch for. I mean, so Meka's a little controlling . . . no big deal. And she's a little particular when it comes to sex. Some men don't even get pussy from their wives so you one up. But this is the same woman that got pregnant with your baby and tried to blackmail you with a million-dollar paternity suit. Then after you write the check, she shows up on the doorstep of you and your new wife with the baby. I don't care what you say, you can't put all that shit behind you."

"But I did," Reo assured him. "I ain't even gon' lie to you. That shit hurt, but I couldn't dwell on the past, man. I would be miserable."

"What are you now?" Nate said, trying to make a point.

Reo paused, then walked back over to the chess table and sat down.

"Look, man," Nate said. "All I'm saying is that's a big hill to climb and get over. Meka pulled some ole' soap-opera talk-show shit on you."

"But losing our baby, man—nothing was worse than that. It's unfortunate that it took that to bring us back together," Reo said sadly. "But after dealing with the death of our baby, none of that other stuff mattered anymore."

"Not even your feelings for Klarke?" Nate asked.

Reo froze. Just hearing that name made his heart beat fast. Had he ever really stopped loving his ex-wife or had he only blocked that out and put it in his past right along with the mess he and Meka had gone through?

"I just wanna be happy," Reo said, shrugging his shoulders.

"You and Mary J. Blige," Nate said, lighting a cigar.

"I'm serious, man. I mean, I'm not unhappy. I don't know how to explain it." Reo thought for a moment. "I just want that feeling of happiness and I want Meka to feel it too. I want us to be happy just like you and Persia."

"Then on the real, don't determine your happiness on the merit of how you see other couples," Nate said seriously. "You'll never be happy if you do that. Hell, there's been plenty of times you've come over here and seen Persia and me kissing and holding hands while only ten minutes before you showed up we were fighting like cats and dogs."

"Word?" Reo asked, laughing.

"Word," Nate replied. "I mean, I love Persia's ass to death, but sometimes, she can work the hell out of my nerves. I just be wanting to choke her ass. Sometimes while she's standing in front of me fussing, pointing that finger, and snapping that neck, I visualize my hands around her throat choking the fuck out of her ass."

Reo laughed as Nate put his hands in the air shaking them as if he had Persia's neck in between them.

"But that same shit about her that gets on my nerves is that same shit that I love about her. I mean, I ain't into a yes chick. I'm confident enough in my manhood that I don't need a weak woman to make me feel strong and like I'm in control. You and I are alike in a lot of ways and that's one of them. Persia and Meka are anything but weak. They are strong, independent women. Some people call women like that bitches, but you know what we call them?"

"What?" Reo asked.

"Wives!" Nate said. "We call them our wives, fool."

"Man, I do love Meka and her bitchy ways. We've been through a lot of bullshit, man. You know that. But I learned that all women have flaws. The grass ain't always greener so you're better off sticking it out with the one you're with. And still, even after everything Meka and I have been through, the lies, the games, the baby . . . we still found our way back to each other and were able to put everything in our past aside. Sometimes I just feel like something's missing," Reo said.

"Something or someone?" Nate said as the telephone rang. He excused himself to go answer the phone. It was a call for Persia, who was out shopping. Nate took a message, then returned to the table.

"Maybe if Meka had friends to do things with," Reo said. "Maybe she would loosen up and enjoy life more. You know? Be a little more carefree. Maybe you can talk to Persia and hint around about her maybe inviting Meka out with her and some of her friends."

Nate damn near spit out the Grand Marnier that was in his mouth. "Persia and Meka?"

"What?" Reo said with a puzzled look on his face.

"Nothing, man, I just mean, Persia and her friends just don't seem like Meka's type," Nate said with a frown.

"You mean Meka doesn't seem like their type," Reo said as if his feelings were hurt. "Forget it, man. If you don't want to do it, just say so. You don't have to make it seem like your wife is better than mine."

"Patna, now you know it ain't even like that," Nate said. "I just thought . . . how would Meka feel about you finding friends for her?"

"She can find her own friends," Reo said in her defense. "She just won't. She's too wrapped up in taking care of the house and all."

"You mean controlling the house," Nate said under his breath as he took a sip of his drink.

"Excuse me?" Reo asked, ready to defend his wife.

"Nothing," Nate said. "I was just thinking . . . never mind what I was thinking. I'll talk to Persia."

"Really, man? Thanks," Reo said, perking up.

"Yeah, I'll talk to her tonight," Nate said with a fake smile on his face. Against his better judgment, he was going to try and hook up Persia and Meka. Nate knew how Persia felt about Meka, that she was a goody-two-shoes stuck-up beyatch. But he couldn't tell his best friend that.

"If given the chance, I know those two could be real good friends," Reo said excitedly.

"Yeah, real good friends." Nate sighed and swallowed down his drink. He then got up and fixed himself another one and drank it down straight.

"Damn," Reo said. "I've never seen you put it away like that before. What is this stuff called anyway?"

"Courage," Nate said as he poured himself another glass. "Courage."

"What do you mean, 'try' to be friends with her?" Persia said to Nate as she slid her satin floral chemise over her head as she prepared to join Nate who was already in bed.

"She's my best friend's wife," Nate said. "And you're my wife. I thought it would be neat if you two were friends also."

"'Neat,'" Persia said, twisting her face. "I'm half white and I don't even use the word 'neat.' Baby, you tryin' too hard."

"Speaking of hard," Nate said with a mischievous look on his face as he caressed his dick.

"You are so crazy," Persia said, rolling her eyes as she twisted her hair up into a bun. "Meka is a member of a book club and I'm a member of a biker's club. We don't have shit in common. Hell, she probably doesn't even shit. Her ass is too tight for anything to come out of it."

Nate couldn't help but laugh. "You my crazy mama," Nate said, hitting Persia on the ass as she kicked her house slippers off and climbed into bed.

"I can't lie, baby," Persia said, pouting. "You know I don't really care for her."

"You were a bridesmaid in her wedding," Nate said.

"I did that for Reo," Persia replied. "He's our boy. I love him. I felt bad that his wife-to-be didn't have any friends besides her sisters to be in her wedding party. Hell, one sister insisted on being just the guest-book attendant."

"You seemed like you had fun being a member of the wedding party," Nate said as he began to rub his hands across Persia's breasts.

"I did," Persia replied. "Her sisters were cool as hell. We kicked it. Got crunked and had a ball."

"Yeah, I remember you lushes at the reception," Nate said. "I think every groomsman got some pussy from a bridesmaid that night."

"Yeah," Persia laughed. "Even the married ones who weren't married to each other."

"Speaking of pussy," Nate said as he moved his hand from Persia's breast across her belly down to her private spot.

"What about pussy?" Persia said as she placed her hand on top of Nate's. "Oh, you mean this pussy right here?"

Persia guided Nate's hand down to her pantyless crotch. His fingers slid up and down her clit, causing her to moan.

"Does that feel good to you, baby? You like that shit?" Nate asked as he thrust his tongue into Persia's mouth, his fingers now inside of her.

"Yeah, baby," Persia said softly. "Yeah."

Nate moved on top of Persia. He pulled his boxers off without breaking their kiss. He took his penis in his hand and began rubbing it against Persia's clit.

"Ooh, baby," Persia moaned. "Put your mouth where your dick is."

Nate smiled before sliding down Persia's body, until he was positioned perfectly between her legs. He kissed her clit, then her left thigh, then her right. He put his middle finger in his mouth, sliding it out slow, then watched her face as he slid it into her. Persia moaned and clenched her pussy muscles around his finger.

Nate began to plunge his finger in and out of her as she crooned, moaned, and groaned. The more Nate watched Persia writhe passionately, the harder he got. His dick leaked pre-cum.

"Oh, baby, I gotta hit that," Nate said as he positioned his dick to enter Persia's wetness. He wanted to be inside of her so badly that he couldn't even finish eating her out.

"Put it in then," Persia begged. "Fuck me."

Nate eased all eight inches inside Persia.

"Damn, you feel so good," Nate said as he began to pump inside her.

Persia kissed Nate's sweaty neck as she grabbed his ass and pulled him deeper inside of her. She began fucking him hard, her clit pressing against his dick as it moved in and out.

Persia pushed against Nate's chest as a signal for him to roll over and allow her on top. Nate was only moments from busting and didn't want to stop, but he intended on giving his baby what she wanted.

Nate was definitely a pleaser. He wasn't satisfied unless Persia got off. And this is why their sex life was so colorful, even after six years of marriage.

They did have a dry spell four years ago when Persia was pregnant with their twin girls. But once she gave birth to the girls, it had been on ever since.

Watching his baby ride his dick was beautiful to Nate. He loved to watch Persia work that shit out. During the ten-second countdown Persia would lean over his chest and bounce her pussy up and down hard on his dick. She made a muthafucka's toes curl.

Nate would cum so much that as soon as Persia lifted her body off of him, juices would drip. Persia's sex had always been the bomb, and this go round was no exception.

"How does it feel, baby?" Nate asked Persia as he pulled her by the hips down onto his dick.

"It feels so good," Persia moaned. "You know I love this muthafuckin' dick."

"Show Daddy how much you love it," Nate said as he pumped Persia. "Show Daddy how much you love this dick."

Persia positioned herself like a frog on top of Nate and began to hop up and down on his dick. The sound of their bodies smacking together turned them both on.

"That's right, baby. Do that shit," Nate said as he watched Persia's tig ol' bitties bounce. "I'm 'bout to cum. Oh shit, I'm 'bout to shoot this nut off up in that."

"Cum on, baby. Cum on," Persia screamed as she released her own juices. As she was climaxing she put her body in full speed. She could feel Nate filling her up with juices of his own. The two moaned in ecstasy as their two bodies went limp.

Persia collapsed onto Nate's chest then rolled over. The two lay there breathing as if they had just raced one another in a marathon.

After a minute Persia looked over at Nate who had just turned to look over at her. The two burst out into laughter.

"Baby, that was good," Nate said.

"Yeah," Persia agreed. "It was good for me too."

Nate leaned over and kissed Persia.

"So, you gonna do that for me?" Nate asked.

"Do what?" Persia questioned.

"Invite Meka to hang out with you and your girls."

Persia sighed then paused for a moment. "Sure, anything for my man," Persia said as she tapped Nate on the chest with her hand then reached over to turn the lamp off. "Besides, a few hours of hanging out with Meka, how bad can it be?"

3

FOR THE SAKE OF
THE CHILD

"Baby killer, baby killer, baby killer," were the taunts Klarke had become accustomed to hearing for the last four years. Klarke knew when she copped a plea for the murder of the baby of her former husband, Reo Laroque, and his ex-girlfriend at the time, Meka, that she would have to spend the rest of her life behind bars watching her back. An inmate locked up for having harmed a child was like a goldfish swimming with sharks. Other inmates, even those who had committed manslaughter and rape, frowned upon inmates who had harmed a helpless child.

It had been Klarke's plea of guilty to first-degree murder that kept her from getting the death penalty in what was sure to have been one of the most highly publicized trials ever. So to protect her family from anymore humiliation than what they had already endured, Klarke pled guilty.

It should have been the hardest thing in the world for her to do, but it wasn't. The day the baby was found floating in the swimming pool in the backyard of Klarke's house, there had been only four other people in the home. Klarke, Reo, Vaughn, and HJ. No one had wanted to even consider the fact that any of them were capable of such a devious act. They thought someone had broken into the house and drowned the baby. But all of those speculations were shattered the day Klarke came forward and announced her guilt to a crime that she had not committed.

Klarke was just as shocked at her admission to the crime as she was the day her daughter admitted to her that she was responsible for the death of the baby. Motherly instinct had taken over. Klarke knew her daughter would be punished by the system, and wrong or right, she couldn't allow it. She couldn't turn her daughter in. So she created her own version of *Freaky Friday* and traded places with her daughter. The three of them, Klarke, Harris—her children's father—and Vaughn, made a pact to never tell a single soul.

Harris had felt that Vaughn needed help and should have accepted responsibility for the crime. Klarke wouldn't hear of it. She knew that if she left Vaughn in Harris's care that there was a chance that he would turn her over to authorities. Just seeing Vaughn every day would have taken its toll on him and he would have eventually caved. That's why she made Harris promise to send her away to boarding school. Klarke knew Vaughn had a better chance if she was sent away. But every day Klarke woke up asking herself if today would be the day Harris turned Vaughn in.

For Klarke's first few months of incarceration, she had been kept in protective custody and out of the general population. The state feared that she would be done grave harm if placed in gen pop. She had even been placed on a suicide watch, so she wouldn't harm herself and her and Reo's unborn child. But Klarke hadn't planned on killing herself. She had planned on enduring. Besides, she had seen how much suicide hurt the ones who were left behind.

Tionne, the woman Harris had forsaken their marriage for over nine years ago, had committed suicide. They had all struggled with her death. Everyone seemed to blame themselves for not making Tionne happy enough in life. Klarke would never do that to the people who loved her. She was much stronger than that.

But Klarke had cried. She had cried for everything she had been forced to leave behind.

She had had to leave behind her beautiful daughter and her son who was growing into a handsome young man. She had to leave behind two wonderful best friends, Breezy and Jeva, who had always been right there by her side whenever she needed them. She had to leave behind the most loving husband any woman could ask for, Reo. He was her third husband and he had proven that the third time was indeed the charm. No man had completed her as Reo had.

But the most difficult thing that Klarke had had to give up was her newborn baby, the one she had given birth to behind prison walls. She was doing a life bid, so the baby had been turned over to Reo. She had signed an agreement forfeiting her rights as a mother to her son and that she would never seek to have any contact with the child. Reo Carmine Laroque, Jr. would never know her as Mommy.

Klarke had felt that it was the right thing to do for her baby and Reo. She had already brought enough sadness and destruction into his life. The last thing she wanted to do was to force her presence in his life anymore. In addition to that, if her son would always know her as the woman behind bars for murder, then she would rather he not know her at all. She did one of the hardest things she ever had to do in her life and all for the sake of her child.

Now that she was being released from prison and her daughter,

Vaughn, was taking her place, Klarke felt as though every sacrifice she had made had been in vain.

She remembered the day Harris had called to tell her that Vaughn had killed the baby.

A Detective Edwards had been questioning Klarke and Reo about the death when his phone rang. When Detective Edwards had answered the call and heard that it was Harris, he mentioned that Klarke just happened to be right there with him. Harris then immediately asked to speak to Klarke. Harris's words had burned through her.

"Klarke! Oh my God, Klarke!" Harris shouted, out of breath. "It's Vaughn. I tried to call you at home. You didn't answer. Your cell phone is off. Oh, my God!"

"Harris, calm down," Klarke said in a mellow tone. "Just calm down and tell me what's the matter with her."

"She did it, Klarke," Harris said as his voice cracked. "Vaughn just told me that she's the one who killed your husband's baby. Klarke, she killed the baby."

Klarke had to maintain her composure. Both Detective Edwards's and Reo's eyes were burning a hole through her. "I'm on my way," Klarke said in a stern tone, trying to maintain her composure. "Just stay calm until I arrive."

It didn't matter that Vaughn was only thirteen and would probably receive a less harsh punishment than Klarke would. No way was Klarke handing her baby girl over to the system. Klarke couldn't imagine her daughter in jail for any amount of time, not six years or six months. After getting the phone call from Harris and running out of the police station, Klarke went straight to Harris's house.

When she walked through the door Vaughn was sitting on the couch and Harris was staring out of the living room window. Harris hadn't even been able to look at his daughter anymore. She knew then that things would never be the same between them again.

Klarke had run over to Vaughn and hugged her. Then she looked into her eyes and saw the innocence and helplessness. This was the child she would die for. The child she would trade her life for. At that moment she knew what she had to do. Klarke asked no questions. She simply told Harris and Vaughn what she felt had to be done.

Harris had been violently against it, but he knew there was no talking her out of it. So he had vowed along with Klarke and Vaughn to keep this between just the three of them. Klarke wouldn't tell her best friends or her sisters. Harris wouldn't tell his family and Vaughn wouldn't tell HJ.

Harris had been too opposed to the plan for Klarke to be 100 percent comfortable that Harris wouldn't do something foolish. That's why she was hoping with Vaughn away at boarding school it would be an out-of-sight out-of-mind deal. Klarke knew Harris well, well enough to know that Vaughn's presence would weigh heavily on him and it would only be a matter of time before he would break. Klarke just couldn't risk that happening. So as badly as Vaughn needed her father at a time like this, Klarke knew that it would be better for her to get away and stay away.

The separation meant that Vaughn and Harris would never have the father and daughter relationship that they once had. But Klarke felt she did what she had to do as a mother.

The morning Klarke was to confess, she vomited all morning long. At first she thought it was her nerves. She later found out that she was almost three months pregnant. With all of the drama, she hadn't noticed that she hadn't gotten her period. All she could think about was her family. She loved them so much. Parting from them was absolutely heartbreaking. Harris had to tear Klarke and Vaughn apart so that Klarke could go meet with her attorney to turn herself in. It was like the scene from the movie *The Color Purple* when Mister was trying to separate Netti and Cealy. Vaughn begged Klarke to allow her to turn herself in, but Klarke wouldn't hear of it. It was so emotional and draining that by the time Harris separated them, Vaughn was literally laid out on the floor. That would be the last time they would all be together. Only two weeks after Klarke's imprisonment, Vaughn was shipped off to boarding school. This provided some comfort for Klarke. She knew that her daughter was gone, safe, sound, and free. And she had remained free until the girl who was hiding in the cloakroom when Vaughn confessed to Sister Beasley snitched.

"Visit," the female correction officer shouted to Klarke, waking her from her beauty sleep. This was the same officer's second time visiting Klarke's cell that day. Earlier Klarke had received an urgent phone call from Harris but was in the showers and the lazy-ass guard didn't feel like going through the trouble of getting her.

"What?" Klarke said, dazed, rubbing her eyes and patting her straight, elbow-length hair down.

"Wake up, sleeping beauty," the guard said. "You've got a visitor."

"It's not my visiting day," Klarke said.

"It's your attorney, damn it, now move it."

Klarke stood up and straightened herself up. She had on a pair of jeans that she had unsnapped for a more comfortable sleep. She snapped her jeans and tucked in her blue prison shirt and followed the corrections officer.

Klarke didn't understand why her attorney would be showing up at the prison out of the blue. She felt it in her gut that something wasn't right.

Klarke was baffled. She hadn't talked to her attorney since the hearing when she confessed to the crime. She hadn't a need to talk with her. Klarke's stomach sank into a knot as she sat down to speak with her attorney.

"How have you been?" Klarke's attorney asked.

"I've been in jail. Does that answer your question?" Klarke asked.

"I see you've adapted to prison life," Klarke's attorney said in reference to Klarke's sarcasm, a characteristic she had never possessed before.

"I'm sorry," Klarke sincerely apologized. "I'm just a little spooked about your being here. What's going on?"

Klarke's attorney took a deep breath. Klarke had a feeling that it wasn't going to be something she wanted to hear.

"I've got good news and bad news for you," her attorney said.

"What it is?" Klarke asked hesitantly.

"Well, the good news is that you're going to be a free woman soon."

"I—I don't understand," Klarke said, taking deep breaths. "No. I don't understand. Why? Why would they let me out? Why would they do that?"

"I think you know why," her attorney said as she watched Klarke begin to fall apart.

"No," Klarke whispered. "No. No. No. This is crazy. Why would they let me out of here? I killed a baby. I'm in here for life. I'm in this motherfucker for life."

Finally her whispers turned into roars.

"Oh, God, no!" Klarke shouted frantically. She got up and walked over to the attorney and got down on her knees. "Where's my baby? Where is she? Don't let them touch her. Don't let them talk to her."

"She's already been talking. She told them about the entire scheme of you confessing to the murder in order to keep her from going to jail. They've taken your daughter into custody for the murder of the baby," the attorney said in one breath as if it would have been less painful for Klarke to hear.

Klarke began to sob. "Why? Why? Why? Oh, God. My baby."

Klarke stood up and walked back over to her chair and sat down.

"She admitted to one of the nuns at her school that she committed the murder and that you were just covering for her."

"That's not true. She wouldn't have done that. She couldn't have. I've been here all of this time and for what? For what?" Klarke threw her hands up and began to moan.

Klarke cradled her head with her hands and rocked back and forth.

"She's lying. The nun is lying," Klarke said after regaining her composure. "Vaughn wouldn't have said that to her. Where is this nun? Let me talk to her. I'm sure I can straighten this all out."

"She's dead," her attorney said.

"Dead?" Klarke asked, confused. "How'd she die?"

"It's being investigated. It seems as though she died right after your daughter confessed."

Klarke allowed her attorney's words to sink in.

"They don't think . . . they don't think my baby had anything to do with that, do they?"

"They're investigating the death. A student overheard the entire conversation between your daughter and the nun. Right now she's the state's only witness. She sounds credible."

Klarke remained silent. She was frozen stiff. It wasn't that she didn't want to speak or move or just scream. She couldn't.

"I'm going to need a statement from you," her attorney said. "The court will probably want to punish you somehow for obstructing justice, but I'm sure I can get you time served or probation." She took a deep breath. "Here comes the most difficult part. Your daughter will most likely be charged as an adult. There has to be an adult determination hearing to decide that, but you know how the state of Ohio is. She could be looking at a life sentence or even the death penalty."

Klarke finally found strength to rise up out of her chair in shock. But before she could say or do anything she fainted.

"Help! Help!" her attorney screamed. A few seconds later a couple COs entered the room and rushed Klarke to the infirmary.

After they checked her vitals, Klarke began regaining consciousness. Before opening her eyes she prayed that everything had been a bad nightmare, that Vaughn was still away at boarding school graduating, preparing to go off to college. But when she opened her eyes and looked over to her left there sat her attorney.

"Are you okay?" her attorney asked.

"No. Please no more," Klarke begged in a helpless tone. There was nothing she could do to save her daughter this time. A part of her wanted so much to be happy that she would once again be a free woman, but not by having her daughter's freedom taken away. It was never supposed to be this way. But now Vaughn would be taking her place in the prison cell and there wasn't a damn thing she could do about it. Or was there?

"I could say that I forced Vaughn to drown the baby," Klarke said to her attorney, who had returned to the prison two days later to give Klarke information on her release. Klarke had been doing a lot of thinking. She couldn't wait to share her ideas with her attorney.

"I could say that I mentally manipulated her into doing it," Klarke said desperately.

"Sweetheart," Klarke's attorney said, putting her hand over Klarke's trembling one. "I know how much you love your daughter. You've spent the past four years proving it. Only a mother could have done what you did."

Tears began running down Klarke's cheek and her attorney was trying her damnedest not to let her own fall.

"But I'm bound by the judicial system," Klarke's attorney said. "I can't knowingly aid you in deceiving the court. I just can't."

Klarke broke down. "Please!" Klarke begged. "Please! They're going to put my little girl in jail. My baby."

Her attorney could no longer keep her tears from falling. "I'm sorry, Klarke," she said as she stood up quickly, grabbing her case file and shoving it into her briefcase. She felt in her heart that if she remained in that room one more minute, that she would find a way to help this desperate woman. Instead, she wiped her tears away with the back of her hand and signaled for the guard to open the door.

"I know it's easier for me to say than for you to do," Klarke's attorney said as she exited the room, "but try to enjoy your freedom."

The door closed behind her attorney. Klarke's last hope had just left her hanging.

"Nooooo!" Klarke shouted as she picked up the chair her attorney had been sitting in and threw it at the door. "Noooooo!"

Klarke had attempted to refuse to back down on her confession of murdering the baby. She knew that if she did, the courts couldn't do anything permanent without evidence to back up either confession. For all they know, Vaughn could have been lying to save her mother. But by the time Klarke realized that was an option, the authorities had gotten to Harris before she could relay her "new plan" to him. He supported Vaughn's confession. As far as Harris was concerned, there was no reason for both of them to be behind bars while the slow wheels of justice turned.

Klarke had already given a statement to her attorney that wasn't favorable to Vaughn. Everything had fallen apart right before Klarke's eyes.

Klarke was escorted through the prison by one of the male prison guards. In her arms she carried a box that held all of her belongings. By the look on her face, one would have thought she had been waiting on death row and her number had finally been called.

"Name?" a female guard asked Klarke before she would buzz her through the locked door.

Klarke rambled off her name for the fifth and final time. They could care less who in the fuck they let in the prison door, but they sure in the hell weren't going to let the wrong one out.

"Number?" the guard asked.

Klarke, almost in a daze, swallowed and said, "50195-083."

"Well," the security guard said to Klarke. "This is it." Klarke tried to force out a smile, but she couldn't. The guard patted Klarke on the shoulder then watched her walk through the door to freedom.

As Klarke stepped outside the sun struck her hard across the face. She raised her hand to block the blow to her eyes. She spread her fingers then peeked at it from in between them. It was beautiful. It didn't seem like the same sun that warmed her skin in the prison yard. This was a much friendlier and pleasant sun.

The feeling was surreal. Klarke couldn't believe she was actually going home. Then she realized that she didn't have a home. The last thing Klarke had thought about was where she would lay her head. She thought it would be on a state-issued pillow behind bars for the rest of her life. Klarke's thoughts immediately changed when she fully focused her eyes. A small grin finally managed to curl on her lips. Harris, Jeva, and Breezy, along with a few members of the media, had been waiting almost two hours for her to come through those doors. The first thing that caught Klarke's attention was the bouquet of fire-red, long stemmed roses that laid across Harris's arms. She knew they were more like guilt flowers than welcome-home flowers. But she had gotten over her initial anger for Harris's caving in to the authorities. Being angry wasn't going to do anybody any good at this point.

Klarke looked up at Harris and smiled sadly. There he stood, ten years Klarke's senior and still looking just as handsome as ever. He wore his hair in a very conservative, low afro, which had a few gray hairs sprinkled throughout since the last time he had brought HJ to visit her. Harris stood five feet eleven inches and had the skin tone of mahogany. He still had pretty much the same physique he had when Klarke had met him over nineteen years ago, with the exception of the little gut that age and a slowing metabolism brought on. But he still looked good and he had been good to her during her stint in prison.

Harris had taken care of all of the children's needs and accepted every last one of her collect calls without complaint. He always made sure that HJ visited her at least once a month, sometimes twice. And like clockwork, the fifthteenth of every month, fifty dollars was put on Klarke's books. But she hadn't been surprised. After all, Harris was the same man who had paid off the balance of her truck note when it had gotten repossessed even years after they had divorced. She knew it was out of guilt more than generosity. He did start the chain of events that had led Klarke up to this point in her life. If he had been a faithful husband and kept his dick in his pants, they would still be a happy family. But nonetheless, the monthly stipend helped Klarke out tremendously.

Standing beside Harris was Breezy and next to her was Jeva. Klarke could tell that Jeva had been crying. Her nose was red and her eyeliner was smudged. But she still looked gorgeous standing there with her long wavy black hair that had been freshly permed, the blond highlights shimmering in the sun. Jeva stared at her, a huge smile covering her face, revealing her deep dimples.

Breezy was smiling as well. And also looking better than ever.

She had lost over twenty-five pounds since Klarke had been imprisoned. Each time she had visited Klarke, Klarke had complimented her on her weight loss. But even before, when she was thick, she was fine and you couldn't make her believe anything different about herself.

Breezy and Jeva were the best friends Klarke could have ever asked for. These were Klarke's girls, her road dawgz. Not only had they made sure that Klarke always had what she needed, but they visited her often and wrote her comforting letters.

Klarke stood there staring at them, completely tuning out the questions the reporters were shouting out to her.

"How does it feel to be a free woman even though your daughter is now in jail?" one reporter asked.

"Did you ever imagine being a free woman again?" another asked. But Breezy's shouting to her turned her attention away from the questions.

"Get your ass over here!" Breezy shouted. One more second of staring at Klarke and she would be crying too.

Klarke smiled then walked over to them. They all embraced.

"I'm so glad that you're back on the outside with us," Breezy said to Klarke, relieved.

"I can't believe this is real," Jeva said as she began to cry. "I can't believe you are actually here with us. Oh, Klarke. This is all so crazy."

"Believe it," Klarke said as she placed her forehead against Jeva's and wiped her tears with her thumb. "And, yes, as crazy as all this may seem, I'm here to stay."

"And here is where you belong," Harris added with a wink, then gave Klarke a small peck on the lips.

"Where's HJ?" Klarke asked Harris. "Where's my baby?"

"He's at home with Sissy," Harris replied. "They're doing a little decorating for you, but shhh, it's supposed to be a surprise."

"You ready to go home?" Breezy asked.

Klarke had not yet discussed, or even thought twice about, where she would go once released from jail. The state gave her time served and didn't penalize her any further for her false confession and she was being released without strings. Her home, the one she had lived in with Harris and the kids for thirteen years and remained in even after marrying Reo, had been sold when she was sentenced to prison.

"You can stay with me, of course," Breezy said quickly.

"Me too," Jeva said.

Harris remained silent at first, allowing his eyes to welcome Klarke to stay in his home. Then he decided to speak up. "Me too, Klarke," he said, looking into her eyes. "You can stay with us, me and the kids."

Klarke appreciated all three of their invitations and decided to take one of them up.

"I really want to see HJ," Klarke said. "So, if I could just come to your house for now, Harris, just for a little while, to spend time with HJ . . ."

"You know you don't even have to ask," Harris said.

"Thanks, Harris," Klarke said.

"Well, I guess that answers that question," Harris said, rubbing his hands together. "Shall we go?"

"Yes, we shall," Klarke said, taking Harris's arm.

They all started to walk away, then Klarke stopped in her tracks.

"Just a minute," Klarke said. She turned around and stared at the jailhouse, the building where she had laid her head for the past four years. The building that would soon hold her daughter.

Tears welled up in her eyes but she didn't let them fall. Harris put his hand on her shoulder. Klarke looked up at him then laid her head on his hand.

"It's going to be okay," Harris told Klarke, his tone reassuring and firm. "It's going to be okay. You did everything you could."

Klarke shook her head but she knew she had to be stronger than ever now. She held her head up high, blew a good-bye kiss to the building, then the four of them walked away. Reporters were still shouting questions to Klarke, only now the questions were far more harsh. They all headed toward Harris's car, but the reporters followed them.

"How could you possibly have thought that you were doing your daughter more good than harm by giving a false confession?" a FOX News reporter shouted.

"How does it feel to be a free woman?" an NBC reporter yelled.

"No comment," is all Klarke responded.

"Did you realize that you were jeopardizing the safety of the public by enabling a killer to remain on the streets?" a radio news reporter asked.

"We heard you've started receiving hundreds of letters from mothers supporting what you did for your daughter. How does that make you feel?" the same radio news reporter asked.

"No comment," Klarke said, hurrying to the car.

"Please, just give me five minutes," a CBS reporter insisted. "Did you feel guilty for raising a murderer? Is that why you took the blame? Did you see it as a type of self punishment for failing at raising a decent law-abiding citizen?"

That final question stopped Klarke in her tracks. Harris tugged at her arm and pulled her on. They all proceeded to climb into the car.

"Just one question, please," the NBC reporter insisted. "How could you protect and love a murderer?"

By this time Breezy was highly frustrated and couldn't take it anymore. "Did you hear what the hell she said?" Breezy yelled. "No muthafuckin' comment!"

They all got into Harris's Lexus and rode off, Breezy holding her middle finger up to the reporters until they were out of sight.

Breezy and Jeva had each driven their cars over to Harris's house. They all wanted to be there for Klarke upon her release from jail but thought it would be better if they all took one car.

On the ride home Klarke didn't take in the trees, the green grass, or the blue sky that most other ex-cons might have paid special attention to. Instead, she stared down at her lap and listened to Breezy and Jeva babble on and on about how they couldn't wait to go to the Cheesecake Factory as a trio like they used to. They used to make it a ritual to go to the Cheesecake Factory every third Saturday of every month, right before they went window-shopping. But this trio didn't partake in the usual window-shopping that most people did. Instead of window-shopping for the latest style in clothing or expensive furniture or jewelry, they were window-shopping for men.

Jeva and Breezy hadn't gone to the Cheesecake Factory, let alone window-shopping, since Klarke got locked up. It just didn't feel right without their partner in crime. After all, the ritual had been Klarke's idea in the first place. Although Klarke was prepared to try to get back to a normal life, cheesecake was the last thing on her mind. Her children were the first.

By the time Harris pulled the car into his driveway, Klarke was more than anxious to see her son. She damn near hopped out of the car before Harris could even put it in park. When HJ saw the car pull up he ran out of the house with Sissy close behind him.

"Mom!" HJ yelled with excitement. "Mom!"

"My baby!" Klarke said, opening her arms wide. HJ ran into her arms and covered her with kisses. "Gosh! You've grown a foot in the last month, haven't you?"

HJ was the spitting image of Harris. A handsome young fella he was indeed. He had his hair braided like Lil' Bow Wow as the sparkling diamond earrings gleamed in each ear. Klarke knew she was going to have lots of trouble with the little girls when it came to HJ.

"Oh, Mom." HJ smiled. "I'm so glad you're home. I'm so glad that you are here. I hated coming to that place to visit you. I'm so glad you're home with us."

"Yeah, me too," Sissy agreed.

"My goodness," Klarke said to Sissy. "You're so big and pretty. How old are you now?"

"I'm nine years old now," Sissy said proudly. She looked exactly like her mother, Tionne, with those big brown eyes and sugar-cone complexion. She looked like little Rudy from the *Cosby Show*.

"Can Auntie Klarke get some love?" Klarke said, opening one arm to Sissy. Sissy had always called Klarke "Auntie." That's who she grew up knowing her as. Sissy had been one year old by the time Klarke found out that not only was Sissy Tionne's, Harris's supposedly so-called cousin's, daughter, but that she was also her own husband's. It killed Klarke finding out, especially since Tionne pretended to be a friend to Klarke, not to mention a cousin to her husband. Klarke had no idea that Tionne was a fake cousin, that she was someone who had just grown up with the family and in their eyes qualified as cousin status.

This was the reason why Klarke never questioned Harris and Tionne's close relationship. This is why she never saw the affair coming. Klarke had even baby-sat Sissy on a few occasions completely unaware that the baby was Tionne and Harris's love child. When the shit hit the fan it was a mess. After weeks of not being able to pull her depressed body out of bed, Klarke finally found the will to get up out of that bed and go over to Tionne's house and beat her ass. Klarke handled it like a ghetto queen—nappy hair, shorts in freezing cold weather, and kids in the car.

Needless to say Klarke soon filed for divorce. Harris moved in with Tionne and they had been a couple all the way up to Tionne's suicide. Harris never married Tionne though. His heart still belonged to Klarke. He was addicted to her. Tionne knew this deep down. She knew that she would never fully possess Harris's heart and it drove her crazy. She was always accusing Harris of cheating on her with Klarke. No matter what Harris did or said to assure her that he wasn't, Tionne still doubted him. This played a big part in Tionne's suicide.

No matter what drama Klarke, Harris, and Tionne went through, Sissy was never mistreated. Klarke loved her before she knew the truth about her conception and she loved her all the same afterward.

"Of course you can get some love, Auntie Klarke," Sissy said in a matter of fact manner.

Sissy hugged Klarke and kissed her on the cheek. "I'm glad you came back," Sissy whispered. "I'm glad for HJ. Maybe one day my mommy will come back too."

Klarke was at a loss for words. She didn't know what to say so she just kissed Sissy on the nose and quickly changed the subject. "Any food in that house?" Klarke said. "I'm starved. I haven't had a decent meal in four years."

"I can't tell," Breezy said, smacking Klarke on her tush. "Looks like an awful lot of junk in that trunk if you ask me."

"Watch it," Klarke joked under her breath. "Felony one . . . I'll cut yo' ass."

They laughed and headed toward the house. They were glad to see that Klarke was able to joke. She hadn't lost her sense of humor.

"Mom, we got all of your favorites inside," HJ said, pulling Klarke by the hand into the house. "We got fried catfish, macaroni and cheese, greens, cornbread . . ."

"When did you learn to cook like that?" Klarke asked HJ. Before he could answer, entering the house, Klarke saw both her sisters, their husbands, and children.

"Surprise!" everyone yelled. "Welcome home" followed.

"Oh my God," Klarke said, putting her hand over her mouth. "Mahogany, Candice. I can't believe it!"

Klarke ran over to her sisters, who were standing side by side, and embraced them. The waterworks were on. The three couldn't stop crying. Klarke's sisters each lived in different states so they hadn't been all that close before Klarke went to jail, but their love was strong. Klarke's sisters, even though they were older, had always looked up to her. She was like the centerpiece of the family, especially after their father died. Klarke's own mother had passed shortly before he did.

Mahogany lived in Atlanta and Candice lived in Boston. Prior to her going to prison Klarke hadn't visited with them like she should have. That was a major regret she had while locked up. Mahogany had flown to Ohio twice to visit her in jail and Candice had visited her only once.

Candice hadn't flown in specifically to visit Klarke. Her husband's cousin, who lived in Chillicothe, Ohio, hosted a family reunion a couple of years ago. She paid Klarke a visit while she was in town. The visit was a complete surprise to Klarke and it kept her on cloud nine for weeks.

Klarke and her sisters had never been extremely close, not even as children. But that had a lot to do with the fact that they didn't grow up in the same household. Klarke only shared the same father with her sisters. Mahogany and Candice were raised in their mother's home. Klarke's father had been married to their mother before he met and married her mother. But she never referred to Mahogany and Candice as her half sisters.

"I missed you, girl," Mahogany said to Klarke.

"I've missed you too," Klarke replied. Klarke stared at her sister as if it was the last time that she'd ever see her. She couldn't take her eyes off of her. It felt surreal being there with her sisters when only hours ago she had been incarcerated. Klarke pulled Mahogany against her and squeezed her tight. Klarke then signaled for Candice to join in on the huddle. Everyone else decided to leave the room and give the sisters a moment to themselves.

After a few minutes of catching up, they rejoined everyone else and dug into the home cooking that Mahogany and Candice had prepared. Jeva had brought two dozen no-bake-cookies, Klarke's favorite dessert, and Breezy had furnished the beverages. They all ate and talked for hours.

At around nine P.M. that evening everyone started to leave. Breezy was the first to depart. She had to go home and get ready for work. Jeva followed shortly thereafter. She had an early photo shoot the next morning.

Klarke's sisters and their families left a couple of hours after that. They were booked at the Clarion hotel for the next couple of nights. They promised to return the next morning for breakfast, which they did. Harris had to work and HJ and Sissy had school, so Klarke ended up spending time with her sisters and their families alone. It was refreshing for Klarke and it kept her mind off of Vaughn. Thank goodness her sisters were there for her. But eventually they had to get back to their neck of the woods and Klarke had to face the world again, alone. It would be difficult, but Klarke prayed that she'd get through it somehow. Unbeknownst to her, it would be one bumpy-ass ride. She would need much more than a prayer.

4

QUEEN BITCH

"That fucking bitch!" Meka yelled to herself after slamming down the phone. "This is not happening. God, please tell me this is not happening. This is not right."

Meka frantically paced back and forth in her bedroom as she talked to herself out loud. Reo was showering in the connected bathroom, singing one of Mario Winan's songs off-key.

Meka was absolutely beside herself after getting the news about Klarke's release from prison.

"I can't believe that bitch is out of jail." Meka continued ranting and raving. "And it's only going to be a matter of time. I just know it."

Meka continued to pace as her blood boiled. She could feel a headache coming on. Her temples were throbbing and her neck was cramping.

"I'll bet a million dollars that she's scheming up a plan right at this very moment to try and use Junior to worm her way back into Reo's life. But what that bitch doesn't know is that I'm the queen bitch when it comes to playing dirty." A mischievous grin crept across Meka's face. "Let that bitch try to fuck with me. She might have met her match with me."

"Who might have met their match?" Reo said, catching the tail end of Meka's spiel.

"Oh shit!" Meka said, freezing in her tracks. She hadn't noticed that the shower water was no longer running. "You scared me. I thought you were still in the shower."

"You look upset and you're in here talking to yourself," Reo said, drying himself off with a towel. "Who might have met their match? Who are you talking about?"

"You're not going to believe this," Meka said. "Hell, I can't believe it." She threw her hands up in the air and began pacing.

"What is it, baby?" Reo said, becoming inpatient. "Just spit it out."

"She's out of jail. Can you believe that? They actually let that bitch out of jail. I don't care who did it. They should all be locked up if you ask me. Oh, but I guess nobody asked me. Who cares about what the mother of the murdered child thinks?"

"Calm down," Reo said, walking closer to Meka. He could see she was shaken up. He pulled her against his body to console her. "Who's out of jail? Who should be in jail? What are you talking about?"

"Oh, baby," Meka said, looking into Reo's eyes. "They let her out. They really let Klarke out of jail."

Reo was speechless. He had mixed emotions that he couldn't explain. Here it was that the woman convicted of murdering his baby four years ago was being released from jail and yet he wasn't nearly as upset as Meka. He was almost relieved. But before he allowed his emotions to get the best of him, he needed to hear all of the details.

"I don't understand," Reo said, dazed. "But she admitted to murdering our baby. She took a plea. There was supposed to be no possibility of parole. When did they let her out?"

"This morning. They said she didn't do it," Meka said. "They said it wasn't her, but that she was covering for her daughter."

"Vaughn?" Reo asked in disbelief.

"Yeah, whatever the fuck her name is."

"That's bullshit," Reo said, waving his hand. "Impossible."

"Obviously not. Even the girl's father is backing the story. Supposedly that's why he had sent her away, to cover up the lie. I guess the whole fucking family was in on it. Those idiots!" Meka shook her head.

"Whoa," Reo said, slowly walking over to the bed and sitting down on it. He couldn't believe his ears. But he should have believed his heart four years ago when Klarke was convicted of the murder. His heart kept telling him that she wasn't capable of doing such a thing, that the woman he had loved like no other woman would go to such extremes to keep a man. It was evident that a woman like herself would go to such extremes to protect someone she loved. He should have known better. He should have followed his heart instead of his head, allowing Meka's hate for Klarke to outweigh his love for her. On the same token, Reo never pegged Vaughn for doing something like that either.

"At this point, I don't know who they want us to believe killed our baby," Meka said, sitting down next to Reo. "Do you think they even know at all? This just doesn't make sense. I say Klarke admitted to it and she should stay in jail. Case closed. But no, now they've opened a whole new can of worms and that bitch is as free as a bird on the streets."

"Just who are you angry with?" Reo asked. "You seem to be more upset about Klarke being out of jail, than the fact that the real murderer of our baby is going to jail."

Meka was caught off guard by Reo's reaction to her actions. She gathered herself and changed her demeanor before replying.

"Oh, no, sweetheart." She tried to assure Reo. "It's not that. It's just that, how could she go all of this time having us believe that the person responsible for the death of our child was paying for the crime? I mean, that was our only sense of relief, as minor as it may have been. So, yes. I guess you could say I'm angry about her being released from jail. She should be punished for her part in covering up the crime. Why didn't we get a say?"

"She has been punished," Reo was quick to say as he walked over to his dresser. "She served four years and eleven days in prison. Not to mention all that she lost. All she gave up. All she had to leave behind."

Reo pulled out the top drawer and fumbled through some boxers and T-shirts.

Meka couldn't believe what she was hearing. Already Klarke had her husband on her side of the fence. Meka shook her head, stood up, and headed toward the bathroom.

"Hell," she said, throwing her hands up. "Then let the bitch walk free. I mean, like you said, she's served her time, four years and eleven days," Meka said, piercing Reo with her eyes as she entered the bathroom. "But who's counting?" She slammed the door behind her.

The loud bang shook Reo. He closed his eyes. It had been four years and eleven days that Klarke had been locked away in prison. He had been counting. Reo looked over his shoulder to confirm that Meka was still in the bathroom. He then pulled the entire dresser drawer he had been fumbling with out. Taped to the back was a letter. He carefully peeled the letter off, unfolded it, and began to read it:

Hey you,

It's been a while, eleven months and two days to be exact. I know because that's how long I've been locked up in this place.

I've been doing a lot of thinking in here. It's not like I have anything better to do. I've come to the conclusion that most people who tell a person they would die for them are full of shit. What is it with society thinking they have to say what a person wants to hear? To die for someone you would have to love them unconditionally. Every love is conditional, with the exception of God's, Jesus's, and a mother's love. Just know that if ever someone tells you they would die for you that it's more than likely a lie. They probably don't mean for it to be a lie, but it is, in fact, a lie with good intentions behind it.

Is there really such a thing as a good lie? I mean some people will lie about the weather outside. They'll tell you the sun is shining with the sound of rain and echoes of thunder in the background.

A lie makes a long story short. I guess that's why men lie to women . . . why women lie to men . . . why people lie to each other. But it's funny how a person will pick the hell out of the truth, huh? Tell someone a lie and they are more apt to roll with it. Lying is hard work though. Do you know how much energy you drain your body of and how much stress you put it through in order to tell a lie? On top of that you have to store the lie in a memory bank so that you don't slip up in the future. A born liar dies a liar.

But you know something? Sometimes lies save lives. The truth hurts so a lie is kind of like a Band-Aid on life. It covers up some foul-ass acts.

I know you have no idea what I'm trying to say. You probably think this is a bunch of jail talk. Well, that's okay. This letter wasn't meant to heal you. It was meant to free me . . . my mind anyway.

I'm hoping you don't see that this letter is from me and toss it out with the garbage before reading it. I know I agreed to let you live your

*life and raise our child as you see fit without any interference, so I
promise I will never contact you again in any form.*

*You know . . . this doesn't hurt as bad as I thought it would. The
entire time I was carrying our child I always knew that it would never
know who its natural mother is. (Look who's waiving the rights to
their child now.) You are a good man and I know you will raise the
baby to be a wonderful human being. I have no worries. Therefore I
can sleep at night and live with myself for the decision I have made.*

So I guess, in short, I just want to say thank you in advance. Until next lifetime, when our souls mate, I'll love you always!

—KAT

When Reo received that letter from Klarke, after she had been
locked up in prison for almost a year, he had no idea what it
meant. Now it all made sense. Reo closed his eyes and shook his
head. She had been trying to tell him when she wrote him that letter. If only he had read between the lines. Maybe he could have
done something. For starters, he could have been there for her.
But now it was too late. Or was it?

5

THE TOUCH OF A MAN

Harris had just taken a shower and brushed his teeth. Wearing nothing but a pair of light blue pajama pants, he headed toward his bedroom to lay down for the night. He padded down the hall in bare flat feet as he dried off his neck with the towel that was wrapped around it. As he passed by Vaughn's old bedroom he could hear a faint weeping. He paused and listened outside of the door. He could hear Klarke's weeping grow louder.

Klarke had been occupying the room for two weeks now and for two weeks Harris had heard her weeping every night when he passed the door. So many times he had balled his fist to knock on the door and ask Klarke if everything was okay, but he knew everything wasn't.

Sometimes being released from jail after so many years was harder than going to jail. Klarke had to start all over with her life, not to mention that she had a daughter in prison and a son who was almost four years old that she was estranged from. Harris didn't know what to do or say to ease Klarke's pain. But he knew he couldn't walk by that door one more night without at least trying.

"Klarke," Harris asked, knocking on the cracked door. "Is everything okay?" When Klarke failed to answer, Harris slowly opened the door.

Klarke was sitting up in the bed, balled up in a fetal position, sobbing. This sight was shocking to Harris, as he had never seen Klarke in such a vulnerable state.

"Klarke," Harris said, approaching her. Klarke cried even harder.

"My baby," Klarke said to Harris. "My baby."

Harris sat down on the bed and put his arms around Klarke. "I know it's hard," Harris said, rubbing his hand down Klarke's hair. "Vaughn is going to be okay."

"It's not just Vaughn," Klarke said, her voice muffled. Her head was pinned between her knees and her arms wrapped tight around her legs. "Harris, I have a son who doesn't know me and it's all my fault. I threw him away, Harris. And Vaughn, she doesn't have to be in jail. I shouldn't have given up. I should have tried something else to protect her. I should have gotten another attorney, one who would cooperate and corroborate my story. But I didn't, Harris. I gave up. I threw Vaughn away too. I threw my children away."

"Klarke, don't say that," Harris said firmly, pulling Klarke's face up by her chin. "You had no idea that things were going to turn out this way. You thought you were doing what was right for your children."

"It hurts, Harris," Klarke said, clutching her stomach. "It hurts so bad. It hurts so bad. I've lost two of my children."

"Oh, baby," Harris said, pulling Klarke against him. "It's okay.

I'm here for you. HJ is here for you and Sissy is too. I know we've been through so much, but I'm always going to be here for you, Klarke."

Klarke looked into Harris's eyes and warmed to the genuine caring in them. She hugged him back. Harris remembered this feeling and how he had longed for it for so long. He thought back to all the times Klarke had wrapped her arms around him when they were happily married and in love. It had been ages since she hugged him. It felt so good.

Harris squeezed Klarke tighter as he reminisced. Before he knew it he was kissing her on the head, then on her nose, her cheeks, and finally on her lips. And Klarke fully realized what she was doing. She was kissing Harris back.

It had been four years since Klarke had been touched by a man. Harris had been with a girlfriend or two since Tionne, but no one, not even Tionne, had ever made him feel the way Klarke did. As far as Harris was concerned, no woman ever would.

Holding Klarke by the face, Harris kissed her deeply and passionately. Harris pulled back and whispered, "Oh, Klarke, I love you so much." He began kissing her again as he eased her down on the bed. "Oh, Klarke. Oh, baby, I've missed touching you."

Klarke moaned as Harris's hands caressed her breasts through her nightshirt. Both of them breathing heavily, Klarke grabbed Harris by his head and pulled him tightly to her as she returned his passionate kiss.

"You feel so good," Harris said, lifting up Klarke's shirt. He placed his hand between her legs and rubbed her through her panties. He then put his hand inside her panties and stroked her clit with his index finger. He lifted his finger to his nose and inhaled deeply. "You smell good." He then sucked her juices from his finger. "And you taste so good."

Harris leaned in and took one hard nipple into his mouth and began to suck, while his right hand began to caress its way back down her stomach. He slipped his hand between her legs and thrust a finger into her. Klarke moaned at the sensation. She was so wet, Harris gasped and hardened almost to the point of pain. A pearly drop of pre-cum leaked from his penis. Klarke slid his pajama pants down and wrapped her hand around him tightly and began to stroke him.

With her clit throbbing in ecstasy Klarke pushed her panties down, out of Harris's way.

"Oh shit," Harris said. "You're so wet. You feel so good. I love you, baby. I've always loved you and I always will." He slipped her panties all the way off and tossed them aside. Then he lay on top of her and pressed himself against her.

Klarke gasped. "Oh God, you feel so good too." Klarke grabbed Harris by the waist, forcing him to thrust himself hard against her clit. She began to rock her hips against him.

Harris bent his head and gently bit her hard nipples. Klarke arched hard as he continued to rock hard against her clit. Then he pulled back and positioned the head of his penis at her opening. He stared down at her as he began to press inside her.

"Oh I love you so fucking much," Harris said, his voice tight, the look in his eyes intense.

"Oh, yes. Don't stop!" Klarke shouted out as she grabbed her ankles with her hands as Harris began to stroke inside of her.

"I won't stop," Harris said, leaning down to press his face in her neck. "Oh, I love you."

Klarke moaned, "I love you too, Reo."

Above her, Harris froze.

Klarke opened her eyes and stared up at the ceiling in horror, realizing what she had just said.

Harris's dick immediately went limp and he slowly pulled out of her and rolled off of the bed. He stood up and pulled his pajama pants back on. He refused to look at her.

"I'm so sorry," Klarke said finally. She sat up, scooped up her panties, slipped them on, and pulled the covers up over her breasts. She pulled her knees up to her chest and stared at him in misery.

"No, I'm the one who should be sorry," Harris said, still not looking at her. "I don't know what I was thinking. I didn't mean to come in here and take advantage of you . . ."

"You didn't take advantage of me, Harris," Klarke said, shaking her head. "You only came in here to comfort me and one thing led to another. That's all."

"You gonna be okay?" Harris said.

"Yeah," Klarke said softly. "I'm fine. I'm fine. You should go get some rest. You've got to be at work at six o'clock in the morning."

Harris turned and walked to the door.

"Go see your son, Klarke," Harris said as he stood in the doorway. "I don't give a damn about any agreement you signed. You have every right to know him and he has every right to know you. You are that boy's mother. So if you won't go see him for yourself, at least do it for the sake of the child."

Harris closed the door behind him, leaving Klarke to stare after him.

6

FAMILIAR TERRITORY

Klarke walked through the corridor of the all too familiar territory. The cement walls painted a terrible yellow seemed to be closing in on her. The mildew smell made her want to hunch over and vomit, but she had to be strong. Klarke held her breath, taking only small breaths every now and then to limit the intake of the stale odor.

"Phone number seven," the guard said to Klarke as he pointed and opened the door for her. Inside the door was a small strip that was no wider than the corridor she had just walked down. It looked like eight phone booths lined up against a heavy plate glass window.

"Phone?" Klarke asked, surprised. "I'm here to visit my daughter, Vaughn Bradshaw."

"Phone number seven," the guard repeated. "Stand over there and she'll be out to talk to you."

The door closed behind Klarke. She just stood there unable to take the next step. She wanted to touch Vaughn, kiss her and hold her. Not talk to her through a piece of glass.

Klarke slowly walked over to phone number seven, passing a gum poppin', project chick with her burgundy hair in a French roll that had pin curls on the side. She also had finger waves going up the front. This chick was styling at least three hairdos from what Klarke could see. She turned around to look at Klarke and smiled, grille full of silver. Klarke pleasantly gave her a half a smile in return.

Klarke stood at phone number seven for about five minutes before she saw Vaughn. Vaughn walked up to the window wearing a blue two-piece prison uniform. Her ankles were shackled. At the sight of Vaughn in prison garb, Klarke's bottom lip trembled, but she didn't break.

"Mom," Vaughn said softly with a smile after picking up the phone. Klarke wanted to reply but she couldn't. She knew that if she opened her mouth to speak she would break.

Vaughn just stared Klarke in the eyes then placed her hand on the window.

"I'm sorry, Mom." Klarke could read Vaughn's lips as her eyes watered. "I know I ruined everything, but I had to tell the truth this time. I had to, Mom."

The tears began to run down Klarke's cheeks. She placed her hand on the window against Vaughn's. She squeezed her eyes closed. This is why she refused to allow HJ to join her in visiting Vaughn. She had been telling him to be strong, but yet here she was, a broken-down mess. She didn't want her son to be a witness.

"Mom, don't cry," Vaughn said. "I'm okay. You know I can hold my own."

Klarke knew Vaughn was tough. She had always been a ball of

fire and mature for her age. It didn't matter that Vaughn had been thirteen years old the last time she had seen her and now she was seventeen. To Klarke, she was her baby. She was the same brown-eyed baby girl she had brought home from the hospital seventeen years ago.

"You look so beautiful," Klarke said, but Vaughn couldn't hear her through the glass.

"What?" Vaughn mouthed, then signaled for Klarke to pick up the phone.

Klarke picked up the phone and held it to her ear.

"I said you look so beautiful," Klarke said, with her hand still on the window against Vaughn's.

"My cell mate calls me Chante." Vaughn gave a halfhearted laugh. "She said I look like Chante Moore, the singer."

Klarke laughed with her. She paused, then took a deep breath. "This wasn't how it was supposed to turn out."

"Mom," Vaughn interrupted. "Can we not talk about all of that? I'm here now and there's nothing we can do to change it. Just pray for me, Mom."

"I pray for you every minute of the day," Klarke assured her. "I love you so much."

"If anybody knows that, it's me." Vaughn smiled. "How's HJ? What's he saying about all of this?" Vaughn now took on a more serious demeanor.

"He's okay," Klarke said. "He's gained a mother and now lost a sister so it's a little hard for him to sort out his emotions."

"Just keep him busy. Keep him occupied so that his mind stays off of things, okay, Mom?" Vaughn said in a tone that was more begging than concerned.

"Of course I will," Klarke said.

"How's Dad?" Vaughn said in sort of *why isn't he here with you* manner.

"He's, he's okay I guess," Klarke said, looking down.

"Tell him I said hey."

"I will."

"Mom?" Vaughn said, as she could see her mother was on the verge of breaking down again.

"Yes, baby?" Klarke said, taking her hand off of the glass to wipe the drippings from her nose with her knuckles, then placing it back on the glass again.

"I really am okay. I would tell you otherwise. I mean, it's not so bad really," she said bravely. "It reminds me of boarding school. The food here is even better than the cafeteria food at Challahan."

"I checked you in some items. I tried to bring you some books but they said all books must be shipped directly from the publisher."

"What books were they?" Vaughn asked curiously.

Klarke dug in her large shoulder bag, pulled out the small paperbacks, and read them off.

"I heard *The Coldest Winter Ever* was pretty good," Vaughn said. "*Please Tell Me if The Grass Is Greener* sounds interesting."

"Yeah, well, I guess I'm just going to have to order them from the publisher to be shipped to you."

"Thanks, Mom," Vaughn said. "What size underwear did you get me? Do you know the only underwear a chick has up in here are the ones she wore in unless somebody brings her some or she steals them?"

"Vaughn," Klarke said. "You don't have to keep making conversation. Silence is okay. Let me just look at you. It's been so long since I've seen you."

Klarke took in every feature of Vaughn's face. It had to last her until the next time she could visit her. Klarke imagined combing Vaughn's hair into long silky ponytails like she had done when she was a little girl. Klarke remembered helping Vaughn brush her teeth when she was just a tot and teaching her to tie her shoes. The craziest moments floated through Klarke's mind as she stared at her beautiful child who had grown into a beautiful woman.

Now when Klarke looked at Vaughn she saw herself. She saw someone just as strong willed. She saw a survivor.

A guard called to Vaughn that her visiting time was up.

Vaughn sighed. "Looks like it's time."

"Oh, baby," Klarke said, putting her hand back up against the glass.

"It's okay, Mom," Vaughn said, smiling sadly, putting her hand up against the glass as well.

Klarke could tell that Vaughn wasn't just trying to make her feel better. She was being true.

"I love you, baby girl," Klarke said into the receiver.

"I love you too."

Vaughn hung up the phone and turned away. At the door leading back to the cells, she turned around and winked at Klarke. Klarke smiled and watched her walk away.

Klarke's visit with Vaughn eased her mind to some degree. She hadn't witnessed a frightened little girl, but a strong young woman instead. Klarke hung up the phone and got up to leave.

Perhaps, now with some peace of mind about Vaughn's wellbeing, maybe Klarke would be able to stop crying at night. But there was just one more order of business she had to fulfill. And knowing what Klarke was up against, she feared that this one wouldn't end so well at all.

7

WINDOW-SHOPPING

Although Klarke's visit with Vaughn had eased her mind to some degree, she still found it difficult to function on the up and up every day. She had her moments. Breezy and Jeva made many failed attempts to get her mind off of things. They tried to get her out of the house by inviting her to the movies, the club, the gym, etc. . . . But Klarke always declined.

Breezy had finally put her foot down by not excepting no for an answer.

"Look, bitch, you been moping around that house for too damn long now," Breezy said to her over the phone. "You're free now and there's nothing you can do about it. I know you probably think that that's mean of me to say, but somebody has to tell your ass the truth and who better to do it than a girlfriend. You ain't did shit with your hair. You wear the same damn outfit every day. If

I see you in that gray sweat suit one more time, I swear to God. And damn it, girl, your ribs are starting to show. Eat something, for crying out loud!"

Klarke allowed for a faint smile to appear on her face. That damn Breezy never was one to bite her tongue. You either loved her because of her openness and fly-ass mouth, or you hated her because of her openness and fly-ass mouth. Either way it went, Breezy didn't give a fuck. She was going to do Breezy regardless. But Klarke loved her.

"Girl, I just can't get motivated," Klarke said.

"Motivated to do what? I ain't asking your ass to run a marathon. I'm just asking you to breathe again. Can you do that for me, Toni Braxton?"

Klarke laughed. She hadn't laughed since her visit with Vaughn. It felt good.

"You are stupid?" Klarke said.

"I'll be that. But, back to what I called you for. You know what this Saturday is, right?"

"No, what is it?"

"It's the third Saturday of the month, hoe," Breezy joked. "Now don't get to acting stupid and make me come up over there. You know dang on well it's the third Saturday of the month and it's going to start being just like old times. Jeva and I are not taking no for an answer."

"Breezy," Klarke said tiredly.

"Breezy my ass. That gives you two days to get *motivated*."

Klarke remained silent.

"Hello, anybody there?" Breezy asked.

"I hear you, damn it."

"All right then. It's a date. Same place. Same time. See you there." Breezy hung up before Klarke could make one last attempt to decline. Klarke hung up the phone and smiled. She had missed spending time with her best friends. There were so many nights that she had laid in her cell dreaming about being able to spend time with them just like old times. Life is too short and unpredictable. Her dream had finally come true and Klarke decided to take advantage of it.

It was the third Saturday of the month, which meant window-shopping time for Klarke, Jeva, and Breezy. Same as they always had, the women planned on meeting at the usual spot, the Cheesecake Factory. There was even discussion about catching a movie as well. They had each gotten plenty of rest the night before to prepare for their long day together. The trio had spent an hour on the phone planning out their wardrobes from their shoes down to their jewelry. They were like teenage girls preparing for the first day of high school.

The women had truly been looking forward to their first time out together in four years. Window-shopping had always been a form of therapy for them. It was the time they dedicated solely to providing company for one another's misery. They chatted about men, money, and have-nots. Usually, by the end of the day, one had felt that the others were far worse off than she was. After an afternoon of window-shopping, their own problems didn't seem so bad anymore.

They had a lot of catching up to do so time was definitely on their side as was the weather. The sun lit up the sky like a candle in a pitch-black room. There didn't look to be a sign of rain within a fifty-state radius. The sky appeared to be just that clear. But just in case, they had already decided that if it were to rain, that they would postpone their outing until Sunday. Dodging raindrops, staining an outfit, and ruining a perfectly styled hairdo was a no-no. Clear skies played the number one role in window-shopping.

One would have thought that these women melted in the rain because even a sprinkle would keep them from hitting the mall. It was as if the weather determined the mood of the day and the attitudes the women would carry with them. But as always, Mother Nature had their backs.

Klarke was the one who had had the hardest time deciding what to wear. Almost every stitch of clothing she had ever owned had been donated to the Salvation Army upon her going to jail. Klarke had given Harris power of attorney in order for him to put her house on the market. Harris packed up the house and its contents and put it up for sale. He saw to it that Breezy and Jeva got the opportunity to come to the house and pick out some items for memory's sake. All of Klarke's jewelry, as well as the miniature elephants she had collected over the years, were placed in a safe-deposit box for Vaughn. Harris had packed everything else up and sat it curbside for pickup. Neighbors and passersby claimed several items for themselves before the Salvation Army truck arrived.

The house sold after being on the market for only two months. Harris set up an account for Vaughn and HJ's education with the proceeds from the sale. Now that Klarke was out of jail, Harris turned over the bank account to her. The house had sold for $175,000, but there was only $100,000 in the account. Harris hadn't mishandled a penny nor had he spent a dime on himself. He had only used the money to pay for Vaughn's boarding school tuition. He had planned on exhausting the entire account with Vaughn and HJ's college tuition fees.

Klarke planned on handling the money just as wisely. But, without a doubt, she had to dip into it to get her wardrobe together. She had already dipped into it to purchase a nice little used Hyundai Sonata that she found to be quite fashionable. God, family, career, and fashion was Klarke's priority list. Even in prison Klarke concerned herself with her appearance. She always made sure that not a hair was out of place, that her lips were moist with lip gloss and that her clothing fit to compliment her nice figure, unlike some of the other inmates who preferred to wear their clothing baggy and their hair in nappy ponytails or raggedy braids. Klarke had always had a wonderful sense of fashion since her teen years, but at thirty-nine, she knew she would have to pay just as much and more attention to her appearance. Under no circumstance would she ever fit the middle-age-woman stigma. So Klarke planned on doing a little more than just window-shopping in order to replenish her closet with the latest fashions.

Breezy had her thoughts set on making a purchase or two herself. The purchase of a quality, expensive outfit here and there was nice, but a good pair of shoes and a handbag was a genuine treat. For most of her adulthood, Breezy had always loved buying nice things, but not with her own dime. That's the role men had always played in her life. But after her tragedy with Guy, the married man she was dating and then blackmailing, she was more than glad to reach down in her own purse and pay her own way.

She could have never imagined in her worst nightmare how using a man for his money could turn her life upside down. When Guy decided to throw Breezy out like yesterday's news to be more attentive to his wife, Breezy's anger got the best of her. She threatened to tell Guy's wife everything about them right down to the abortion she had with his child. When Guy saw that Breezy meant business and was willing to destroy his life with his wife and children, he gave in to her demands, promising to provide her with a nice monthly allowance to at least cover her rent. And she didn't even have to come up off any pussy. The entire scheme backfired and eventually led to Guy being jailed for the murder of Breezy's father. It was like salt in a wound for Breezy. Her father had only been out of prison for a month or so after serving a fifteen-year sentence, a jail term that he would have never have had to serve if it weren't for her. Upon release from prison he moved in with Breezy. He ended up taking a bullet that was meant for Breezy. It ate Breezy up, knowing that she would never be able to tell him the truth.

In Breezy's freshman year of college, after turning up pregnant by a boy she had been dating named Judge, Breezy told her father that he had raped her. She was scared and didn't know what else to do so she felt she had to lie. Telling her daddy that she was pregnant broke his heart. Breezy couldn't be the cause of that so she thought quickly and cried wolf. She had no idea that her father would play judge and jury and shoot the accused in the head, instantly killing him. Her father would be found guilty of the vigilante killing and sentenced twenty-five years to life. And all of this stemmed from Breezy's dishonesty.

Years went by before Breezy ever told a single soul. The demons taunted her so she finally confided her dirty little secret to Jeva, who convinced her to tell her father the truth. The day Breezy was prepared to tell her father the truth about her pregnancy in college was the day she found him murdered. Breezy was devastated. She had no one else to blame but herself, although she managed to find room to blame her mother as well.

Her mother had divorced her father while he was incarcerated. This added to the grief. Breezy's relationship with her mother had been estranged ever since the divorce. That's pretty much why she was so close with Klarke and Jeva. Their female companionship made up for and was a distraction from that which she missed having with her mother. And with Klarke having been away, Jeva soon became the center of Breezy's attention. And a good friend she had been indeed.

Jeva was the most caring friend anyone could have asked for. She was a little on the dizzy side, but she was sincere in her friendships.

That's why Breezy was especially anxious to spend the day with the best girlfriends in the world.

In final preparations for the day's window-shopping event, Jeva had gone to the gym early in the morning in hopes of fitting a little more comfortably into the blue floral chiffon dress she had planned on wearing. After breaking up with her fiancé, Lance, Jeva had picked up a few extra pounds, twenty to be exact. She treated her daughter, Heather, and indulged herself, in shopping and food to keep their mind off of him. Whenever Heather asked about the man she knew as Daddy, the more shopping or eating they did. The questions about Daddy were soon replaced with the latest Baby Phat gear or Barbie gadget.

The more Jeva ate, the more she had to shop to accommodate her increasing figure. She went from a size four to a size ten easily. Since she stood only five feet tall, the extra weight couldn't be hidden. Eventually Jeva joined a gym and got right back into her size fours. Exercising made her feel healthy and good inside which made her look just as good on the outside. She wanted that feeling to last so she maintained her membership at the gym even after she shed her body of those twenty extra pounds. And boy had it paid off. She looked better than ever. If only that damn Lance could see her now.

Jeva had been with Lance for six years before they broke up. He had been the only father her now ten-year-old daughter had known. Actually, as far as the rest of the world was concerned, Lance was Heather's father. Before Jeva became a photographer she made her money as a stripper. She met Lance one night in the club she was dancing at. She was almost three months pregnant when she met him. Lance had only come into the club that night to celebrate one of his friend's birthdays. He had no idea he was going to fall for one of the dancers.

The two dated outside of the club and formed a relationship. It just so happened that he was in the process of buying a new home when she met him. After only two months of knowing one another, Jeva moved in with Lance. He had been living with his mother up until then.

By the time Lance closed on the house and moved Jeva in with him, he was well aware of her pregnancy and that there was no possible way the baby was his. But Lance could have cared less. By then, he was head over heels in love with Jeva. She was absolutely beautiful with her long straight black hair that hung down to her butt. Her dark brown slanted bedroom eyes were what hypnotized Lance in the first place. And those deep-pitted dimples made her look like a happy little schoolgirl that he couldn't wait to get home and spank. Any man in the club that night would have been happy to have this exotic, half-Caucasian and half-Hispanic (Colombian) *mami* on their arm. But Lance went home with the "W" that night and a proud winner he was, up until the time his mother and boys talked about his ass for falling for a stripper. So Lance soon went from wanting to be Jeva's husband to just being her husbfriend.

Lance was working as a maintenance man and was receiving health benefits. He and Jeva agreed that he would tell his insurer that the baby she was carrying was his so that the medical bills would be taken care of. It was their private deal. They never told anyone. At the time, Jeva didn't know Klarke or Breezy, but even once she met them and became close friends, she still never whispered a word. Although girlfriends tell one another everything, there is always that one thing that they keep buried deep within them. Some things are simply better left untold. Jeva hated that she could never share that one issue with her friends. Sometimes it would bother her and put her in a funk, but she had to fight it out with her own conscience.

Being adopted herself and being deprived of knowing her own

biological parents, Jeva feared that no one, not even her best friends, would understand her turning around and putting her daughter through almost the same predicament. Jeva had nightmares of her daughter ending up on talk shows searching for her biological father.

All of the women's past blues and heartaches were just that, the past. They made a pact to move forward in life, beginning with their first window-shopping outing. Back in the day, window-shopping was just that, window-shopping. The women were looking because they had no money . . . looking for men with money, that is. But with all of the drama these women had been through with the opposite sex, men were the last thing on their minds. At least that's what they wanted one another to believe. But their true agendas would soon surface.

Breezy and Jeva had arrived at the Cheesecake Factory promptly at the agreed-upon meeting time, 11:30 A.M. Klarke arrived about ten minutes thereafter. Yep, it was just like old times. Being fashionably late was Klarke's forte. She had always purposely arrived late to make sort of a grand entrance. The girls had long gotten used to her personal habit. Breezy and Jeva didn't mind though. This gave them a chance to put their name on the waiting list to be seated. Usually by the time Klarke arrived they hadn't even been seated yet. Saturday brunch was one of the busiest days for the Cheesecake Factory so a fifteen-minute wait was always expected. Just as Klarke had come waltzing into the restaurant wearing some Old Navy drawstring capri khakis that tied just bellow her calf and a pink three-quarter-sleeve snap-button tee, their table had been prepared for them.

"Williams, party of three," the host called out to the dozen or so folks waiting to be seated.

"Right here," Breezy answered, waving her hand.

"Follow me please," the host said.

Klarke, Breezy, and Jeva followed behind the host to a booth in the rear section of the restaurant.

"Ladies, Holli will be your waitress today and she'll be right with you to take your drink orders," the host said as she handed the women each a menu and turned to walk away.

"Excuse me," Jeva said to the host. "By any chance do you have a waiter named Chauncy that works here?"

The host thought for a second and replied, "No, I don't believe we have a waiter by that name."

"Okay," Jeva said, slightly disappointed as the host walked away. "Just checking."

"Cheer up, sad sack," Breezy said, winking at Jeva.

"I just wanted everything to be just like it used to be right down to our regular waiter, Chauncy."

"I'm just glad to be sitting here with you two and not with Belina the Butch." Klarke laughed and Breezy and Jeva joined in with her.

"Were you fighting the dykes off, Klarke?" Breezy asked.

"Breezy!" Jeva exclaimed, closing her eyes.

"What?" Breezy replied. "She's out now. We can talk about it."

"Talk about what?" Klarke asked before their waitress came over and interrupted.

"Hi, I'm Holli and I'm your server," she said in the perky white girl cheerleader voice that she was. "Can I start you ladies off with something to drink?"

"Yes," Breezy said. "And we already know what we want to order."

The waitress proceeded to take the women's drink and food orders, then left them to continue their conversations.

"Okay, Bria Nicole Williams," Klarke said sternly to Breezy. "What was it you were saying?"

"Nothing," Jeva answered for her.

"Girl, stop tripping," Breezy said, snapping her neck. "We've been dying to find out just how much coochie bumpin' goes on in a women's prison."

"You are a freak," Klarke said, looking around to make sure no one was dippin' and dappin' into their conversation.

"Seriously," Breezy continued. "I mean, now that you're out, you can tell us all of the dirty deeds that go on behind bars."

"I don't know what you're talking about." Klarke played stupid as the waitress sat her Shirley Temple down in front of her and gave Breezy and Jeva their ice waters with lemon.

"Your meals will be right out," the waitress said, walking away.

"Come on, Klarke. You can tell us," Breezy said, licking her lips. "Did you get . . . umm . . . let's say . . . satisfied while you were in the clink?"

"Breezy!" Klarke blushed.

"Stop playing," Breezy ordered. "Getting your pussy licked is getting your pussy licked. When it comes to that, it don't matter who's doing the lickin'."

"Okay, that's enough." Klarke laughed.

"I can't believe you," Jeva said, almost embarrassed.

"Did you get your carpet nibbled on or not?" Breezy asked, rolling her eyes.

Klarke rolled her tongue against her jaw and took a sip of her Shirley Temple.

"I knew it, I knew it!" Breezy said.

Just then a tray of food was placed beside their table. Jeva's order was placed down in front of her first.

"Thank you," Jeva said, looking up. She couldn't believe her eyes when she saw who had carried their trays out. "Chauncy!"

"That would be me," Chauncy said with a crooked smile, one partial dimple appearing.

"I asked the host if they had a waiter named Chauncy and she said no," Jeva said, touching Chauncy's hand.

"Well, they don't," Chauncy said, proudly straightening his tie. "I'm the general manager now. I'm in charge of all of this." Chauncy put his hands up and looked around the restaurant.

"Congratulations," each of the women said to Chauncy.

"That's wonderful." Jeva blushed. Jeva had always found Chauncy to be a cutie pie, but whenever she mentioned these feelings, Klarke and Breezy were quick to remind her that he was just a waiter. What lifestyle could he possibly have provided for Jeva as a waiter?

"Thank you," Chauncy said with a bow. "I missed seeing you girls."

"Sure you did," Breezy said, popping a piece of popcorn shrimp in her mouth from the plate Chauncy had laid in front of her. "You missed our tips."

"That too." Chauncy winked. "But anyway, I'm glad to see you all again." Chauncy turned to Klarke. "I read in the newspaper about your release. I'm sorry about your daughter. I'm sure the circumstances make it difficult for you to embrace your freedom. Nonetheless, I'm honored to serve you today. Ladies, this one is on the house."

"In that case," Breezy said, damn near choking on a French fry, "screw this ice water. Can a sistah get a glass of wine?"

Chuckling, Chauncy replied, "I'll see to it that your table gets a bottle of our best wine. And again, it's good seeing you ladies back in our establishment."

Chauncy winked at Jeva and walked away.

"I can hardly believe you did that," Jeva said to Breezy. "The man was giving us our meal free and you go begging for wine."

"Closed mouths don't get fed," Breezy said, dipping her fork into Jeva's plate, scooping up a bite of her baked potato. "Sometimes if you don't speak, then you don't eat."

"Oh, Breezy." Klarke laughed. "I love you."

"And I love you right back," Breezy said, puckering her lips and making a kissing motion. Just then their server brought over a bottle of merlot and poured each of the ladies a glass.

"Raise 'em up, girls," Breezy said, lifting her glass to toast. "To window-shopping."

"To window-shopping," Klarke and Jeva said as the ladies clinked glasses.

The women demolished the entire bottle of wine. Laughing, talking, and buzzing through the entire meal. Chauncy had even sent their waiter back to the table with a second bottle of wine, which the women declined. They already had to walk off the bottle they had just drunk so that they would be able to drive at the end of the day. One more drink and they wouldn't have been able to walk, let alone drive.

"Y'all ready to fly this coop?" Klarke said, sucking up that last sip of her Shirley Temple.

"Yeah, let's do the damn thang," Breezy said, unbuttoning the top button of her white Guess jeans, then untucking her Guess T-shirt to pull down over her unbuttoned pants. "After about an hour of walking through the mall I should be able to snap my pants up again."

"We know damn well we wasn't supposed to eat that much food," Jeva said, rubbing her stuffed belly.

"Fuck it!" Breezy said. "We gettin' too old to worry about struttin' down the mall like peacocks. Face it, ladies, it's time to waddle like turkeys."

"You stupid." Klarke laughed. "Let's stop off at the ladies' room, then head out."

"You guys go ahead," Jeva said. "I can't move. Give me five minutes."

Klarke and Breezy went to the ladies' room and touched up their makeup. They met Jeva back at the table.

"You ready, girly?" Breezy said to Jeva.

"Readier than ever," Jeva said with a huge smile. "Let's go."

The three each left a ten-dollar tip. Since the meal was free, it only seemed fair to splurge on the tip. They waved at Chauncy, who was handling business at the bar, and thanked him for the free meal.

"I guess it's time to go look at things we won't be taking home with us," Jeva said.

"Actually," Klarke said, "I need to do more than window-shop. I actually need to take some things home. I don't have any clothes."

"And it's time for my monthly pair of shoes," Breezy said. "I need something to match this bag."

"That purse is gorgeous," Klarke said, referring to Breezy's Louis Vuitton backpack. "I want to work where you work if your salary permits a Louis Vuitton budget."

"Chile, please," Breezy replied. "This is a knockoff. I got it at a purse party last year. It damn near looks like the real thing though. It's hard telling the difference between a fake Louis and a real one."

"That girl spends so much money on fake Louis, Prada, Gucci, and Coach purses that she could have just gotten real ones by now," Jeva added. "I mean she literally has a graveyard of knock-off purses with stitching unraveling and whatnot. They have a two-year life, tops."

"I'd rather have a choosing of several knockoffs than two or three real ones. You know I prefer a lot of something to keep me happy rather than just one of something to give me part-time bliss," Breezy said in her defense. "Not all of us have trust funds to live off of."

"I have a job, thank you," Jeva said, rolling her eyes.

"You go to the park here and there and take pictures of birds," Breezy said. "That's a hobby. Now running off to star-filled award shows and shit to take pictures, that was a job."

"I just shot the cover for *Toledo Magazine*, thank you very much," Jeva said. "I was up at the crack of dawn shooting photos of that damn Victoria Secret model. That was work, sweetheart."

"Forget the purse," Klarke said, becoming agitated by Breezy and Jeva's debate. "I see nothing has changed while I was gone. Whatever did you two do without me here to referee you?"

"Believe me, you don't want to know," Breezy said in a mischievous tone. "You really don't want to know."

As the women strolled through the mall they came upon Nordstrom. Nordstrom had always been Breezy's favorite store for shoes.

"Nordstrom is having a twenty-percent-off shoe sale," Breezy said. "You know I'm a shoe diva so let's head on over there."

Breezy led the way into Nordstrom. The shoe department was right there at the entrance so Breezy dove in as Klarke and Jeva looked around the shoe selection also.

Breezy quickly fell in love with a pair of Etienne Aigners and a pair of Anne Kleins. She had a hard time deciding between the two. Klarke and Jeva were no help with their indecisive asses. Cost was usually the deciding factor, but both pairs had the same sticker price, one hundred and seven dollars. Her monthly shoe budget was a hundred dollars and she had done well at never going over her budget. This time would be no different. After a game of enee meene minee moe and I struck a match and it went out, Breezy chose the Etienne Aigners.

After making her selection, Breezy went and stood in line. She waved down Klarke and Jeva who joined her.

"Let me see what you got," Klarke said to Breezy. Klarke admired the shoes.

"Aren't you going to buy some shoes too?" Breezy asked Klarke. "You said you had to hook your wardrobe up. Shoes make an outfit, suga."

"Oh, I plan on getting shoes," Klarke replied. "But not from here. Even on sale, these shoe prices are out of my range. Take me to Payless." Klarke wasn't cheap or flashy. She was reasonable. Wanting big things with little money is what started the chain of disaster in her establishing her relationship with Reo. Klarke didn't allow fate to unite her and Reo, no, she just had to add her two cents to God's dime.

During the time Klarke pursued Reo, his name had been in every newspaper, magazine, and on every talk radio and television program, including *Oprah*. His book sales were record-breaking and were being optioned as movies. While Klarke was in prison, one of his books had even made its way to the big screen, *The Root of All Evil*. Klarke would sit and imagine being the wife of this bestselling author, being showered with diamonds and pearls. Never having to work for peanuts another day in her life. But what were the odds of her meeting him? She took it upon herself to increase the odds.

Klarke started out by doing her own research on Reo. Before he got his book deal with a major publishing house, he had self-published. He had been a client of the book-printing company that Klarke worked for at the time, Kemble and Steiner. She got all of his personal information from his customer file, which included a credit application. His private email information was on one of the forms. Although it seemed far-fetched at the time, Klarke came up with a plan that she knew would work. She sent

Reo an email pretending to be someone he had met in a Boston airport. From Reo's viewpoint, the email was accidentally sent to him, but instead of just deleting the email or letting the sender know that she had the wrong email address, Reo played a game of cyber charades, pretending to be that person in the Boston airport. One thing led to another and before Klarke knew it, she was saying "I do" to Reo in a beautiful, intimate, Las Vegas wedding. She never thought in her wildest dreams that Reo would ever find out, but during the investigation of the murder of his baby, the issue was brought to light. The same day Reo found out about Klarke's scheme was the same day Klarke found out about Vaughn's connection to the baby's murder. When Klarke saw the look in Reo's eyes she knew she had lost her man forever, so confessing to the murder was that much easier.

The saying that the love of money is the root of all evil proved valid. Klarke's obsession to achieve the means to live a cozy lifestyle took over her life. She centered all of her attention on roping in Reo, so much that she never even noticed how the entire situation with Reo's baby's mama drama was affecting her daughter. That's why Klarke vowed never to get caught up in the material world again. And if that meant passing up a pair of Nordstrom pumps, then so be it.

"If Star Jones can wear Payless, then so can I," Klarke joked.

"Now you know Star Jones don't wear no Payless shoes," Jeva said.

"She said that she does," Breezy said. "And big girls don't lie."

When it was finally Breezy's turn in line, she handed her shoebox to the nice-looking gentleman at the register. At first he only looked like a familiar face to Breezy, but she soon realized where she knew him from.

"Did you find everything you need?" the clerk said pleasantly, taking the shoebox from Breezy. Before Breezy could answer he looked up at her and immediately recalled his last encounter with her. His entire demeanor changed. No longer the nice helpful clerk, he smacked his lips and flopped the shoebox down on the counter and proceeded to ring up the shoes.

"You again," Breezy said, recognizing the clerk as some gay guy she had gotten into a bit of a tiff with way back when while shopping in Nordstrom with Klarke and Jeva.

"Um," the clerk said, snapping his neck. "You took the words right out of my mouth. *Anyway* . . . your total is ninety dollars and seventy-one cents."

Breezy looked at Klarke and Jeva with a "Can you believe this?" look in her eye. She took the Louis Vuitton backpack off of her back, unzipped the outer pouch, and pulled out a hundred-dollar bill. After snapping the crisp bill, she handed it to the clerk with her index and middle finger, then rolled her eyes.

The clerk snatched the hundred-dollar bill, then held it up to the light and examined it. He took a special marker from off of the register and ran it across the bill. Once again he held it up to the light to examine it.

All of the onlookers in line were looking at Breezy like she possibly could have been trying to pass a counterfeit bill. Breezy was embarrassed and pissed. "Is all that fuckin' necessary?" Breezy shouted. "Aren't you taking your job just a little too seriously? I mean it's not like if it were a counterfeit bill that they are going to take it out of your paycheck. I'm sure they'll still pay you minimum wage regardless."

"Hold up, Miss Thing," the clerk said with hands on hips, eyes closed, and head wobbling. "You are way out of line. I am simply doing my job."

"Well maybe you need to get a life or get a new job because it is not that serious," Breezy said. "Why are you still working in a shoe store after all of these years anyway? Who are you, Al Bundy?"

Klarke and Jeva, who would normally be embarrassed by Breezy's fly-ass mouth, busted out laughing.

"No, Miss Thing did not just try to go there," the clerk said.

"Try to go there," Breezy huffed. "I'm gone. Went there and now I'm back."

"Well, I'll have you know that I do take my job very seriously. And part of my job is to make sure that I don't receive counterfeit currency," the clerk said, looking down at Breezy's backpack. "And I figured since you pulled this hundred-dollar bill out of that fake-ass Louis Vuitton bag, that the money you pulled out of it was fake too."

Once again Klarke and Jeva fell out laughing.

"You know what, Chante?" Breezy said to the clerk.

"It's Shasta," the clerk said, pointing at his badge. "Read the name tag. Shasta. S-H-A-S-T-A."

"Oh, pardon me, Shasta," Breezy said, being sarcastic. "But like I was getting ready to say, that comment you just made, the fake bag, the fake money."

"Yeah, and?" the clerk said to Breezy, staring her down.

Breezy stared him down right back, paused, then let out a sigh of defeat. "I'm gon' give you that one. You got me on that. The 'w' is yours. I bow out gracefully."

The clerk looked at Breezy, then cracked a smile. "Girlfriend, that Al Bundy comment was cute too. Not as lovely as my comment, but cute."

The clerk placed the hundred-dollar bill in the cash register and handed Breezy her change. He bagged up her shoes and handed them to her.

"Please come again," the clerk said with a diva wink.

Klarke and Jeva laughed their way out of the store. This was definitely the highlight of the day. As the women exited the store, Klarke managed to control her laughter long enough to say something to Breezy and Jeva that had been on her mind.

"I have something I've been meaning to say to you two," Klarke said.

"Okay, but can we sit down right here on this bench?" Breezy said. "My dogs are killing me."

Breezy and Jeva sat down and Klarke stood up in front of them. Breezy took off one of her shoes and began rubbing her feet through her trouser socks.

"I just want to thank you both for looking out for me the last four years." Klarke spoke softly. "I know I never expressed it before, but I really appreciated everything y'all did for me while I was locked up. The letters, the toiletries, the visits, accepting all those collect calls."

"You are our girl," Breezy said. "What did you expect?"

"I know," Klarke said. "But when you are down and out, you find out who your true friends really are."

"We know you'd do the same for us," Jeva said, putting her hand out.

"Thanks," Klarke said, taking her hand. "And, Jeva, thanks for using up tons of VCR tapes recording all those television shows for me, even though I couldn't use them."

"I can't believe she actually thought you had a VCR in your cell and could just pop in a tape at your leisure," Breezy said, sucking her teeth.

"Well, I didn't know," Jeva said in her defense. "They have cable so I figured they had VCRs too."

"Looks like your kind deed wasn't in vain after all," Klarke said, dropping Jeva's hand. "If you still have them I'd like to see what I missed out on."

"Sure, Klarke," Jeva said, looking over at Breezy, giving her a smug look. "You know I record everything anyway."

"But, anyway," Klarke continued. "I just wanted to say thanks. I don't know how I would have ever survived in the joint."

"You knew you could count on us," Jeva said. "You can always count on us."

"And if not us, you knew Harris was going to be there for you," Breezy added.

"Yeah, he kept my books up. At least fifty dollars a month faithfully," Klarke said.

"You all the way in the clink and he still trying to trick. Girl, you know you got to give him some now that you're out?"

"Breezy," Jeva said, shocked by her candidness. Breezy's mouth was something you never got used to.

"You are so bad. You aren't ever going to change, are you?" Klarke smiled at Breezy.

"Bad girl for life," Breezy said with a wink. "But don't be trying to change the subject. You're coming off of a four-year drought. Your kitty got to be purring."

"Granted, Harris has been there for me through thick and thin," Klarke said. "But that's over now. Besides, I've contacted a real-estate agent and I'm going to go look at a few places next week, which means I need to go job hunting also. I can't live off of that money from the sale of the house forever. So, I'll be out living on my own before you know it."

"Yeah, but you could be staying with Breezy or me temporarily," Jeva said.

Klarke was at a loss for words. Jeva was right. Why in the hell was she living up in Harris's house? Yeah, she wanted to spend time with HJ, but she could do that at Breezy or Jeva's house just as easily.

"Look, you do what you need to do to take care of your business," Breezy said. "No matter whose roof you are living under, handle yours. You have a daughter and two sons to worry about."

There was instant silence. Breezy closed her eyes, realizing what she had just said. Jeva looked down and sucked in her lips.

Neither wanted to witness the despondent expression on Klarke's face.

"Sorry, Klarke," Breezy said.

"It's okay," Klarke lied.

"You gotta do something," Jeva said, taking a chance at crossing the line. "You do have two sons. I don't care what kind of document you signed. I know you, Klarke. I know how much you love what's yours. I can't see you living happily ever after while living only two hours from a son that you can't see."

"I know. But what do I do?" Klarke replied as she squeezed in between Breezy and Jeva and sat down.

"Well, first you are going to have to get around that Meka character," Jeva said. "I'm sure she's still buzzing around like a buzzard trying to sink her claws into Reo."

"Forgive me for saying this, but Vaughn killed the wrong person," Breezy said.

Klarke's eyes widened and her mouth dropped open.

"I'm sorry," Breezy said. "I've been trying to work on that 'think before I speak' thing for years, but it just don't work for me."

"This is a sensitive matter for Klarke," Jeva said. "So maybe you should work on it a little harder."

"I said I'm sorry, damn!" Breezy said.

Klarke watched Breezy and Jeva go back and forth like an old married couple.

"But anyway, back to what we were talking about," Jeva said. "Klarke, you've got to talk with Reo. With the truth surfacing, he's got to understand that you only made the choices that you made out of love. He has to let you see your son."

"That's what Harris said too," Klarke said.

"You talked to him about it?" Breezy asked in surprise.

"I live with the man, of course we talk," Klarke snapped.

"Looks like I pushed a hidden button," Breezy said, rolling her eyes. "Wonder if I'm the only one pushing your buttons."

Klarke rolled her tongue against her jaw and looked up, pretending to ignore Breezy. But they saw right through her.

"You hoe," Breezy said, nudging Klarke with her elbow. Klarke tried to keep a serious mug, but a smile crept through. "You fucked Harris. You fucked him."

"Shhh," Klarke said, putting her index finger over her lips. "You trying to tell the entire mall my business? And besides, I didn't really fuck him."

"Did he stick it in?" Breezy demanded to know.

"It wasn't like that," Klarke said.

"Did he penetrate, damn it?" Breezy insisted on knowing.

"Will you just let me explain?" Klarke said.

"Oh, my God, Jeva," Breezy said, putting her hand over her mouth. "She's been holding out on us. This hoochie thinks she's Peaches and that Harris is Herb. They reuniting and shit and she ain't said a word."

"Will you relax?" Klarke said. "Will you stop jumping to conclusions like you're auditioning for a role on *Three's Company*? We didn't do it. I mean, yes, he stuck it in, but I couldn't. I couldn't do it, y'all. My body doesn't crave him."

"Just who does it crave?" Jeva asked.

"Does it matter?" Klarke said, standing up. "I'm tired of sitting here. Come on, let's go."

Breezy picked up her Nordstrom bag and stood up.

"Wait a second," Jeva said, digging in her purse. "Let me put some lip gloss on real quick." As Jeva dug down in her purse a Cheesecake Factory business card fell out and onto the ground. "Ooops," Jeva said, hurrying to grab it.

"I'll get it," Breezy said, beating Jeva to the punch by scooping up the card. "Chauncy's cell, Chauncy's home in Chauncy's handwriting," Breezy said as though she was a teacher reading a lesson plan. "So this is why you didn't want to join us in the ladies' room."

It was starting to become clear to Breezy that Jeva's plans for the day had included a little more than just window-shopping too.

8

SPEAK OF THE DEVIL

Reo sat in his study at his desk typing at his computer. His agent had suggested that he start working on his autobiography. As hard as it was for Reo to pen some of the most painful issues his life had entailed, it was also a form of therapy for him. And that's why he was so quick to oblige. Since his wife had been a major part of his life way back since high school, he often bounced ideas off of her and welcomed her input.

Reo had just printed out the first chapter for Meka to review. She sat beside him scanning down the pages as Reo started typing away on the second chapter.

"So do you think she'll try to get back in your life?" Meka interrupted Reo's thoughts. She could hardly stay focused on any one subject matter since finding out that Klarke had been released from prison. Whether Klarke had murdered her baby or not, she hated her. She hated that she had gotten Reo to marry her after only a short period of time, compared to how much time she had invested in Reo. "I mean, to try to see Junior, that is."

Reo knew that Klarke trying to see Junior was the least of Meka's worries. Meka was the type of woman who would hand over Junior in a handbag, willingly, if it meant Klarke staying out of their lives forever. It was the thought of Klarke trying to see Reo that truly stressed Meka.

"I don't know," Reo replied as he stopped pounding the keys on the keyboard to stare off into space. "Knowing that KAT didn't have anything to do with the murder of our child changes everything."

"Changes everything like what?" Meka asked, slamming the papers against her lap. "And her name is Klarke."

Before Reo could reply, their nearly explosive argument was interrupted by a quaint knock on the door. It was as if the caller had almost hesitated before knocking, but decided to do so anyway.

Meka sighed. "I'll get it." She stood up and placed the papers down on the chair, but before storming out of the room she said, "But our discussion is not over by any means. We'll finish discussing this matter just as soon as I return."

Meka walked out of the study and headed down the hall of their ranch-style home. It was the same home Reo had purchased for himself after he received his first major book deal. Meka had made some interior changes since she had moved in. There seemed to be some sort of floral theme going on. Every hanging mirror, just about, was garnished with some wild flower or another. Even the kitchen place mats had sunflowers printed on them. The living room furniture set had a floral pattern as well. The overkill of a woman's touch didn't bother Reo though. As a matter of fact, he hardly noticed it, since he spent more time away on book signings than he did in his own home.

"Who is it?" Meka yelled as she turned the bolt to unlock the door. When Meka, not waiting for the person knocking to respond to her query, flung open the door, she couldn't believe her eyes. The nerve of this uninvited guest to show up on her doorstep. And on top of that, the nerve of her to look as though she had specially dressed for the occasion.

"It's me," Klarke said through the security-screen door with a smirk on her face. She stood outside on the doorstep looking like she had just been ripped from the pages of a magazine. Her makeup was flawless, not too much and not too little. It was just enough to make her skin look a perfect light bronze. She had on a light brush of pink eyeshadow over top of the three silver strokes of eyeshadow. The two light coats of mascara made her eyelashes look a mile long. She wore just a hint of pink rouge on her perfect cheekbones. The pink shimmery lip gloss on her full pouty lips brought out the pink in her pink-and-white Reeboks that Klarke had purchased specifically to match the solid pink one-piece terry cloth pants designed by J-Lo that she was wearing.

The day before, Klarke visited Scizzors, the beauty shop she had gone to a few times before she went to jail. The stylist, Terri Deal, had dyed Klarke's hair a dark brown and cut it into multiple long layers that flowed down her back. It was whipped into a feathered Farrah Fawcett do. Klarke held a striking resemblance to the beautiful Lisa Raye. By no means did Klarke look as though she was pushing forty. As a matter of fact, she looked as though she was barely legal.

"Is Reo home?" Klarke asked, innocently batting her eyes as if she had every right to be on their doorstep. "Tell him it's his baby's mamma."

"Speak of the devil," Meka said as she stared Klarke down with the most evil expression she could muster up.

"And the devil appears," Klarke replied with a wink.

"You've got some nerve showing up at our, me and my husband's, home," Meka said to Klarke, almost through her teeth.

Klarke was in somewhat of a state of shock. She had no idea that Reo had gotten remarried, and to Meka no less, while she was in jail. She figured that mourning the loss of their child together had made them close again, but marriage? Klarke couldn't help but consider whether if she had known Reo's intent was to marry Meka, that she might have thought twice about signing the divorce papers he had served her while she was locked up. Although Klarke wanted to just fall out and cry, run away in defeat even, she just swallowed and maintained her composure.

"I don't want to cause any trouble for you and Reo," Klarke said softly, with Meka cutting her off.

"The hell you don't!" Meka said, bobbing her head.

"Really, I don't," Klarke said innocently.

"I see right through you," Meka said, snickering under her breath. "Do you think the fact that you didn't directly harm our child changes anything? Are we supposed to look at you as some martyr now? Do you think all of this gives you the green light to just show back up into our lives unannounced?" Meka said, pointing her finger at Klarke through the security-screen door. "Your daughter, the child you were expected to raise properly, murdered our daughter. No matter what excuses you try to make up or what you say, I know that the apple doesn't fall too far from the tree. You are not to be trusted. So don't show up here with your violin expecting us to weep to your sad serenade."

Klarke stood outside on the porch silently as her eyes welled up with tears of pain and anger. It had taken so much courage for her to come to Reo's house. She wanted to turn the car around a thousand times as she drove from Toledo to Columbus. At that very moment Klarke knew she had made a mistake showing up at Reo's house. She had no right to come turn his life upside down.

She had entrusted Junior with him because he was a good man. That hadn't changed.

"You're right. I'm sorry," Klarke said as she turned to walk away. She had no right at all to be there.

"Wait a minute," Meka called to Klarke, stopping her in her tracks. Meka unlocked the security-screen door, cracked it, and poked her head through it to have one more go at Klarke.

"If you're thinking about trying to renege on your agreement of staying out of Junior's life, just remember, you signed papers terminating your rights as his mother. I'm his mother now. I'm the one he calls Mommy!" Meka quickly pulled her head back and slammed the front door proudly in Klarke's face.

Klarke ran to the car in tears. Meka had gotten the "W." She had broken Klarke down and Meka knew it as she brushed her hands together as if she had just taken the garbage out to the curb. Meka looked at herself in the oval mirror surrounded by ivy and smiled at her reflection before returning to the study to join Reo.

"Who was that at the door?" Reo asked Meka as she entered the study.

"Some kid trying to sell me chocolate candy bars," Meka replied as she walked over to the chair, picked up the papers, and sat down.

"Did you buy any?" Reo questioned.

"You know what chocolate does to my face," Meka replied with a smile.

Once again the doorbell rang. Meka quickly jumped up from the chair. "I'll get it. It's probably that kid again. You know they don't take no for an answer now days. They're like little Jehovah's Witnesses."

Meka rushed out of the study and down the hall.

"Hey," Reo called to Meka. "If they have the caramel-filled ones, go ahead and buy me a couple."

Meka knew it was Klarke again, probably coming back to beg and plead. Meka swung open the door and began to scold.

"Did you not understand—," Meka tried to blurt out, but Breezy quickly put a halt to her words. Breezy pulled open the security-screen door that Meka had failed to lock in her rage with Klarke. She grabbed hold of Meka's hair, snatching her out of the door and twisting her down to the ground. Meka began to scream as Breezy tried her hardest to pull every strand of Meka's hair out of her head.

"Talk shit now, bitch," Breezy said, snatching that bun right out of Meka's hair. You couldn't even see her face as strands of hair went every which way.

"Get off of me. Stop it!" Meka screamed, clawing at Breezy's hands.

"Oh, you want me to stop?" Breezy asked as she twisted Meka's hair around her hand in a tight grip. "Say uncle. As a matter of fact, say mommy. Call me mommy, bitch. Let's see who calls who mommy around this muthafucka."

"Breezy, don't!" Klarke said, catching up to her and pulling her off of Meka. "She's not worth it, girl."

Breezy looked up at Klarke, breathing heavily. It took her a minute to come to her senses, but eventually she did. Breezy turned Meka's hair loose and stood up.

"Don't you ever fucking say the wrong thing to my friend again . . . ever!" Breezy screamed, pointing at Meka as tears of anger began to roll down her face. "She's more of a woman than you will ever be. It wasn't too long ago when you were the mother putting a price tag on her child. How easy we forget."

Meka lay on the doorstep rubbing her sore head.

"Baby, what's going on?" Reo called from down the hall as he rushed to Meka's aid. Reo came around the corner to find Meka's body against the screen door. She was lying on the ground. Reo immediately noticed her discombobulated hair and the strands scattered about that Breezy had managed to pull from the root of Meka's scalp. Reo kneeled down and tried to help Meka up, but she angrily pushed him away.

"Leave me alone. I'm okay. You just go call 911," Meka said, standing up and stepping inside the door to where Reo was standing. "I want those bitches arrested for assault and battery!"

By this time, Breezy and Klarke were making their way back to the car.

"Who? Who did this to you?" Reo said as he quickly walked outside of the door to seek out the culprits.

Klarke had managed to drag Breezy back to the car and forced her into the passenger seat, Breezy begging Klarke the entire time to allow her just one more blow at Meka.

"You only came along for moral support, remember?" Klarke said to Breezy. "Now we done probably caught a case."

Klarke and Breezy knew they had to get out of there before the police did decide to show up. In a prestigious neighborhood, such as the one Reo and Meka resided in, they knew it wouldn't be long before they heard the roar of the sirens.

Klarke ran around to the driver's side. As she opened the car door she looked up, only to lock eyes with Reo who was standing on the porch. When their eyes met it was like a bolt of lightning had struck.

Klarke stood frozen, unable to move.

Klarke wanted to throw herself at Reo's feet and beg for his forgiveness. She wanted him to forgive her for all of the lies and deception she had subjected him to. She wanted him to tell her that he had forgiven her for all of the games she had played. She wanted so much for him to know that although she had used shady tactics to plan their initial encounter in forming a relationship, that their loving each other was fate. She wanted to remind

Reo of how much she loved her children, how she would do every-thing within her power to protect them from anything, including jail. As a father he had to know how strong a bond a parent has with a child. He too would have done the same thing if he had been in her shoes. What parent wouldn't sacrifice their own free-dom for that of their child's if they had the chance?

Reo couldn't explain the feeling that came over him when he looked into KAT's eyes. It was almost as if she hadn't been locked away in prison at all, but more like she had been away on a long vacation and had finally made her way back home to him. He wanted to greet her with a warm kiss, roses, and a bottle of her fa-vorite alcoholic beverage, Alizé. But he had a new life now that had no place for her. There was no place for KAT in Reo's life, but he couldn't say the same for his heart.

Realizing that the police would probably arrive shortly, and as Klarke had no intention of ever going back to jail again, she quickly got into the car. She fumbled getting the key into the ignition, then started the car. She pressed the gas and the car engine roared. Klarke looked at Reo one last time, who hadn't moved an inch. She then looked straight ahead and drove away, mumbling those famous last words under her breath, "I'll be back."

Klarke woke up out of her sleep in a cold sweat. Her pale pink satin nightgown was clinging to her. Something had jolted her from her sleep.

Breathing heavily, Klarke turned on the lamp on the night-stand. She looked up at the photo clock hanging on the wall. The numbers were printed over a picture of Harris, Tionne, and the three children, Vaughn, HJ, and Sissy.

Klarke put her head down, rubbed her eyes, then looked back up at the clock. It was 3:15 in the morning. Klarke had only been in a deep sleep for the past hour. The earlier events at Reo and Meka's house had had her antsy and upset. She had been tossing and turning all night.

Klarke had been thinking about Junior. If only she could have gotten one peek at him in the flesh. She longed to see his little face. Maybe then she would have turned her car around and gone back home. Then she wouldn't have had to be subjected to Meka's horrible words. That's what she kept trying to convince herself of anyway.

Just then Klarke jumped up out of bed and walked over to the closet. She pulled out the cardboard box that had carried her belongings home from prison. She plopped down on the floor right there at the closet and began rummaging through the box. She flipped through various documents as well as letters from Breezy, Jeva, Harris, Vaughn, HJ, and her sisters. She pulled out one letter in particular and began reading it.

Dear Klarke,

    I really don't know how to open this letter, what words to say or how to say them. So I guess I should just say what I'm feeling. I think if my wife and son knew I was doing this, they'd chew me a new hide. Maybe they wouldn't. Hell, maybe they've even been writing you too. Who knows? As a man of God I just have to do what I feel is right.

    What you've been accused of, what you pled guilty to doing, by having your freedom stripped from you, you are paying your debt to society. But ripping a child away from his mother isn't a fitting punishment.

    Therefore, I'm enclosing a picture of your boy. Isn't he handsome? He has your eyes.

    Look at his picture every day and it will make your nights easier. Sleep with his picture every night and it will make your days easier.

*Talk to him and never forget to include him in your prayers. I figured,
since you two will never know each other personally, you could at least
be soul mates.*

Mr. Laroque

Klarke's eyes watered as she read the first of the few letters Mr.
Laroque had mailed her while she was in prison. Every year, one
week after Junior's birthday, Mr. Laroque would write to Klarke
and enclose a picture of her son at his birthday party.

Mr. Laroque saw to it that Klarke didn't exclude her child from
her life. His act would be a priceless part of her survival while incarcerated. That, and knowing that her other two children were
doing well, kept Klarke's spirit alive.

As Klarke finished reading the letter she placed it back in the
box. She knew that she needed to thank Mr. Laroque for saving
her. He needed to know just how much what he did meant to
her. And on the same token, perhaps she could get him to talk
to Reo for her. Reo and his father had always had the perfect
father and son relationship. If anyone could help her, it would
be him.

Suddenly Klarke felt hope. She packed the box away and
headed back to bed. In the morning she would work on contacting
Mr. Laroque. She turned off the light, tucked herself back into
bed and slept like a baby for the rest of the night.

The first thing in the morning Klarke got HJ and Sissy off to
school. She ironed their clothes and prepared their school lunches
while they ate bowls of cereal and toast for breakfast. Harris had to
be at work at six A.M. so he left the house before any of them even
rolled over in bed. For old time's sake though, and to show her

gratitude to Harris for giving her a place to lay her head until she got back on her feet, she had ironed his clothes and prepared his lunch the night before.

Klarke fixed herself a hot cup of coffee, then sat down at the long glass dining room table with the cordless phone, pencil and paper in hand. Klarke began her search for Mr. Laroque by calling the Columbus information operator. She was disappointed to find that the number wasn't listed in the public directory. Recalling that Mr. Laroque had made a living as a college English instructor, Klarke decided to go online to see if she could come across anything.

Klarke went to HJ's room so she could use his computer. She signed onto the computer as a guest user and initiated her search.

After about an hour of looking up staff information for the local colleges in Columbus, Ohio, Klarke finally found a listing for Mr. Laroque. He was an English literature instructor at one of the downtown community colleges. The phone number for the English department was listed, so Klarke wrote down the phone number, then logged off of the computer.

She pulled the phone, which was in the shape of a race car, closer to her. Klarke sat there with one hand on the phone and the other hand holding the piece of paper she had written the phone number on. She stared at the phone number for a few minutes before she took a deep breath, picked up the receiver, and dialed the phone number.

"Columbus State Community College," a woman's voice said. "How may I direct your call?"

"Mr. Laroque," Klarke said nervously. "He's an English instructor there."

There was silence on the phone.

"Hello," Klarke said.

"Yes, I'm sorry," the woman said as she swallowed the knot in her throat that seemed to be choking her up. "Mr. Laroque is no longer with us."

"Oh," Klarke said with disappointment. "Well, do you happen to have the number where he works now?" Klarke asked.

Once again, there was silence on the line.

"Hello," Klarke said becoming frustrated.

"No, you don't understand," the woman said as her voice began to crack. "Mr. Laroque went into cardio arrest last evening while instructing his night class. The doctors were unable to resuscitate him. We lost him."

Klarke dropped the phone as she sat there in shock. She started taking deep breaths as she felt a lack of oxygen. After a minute or so, she opened her mouth to wail, but not a sound came out. Tears began to drop down her face like a waterfall.

How would Mr. Laroque ever know how much his letters meant to her? Why didn't God give her a chance to thank him, to tell him how she felt? Who would help her now?

Klarke stopped thinking about her own sorrow long enough to start thinking about what a hard time Reo must be having. She knew that Reo and his father were very close. He was probably devastated. Klarke wished that she could be the one there for him, to hold him and tell him that everything was going to be all right. It sickened her knowing that it would be Meka's shoulder he would cry on.

Klarke picked up the phone and began pounding it against the receiver. "No, no, no," she screamed. "Noooo!"

"Are you going to go to the funeral?" Jeva asked Klarke as they sat in the Cheesecake Factory with Breezy.

Klarke didn't respond. She just sat there making tracks with her fork in her piece of cheesecake.

"Yeah, right!" Breezy answered for her in a sarcastic tone. "She'll be the one sitting right in between Reo and his bride."

"I can't believe he's gone," Klarke said in a daze as her bottom lip began to tremble. "I wish I could call Mrs. Laroque or something. I wish there was something I could do."

"I don't think Reo would mind you paying your respects," Jeva said, taking a bite of her cherry cheesecake.

"Yeah, maybe you're right," Breezy said, reconsidering. "Losing a father is hard. Klarke, both you and I know that. And Jeva, you've never even been privileged enough to even meet your biological father. It just doesn't seem fair."

Breezy couldn't finish her thought without getting choked up. Jeva got up and walked over to Breezy and put her arms around her and hugged her tight.

"Thanks, babe," Breezy said in a soft whisper. "I needed that."

Jeva kissed Breezy on the nose and smiled. All the while Klarke stared at them with a peculiar look on her face. She had seen Jeva comfort Breezy before. That wasn't unusual. This time, though, there appeared to be something more intimate about the way she was comforting her.

Klarke couldn't worry herself with speculations. For now, she had enough to worry about. She needed to decide whether or not to drive to Columbus to pay her respects to Mr. Laroque. And after that she needed to find out exactly what in the hell had gone on while she had been away. It was clear to her that Breezy and Jeva hadn't told her everything.

Klarke was sure she was the most inconspicuous mourner at Mr. Laroque's burial. She had managed not to be spotted at all during the funeral services at the church. She did so by dressing incognito.

Klarke wore a black skirt suit. It was the same suit she wore to court the day she falsely pled guilty to the murder of Reo's baby. The suit was returned to her when she was released from jail. She hadn't yet purchased anything that was appropriate to wear to a funeral. She covered her legs in ultra sheer jet-black panty hose and a pair of three-inch killer pumps. Her large, velvet black brim hat had a piece of black lace attached to it that draped down over her face.

HJ didn't stand out either. Breezy had offered to ride along with Klarke again for support, but Klarke knew better this time around than to accept her offer. HJ would do just fine. Klarke debated over and over whether or not to bring him. She knew that if Meka spotted her, that there was the potential for things to get real ugly, real fast. But she was confident that she had taken enough measures for them not to stand out.

HJ fit in with all the other teenage boys there who were dressed in dark slacks with a white dress shirt and clip-on tie. Klarke hoped that by bringing him along, just in case she was spotted by Meka, that Meka would be less likely to be confrontational if she saw that she had her son with her. She would see that Klarke wasn't there for any trouble, but to sincerely pay her respects to Mr. Laroque.

The family was so distraught that it broke Klarke's heart. Two gentlemen supported Mrs. Laroque. Reo looked like he was still in shock. Meka stayed close to him, holding his hand. Klarke pushed away the thought that she wished it were her comforting Reo.

Klarke knew that her presence was risky, but she just had to pay her respects to Mr. Laroque. This was her way of saying thank you to him. It was the only way that would allow her some sense of closure.

When Reverend Sandy stood before the church, she could barely perform the eulogy, but what was truly heart wrenching was when Reo got up in front of the church and read a poem he had written for his father:

It hurts that you're gone, but I can't live in the past
I see you gone and all I can say is that you're free at last
When I wake up I just wish that you were there
But having that feeling of you not being here I just can't bear
Sometimes I just sit at home in a daze
I know that I will be able to see you again someday
It shouldn't have been you in that casket
For us to see all of your friends and family during this time is tragic
I am writing this straight from the heart
God does things for a reason. That's why he took us apart
You left behind for us many good things
But you left one bad thing and that is this pain
When you died it was a big shock
It hit everyone hard just like a rock
Now I have to carry the world on my shoulders
Every day that you're gone, it just gets colder

After the church service, everyone drove to Greenlawn Cemetery for the burial. At the burial site there were five chairs placed in front of Mr. Laroque's casket. Mrs. Laroque occupied the first chair and to her right was a woman who looked just like her, only younger. It was pretty safe to say that the woman was her sister. On her right sat Reo. He was so broken up that he still didn't even have the strength to comfort his mother. He stayed hunched over the entire time as if he had bad stomach pains from food poisoning. Every now and again he would look up at the casket and then completely lose it.

Sitting beside Reo was Meka and beside her was a small boy. It had to be Junior. From where Klarke was standing she could only get a side profile of him. She probably hadn't noticed him in the church because he was so small and she had sat in the very back pew. Junior was just sitting there like a well-groomed soldier. He was too young to understand fully what was going on, but to comfort him Meka would often kiss him on top of his little afro. But she mainly tended to Reo by kissing him on his cheek and rubbing his back. Klarke forced herself to look away.

The casket was lowered, Reverend Sandy said a few final words, then dismissed the guests. The mourners began to disperse to their cars.

Suddenly, a tap on the shoulder startled Klarke.

"What the hell are you doing here?" Meka said in a harsh whisper. "I can't believe you used the death of Mr. Laroque to try and worm your way back into Reo's life. That's low for even you, Klarke Taylor."

"It's Laroque," Klarke corrected Meka.

"Excuse me?" Meka said.

"The name is Klarke Laroque." Klarke enjoyed throwing that fact in Meka's face. "For one minute did you ever stop to think that I might be more interested in my Junior than your husband? But never mind that. I'm only here to pay my respects to Mr. Laroque. That's my sole purpose for being here. But trust me, I won't mind adding kicking your ass to the agenda."

"You dirty—" Meka said before being interrupted by HJ.

"You're the woman in my dream," HJ said to Meka after having stared at her ever since she approached them.

"Oh," Meka said, startled by HJ and embarrassed that she was fixin' to act a fool in front of the boy. Once she had spotted Klarke, Meka hadn't seen anyone or anything else. That's why she hadn't paid any attention to the fact that HJ was standing there. Meka looked down at him in surprise, but played it cool. "You are such a sweetheart. I get that all of the time."

Meka collected herself. Klarke's strategy of bringing HJ along had worked.

By now, a few folks at the burial were starting to notice the small spat between Klarke and Meka. For fear that Reo would soon notice and decide to approach Klarke to perhaps thank her for showing up to pay her respects, Meka decided to cut her conversation with Klarke short. She knew that her husband was devastated and vulnerable. No way was Klarke going to get any Cuba Gooding Jr., Boyz N the Hood pity affection from her man.

"Look, *my* husband needs me right now," Meka said, smoothing the jacket of her navy blue pinstriped pants suit. "I trust you'll have a safe drive back to Toledo."

Meka smiled at Klarke then looked down at HJ and gave him a wink accompanied by a smile. She then walked back over to Reo just in time to help him up out of his chair so that she could aid him in the walk back to the limousine.

"Hey, Mom," HJ said. "That woman—"

"Not now, HJ," Klarke said, cutting him off by putting her hand up in the air. "We need to go."

Klarke grabbed hold of HJ's hand and proceeded to her car. Seeing Reo and Junior and not being able to be near them was too painful. She had to get out of there.

Once Klarke and HJ got into the car Klarke placed her hands on the steering wheel and then placed her head on it.

"You okay, Ma?" HJ asked in a comforting tone.

Klarke looked over at her handsome young son, the spitting image of his father.

"I'll always be okay just as long as I have you by my side."

HJ leaned over and kissed his mother on the cheek. Klarke smiled at him, put the key in the ignition, and started the car. She slowly began to drive away.

By the time Klarke drove by the family's limo, Reo was settled in. He looked up and saw Klarke driving by. Klarke was looking straight ahead and didn't see Reo.

Reo smiled. It was the first time he had smiled since his father had passed. Something about knowing that Klarke had been there for him gave him some peace.

Her presence there reminded him that she was the same woman he had managed to so easily fall in love with years ago. She was the same woman that he would never stop loving.

9

MY BROTHER'S KEEPER

It was official. Vaughn was going to be charged as an adult. The entire situation was absolutely numbing. This is exactly why Klarke had confessed to the murder in the first place. The state of Ohio, a state that recognized and utilized the death penalty, didn't go easy on youth. An eye for an eye. A life for a life.

At the adult determination hearing, when the judge read his decision, Klarke fainted. Thank goodness Harris was there to catch her fall. Vaughn, on the other hand, simply smiled at the judge while shaking her head. None of this seemed to be fazing her the least bit. With her fate in the white man's hands, this is exactly the decision she had predicted the judge would make. Actually, she had bet some white girl in lockup, her cell mate, that they would try her as an adult. Her smile was that of the winner of a twenty-dollar bet.

When the bailiff was handcuffing Vaughn, she saw her father trying to revive her mother. Harris looked up and for a moment their eyes locked. Vaughn glared at him, silently calling Harris every sorry excuse for a father, forcing Harris to look away. Then the bailiff yanked Vaughn around and escorted her out of the courtroom.

Vaughn walked ahead of the bailiff, damn near tripping over her own feet as she looked back at her mother who had now regained consciousness. Vaughn hated what this had done to her mother. Klarke had been more at peace sitting behind bars for life for a crime she hadn't committed than she was watching her baby girl be hauled off in handcuffs. Vaughn wished that she could turn back time. She wanted to go way back, all the way back to when it was just her mother, father, HJ, and herself. When life had been good.

When Vaughn returned to her cell, she laid on her one-inch-thick cot and stared up at the ceiling for the rest of the day, but not before seeing to it that her cell mate made good on her bet. A week later Vaughn was transferred to Marion Prison for Women, where she would await her trial.

Marion Prison was nothing like the county. Vaughn had only been there eight days and yet it felt more like eight years.

HJ entered the prison visiting room where his sister, whom he hadn't seen in years, was sitting waiting on him. He had asked Klarke to take him, but she told him to ask his father. Harris had not yet been to visit Vaughn, and Klarke thought this would be a good way to get him up there. Harris agreed to take HJ, but he himself waited out in the car while HJ went in to see his sister.

All Vaughn knew was that she had a visitor. She thought it was going to be her attorney because Klarke had just visited her along with Breezy and Jeva.

When Vaughn looked up and saw HJ standing there in the doorway she trembled. She couldn't believe her eyes. Vaughn was overwhelmed with joy. Every moment they had ever shared together flashed through Vaughn's mind. Them sitting at the kitchen table, her doing homework and him gobbling down Ho Hos. When they had gotten their first Bibles. The times that she had popped him upside the head when he got on her nerves. Tears filled her eyes. He was her best friend.

Now slim and slender, Vaughn recalled how she used to poke HJ in his chubby belly and call him the Pillsbury Dough Boy. She had missed him. His letters had kept him close in her heart, but nothing compared to seeing him in person.

Overcome by emotion, Vaughn didn't even realize that tears were steadily making their way down her face. Now how did that look? Here she was the big sister, bawling like a baby. Vaughn buried her face in her hands in embarrassment.

"Vaughn," HJ said as he rushed over to hug his sister. He closed his eyes and squeezed her tightly. "I love you. I rehearsed a thousand times what I was going to say to you once I got here, but all I can say is I love you."

"I love you too," Vaughn said as she hugged him back. "I've missed you so much," she said, looking up at HJ.

"Me too," HJ said, looking down at Vaughn and wiping her tears away. Vaughn only cried harder.

"My little brother. I love you so much."

"I'm scared, Vaughn. I don't want you to go to jail forever," HJ said. "First Mom and now you. None of this is right. I should just—"

"Shhh, little brother, shhh," Vaughn said, comforting him.

"It's not fair. You're not the one who hurt that baby. I was there, not you. I should be the one locked up," HJ said.

"Stop it!" Vaughn said sternly, grabbing HJ by the arms. She shook him. "We were all there. We were all in that house with the baby that night, so if that's the case, then we all should be in jail."

"But I was there at the pool," HJ said sadly.

"Do you remember doing it?" Vaughn asked HJ, knowing that he couldn't remember a thing. Vaughn grabbed HJ by the chin and looked him dead in the eyes. "Do you remember putting that baby in the pool and drowning her?"

"No. I just remember going to bed and then waking up standing next to the pool, wet," HJ said, confused. He slowly continued as he tried to recall that horrible night that changed their lives. "The baby was in the pool floating and I was just standing there. I was just standing there. I don't know how I got there. I can't remember, Vaughn. I remember you making me take off my wet pajamas and you buried them down in the flower bed. I don't know how I got wet. I think I remember you getting me dressed in some dry pajamas and then you put me back to bed. Or was I dreaming?" Vaughn just looked at him, her expression grim. She just listened to HJ go on and on. "I was crying. You told me everything would be okay, that you would take care of everything. That's all I remember, Vaughn. I've tried. I've tried really hard to remember what happened that night, but I can't remember. I just can't remember."

"See?" Vaughn said, holding onto HJ by the arms and smiling at him. "You can't say you did something that you really don't remember doing, can you?"

"But—"

"No buts," Vaughn said sharply. "Besides, does it really matter? Mom's free. Now she's there to take care of you far better than I ever could."

"I just wish Mom never met Reo," HJ said angrily. "Then none of this would have happened. Why did he have to be such a liar? I thought he was going to be different. He should have told

Mom he had that baby. Then maybe she never would have married him and that baby never would have been in our house." HJ bowed his head and nodded.

"None of that matters now," Vaughn said, putting her hand on HJ's shoulder to comfort him. "We can't blame Reo. He was nothing but kind to us, HJ. He was like a father. You know that."

"Fathers don't leave their kids," HJ said, jerking away from Vaughn. "After Mom went to jail we never heard from him again."

"Look, HJ," Vaughn said softly. "I don't want to talk about Reo, the baby, or anything else. That's not what this visit should be about. I want to talk about you. I've missed you."

"I've missed you too," HJ said, smiling.

Not speaking about it again, Vaughn and HJ visited with one another for the next hour and fifteen minutes. They laughed and reminisced. Vaughn shared some boarding school stories that she hadn't written to him about and HJ shared some school stories that he hadn't told her.

The guard, touched by the brother-sister reunion, allowed them more time than usual. Eventually, though, she had to tell HJ that he had to leave. Vaughn got in her last hugs, then she and HJ knelt down to pray:

"Dear Lord, thank you so much for all of the blessings you have bestowed upon us. Thank you for watching over our family and keeping them safe and sound and free from harm. Dear Lord, most of all we just want to thank you for allowing me to play such an important role in my brother's life. Thank you for giving me the strength and the will to take care of him no matter what.

"Dear Lord, we ask that you please give HJ the strength to go on through life. Please guide him and let him know how lucky he is to be loved so much.

"We say this prayer in the name of your son and our savior, Jesus Christ. Amen."

"Amen," HJ repeated.

Vaughn took a deep breath. "I don't want to scare you, but I don't want you to be surprised. The court is going to charge me as an adult. That means I can be sentenced twenty-five years to life or I might even get the death penalty," she told HJ.

"Don't say that, Vaughn!" HJ said angrily.

"Listen to me, HJ! You're not a little kid anymore. You're fifteen years old. You're a young man. You have to know what's going on."

HJ hugged Vaughn one last time. The guard came into the room, signaling that the visit was officially over. Vaughn stood up from the visiting table and HJ watched the guard escort his sister away.

"Hey, HJ," Vaughn said, turning around.

"Yeah?" HJ replied, choking back tears.

"Don't stop sending me those prayer letters," she said smiling. "I need them in here now more than ever."

"I won't, Vaughn," HJ said as he smiled and looked down. "I don't know the next time I'll be back to visit, but hopefully it will be soon. But in the meantime, lots of prayer letters."

"As long as we pray together, we'll be just fine." She walked away with a smile.

Back in her cell, Vaughn couldn't stop thinking about HJ and their conversation. She had fed HJ hideous stories about how Reo's new baby would destroy their happy lives the same way she had fed him stories about how Harris's child with Tionne would destroy their lives. Vaughn's words had come true the first time, so why would HJ think they wouldn't come true the second time around? As far as Vaughn was concerned, HJ had only done what she wanted to do but hadn't had the nerve to do. Ironically, that very night she had contemplated ending it all. But God told her that that wasn't the answer to the situation.

But Vaughn refused to stop believing. She still believed God would take care of her.

Besides, a few years in jail wasn't too bad, Vaughn thought. She was sure she could find something to get into to keep herself pre-occupied for the next few years. A wicked smirk covered Vaughn's face. She was positive she could.

Harris sat at the kitchen table reading the newspaper and eating a plate of spaghetti and meat sauce that Klarke had made for dinner. Her spaghetti had been his favorite dish when they were married, next to her anyway.

"Any good news in that paper?" Klarke said, walking to the re-frigerator to pour herself a glass of soda.

"Three more U.S. soldiers died over in Iraq," Harris told her as he continued to read the paper.

"That's not good news," Klarke said, pouring a glass of Faygo red soda. She took a sip. Harris just grunted distractedly.

"How's the spaghetti?" she asked, sitting down at the table with him.

"Just how I remembered it." Harris smiled.

Klarke smiled back. "That's good."

Harris put the paper down and looked at Klarke.

"What's with the small talk?" he asked. Although the two lived under the same roof, Klarke had pretty much ignored him since the night they almost had sex. But she had been busy trying to get her life back in order. And on top of that, she didn't want to give him any ideas about him and her.

"You're on to me, huh?" Klarke said. She took a deep breath. "I found a place."

"Oh yeah?" Harris said, looking down at his plate. "Where about?"

"Over near Westgate. It's a nice three-bedroom apartment."

Harris immediately looked up. "Three bedrooms, huh?"

"Um-hm. A room for myself, HJ, and Vaughn."

Harris shook his head.

"What's that about?" Klarke asked angrily.

"Nothing," Harris said, returning to his spaghetti.

"Look, I don't know how things are going to turn out with Vaughn, but she's always going to have a place in my home."

"So what are you trying to say, Klarke?" Harris said, slamming down the fork and pushing the plate away.

"She's your fucking daughter too, that's what I'm trying to say," Klarke said. "So why do I feel like a single mom when it comes to her? I'm the only one visiting her, taking her things, putting money on her books."

Harris picked the paper back up again.

"HJ and I went to visit Vaughn today at the jail," Klarke said in a calmer tone.

"How is she?" Harris asked after a while.

"She's hanging in there."

"That's good," Harris said, still not looking up from the newspaper he was reading.

"She asked about you. She asked how you were doing."

Harris didn't respond.

"When are you going to go visit her?" Klarke asked, exasperated.

"I really can't say. I have so much going on with work and all."

"What are you afraid of?" Klarke said, becoming frustrated all over again.

"Afraid? I'm not afraid of anything," Harris said, grimacing.

"Then I don't understand why someone who claims to love his daughter so much—"

"I do love my daughter!" Harris shouted, slamming down the

paper. "If I didn't love her then I wouldn't have done everything I did to keep her from going to jail four years ago. It was hard. It was damn hard not seeing her, being with her."

"You could have still kept in touch. Wrote her. Talked to her on the phone. Harris, you didn't even send her birthday cards or anything. That hurt her and reading it in the letters she used to send me hurt me too. We agreed that she needed to be sent away, but to alienate her. Do you know that girl knows the exact number of times she had contact with you while she was in boarding school and she remembers every excuse you made for not seeing her? And I don't know what your excuse is now. I mean the cat is out of the bag. There's no temptation of turning her in to the authorities. The authorities already have her. So tell me, Harris, when are you going to see your daughter?"

Harris got up from the table with his plate still half full of spaghetti in hand. He carried it over to the sink and scraped the scraps into the garbage disposal. Klarke sighed. He wasn't hearing her. It was as if she hadn't spoken a word.

"I'm going to bed," Klarke said, picking up her glass of soda. "Vaughn has another visiting day coming up on Wednesday. Visiting hours aren't over until six."

Harris almost didn't recognize Vaughn when he saw her sitting at the table in the visiting room waiting for him. Her hair was in jailhouse braids straight down her back and she was wearing that Godforsaken felony-orange jumpsuit. Harris took in every inch of her. She wasn't wearing earrings. Klarke had taken her to get her ears pierced when she was five months old and since then he had almost never seen her without a pair of nice dainty earrings. It would have softened her hard appearance. His heart broke as he looked at his little girl sitting there looking like a hard-core criminal.

It was like déjà vu, walking across that crowded room. It seemed like only yesterday that he had made the same exact trek to visit Klarke.

On his way over to Vaughn, Harris passed a vending machine. He stopped, pulled a couple of one-dollar bills out of his wallet, and made a purchase.

"Vaughn," Harris said when he reached her.

Vaughn stared up at her father, not sure what to do. So she waited for him to make the first move.

"Honey," Harris said, opening his arms for a hug.

Vaughn hesitated, sighed, then stood up to hug her father. She hadn't felt his arms around her in a long time. She pulled back and sat back down in her chair. Harris pulled out a chair from the table and joined her.

"I bought these for you," Harris said, placing the pack of Skittles he had just purchased from the vending machine on the table.

Vaughn looked down at the Skittles, then up at her father. Did he actually think a pack of Skittles was going to make up for the past?

"You didn't even miss me when I was away," Vaughn said, rolling her eyes and shaking her head. She had always told herself if and when she ever saw her father again, that she wouldn't bite her tongue. She had a few questions and, damn it, he better have the answers.

"That's not true," Harris said defensively.

"Then how come you never let me come home? Even when classes were out at school you never let me come home. You didn't want me there anymore." Vaughn sadly looked away as her eyes began to water.

"Vaughn, that's not true," Harris said, reaching out to touch Vaughn's hand. She pulled her hand away.

" 'Not this time, Vaughn,' " she said, imitating her father. " 'I'm on mandatory overtime at work. Not this time, Vaughn.' 'The weather is too bad to drive in. Not this time, Vaughn' . . . 'Not this time, Vaughn.' "

Vaughn broke down in tears and Harris tried to blink his own tears away. He knew his daughter was right and that he had been so wrong.

"I understand that you're hurt," Harris said, once again putting his hand on top of Vaughn's.

"Hurt?" Vaughn said, snatching it away. "I'm pissed!"

Vaughn took deep breaths, trying to control herself. She wiped her tears away, then smiled wickedly. "They got some shrink prick fuckin' with my head," Vaughn told him. "They wanna know if I'm crazy. If I was crazy then, when the murder happened, and if I'm crazy now. They wanna know why. They wanna know why I took the life of an innocent baby. They even wanna know if you used to touch me when I was a little girl. If you used to fondle me, touch me in my private parts."

Vaughn paused. Harris had a disturbed look on his face.

"Didn't Mom tell you?" Vaughn asked. "My stupid attorney is working on changing my plea to not guilty by reason of temporary insanity. She's going for a jury trial."

"I didn't know that," Harris said, putting his head down.

"Can you imagine what would happen if I told them yes?" Vaughn giggled. "That your touches were bad touches."

"That's not funny, Vaughn," Harris said, his voice low and anxious.

"Little girls who get touched by their daddies then grow up and commit murder get sympathy from the jury, don't they?" Vaughn said, watching for his reaction.

"You are sick," Harris said with disgust.

Vaughn laughed even as tears filled her eyes. "That's all I wanted to hear you say, *Dad*," she said. "I've known that's what you've thought about me all along. Did you really think I didn't know why you never wanted me back at the house?"

Harris remained silent.

"You thought I'd hurt them," Vaughn said, sniffing. "Didn't you? You thought I'd hurt HJ and Sissy?"

"Vaughn, stop it!"

"Come on, Daddy, just say it. I won't be mad. I promise. Just say it. Daddy, I just want to hear you say it. I just want to know that that's the reason why you didn't want me to come home. Not because you didn't love me . . . not because you didn't love me." Vaughn began to cry harder.

Harris got up, rushed to her, and wrapped his arms around her again. He squeezed her as tightly as he could. "I did love you, baby. I do love you," Harris said, not letting Vaughn pull away. "I'm sorry. I'm so sorry and I will make it up to you. Daddy's here for you now. Please forgive me. Please."

"I needed you, Dad," Vaughn said.

"I know, baby. I know."

Slowly, Vaughn put her arms around Harris and hugged him back.

Finally they let go of each other and Harris sat back down in his chair.

"Daddy, I know what you think about me," Vaughn said.

"Vaughn, don't . . ."

"Just listen, please," Vaughn said. "I just want you to know, you and Mom both, that you raised wonderful children, no matter what any judge or jury could ever say. We were taught to love and to look out for one another. And although I'm locked up, I'm still going to get an education in here. I'm working in the library. I'm still going to live, Daddy. I'm still going to live and make you proud. I know you blame yourself. Looking at me would have been a reminder of your failure. But, Daddy, you didn't fail with me. You didn't."

No matter how comforting Vaughn wanted her words to be to her father, Harris still couldn't help but blame himself. It was his fault that they were no longer the happy family Vaughn had grown up in. When he had cheated on their mother he had cheated on his children.

If it had not been for his affair with Tionne, they would have still been together and there would have been no Reo, no baby's mama and no baby. His daughter wouldn't be behind bars.

It was hard for him to wake up in the morning and at night it was hard for him to sleep. He always felt that once he closed his eyes, God would take him away as punishment for all of his dirt. Little did Harris know that it wasn't God he needed to worry about.

10

SUNDAY BRUNCH

———————————
———————————

———————————

Dear Breezy,

This is only the hundredth letter I've written you. Believe me, if I thought what you think I did to your father, I wouldn't answer any of my letters either. But if you would just come visit me one time so I can really talk to you, you won't regret it.

Baby girl, you and me kicked it for a long time, long enough for you to know that I'm no killer. I would never take the life of another human being. I know I've lost my temper at times, but I'd never lose my damn mind. You know I'm not capable of doing anything like that.

Things are much too complicated for me to try and write it all in a letter. That's why I've been begging you to come and visit me. I'd rather talk to you in person. Sweetheart, you know how much I loved you. I still love you, even after all of these years.

You can throw this letter out just like you've probably done with *all the others, but guess what? I'm going to keep writing you. I'm going to use my entire commissary for the rest of my life on stamps until I get you here. Baby, I can't breathe, sleep, or eat knowing what you think about me.*

Don't you want to know what really happened? Don't you want to know the truth? Coming to visit me, if nothing else, will bring you closure.

Every night I pray that things could have turned out differently between us. If you could have just given me time, I would have eventually left my wife for you. You know I had a lot to lose in that relationship and that I had to walk on eggshells to make things right for us. But you, being the strong-willed, no-nonsense type of woman that you are, just wouldn't let me do what I had to do to make sure that our life together was going to be smooth.

Please, Breezy. All I'm asking for is just five minutes. I just have to get this off of my chest. You have no idea what being in here for a crime I did not commit is doing to me. I don't care what anyone else thinks of me. You are the only one I care about.

Please, Breezy. Come see me, just five minutes. Just five minutes is all I'm asking.

Love, Guy

"Ain't this 'bout some ol' Keith Sweat jailhouse talk?" Breezy said to herself as she balled the letter up and threw it across the room. It landed on the living room hardwood floor and rolled under the gold queen bench. Now that she had performed the first part of her daily routine, kicking her shoes off and then going through the day's mail, it was time for a long hot shower.

Breezy picked up the Nine West mahogany loafers with three-inch heels she had kicked off and carried them to her bedroom. Breezy lived in a spacious studio apartment. It was a bachelorette pad to die for. She had lucked out because of Jeva. A model Jeva shot some pictures of used to live there. He had just signed a five-year lease when he landed a huge modeling contract in Europe. He needed someone to sublease ASAP. The old lady who owned the property had been allowing him to lease it for next to nothing, but had locked him into a long-term lease. He mentioned his predicament to Jeva. Breezy had been living with Jeva at the time. It was right after her father had been murdered. The police had taken Breezy in for questioning, but then decided to hold her on suspicion, accusing her of having something to do with the murder of her father. It was an awful time for Breezy. The police had destroyed her apartment and its contents searching for evidence to make a case against her. They found nothing, so after holding her in jail for seventy-two hours, they had to let her go.

For those three days in jail, though, Breezy's picture was flashed on all of the local television stations. She even ended up losing her job. Jeva was kind enough to take her in until she could get back on her feet and find a place to stay.

Breezy had only lived with Jeva for a few months, but there were some weird feelings going on between them that neither one wanted to confront, so it was time for Breezy to go before their friendship was permanently affected. So that same day Jeva found out about the apartment, Jeva had relayed the information to Breezy and she went to check out the place the very next day.

It was the bomb to say the least. The studio felt like home to Breezy the moment she stepped through the double metal doors. He had obviously hired a professional decorator to lay it out. It was an MTV *Real World*–type setting. He had oil paintings that you had to be high or drunk to figure out what the picture actually was. There were beautiful vases throughout with a variety of silk flowers in them. Everything was simple but sophisticated. Like the solid oak chest that served as the living room table and the high diner-like table with long legged chairs that sat in front of the long vertical window. And when Breezy found out that he was leaving the apartment furnished with everything in it except for his clothing, she knew she had to have the place. His bachelor pad soon became her bachelorette pad.

Breezy sighed as she sat down on her round king-size bed with a safari-print comforter. It had been a long day at work that had spilled into overtime. Being stuck on a drawn-out phone call with a claimant had put her behind in her daily workload. Being an insurance claim adjuster had its moments. She had decided to stay late and get caught up rather than be greeted by a mile-long list of things to do in the morning.

She dropped her loafers and noticed that there was a scuff on one of the heels. She picked the shoe up and rubbed the scuff with her index finger and then admired the heel. It felt good to be able to wear three-inch heels, Breezy thought. Before, when she was heavier, she wouldn't dare wear anything over two inches, and that was pushing it. It was hard work towing all that ass barefoot, let alone on stilts. She put the shoe back down, stood up in full view of her full-length vanity mirror, and slid her tan Lerner New York side-zip slacks down to the floor and stepped out of them. She admired herself briefly in the mirror, turning from left to right, then all the way around. She damn near broke her neck to get a glimpse of her ass in the mirror.

"No more cottage-cheese ass," she said, smacking her firm buttocks. That Stairmaster she had ordered through Fingerhut had paid off wonderfully. Even when she was a thicky thick girl, Breezy loved the hell out of herself, but now that she was as solid as Beyonce, couldn't nobody tell her shit.

Breezy stood in the mirror and pulled her mahogany ribbed tee over her head like she was performing in a commercial (or a porno). She unsnapped her chocolate silk 36-D bra and admired her pretty brown coconuts. She caressed them and, just for the hell of it, licked her left nipple, only because it looked so tasty and because she could.

Breezy pushed the matching chocolate silk thong down her flawless legs and stepped out of it. It met the bra she had dropped at her feet in a small puddle of silk. Breezy took one more look at herself, winked, then headed for the shower.

The hot water relaxed her and the steam seemed to caress her body. Her hands felt like a stranger's as she closed her eyes and caressed her pretty brown browns. She threw her head back and allowed her fingers to answer the call of her pussy.

She massaged her throbbing clit then plunged one finger inside of her then a second finger, then three and then four. She may have lost weight but she still had that big pussy that every man she had allowed inside of her got addicted to. She was addicted to it herself. She masturbated in the shower about three nights a week and used a sex toy from her bag of tricks the other four nights of the week.

Breezy had kicked it with a man or two or three over the past couple of years, but none she would even consider making her man. She only gave in when she was just absolutely craving the touch of a man. With all the drama with Guy, losing her father, and Klarke going to jail, dick was the last thing on her mind. And then there was her *thing* with Jeva that was just taboo. They had made an unspoken pact not to talk about their *thing*. Besides, whenever she did let a man into her kingdom, he was never up to the challenge. Breezy soon learned that the old saying about if you want something done right, do it yourself, was true.

Breezy began to move her fingers faster and faster as she hurtled toward her climax. When she was right on the edge of climaxing, she placed her hand on her clit and crossed her legs, locking it there, and flexing herself against her hand. She moaned and trembled as she came. The juices flowed down her thigh and mixed with the water. Breezy took a deep breath, then opened her eyes.

"I love you," she said to herself in a low, husky tone. She stood under the water for a few more minutes, then turned the water off and stepped out of the shower.

The Etienne Aigner shoes Breezy had purchased from Nordstrom were killing her feet. She had tried to break them in, but they still hurt.

It was Sunday afternoon and Breezy had nothing but time on her hands, so she decided to run up to the mall and exchange the shoes. She wet her shoulder length curly bob and put some Wet-N-Wavy styling gel in it. She didn't put on a full face, only some MAC clear lip gloss and eyeliner. She threw on a pair of DKNY jeans with a white DKNY long-sleeve T-shirt. She slid on a pair of white footies, her K-Swiss, and headed out the door.

The mall parking lot was stacked. Everyone must have raced straight from the church parking lot to the mall parking lot. Breezy circled the main entrance parking area four times before finding a space. She parked her five-year-old Mercedes—that was still in mint condition and with very low mileage—clicked the remote alarm, and headed into the mall. As soon as she walked into the mall she noticed a familiar figure walking toward her as he headed to exit the mall.

"Look what the wind done blew in," the gentleman said with his sparkling pearly whites. "Or should I say 'breeze'?" He winked and gave her a sexy smile. The two-karat diamonds in his ears winked at her too.

He looked Breezy up and down, waiting for a reply. Breezy could hear her heart pounding in her chest. She hadn't seen this man in forever and a day. As a matter of fact, the last time she had seen him was when he had stormed out of her apartment. They had always argued, made up, and broke up only to make up again throughout their relationship. But he had gotten tired of their rocky relationship and decided that staying broken up was just better than staying together.

"I didn't even know you still lived here," Hydrant said. "I was sorry to hear about your father."

"Thank you. It was a hard time for me, but fortunately I had all of the people who cared about me there for me," Breezy said, making it clear that he hadn't been one of those people.

"So you doing all right?" Hydrant asked, ignoring her unspoken statement.

"Yeah, I am. Thanks for asking."

It was obvious to Breezy that she was still deeply affected by Hydrant because her palms were sweaty and she couldn't stop blushing.

"So, Kristopher, what have you been up to?" Breezy said, trying her hardest to stop blushing.

"Call me Hydrant," he said. "Everybody does now, but only you know the true meaning behind it." He smiled.

Breezy put her head down, trying to hide a huge grin. She did know because she had given Hydrant the nickname. From the moment she laid eyes on his dick it reminded her of a big ol' fire hydrant. And he was the only man in the world who could ever put out her fire.

That was the text message she would leave on his cell phone when she wanted a booty call: HYDRANT. He knew what it meant and he knew to come running.

One day he was at a family cookout when Breezy called and left the text message. He had laid his phone down and had forgotten all about it until his wheelchair-bound loud-mouth auntie started rolling around the yard with his phone yelling "Hydrant! Who is

Hydrant? What's Hydrant mean?" From that day on, everybody started calling him Hydrant instead of his birth name, Kristopher.

"You do remember, don't you?" Hydrant said, bending his six-foot-nine-inch body down so he could see Breezy's face. "It hasn't been that long, has it?"

"Oh, I remember all right," Breezy said, lifting her head. Hydrant stood up straight again.

"So, how have you been?"

"Fine."

"I didn't ask you how you looked. I asked you how you were doing."

Breezy laughed at Hydrant's old corny line. It was the same line he had used on her when she met him six years ago at a First Friday networking affair.

"I see you haven't forgotten all of your Will Smith, *Fresh Prince of Bel-Air* lines."

"You lookin' good, ma," Hydrant said, licking his lips. Any other man in the world could lick his lips, besides LL Cool J, without making Breezy's panties wet, but Hydrant had her ringing her shit out.

"You too," Breezy said, reaching out to his huge biceps. "Been in the gym I see."

"Nah, that's from work," Hydrant said. "I work for the Toledo Fire Department now."

"Get out of here," Breezy said, hoping Hydrant didn't see the dollar signs in her eyes. Although she had buried her gold diggin' shovel years ago, every once in a while she had the strange urge to polish it up again. But then she thought about all the trouble her pursuit of the almighty dollar had gotten her into and knew it wasn't worth it.

"Seriously. I started training a couple of months after you and I . . . uh . . . you know," Hydrant said awkwardly. "I didn't make it the first go round, when I tried for the fire department, but I didn't give up. In addition to that, you know my mama, she kept pushing me and wouldn't let me give up."

"Yeah, Ms. Long always was a ball of fire."

"And she was tired of me living with her." Hydrant chuckled. "She wanted me to get a good paying, steady job so that I could take care of myself."

"And throw her some loot on the side too," Breezy added with a giggle.

"You know Mama. She got to get hers too. She always told my sisters and me that if we ever found a dollar on the street, that fifty cents of it was hers without question."

Breezy and Hydrant joined each other in laughter.

"A firefighter. So no wonder I haven't seen you around. You've been too busy putting out fires."

"Yeah, well, I always have Sundays off. You know?"

I do believe this nigga is trying to hook up, Breezy thought. "Is that right?"

"Yeah." Hydrant cleared his throat. "I usually spend it with my little girl, but her and her mother are out of town this weekend."

"Oh," Breezy said, forcing herself to keep smiling while what she really wanted to do was stop wasting her fucking time and move on. She had vowed that when she did get a man in her life, he wouldn't have any kids. That was one of the things that attracted her to Hydrant before, the fact that he had no baby-mama drama. "You have a little girl?" Breezy could barely get the words out.

"Um-hm. I got married and had a baby."

Breezy swallowed hard.

"Married, huh? Well, that's great. It was good running into you. Maybe I'll bump into you again. You take care," Breezy said, turning to hurry toward the exit door.

"Wait," Hydrant said, grabbing Breezy by the hand. "Weren't you coming into the mall?"

Breezy paused for a minute. "Oh yeah," she said with a dumb laugh.

"Marriage isn't a contagious disease, you know, Bria," Hydrant said, looking deep into her eyes, still holding her hand.

"Look, Hydrant. I'm not into married men. The drama that comes along with them I wouldn't wish on the devil."

"Well if you had let me finish before trying to run off like Cinderella one minute before midnight then you would know that I'm not married anymore."

"Oh, I'm sorry to hear that," Breezy said, smiling.

"Like hell you are." Hydrant laughed, amused by the smile on Breezy's face.

"Seriously. It must have been hard on your little girl. How old is she?"

"She's only two."

Damn. That's sixteen more years of child support he has to pay out of that firefighter's income. Hell, twenty if the little crumb snatcher goes to college, Breezy thought to herself while adding up how many pairs of shoes from Nordstrom all that child support could buy her.

"She's Daddy's little girl," Hydrant said with a big smile on his face.

I'm not even about to compete with a two-year-old, Breezy thought. "How sweet," Breezy lied.

The two just stood there. Neither knew what to say next.

"Well," Breezy sighed. "It was good running into you. Hopefully I'll see you again."

"How about next Sunday?" Hydrant blurted out, barely allowing Breezy to finish her sentence.

Breezy thought to herself for a moment. She had never dated a man with kids, a man with kids who didn't have a wife at home to take care of the little rug rats. Maybe it wouldn't be so bad. Breezy decided to give it a shot.

"Sure, what time?" Breezy said.

"Why don't I give you my home phone number? You can call me so we can set up a place and time." Hydrant pulled his wallet out and dug for a piece of paper. "Do you have a pen?"

Breezy gladly dug down in her Louis Vuitton knockoff. She was all smiles. *Yes! He's giving me his home phone number. No pager, no cell phone, and no mama's phone number. He's giving me his* home *phone number.*

Breezy handed him a pen she had swiped from the office and watched Hydrant write his phone number down. He then handed her the piece of paper.

"I put my address on there too. If you agree, I'd like you to come to my house so I can cook for you. How does that sound?"

"Delicious," Breezy said, not realizing that she was licking her lips. "I'll bring dessert."

"I was hoping you'd say that," Hydrant said with a mischievous mile.

Chatting with Hydrant felt just like old times, like they had never been apart. They always did groove. That hadn't changed.

"I'm looking forward to next Sunday, Hydrant," Breezy said, nodding her head slowly.

"That makes two of us." Hydrant winked and exited the mall, leaving a horny, soaking-wet pantied, Breezy behind.

"I don't care what anybody says," Breezy said, laying her fork across her plate, signaling their waiter that she was finished with her meal. She, Jeva, and Klarke were at the Cheesecake Factory again. "Mr. Clean is sexy and I know I'm not the only woman on earth who thinks so. Hell, I bet if we go ask Chante—I mean

Shasta—he would even probably do him." Breezy sipped on her Long Island iced tea.

"It is time for you to get a man for real," Jeva said, putting up her hand. "Or stop drinking those Long Island iced teas, girlfriend."

"And I thought I needed a man," Klarke said, setting down her Shirley Temple.

"So y'all honestly don't think Mr. Clean is sexy?" Breezy said seriously.

Klarke and Jeva looked at one another, then the two burst out laughing.

"See, I knowed it!" Breezy said with a victorious smile on her face.

"Okay, okay," Jeva said, surrendering. "After Victor Newman on *The Young and the Restless*, Mr. Clean is the second sexiest actor alive, even if he is animated."

"Mr. Clean is lightweight fine," Klarke agreed.

"For a white man, he is," Breezy added.

"Mr. Clean is not white," Jeva said. "He's Latino or mixed with something, but he's not white."

"We are not about to start off our window-shopping ritual with a debate over a cartoon character's nationality." Klarke laughed. "I swear you two argue like you were a couple."

Both Breezy and Jeva fell silent. Jeva ran her fingers through her hair and pretended to look for split ends. Breezy looked around the restaurant.

"I haven't seen Chauncy," Breezy said, suddenly changing the subject. "Isn't he working today?"

"Uh, no," Jeva answered. "There's some general manager's training in Miami or something like that."

There they go again, Klarke thought, watching them carefully. *I know I'm not crazy. These two are hiding something. Something is going on and I'm going to get to the bottom of it right now.* Klarke opened her mouth to just blatantly ask Breezy and Jeva what in the hell was going on between them, but Breezy began speaking before she could.

"Speaking of finding a man," Breezy said, clearing her throat, "guess who I'm joining for Sunday brunch tomorrow?" She smirked.

"We getting too old to be guessing," Klarke said, deciding to let it drop. "Just tell us."

"Mr. Kristopher Long, also known as Hydrant," Breezy said as she sat back and waited for their reactions.

"Get out of here!" Jeva said excited. "You and Hydrant?"

"Talk about a blast from the past," Klarke said, taking a sip of her Shirley Temple. "How is Hydrant? I always liked him. He was a cool brotha."

"Yeah, but his pockets weren't deep enough for Breezy," Jeva said, turning up her lips and rolling her eyes. "And does he still live with his mom?"

"As a matter of fact he doesn't. He has his own place and he is on the payroll of the Toledo Fire Department," Breezy said proudly, then began making fire engine siren sounds.

"Well go ahead, Hydrant," Klarke said, giving Breezy a high five. "He got himself intact. See, Breezy, I told you that you just have to give a brotha some space so that he can take a minute to get his stuff together. But noooo. You had to have him and you had to have him right then and there. I told you that all you had to do was let him handle his business and if it was meant for y'all to be together then that's what would happen."

"You could see Hydrant's potential a mile away," Jeva said, nodding. "He was a good guy."

"All right already," Breezy said, rolling her eyes. "Enough of the preaching. I've learned from my mistakes." Breezy paused and thought for a moment. "Boy have I learned."

"Then why do you have that look of doubt in your eyes?" Jeva asked.

"Well," Breezy said, taking a deep breath. "It seems that while Hydrant was running around putting out fires, someone was putting out his."

Jeva's mouth dropped open. "Oh, girl," Jeva said. "He didn't get married, did he?"

Both Jeva's and Klarke's ears were at attention, awaiting the juicy gossip.

"Yes he did," Breezy said, rolling her eyes. "But he's divorced now."

"Oh," both Jeva and Klarke said with a sigh.

"We thought we were about to hear some dirt," Jeva said, sitting back in her chair.

"If he's divorced, then what's the problem?" Klarke asked, sipping on her Shirley Temple.

"He now has said child by his ex-wife," Breezy said, rolling her eyes up into her head again. "A two-year-old daughter. A baby means there's a baby's mama lurking somewhere with plenty of drama."

"Well, at least he had the baby before you and him instead of during you and him," Klarke said. "That will make it much easier for you to get along with both the child and the mother."

Breezy almost choked on her drink. "Get along with the baby's mama?" Breezy said with attitude. "I'm not trying to look at, let alone get along with, someone who has fucked my man."

"That's ridiculous," Klarke said, almost laughing. "That woman hasn't done anything to you. So what if you two had a man in common. It wasn't at the same time. And it's who he's with now that matters, not who he's been with."

"See, Breezy ain't like the rest of you women out there," Breezy said, talking in third person. "All that befriending and getting along with the ex is for the birds. An ex is, and should remain just that, an ex. Everybody ain't gotta be all friendly and cordial over a cup of coffee and shit. Damn what Will and Jada or Rodney King says. Not all of us should just get along. I don't mean to speak ill of the dead," Breezy added while inhaling a fork full of cherry cheesecake. "But the way you stayed cool with Tionne even after finding out she was your husband's mistress and the mother of their love child . . . fuck that. That shit would have never gone down in Breezy Land." Speaking with a slightly full mouth, Breezy continued her lecture. "And I know, girlfriend, I know after laying in bed for weeks in heartbreaking anguish you found the strength to get up and go beat her down. And maybe that was some sort of closure for you. But a bitch like me would have beaten her down every time I saw her. Hell, I would have gone to her funeral just to kick her ass one last time before they put her in the ground."

"Bria Nicole Williams!" Klarke said, trying not to laugh. "You are going to hell, girl."

"See you there then." Breezy winked while finishing off her drink. "I'll see you there."

At thirty-something years old, Breezy felt too damn old to be running around like a high school girl preparing for her first date. Breezy had been with three boys in high school, fifteen men in her adulthood, and had even French-kissed a girl. She was anything but a virgin to this dating game. Hydrant was one of those fifteen men, but Breezy still felt as though it was her first date ever with him.

Their history together made Breezy even more nervous than she would have been if it was their first date ever. Hydrant was a good man. He always had been and Breezy wasn't about to let him slip through her fingers again. She knew in her heart and her head that she had been unfair to him in their past relationship. The almighty dollar had been her motive for past romance and pride was to blame for allowing Hydrant to walk out of her life. It's better late than never, but Breezy eventually learned (the hard way) that the love of a man with money was the root of all evil. It was time to love a man for exactly what he was . . . a man.

Although Hydrant couldn't afford Breezy's demanding lifestyle back then, he was a hard-working man when it came to making his money. Sometimes after working for hours he would come to Breezy's place, cook dinner for her, then clean up. He knew Breezy was high maintenance, but he loved her. He hoped that what he did in chivalry would make up for what he couldn't do financially.

At the time, Hydrant had been working for his uncle laying concrete for contracts through the City of Toledo. Hydrant was working as an independent contractor. He made enough money to pay the rent at his mom's place and his bills, plus take Breezy out to dinner here and there. But back then Breezy was polishing up her shovel every night to go diggin' for gold. And when she knocked Guy upside the head with her shovel, Breezy found herself performing a juggling act by dating both Hydrant and Guy at the same time.

Guy was a supervisor for the post office and had been there for sixteen years. His wife held the same position at a different location in the city for only three years. Guy earned more than twice as much money as his wife. And fortunately for her, Guy was one of those men who believed that if the man could, then he should be the sole caretaker of his family, no matter how much the wifey made. So he paid the majority of the bills, leaving his wife's paycheck pretty much hers to play with.

Between work, wife, and his two children, Guy's time was spread thin. Breezy pretended that his lack of attentiveness toward her was a big deal, so Guy pacified her with dead presidents. Money was time and since he didn't have the time he thought Breezy needed, he supplied her with money.

Guy's wife was fully aware of his indiscretions with other women. You could call it women's intuition. She was getting what she wanted out of the marriage so she didn't make too much of a fuss just as long as he didn't put it in her face. Sooner or later Guy would get sloppy and mess up. His wife would find out about the women and scare them off with a phone call or two, but she met her match with Breezy. Breezy didn't scare easily. Breezy's name had just turned up one too many times. When Breezy finally called Guy's cell phone and his wife answered, that was the straw that broke the camel's back.

Guy had to put on a front for his wife and play it off as if Breezy was some crazy deranged broad who was trying to seduce him. He called Breezy every hoe in the book in an attempt to spare his wife's feelings. He immediately made his way over to Breezy's house after the phone call to apologize and at the same time inform her that they had to lay low.

At first, he did most of the talking through the front door because Breezy refused to open it and let him in. He tried to sweet talk her, but shit wasn't that easy in Breezyville. Although Guy thought he was going over to Breezy's house to regulate the relationship, Breezy flipped the script completely. Guy ended up breaking in her door to get at her. But again, Breezy didn't scare easily. By the time Guy left her house he had agreed to pay Breezy's rent just as long as she didn't confront his wife about the naughty details of their relationship, right down to an abortion he paid for Breezy to have when she got pregnant with his child. Guy had been fucking with Breezy long enough to know that she didn't make idle threats.

It just so happened that a nosy neighbor who lived across the hall from Breezy had witnessed the fight that night. The eyewitness testimony was the nail in the coffin as to motive when Guy was put on trial for the murder of Breezy's father. The theory was that Guy was really after Breezy. He was going to shut her down once and for all. No way was he going to continuously allow her to blackmail him. Breezy's father had just been released from jail and had moved into her apartment with her. When Guy entered the home at an attempt to take care of Breezy, her father startled him. Unfortunately, the unexpected guest took a bullet that was intended for Breezy.

Breezy tried attending the hearings but the judge seemed to kick her out every day of the trial. She couldn't control her temper. Listening to the defense make up some far-fetched theory about Guy being set up infuriated Breezy. She wanted Guy to man-up and take his punishment like a man.

This was the turning point in Breezy's life. She had been defeated in the worst way possible. She had gone through life fighting demons and finally it seemed as though they had prevailed. Breezy had vowed that no man was ever going to hold a dominating position in her heart. But the way she was feeling as she prepared for her date with Hydrant, perhaps God was sprinkling a little kryptonite along her path.

Although Guy was the money man, Hydrant provided Breezy with the sensitivity she needed to feel like a woman. Not only that, but they were one another's equal in bed. Breezy's pussy existed for Hydrant's dick, but her pockets had existed for Guy's wallet. Can you say Dolce and Gabana, Gucci, Prada, and briquettes? Guy was a Rolex and Hydrant was a Timex. I guess you could say Hydrant was in Breezy's life at the wrong time.

Things were different now though. Breezy was older, wiser, and too damn tired for games. She was determined to be serious about having a wholesome, healthy relationship with a man once and for all. That's why it was so important that she convince Hydrant that she was a new woman.

"My sunshine has come," Breezy sang along with Angie Stone's CD as she brushed her teeth. "And I'm all cried out."

After one last rinse and spit, she wiped her mouth off and looked at herself in the bathroom mirror. Breezy used her fingers to break up some of her curls, then picked a piece of lint off of her cream-colored ribbed Polo turtleneck sweater. Breezy stared at herself in the mirror.

"I don't know what I've done to deserve a second chance with Hydrant, Lord," Breezy prayed. "But thank you, God. I won't let you down this time."

Breezy lined her lips with a brown lipliner, then put on some of her MAC lip gloss. She had already beaten her face with the appropriate cosmetics but had waited to do her lips until after brushing her teeth.

She grabbed her little leather jacket to accommodate the early April weather, then headed out the door.

"Sweetheart, prompt just as I remember," Hydrant said, smiling that beautiful smile when he opened the door.

"Good evening," Breezy said as she walked through the door of Hydrant's three-bedroom split-level home. Handing Hydrant the strawberry shortcake cups she had in her hand, she stepped up into the place like it was hers, like she had been there a thousand times. She immediately noticed the lavender, beige, and pink color scheme in the sitting area and knew instantly that it had the touch of a woman, that woman more than likely being his ex. "Nice *casa.*"

"I'm glad you like because *mi casa su casa*," Hydrant said, taking Breezy's hand and planting one juicy helluva kiss on her middle knuckle.

Will he stop with the sexy shit already? Breezy thought. *I'm not trying to fuck this man tonight. There will be no hit and runs on this pussy.*

"Something smells good," Breezy said, sniffing.

"Cool Water," Hydrant said, sniffing his wrist. "It's my favorite cologne."

"I meant the food," Breezy said, smacking her lips.

"Oh," Hydrant said, embarrassed. "That's brunch. It's my specialty . . ."

"Broccoli and ham quiche," Breezy said, finishing Hydrant's sentence.

"You remembered?" Hydrant said, impressed.

"There's a whole lot of things I remember about you, Hydrant," Breezy said, sitting down on the lavender, beige, and pink-striped sofa.

Hydrant followed suit and sat down next to Breezy. The sexual tension between the two was so thick that they could hardly see each other through it.

Hydrant cleared his throat and offered Breezy a glass of wine, which she declined. Alcohol would only enhance the explosion of her out-of-control hormones. Hydrant helped himself to a glass, though.

"It's been so many years between us and yet I feel like we've never been apart," Hydrant said, sipping his wine.

"I know," Breezy said, looking down. Breezy thought about the argument she had had with Hydrant the night they broke things off for good. She might as well have had TLC's "No Scrubs" followed by the Destiny's Child song "Bills Bills Bills" playing in the background. That was pretty much the theme of the argument. Hydrant felt that the best way to make Breezy happy was to allow her to do her thang . . . to get a man who had pockets deep enough for her to deep-sea dive in. "I'm so sorry things had to go down like they did between us back in the day."

"Are you really?" Hydrant asked, licking his lips.

"Yes."

"Then why did you let me walk away, out of your life?" Hydrant asked in a sincere tone. "Why did you let me walk out that door and not so much as call my name?"

Breezy felt a rush of guilt. She had really cared about Hydrant, but back in those days she was on some crazy shit. Breezy mustered up enough courage to respond.

"Pride, I guess," she answered.

"Pride should be a sin," he said.

"I really did want you to come back, Hydrant, I just—" Breezy started getting dramatic as Hydrant placed his index finger over Breezy's shiny lips.

"Uh, uh. Don't," Hydrant said, almost in a whisper. "Listen, ma, this shit right here with me and you? It's about now. Fuck the past. Things are going to be different. We're going to be up front and open with one another about everything. No apologies and no regrets. All right? Is that all right with you?"

Hydrant said that shit with bass in his voice. Breezy loved it when a man, Hydrant in particular, put her ass in its place. She liked a man with a little bit of thug in his blood, not no man knocking her upside the head and shit, but an MC Lyte roughneck type of brotha. Hydrant was that type of brotha all day long.

"Well, since we're being open and all, there's something on my mind that I'd like to say," Breezy said, looking deeply into Hydrant's hypnotizing eyes.

"Speak on." He winked, taking a sip of his wine.

Breezy took the glass from his lips and placed it on hers. She guzzled down the remaining swallow, then spoke. "I appreciate brunch and all, but to be honest with you I don't want it." Breezy stood up.

"Well, damn, ma!" Hydrant said, shocked. "Was it something I said? Do I stink? You don't like the smell of Cool Water?"

Hydrant sniffed up under his left armpit and then his right one.

"I just don't have time for games," Breezy said.

"Games," Hydrant asked, looking up at her, confused. "Who's playing games?"

"You are!" Breezy said, standing over Hydrant. "You invite me over here, cook up this brunch, and make small talk with me."

"Breezy . . ."

Cutting Hydrant off, Breezy plopped down on Hydrant's lap in a straddling position. "Baby, let's just both stop playing games."

Hydrant wasn't the least bit surprised at Breezy's actions. This was the Breezy he knew, the blunt, in-your-face, down-ass chick that made his dick hard.

"All right," Hydrant said, licking his lips. "The games are over. I know why you're here and you know why you're here. Let's make love."

"Boy, stop playing. I don't want to make love to you," Breezy said seriously.

"Who's playing?" Hydrant said, looking around the room. "Just because we haven't seen each other in a while doesn't mean we have to start all over with how we feel about one another. It's our first date in years, but not our first date ever. We've been here before. I mean I know it's been a while since we've seen each other, but I won't think any less of you, as I'm sure you won't of me. It'll be like us picking up where we left off."

"Shhh, shhh, baby, it's not that." Breezy smiled, pulling Hydrant's Sean John sweater over his head. "I don't want to make love to you because I'm afraid you're gonna think I'm a hoe. Hell, you already know I'm a freak. I don't wanna make love because I wanna fuck!" Before Hydrant could respond, Breezy's tongue was down his throat.

"Girl, I put it on his ass," Breezy bragged to Jeva on her cell phone as she drove home from Hydrant's house. "The brotha was snoring, butt-naked on the couch when I left. The quiche burnt and all."

Jeva couldn't stop laughing. "Now what in the hell is he going to think when he wakes up and finds you gone?"

"Girl, I don't know," Breezy said. "I just got scared, you know. I felt like I might have blown it. I should have waited, but I couldn't. I wanted his ass sooo bad. I told my black ass that I wasn't going to give him any. I jumped on that dick like a pogo stick. And raw at that. Damn it! What was I thinking?"

"Girl, I know what you mean," Jeva said. "I had the talk with Chauncy on our very first date. He knows I'm not doing the casual sex thing. I've been celibate since Lance and the only man who's going to get a whiff of this milkshake is my husband, not my husbfriend, and not my husband-to-be, but my husband. But with you, girl, it's a little too late for all of that now. If I were you I'd be turning that car around and going straight back to Hydrant's house."

"And just why am I supposed to say I left?"

"You better stop off at a gas station and pick him up a three-dollar bouquet of flowers or something," Jeva suggested. "If you don't go back, you'll regret it."

Breezy sighed. "No apologies. No regrets."

"What?" Jeva asked.

"Oh, nothing," Breezy answered.

"So what are you going to do?" Jeva asked. "If you don't turn that car back around then you can forget there ever being anything more between you and Hydrant because you are both stubborn. You're not going to call him and he's damn sure not going to call you."

"That's the thing," Breezy sighed. "I don't know if there's ever really been anything more than just sex that me and Hydrant share. If that's the case, I don't know if I even want more."

"Well the clock's a tickin'," Jeva said.

"I hear it," Breezy said. "I hear it loud and clear. Look, I need a minute to think. I'll call you later."

Breezy hung up the phone and stopped at a four-way stop sign. In those few seconds she pondered over whether once again she would allow pride to block her blessings. She had just thanked God that Hydrant was back in her life. She promised God that it would be different this time, that she would take time to appreciate everything Hydrant had to offer and not just sex. At times she used to believe that the only thing she and Hydrant had in common was sex. But she set out this time to prove to herself otherwise. She wanted to prove to herself that she could have a relationship with a man based on something other than money and sex. But after her actions, perhaps she was just kidding herself. Maybe she was meant to spend the rest of her life alone.

11

SIX DEGREES OF SEPARATION

Jeva's palms were so sweaty that she could barely keep the phone receiver from slipping out of her hand. She had been holding it for seven minutes, thirty-eight seconds, and counting. Jeva took deep breaths when she felt as though she was going to faint. Her hands trembled and it felt as though every ounce of blood in her body had rushed to her head. She could hear her heart beating loud and clear. She felt ten times more nauseous than when she had been pregnant with Heather, and it was far worse than the feeling she had the day she laid on the clinic bed to abort Lance's baby.

Jeva had just finished watching an episode of *Maury Povich*. It was about paternity tests. There were women on the show who had lied to their mates and their children about the true paternity of their children. It was horrible. There were men who had raised children for years only to get the results of the paternity test proving that they were not the fathers. It was devastating. Not only were the men heartbroken, but Jeva could only imagine how the children were going to feel once they found out. And the women, some were just as shocked as the men while others had known all along that they had been living a lie.

Jeva had found herself crying through the entire show. There she was, one of those women living the lie.

Taking another breath and trying not to throw up, Jeva began dialing the phone number. This time she dialed all seven digits, actually giving the phone a chance to ring this time.

"Hello," a man's voice answered pleasantly.

Jeva froze.

"Hello?" the male voice said again, this time with slight agitation.

"Uh, hi, hello," Jeva said nervously.

"Hi. Who is this?" he asked, his voice much more friendly now.

"It's . . . it's me," she said.

"Jeva, is that you?"

"Yes. Yes, it's me, Jeva."

"Oh, how are you?" he asked, now relaxed.

"Fine, I guess."

"Hold on and I'll—"

"No, no. I need to speak with *you*," Jeva said quickly.

"Oh, okay. What's up?" he asked warily.

"I can't do this anymore. I can't keep this inside any longer. I know the last time I told you I would never bother you again, but my daughter—our daughter, deserves better. She deserves to know the truth," Jeva said in one breath.

"This can't be happening. This isn't fucking happening, not now!" he said, his voice low and angry. "Why, Jeva? Why do you do this? Why now?"

Jeva fought back a wave of nausea. "I know how you must feel and I'm sorry for doing this to you, but I'm dying inside. This entire situation is eating away at me. It has been for years. You have to understand where I'm coming from. Being adopted and growing up not knowing who my biological parents were has haunted me for my entire life. It still haunts me. Heather deserves better than what I got. She deserves to know you. She deserves a father just as much as any other child."

"Jeva, there has to come a time when you're going to have to let this adoption issue go. And as far as Heather is concerned, she has a father. Lance is her father. You can't just up and flip the script on that child now. Do you know how confused and hurt she'll be? And, Jeva, I do sympathize with your circumstances, but I won't take on the role of father to her. As selfish as it sounds, I just won't do it after all of these years. I won't do this to my children again."

"Heather *is* one of your children," Jeva said angrily. "Look, I'm not asking for you to be her daddy, Larry Bird. I just wanted to warn you that I think my daughter, I think everyone involved, needs to know the truth and I'm going to be the one to tell it. I mean it this time. I have to."

"So what are you trying to tell me?" his voice said, growing angrier. "Is the *Maury Povich Show* going to be giving me a call or what? You can do what you want, Jeva, but I won't let this happen without a fight. I mean, how do I even know she's really mine? You were a stripper for God's sake."

"And I was a virgin."

"Come on, do you still expect me to believe that? Every time a woman sucks a different man's dick she tells him it's her first time. A virgin stripper. Yeah, right!"

"Believe what you want. But you know the truth deep inside

and I'm sure it's been eating away at you the same way it's been eating away at me."

"Actually, I haven't thought twice about it," he said. "With all the other shit that's been going on in my life, I honestly never looked back at the situation."

"Afraid you were going to turn to salt if you did?"

"What?"

"Nothing. Anyway, I just wanted to give you a heads up is all," Jeva said. "Heather will know the truth. With or without your co-operation. Good-bye."

"Jeva, no, wait!" he said, catching her before she hung up the phone. "You can't. You can't do this, Jeva. No matter what your heart is telling you to do, it's just not the right thing. Think just for one minute the pain you would cause Heather. And what would you have accomplished? I'm not going to be a daddy to that child, ever. It will only hurt her more knowing she has a father who doesn't want to give her the time of day. I can't become a part of her life, not this late in the game. I'm sorry. I'm so sorry about all of this, but it was your decision to have that baby. Not mine."

"It was your decision to fuck me," Jeva said in a matter-of-fact tone. "And you were a married man at the time. You could have gotten your wife to fuck you instead of me."

"Damn it, you were a stripper in a strip club. I just wanted my dick sucked to keep it real. That's all I paid you for. It was your choice to take it a step further and fuck me for free. I'm sitting there with a hard dick with pussy in my face. I'm only a man. What did you expect?"

"I give men more credit than that," Jeva said.

"Look, Jeva, I don't mean to hurt your feelings, but it's the truth. And if you are going to tell your daughter the truth, you are going to have to tell her the whole truth."

Jeva began to cry. Telling her daughter who her real father was would mean telling her how she had been conceived. Maybe some secrets were better left untold.

"Jeva, you okay?" he asked, now concerned, but Jeva was too choked up to respond. "Heather is happy now, isn't she? Don't take that away from her. If it's money you need . . ."

"You know I don't need your money," Jeva said, cutting him off. "I just feel like I'm betraying so many people." Jeva began to cry harder. "She's my best friend."

"You didn't know her when you and I got together," he said, his tone comforting. "Who could have predicted in a million years that you two would ever meet one another, let alone become the best of friends? You can't keep beating yourself up about this, Jeva. It's the past. You made a decision that you felt was right for you and your daughter. It was the right decision, Jeva. There was nothing lost and nothing gained, but if you tell now, imagine all that you will lose. Heather will never look at you the same. Your daughter will hate you, Jeva. And don't even think about what this will do to your friendship. You'll be alone."

Jeva thought long and hard before replying. She took a deep breath and then sighed. "You're right. You're so right. If it isn't broke, don't fix it. I don't know what I was thinking. I just feel so alone sometimes and then this guilt thing comes over me, especially with Lance out of our lives now. I've just been having so much more time to think about the whole mess of a lie."

"I know, baby, but you're okay. You're a great mother. You are all that Heather needs. Don't make her suffer any more over this. She's already had one father walk out on her. When Lance walked away from you, he walked away from Heather as well. But when he walked away, he took the truth with him. Leave it alone, Jeva. Don't open up this can of worms," he said with his eyes closed and his fingers crossed on his end of the phone.

"Thank you. Thank you for talking some sense into me," Jeva said, wiping away her tears. "You're right this time. But that doesn't surprise me. You've been right all the other times too."

"Well, fortunately I only have to talk sense into you every few years or so." He chuckled. "So I shouldn't be hearing from you again until two thousand and . . ."

"Ha, ha," Jeva said with a fake laugh. "Thank you for being so understanding. Considering what happened the last time I called, I'm surprised you're being this understanding."

He shrugged off Jeva's last comment. "So are we okay? Are things okay?"

"Yes, yes they are," a calmer Jeva said.

"Okay, good," he said with a sigh of relief, wiping the perspiration that had formed on his forehead with the back of his hand. "Take care of you, okay?"

"I will," Jeva said with a smile. "You take care of you too."

"I will. Good-bye, Jeva."

"Good bye, Harris."

Jeva hung up the phone feeling okay about her change of heart. Only on a couple other occasions had she phoned Harris wanting to come clean to everyone about the the that fact that he was Heather's biological father. Only Harris and Jeva had known the truth. But unbeknownst to Harris, the last time Jeva called it just so happened that Tionne answered the phone at the same time he did. Instead of hanging up the phone, she remained on the line and listened to their entire conversation.

Harris was shocked when he discovered that Tionne had overheard Jeva's and his entire conversation. Tionne was so emotionally distraught by the conversation that she actually put her hands on Harris. She slapped him. She kicked him. She bit him. Harris refused to hit her back. He took his beating like a man. He did threaten to call the police on Tionne if she didn't control herself.

By then he had a bloody nose and scratches all over his hands and neck. Tionne threatened to tell Klarke the dirty little secret he had withheld from her. She actually hit *69 and called Jeva back, making the same threat to her.

This scared Jeva and Harris to death. Tionne could see it in Harris's eyes. At that moment she saw just how much Harris still cared for Klarke. He cared more about Klarke not knowing than he did about Tionne knowing. This only motivated Tionne more into telling Klarke. That would have ruined all chances of Harris ever patching things up with Klarke. But Tionne figured that she would have nothing to gain. Harris would walk out on her in a heartbeat. That's when Tionne knew that she had completely lost Harris's heart to Klarke, if she had ever really had it at all.

Harris got Tionne to end the conversation with Jeva, promising she wouldn't tell Klarke. He then got down on his knees and begged Tionne not to tell anyone. He even agreed to marry her. Tionne was insulted, but agreed. That's just how much she loved Harris. She was willing to be with him even though she wasn't the one he longed to be with.

Little did Harris know, but Tionne had actually paid Klarke a visit with the intention of telling her the truth anyway. She wanted to use the ammunition to make sure that Klarke would never be a threat to her relationship with Harris. She knew she had the atomic bomb. Besides that, Tionne had always suspected and accused Harris of still messing around with Klarke even after their divorce. Harris denied it, but when Tionne found a receipt showing that Harris had paid off the balance of Klarke's Rodeo truck, she knew something was still going on between the two.

To Tionne's surprise, when she arrived at Klarke's house to spill the beans, Klarke convinced her that without a doubt, there was no room in her life or heart for Harris. And although Tionne had planned on hurting Klarke, shattering her world with the dirt she had, she couldn't bring herself to do it. It was evident that no matter what Tionne did, said, didn't do or didn't say, she would never be the woman Harris truly wanted in his life. Tionne would have achieved nothing by betraying Harris so she took Harris and Jeva's secret to her grave.

Dealing with Tionne's death was hard enough for Harris, but knowing what pushed Tionne over the edge ate him up inside. If only Jeva had gotten that abortion like she had promised Harris she was going to do when she told him that she was pregnant.

When she first turned up pregnant with Heather, she didn't know what she was going to do. Getting an abortion had never even crossed her mind. She never thought in a million years she would see the stranger she had made love to in the Champagne Room. She had given him her pager number but he had never paged. She had given something precious to him, herself, and yet he had never even returned to the club to do as little as buy her a drink. Harris was the first person Jeva had ever given a private dance to. And instead of seeing to it that the customer got caught up in the fantasy of it all, Jeva got caught up herself.

What started off as a lap dance went from a twenty-dollar blowjob to consensual intercourse that resulted in a pregnancy. Ironically, Jeva was a virgin prior to her encounter with Harris. He was her first. Jeva had been saving herself for that knight in shining armor that would rescue her from the life of a stripper, take her away from the grimy business, and make her his bride. She wanted to be rescued like one of the characters on a soap opera she watched, *The Young and the Restless*. She was going to be Nikki, a character who came on the show as a strip-tease dancer, and Harris was going to be her Victor Newman, the rich and powerful character who married Nikki and took her away from the life. Jeva had even given herself the stage name Nikki, modeling after the character.

After five minutes with Harris, his smile, and his mature ways, Jeva felt that he was going to be the man she married. He was going to be the man she gave her virginity to and she wasn't even afraid, despite the fact that one of her foster mothers had done a damn good job of scaring her off from having premarital sex.

The foster mother used to actually check Jeva's and the other three foster girls' private areas whenever they returned home from school or any other type of outing of which she hadn't accompanied them. Jeva was only eleven years old at the time and wouldn't have known what a dick was if it had slapped her across the face. This had to have been her fifth foster home that she could remember. No one had cared enough about her to have the talk with her so sex was a taboo subject matter.

The "Panty Check," which is what the girls called it amongst themselves, occurred almost daily. The foster mother would pull on a pair of surgical gloves that she purchased in bulk boxes of one hundred, and call the girls into the bathroom one by one. One of the Hello Kitty beach towels, from a set of eight, would be laid across the black-and-white bathroom floor tiles. The girls knew to drop their panties and hand them to their foster mother. The girls would then lie along the towel while their panties were examined. The foster mother sniffed and checked for suspicious stains. Once the girls passed the panty check, their tiny clitoris would then be pushed to the left and then to the right. The foster mother would slightly open their vaginal hole and peek with her flashlight. Lastly she would sniff.

"You little bitches ain't gon' ruin my business by being able to tell the state you turned up pregnant under my watch," she would say to them. Jeva had learned that being a foster parent was treated as a business, extra income, by most of the homes she was placed in.

Although the panty check never hurt Jeva, it was very scary at first, but then it just became natural. For all she knew, all little girls experienced the panty check. Sometimes, afterward, the foster mother would sit the girls down over cookies and milk and explain to them that they were sexual beings and that men preyed upon them and that premarital sex was evil, an act only approved by the devil. She went as far as showing the girls a picture of several devil-like characters holding a woman down and forcing sex upon her. But Harris didn't look like any devil that night in the Champagne Room.

But Jeva had always been a dreamer. She ignored the fact that Harris was one of the types of men the veteran dancers had told her to keep an eye out for. His type would make you believe you were in a real relationship. He'd pay all the bills for a few thrills. But Jeva had worked up an entirely different scenario in her head. She would show Harris that she wasn't one of those gold-digger dancers. That she was an innocent young thing out on her own, looking for love. And that perhaps she was exactly what he was looking for out on the streets. Harris would be her Victor Newman and she would be the woman who brought him straight home after work instead of to the strip clubs. Little did she know that he already had a woman who should have brought his ass home after work, Klarke.

When Jeva missed her period she immediately visited the downtown Toledo Planned Parenthood clinic where her worst fear was confirmed. She was pregnant. But once again, Jeva thought that if she could just find this man and let him know that his offspring was growing inside of her, then he would be thrilled, to say the least.

Jeva cased out the strip club even on her off nights. She hardly made any money. She couldn't be attentive enough to prospective customers for eyeballing the room for Harris. But two months after finding out she was pregnant, lo and behold, Harris and a couple of his buddies from work stopped in. When Jeva saw him enter the club she left the guy who had just bought her a fifty-dollar drink sitting alone at the bar. She ran back into the dressing room to put on her street clothes. She didn't want to try and convince the man whose baby she was carrying that he could turn a hoe into a house-wife while wearing a sequined halter top with a matching G-string.

After getting dressed, Jeva approached Harris and asked him to join her in the Champagne Room. There she told him about her pregnancy, even showing him the cessation date provided by Planned Parenthood. Harris was sick. He literally vomited on Jeva's four-and-a-half-inch sequined stilettos. He damn near cried, ram-bling on and on about his wife and kids. This made Jeva sick, re-turning the favor of vomiting on his Stacy Adams.

It was clear that Jeva's fairy tale wasn't going to come true. Alone in the Champagne Room, she cried for an hour, gripping the three hundred dollars Harris had left her to pay for an abortion. Jeva had sworn to Harris that she would get the abortion. In the heat of the moment, Harris made it sound like the right thing to do. When it came down to it, though, for Jeva, abortion wasn't even an option at the time. She was going to have that baby. Jeva knew she had a long road ahead of her. She had no money and no health insurance. Soon her tummy would grow and she wouldn't even be able to helicopter down the pole for those measly five-dollar tips. She needed to make all the money she could and fast.

Jeva stuffed that three hundred dollars Harris had given her into her purple Crown Royal bag, put her G-string back on, and went to make that money. Almost Godsent, or so Jeva thought, as Jeva exited the dressing room she literally bumped into Lance. He was wandering about like a lost puppy while looking for the rest room. He had just moved to Toledo with his mom from De-troit and it was his first time out in the city.

Lance could tell Jeva had been crying and offered her a shoulder.

He spent the entire one hundred dollars he had brought to the club buying Jeva drinks and tipping her, in between her telling him of the awful predicament she was in.

Lance had just gotten a job as a maintenance man. He was no Victor Newman, but that didn't matter to Jeva. He was attentive, understanding, and not once did he judge her. He offered to help her in any way that he could. Jeva could tell that he meant it. Being new to the city, Jeva was comforting to Lance and Lance was definitely a comfort for Jeva. It didn't take much convincing on Jeva's part to get Lance to agree to commit to the role of being Heather's father. As a matter of fact, it was his idea. Before Jeva knew it, she and Lance were living together, decorating a nursery.

When Heather was born, she had a smooth bronze complexion, just like Lance. People would automatically say that Heather looked like him.

Jeva and Lance were able to live happily ever after for six years before an ugly breakup. It had taken almost that long for Jeva to get Lance to propose to her. They broke up only months before the wedding. Jeva found out that Lance was pretty much marrying her to benefit from a trust fund her biological parents had set up for her. Not only that, but he was cheating on her with Heather's babysitter and had even slept with Breezy when the two first became friends. Jeva found out about his cheating the same day he proposed. It was during her twenty-ninth surprise birthday party that Lance had thrown for her. Even after overhearing Breezy and Lance discuss their indiscretions through a closed bathroom door, Jeva was still willing to go ahead with the wedding. So she didn't peep a word of it to Breezy or Lance. After all, she hadn't peeped a word to Klarke about her and Harris either. Perhaps that's why she was able to forgive Breezy. Eventually, after she and Lance's breakup, Jeva did tell Breezy that she knew about her and Lance.

It was easy for Jeva to forgive Breezy because of the secret she herself was keeping about having slept with Harris. She knew how easy it was to get caught up in a web of deceit. Losing Lance was a blessing in disguise, but unfortunately, when Lance walked out of Jeva's life he walked out of Heather's too. As far as anyone knew, Lance was Heather's daddy. Jeva had never dared to tell a soul. Jeva knew, just like in the children's story book she always read to Heather, *The Secret Olivia Told Me,* by J. M. Jossel, that once you told a secret, it wasn't a secret anymore.

Heather eventually started asking for Lance. She didn't understand why her father didn't come to visit her. Jeva had ditched and dodged the subject matter with her as best she could. Heather understood that her parents had broken up, but she didn't realize that parents could break up with their children. To fill the void, Jeva spoiled Heather rotten, giving her everything her little heart desired. She figured that if she kept her happy, she'd keep her from asking questions that Jeva grasped for answers to. But how much longer could Jeva pull off the charade?

As Jeva jogged on the treadmill at the Scandinavian Health Spa, she couldn't help but notice the girl next to her struggling to figure out how to get her treadmill working. The girl looked familiar, but Jeva couldn't place her.

Jeva wanted to help the girl out, but she only had seven minutes left of her workout on the tread and she didn't want to stop her flow. J-Lo's vocals were flowing through her headphones, motivating her to keep going. It was on the next to the last song of the CD. She didn't need the groove of her Latina sista disturbed.

Being half Hispanic, Jeva tried to patronize the Latina and Hispanic artist. Since she grew up in foster homes with mostly white families, she didn't know much of anything about her Hispanic background. She felt she could learn a little bit about herself through the artists. She must have watched Jennifer Lopez portraying Selena over a hundred times. She was one of the many who still blasted the old Gloria Estefan and the Miami Sound Machine CDs in her Corvette.

After a few more moments of watching the chunky girl struggle, Jeva became annoyed with her. Her tummy fat was finding its way over her navy blue Ralph Lauren sweatpants. There was fatty skin bulging from underneath her sports bra that could clearly be seen through the Nautica T-shirt she was wearing. She was cute, though. She was Jeva's complexion with pretty brown eyes. She had partial dimples, not as deep as Jeva's, and her body could easily be molded into a sexy figurine with six months of dedication at the gym.

Jeva continued her workout as she looked the girl up and down. The frustrated and somewhat embarrassed girl was tapping her Tommy Hilfiger slide-on sneakers as she fondled with buttons on the face of the treadmill.

She's representing three different millionaires, Jeva thought to herself, shaking her head. *Why am I hating on her? Let me just help this girl out.*

Jeva removed the headphones from her head and placed them on the face of the treadmill. She hit the pause button on her treadmill and walked over to go show the girl how to turn hers on.

"The best way to do it is to just hit the quick-start button," Jeva said to the girl as she pointed to the button.

"Oh, thank you so much," the girl said with a smile. She pushed the button and used the white hand towel she had around her neck to wipe the sweat she had worked up just trying to get the piece of equipment started.

"Is this your first time working out here?" Jeva asked as she headed back to finish up her few minutes on the treadmill.

"Yeah. I used to walk around the track at my old job all of the time," the girl said. "Back home in Nevada I was able to walk year round. Here in the Midwest it gets way too cold."

"You're from Nevada, huh?" Jeva asked.

"I'm from here originally," the girl said, increasing the pace on the treadmill. "I lived here for the first year or so after I was born, but then my parents up and moved my brothers and sisters and me to Nevada."

"Oh," Jeva said, slipping her headphones back onto her head. "Well, enjoy."

Jeva hit the start button again and resumed her workout. After she cooled down and stretched, Jeva headed to the women's locker room to prepare to go into the steam room.

She peeled her sweaty Jerzee jogging suit off and wrapped herself up in a body towel. Once in the steam room, Jeva sat down, closed her eyes, and relaxed. She knew she only had a few minutes before she had to shower and get dressed. The maximum time children were allowed to stay in the Kids Klub was two hours, which meant that she had about thirty minutes to zone off into another world before having to claim Heather.

As steam filled the room Jeva could hear someone enter. When she opened her eyes it was the girl from the treadmill.

The girl noticed that Jeva's eyes were open. "Hello again," the girl said in her chipper voice.

Jeva nodded, smiled, then closed her eyes again. She hated to be rude because the girl was friendly. But Jeva was going on thirty-four years old. She didn't need any new friends in her life. Besides, there was something about this girl. She seemed like the needy type. And on top of that, she was phony. She had long, blond, bleached hair, and was tan, compliments of Tan and Wash. Damn prima donna. She didn't even have the decency to dye her dark brown eyebrows. It was obvious she wasn't a natural blonde. What was she hiding up under that bleach?

"Thanks for helping me out there," the girl went on. "You look like you come here often. I mean your figure and all. You look great."

Jeva kept her eyes closed, refusing to respond to the girl's comments. But that didn't stop her from babbling on.

"I really want to get my body looking right," the girl said, still not getting a response from Jeva. "I bet you come here several times a week to stay in such good shape."

Jeva sighed, realizing two things. One, she was being a total bitch by ignoring the poor girl and two, the girl wasn't going to stop talking no matter how much Jeva ignored her.

"Three times a week," Jeva finally responded. "I come here about three times a week for two hours."

"It shows. If you don't mind, maybe sometime we can work out together. You can show me your regimen."

Damn! Jeva thought to herself. She really wasn't up to making new friends.

"That would be nice," Jeva lied, with a straight face. She rolled her eyes up, but made sure the girl didn't see her.

"We'll have to exchange information," the girl said with the enthusiasm of a pep-rally cheerleader. "By the way, my name is Maria."

The girl smiled and held out her hand to Jeva. Jeva gave her a smile in return.

My name is Jeva," she said, rising to shake Maria's hand.

"Pleased to meet you," Maria said.

"Did you get a good workout in, Maria?" Jeva asked, with an "if you can't beat 'em, join 'em" attitude.

"As good as it was going to get," Maria replied with a chuckle. "Hell, just that little bit of walking on the treadmill I did made me work up an appetite."

"They sell health food here," Jeva said.

"Health food?" Maria said, turning up her face. "Normally health food means food with no taste. Isn't there anything else nearby to eat?"

Jeva thought for a moment.

"Nothing but a Starbucks." Jeva paused then quickly said, "Oh, and there's a Cinnabon down the street."

"Oooh, I love Cinnabon!" Maria said. "With extra icing."

"That's how I like it too," Jeva said.

The two girls paused briefly before Jeva said, "Looks like I'm all done."

Maria, on the same page as Jeva, laughed and said, "That's what I'm talking about. Girl, where you been all my life?"

The two jumped up and exited the steam room. They each showered and chatted as they got their street clothes on. Maria told Jeva a little about her three brothers and sisters and Jeva told Maria about Heather and the fact that she was adopted. Maria accompanied Jeva to retrieve Heather from the Kids Klub.

"Mommy," Heather said when she saw Jeva enter the Kids Klub.

"Did you have fun?" Jeva asked as Heather walked over to her.

"Um-hm," Heather said with a huge smile on her face.

"This is your girl?" Maria asked, shocked at how brown-skinned Heather was compared to Jeva. Jeva always got that look, especially from white women. They would usually ask something stupid like "Are you her nanny?" But sistahs were bold. When Jeva would pass by them on the streets holding Heather's hand, she wasn't two steps past them before she could hear them mumbling "You know her daddy's black."

"Yes, this is my little *mami*," Jeva said proudly.

"*Hola, mi chocolate chiquita*," Maria said, bending down, kissing Heather on each cheek.

"*Gracias*," Heather said with a huge smile.

Jeva stood back and watched the interaction take place between Heather and Maria. Heather was a very loving child, but she never even took to Breezy or Klarke the way she was taking to Maria.

"Heather, this is Maria. I just met her in the gym today. We were going to go over to Cinnabon. How does that sound?"

"Fine," Heather said, rubbing her tummy.

"Then what are we waiting for? *Vamonos!*" Maria said.

"You like speaking Spanish, huh?" Jeva asked. "Your accent is so natural. We speak a little somethin' somethin'. Just the basics."

"I consider English my second language," Maria said. "I was born in the States, but *mi madre* spoke only Spanish to us, mainly while yelling." She laughed.

"I know what that must have been like," Heather said, making a joke.

"All right now." Jeva pretended to threaten her. Jeva turned to Maria to ask her how her mother came to speak Spanish, but was interrupted by the child-care provider in charge of the Kids Klub.

"Heather, don't forget your jacket again," the child-care provider said, pointing to a little cubby hole that housed Heather's pink-and-powder-blue Baby Phat jacket.

"Oh, thank you," Jeva said, grabbing it and slipping it on Heather.

"Let's go," Heather said. "I mean *vamonos!*" She turned to Maria and smiled. Maria grabbed Heather's hand and they headed out of the Kids Klub. Jeva followed in complete amazement. She couldn't believe how well Heather was taking to her new associate. There was definitely something about her. But what was it? Jeva was going to make it her business to find out.

Jeva was sitting on her living room floor with photos spread out when the doorbell rang.

"*Un momento,*" Jeva yelled as she unfolded her legs from her Indian-style position and proceeded to answer the door. "Hey, Breezy. What's up?"

"Girl, same old, same old," Breezy said, entering. She walked straight over to Jeva's love seat and plopped down, kicking her shoes off.

Breezy sighed. Jeva could tell there was something on her mind so she decided to fish.

"Have you talked to Hydrant?" Jeva asked.

"No, not yet," Breezy said sadly.

"You and your pride," Jeva said, shaking her head. "That's going to be your downfall. You better call that boy."

"Jeva, I can't. I don't know what to say."

Jeva could see that Breezy's situation with Hydrant was really bothering her. She walked over and sat down next to Breezy on the love seat. She put her head on Breezy's shoulder.

"You know I love you, right?" Jeva said.

"Yes," Breezy answered.

"But you know you're wrong. You done went over that man's house, fucked his brains out, and left him butt-naked on the couch without as much as a phone call. Imagine what you would feel like if a man did that to you."

"I know, but I just felt so icky. Like a hoe, giving it up before dinner even."

"You and Hydrant have too much history to let that bother you."

"Easy for you to say," Breezy said, pushing Jeva's head off of her. "You been using pussy as a waiver with Chauncy. I don't have a waiver anymore."

Jeva laughed. "Girl, I'm not using pussy. One night I was just sitting here listening to the Yolanda Adams CD I just bought and a song came on titled 'Talk to Me.'"

"After all these years I didn't know you listened to gospel

music," Breezy said, surprised. "You're usually listening to J-Lo, Nina Sky, or somebody. Besides, I thought only black people listened to Yolanda."

"Excuse me," Jeva said, clearing her throat. "That is coming from a girl whose favorite song is 'Gypsy' by Stevie Nicks."

Breezy chuckled and Jeva continued.

"Girl, before I knew it I was sitting here crying and the words to that song became my own. I knew right then and there that I had to start living right. I mean, I'm not perfect and there are still some things that I feel like I'll never be forgiven for, but it's never too late to start fresh today. I'm going to try to change my life one thing at a time, the first thing is honoring my body."

"I feel you," Breezy said. "But, still, that doesn't help me any."

"You can start by getting rid of the one thing that has always controlled your life."

"And what's that?"

"Pride," Jeva said, grabbing hold of Breezy's hand. "That damned overbearing pride of yours."

The doorbell rang, causing both Jeva and Breezy to jump. Jeva looked at Breezy with a puzzled expression.

"Who in the world?" Jeva said as she walked over to the door and looked through the peephole. "Oh, it's Maria, that girl I was telling you about that I met at the gym."

Jeva opened the door and Maria was standing there with an older white man. He had graying hair, and was very sophisticated. He was wearing a black suit with a crimson silk tie. He was evenly tanned, giving him a smooth bronze complexion. Without the help of the summer's sun, he would have probably been as pale as a ghost.

"Hey, Jeva," Maria said, hugging her.

"Well, hello," Jeva said. "I didn't know you were going to be stopping by."

"I'm sorry for not calling first, but my *papi* is in town," Maria said, putting her arms around the man. "We're on our way out to dinner and I wanted him to meet you. Dad, this is Jeva Price." Maria stepped to the side and stared at her father's facial expression.

"My little girl can't stop talking about you," the man said, holding out his hand to shake Jeva's. "I just had to meet this Jeva person."

"Well, the pleasure is all mine, sir, of course," Jeva said, shaking his hand.

There were a few awkward seconds as Jeva waited for Maria to interject. But Maria just stood there as if she were waiting on a specific reaction between her father and Jeva.

Jeva cleared her throat. "Would you two like to come in for a minute?"

Maria paused, looking away from her father and at Jeva. "Actually, we wanted to know if you would like to join us for dinner," Maria said. "Is that okay, Dad?"

"Certainly." He smiled. "A friend of yours is a friend of mine."

Again, Maria paused, as if expecting some other type of reaction from her father.

"Well, I'd love to, but I have company," Jeva said, opening the door wider so that they could see Breezy sitting on the love seat. "This is Breezy."

Breezy looked up, smiled, then waved at Maria and her father. Breezy had the same feeling that Jeva had the first time she saw Maria, that something was familiar about her.

"Breezy, this is Maria and her father," Jeva said.

"Mr. Fendell," Maria's father spoke, introducing himself. "Lovely to meet you." He walked over to Breezy and held out his hand.

Breezy paused but then shook his hand. "You kids go ahead

and have fun," she said, getting up in a hurrying manner and slipping her shoes back on.

"It's good to finally meet you," Maria said, walking over to Breezy to shake her hand. "Jeva has told me lots about you. We'll all have to go out sometime."

"Yes. Yes, we will," Breezy said insincerely.

"As a matter of fact," Maria said, "we can all go out right now. How about joining us for dinner?"

Breezy wasn't feeling it. She wasn't into meeting new people—as a matter of fact, she was lightweight upset that Jeva was trying to pull someone new into their clique. But she remained cordial.

"Oh, I couldn't," Breezy said. "I've got so much to do. I haven't even been home yet from work and I have to go, uh, umm, uh . . . feed my dog."

Jeva looked at Breezy, confused. She knew damn well Breezy didn't have a dog, but she figured this was Breezy's way of not wanting to hurt Maria's feelings.

"Yep," Jeva said to Breezy. "You better get going. I'm sure Fe Fe is starved."

"Then we'll all definitely have to go out some other time," Maria said.

"Yes, yes, we will. Some other time," Breezy said, walking toward the door. "Well, it was nice meeting you, Maria," Breezy said, squeezing between Maria and her father to leave. "And uh, Mr. Fendell. I'll call you later, Jeva," Breezy said, hurrying off.

"Yes, call me," Jeva said as she waved bye to Breezy.

Maria threw her arms up and said, "Looks like you can join us after all."

"Looks like I can. It is okay if Heather joins us as well, isn't it?" Jeva asked.

"Of course," Maria said.

"Then I guess it's a date." Jeva smiled. "I'll just run upstairs and get Heather together really quick. Have a seat and get comfortable. We'll only be a minute." Jeva headed up the stairs. Halfway up she stopped and turned around.

"By the way," Jeva said, "where are we going to eat?"

"The Cheesecake Factory," Mr. Fendell answered.

"What a coincidence," Jeva said. "That's one of my favorite spots."

Maria looked at her father, then said to Jeva, "Daddy always says that there's no such thing as coincidence. Everything happens for a reason."

"Hmm," Jeva said as she headed up the steps again. "I'll be sure to keep that in mind."

It wasn't even the third Saturday of the month. Actually, it was the middle of the week and Klarke, Breezy, and Jeva were at the Cheesecake Factory. They weren't indulging in any food, only drinks. It was actually a pity party for Klarke. She had turned in twelve applications and had been on seven job interviews without success. She needed a job.

"What the hell am I going to do?" Klarke asked as they sat at the bar.

"Don't give up," Jeva said. "There is a job out there with Klarke Taylor written all over it."

"Laroque," Klarke corrected Jeva.

"Oh yeah, Klarke Laroque. Hey, there's my Chauncy," Jeva said, excited when she noticed him across the room.

"Speaking of Chauncy, the other night I know you invited him to your house to watch a movie. I tried calling to see how it went, but never got an answer. I called all night and even in the morning," Breezy said with a suspicious look on her face.

"You know I turn the ringer off when I have company," Jeva said.

"My point exactly," Breezy responded. "I'm guessing he spent the night."

Both Breezy and Klarke waited patiently for Jeva to respond.

"You're guessing right," Jeva said proudly.

"I knew you were going to give in and do it to that man. I knew you were," Breezy said.

"Do what?" Jeva asked, dumbfounded.

"It, man. Did y'all do it?" Breezy asked.

"Uh, uh," Jeva said firmly. "I am done with casual sex. I'm staying a virgin for real this time. I already told you that."

"For real this time?" Klarke said, laughing as she took a sip of her drink.

"You know damn well you fucked him," Breezy said.

"I did not and shhh. Here he comes," Jeva said nervously as Chauncy approached their table with a bottle of wine in one hand and holding three wineglasses by their stems in the other.

"For my favorite ladies," Chauncy said as he placed a glass in front of each of the women and poured them a glass.

"Oh, none for me, thank you," Breezy said.

Everyone stopped and looked at her in amazement. Breezy had never been known to turn down anything free.

"What?" Klarke said in disbelief. "Since when did you stop drinking?"

Breezy sighed and turned her attention to Chauncy. "So, Chauncy, Jeva tells us you guys have been hitting it off just swell."

Klarke laughed under her breath.

"Uh, yeah," Chauncy said, embarrassed. "We have."

Jeva lowered her head and smiled, biting her bottom lip. Breezy was watching how the two were acting as if they had something to hide.

"Well, I just wanted to come over and say hey," Chauncy said. "As you can see, we're pretty busy in here so I need to get back to work. Jeva, love, I'll see you tonight." Chauncy kissed Jeva's hand. "Klarke, Breezy, as always, it was a pleasure to be in your company."

As Chauncy walked away, Breezy mumbled, "Seems like the pleasure was all Jeva's. Girl, the physical attraction between you two filled up this whole goddamn place. Who are you kidding with this you-didn't-sleep-with-him business?"

"I didn't," Jeva said in a high-pitched voice. "Just because you were all on Hydrant like a dog don't mean the rest of us are out bumpin' and grindin'."

"Amen," Klarke said, with a look on her face that suggested she wished she were getting hers on.

"Not another man is getting a sip of this milk without buying the cow, and I mean it!" Jeva declared. "Sex is overrated. This lust shit is for women in their early twenties who don't know any better. But this cat right here," Jeva pointed to her crotch area, "will only be purring for one man, and that's my husband."

Klarke and Breezy took in every last one of Jeva's words that she had managed to relay in a sincere, to-the-point tone. But Breezy could see right through her little good girl act.

"You might be fooling Klarke with that celibate talk, but, hoe, I know you spread them legs like an eagle's wings."

The women all burst out laughing.

"Y'all are too much for me," Klarke said, sipping her wine. She then held her glass up in the air to make a toast. "To those who aren't getting any, to those who are, and to those who wish they were."

"Hear, hear," Jeva and Breezy said. "Hear, hear."

12

BLAME IT ON REO

"Get on top," Reo told Meka as he rolled over onto his back. He had just finished off a few minutes of foreplay, which consisted of a kiss here and a rub there. With only a pair of boxers on Reo pressed his body against Meka's, which was covered in a knee-length, wine-colored nightgown that had slits on each side up to her thighs. Slowly Reo ran his hand up her body, pushing the gown up, trying to get it over her head.

"I don't feel like it," Meka said, accepting the warm juicy kisses Reo had started planting on her neck and all over her face. For three days straight she had sexed the hell out of him. Ever since Klarke had turned up on the scene, Meka had been motivated to perform sexual acts that she never thought she would perform, sober anyway. She felt as though she was beginning to get burnt out on sex. She wanted to turn her face away from Reo's kisses, but forced herself to lay there and accept them as if they were worth a million bucks. Just as long as he wasn't kissing on Klarke.

"Come on, girl. You know it's been good," Reo said as he began to wriggle out of his boxers after finally getting the gown over her head. Meka rolled her eyes up in her head and ignored his comment.

"Just put it in," Meka ordered as Reo rubbed Simmy against her clit. As always, Reo followed her directions. He slowly inserted himself into Meka, one inch at a time until he was almost fully inside of her. Meka wiggled and twisted if Reo tried to put Simmy all the way inside of her. She claimed to have a petite pussy and would whine that Simmy was hurting her. But as far as Reo was concerned, it was as big as a house, especially after two babies. But still, he withheld a couple of inches.

It took Reo a minute to get into the rhythm because Meka kept fucking up his flow by trying to position him so that his body was perfectly centered on top of her.

Finally the shit was feeling damn good to Reo. Meka's walls were warm and soft like cotton. The more he stroked, the better it felt, and the quicker he would cum. But he didn't want to cum just yet so he slowed down.

"Why are you stopping?" Meka said with an attitude.

"I was about to cum," Reo said, breathing heavily.

"Isn't that the point?" Meka asked. She wanted him to hurry up so they could be over with it already.

"You just feel so good. I want to make it last forever," Reo said as he increased his pace once again.

Meka, who had pretty much been lying there the entire time, decided to put her hips into motion. Every time the thought of him being with Klarke instead of her popped into her head, she became motivated to give in to her man's needs. She humped Reo back hoping that her minor contribution would make Reo go ahead and bust one. She even threw in some fake moans and groans to make Reo think that he was really doing the damn thang.

"Oh shit," Reo said.

Meka looked at Reo's face and knew he was about to cum. He had that ugly look on his face. The left side of his face twisted up and he gritted his teeth together and huffed and puffed.

"Don't cum inside of me," Meka reminded Reo. Only once every blue moon did Meka allow Reo to nut inside of her. She hated the feeling of his bodily fluids inside her. The last time she allowed him to release inside of her she had forgotten to insert her diaphragm and ended up pregnant. She'd been on the pill ever since.

"Just let me cum inside of you this one time," Reo begged as he began to dip in and out of Meka faster and faster.

"No," Meka said, putting a halt to her hip rolling. "I let you cum in me the last time we did it."

Now was no time to argue. Reo was seconds away from nutting and he wasn't about to let Meka's attitude take away from the feeling.

"I'm about to cum, baby," Reo said. "I'm about to cum."

"Pull out," Meka reminded him as she grooved her hips a little bit, watching Reo's face the entire time. His eyes were closed.

"Oh, you feel so good. Fuck me back. C'mon, don't just lay there. Fuck me back."

Meka looked at Reo as if he was crazy. He knew better than to talk shit to her while having sex. But she decided to let it slide and continued to slowly hump him back. The sound of their bodies smacking together did it for Reo.

"Oh shit," Reo said pulling himself out of Meka and squeezing his hand tightly around Simmy. He slid his hand up and down, up and down as he squirted on the bed.

Meka scooted out of range. "You didn't get any on me, did you?"

Reo continued to empty himself.

"That was a lot," Meka said, watching him. "I made you cum a lot this time."

Reo paused and chuckled. "I pretty much made myself cum. Don't you see me here jacking my shit off?" Reo said.

"That's insulting," Meka said, sitting up. "What am I now, some hole you use to just stick your thing in to get yourself going?"

"You said it, not me," Reo said, getting up off the bed. He picked up his boxers and wiped himself off, looked at Meka, then walked into the bathroom to take a piss.

"You got any more drink up in this house?" Nate asked Reo. The two were halfway through their game of chess.

"Damn, man," Reo said, holding up an empty bottle of J. Roget. "You pretty much drank this one by yourself. What's the deal?"

"Just thirsty I guess," Nate said, getting up from the couch, heading for Reo's kitchen. "I know where you keep it. I'll check."

Reo studied the chessboard until Nate returned with the second bottle in hand. It was already opened.

"Whose turn is it?" Nate said as he poured himself a glass of J. Roget, damn near drinking it while he was still pouring it.

"Dude, what's really going on?" Reo said, laughing.

"Man, you mean to tell me that you ain't worried?" Nate said, drinking down his glass.

"Worried about what?" Reo asked.

"Meka and Persia."

"They're big girls."

"I know that, but they're complete opposites. Aren't you afraid of what could be going on?"

"They're at your house watching the second season of *Sex and the City* and nibbling on wingdings and meatballs. What could possibly go wrong?"

"Uh-hm. You don't know my Persia," Nate said, gulping down another glass.

"Yeah, seeing how she got your black ass in check, no telling what poison she's feeding my baby."

"Nigga, please," Nate said, catching himself. He knew Reo hated the casual use of the word "nigga" no matter what color the person saying it was. "I mean, negro."

Reo twisted his mug up as if to say Nate's second choice in words wasn't any better.

"Anyway," Nate continued. "Didn't nobody put me in check. Persia is a good woman. I had to be a reflection of my girl. But before I met her, I used to be the ladies' pet and the men's threat." Nate grabbed himself and posed. "Hell, if I wasn't a married man, I could have gotten your wife to marry me instead of marrying you."

"Please," Reo said, taking a sip of the fresh glass of J. Roget Nate had just poured him. "KAT wouldn't have looked at you twice." Reo started laughing, but Nate just sat there staring at him. Reo finally realized what words had just escaped his mouth.

"Damn," Reo said, sighing and shaking his head. He stood up to get his head together.

"You all right?" Nate asked.

"Yeah, yeah, man. I'm cool," Reo said, gulping down his drink. "Pour me another glass."

Nate obliged as he watched his best friend pace the living room floor. "This is the third time in two months you've called Meka KAT. The last time I didn't call you on it, but I know you knew."

"My head is just all fucked up, man," Reo said. "It just seems as though Meka and my relationship is so sometimey. Granted, I haven't gone on as many book signings as I had been in the past. Especially since my pops passed. But by the same token, I've been spending a lot of time at my mom's house. She needs me."

"You don't need to make excuses for me," Nate said.

"Who said I'm making excuses?" Reo snapped.

"Aight, partna'. Calm down," Nate said, walking over to Reo and putting his hand on his shoulder. "I know you and Meka have your problems here and there, and I know you are really not trying to hear what I'm about to say, but you're gonna hear it anyway. This is your entire fault. I hate to say it, man, but this is all your fault."

"With best friends like you . . . ," Reo said, not finishing the old cliché.

"I'm serious, man."

"Yeah, yeah. Just blame it on Reo. Blame it all on Reo."

"You married one woman while you were still in love with another woman," Nate said.

Reo paused. "What was I supposed to do, man?" Reo asked sincerely. "What was I supposed to do? KAT was gone, out of my life for the rest of my life. I mean, she pled guilty to the crime. How was I supposed to know she didn't really do it? How was I supposed to know she would get out again someday?"

"You weren't supposed to know," Nate said. "You were just supposed to be there for her. You took vows, man."

Reo took a gulp of his drink. "I've known Meka forever. I grew immune to her and her ways. And I do love her. I do."

"Sounds like it's not me you're trying to convince," Nate said. "You've never heard me say that I've doubted how you feel about Meka. It's just a shame that you claim to love Meka, but you're in love with KAT."

Reo sighed. "You always could see right through me, Nate."

"I don't have to see right through you. You're a good man, my friend," Nate said, patting Reo on his shoulder. "You wear your heart on your sleeve is all. So just think, if I can see it, don't you think Meka can see it too?"

Meka was the first of the invited guests to arrive at Persia's house. Persia had invited Meka, as a favor to her husband, to join her for girlfriend day, which was the day she and her friends got together to watch past episodes of *Sex and the City.*

"I'm glad you could make it," Persia lied as she let Meka in the door. "The others aren't here yet, but they will be soon. They're always late."

"That's the thing with black people," Meka joked. "They always want their check on time, but yet they're always late for work."

Persia let Meka laugh that one off alone. She hoped she'd get talk like that out of her system before her friends arrived or there could be trouble.

"I brought some wine and some appetizers," Meka said in a jolly tone. "It's white wine. Dark wine just doesn't taste as smooth. It's as dry and rough as a dark-skinned person after a swim."

Persia stared at Meka in disbelief. Did she think that just because they both had fair complexions it was okay to make fun of dark-skinned people? Persia wasn't feeling it. Nevertheless, she figured Meka would have enough sense not to behave so shamefully in front of her guests.

"I see you have meatballs and chicken drums," Meka said. "They look delicious, but I brought something else."

Meka uncovered a tray of little chicken squares with pineapples and toothpicks stuck through them.

"They're chicken breasts. White meat." Meka smiled. "Aren't they adorable? I bought them just like this from Meijers Deli."

The doorbell couldn't have rung soon enough for Persia. She excused herself and went to open the door. It was her friends Marsha and Kimmi. They were sisters. Persia invited them in and walked them into the kitchen so that they could set out the items they had brought with them.

"Meka," Persia said, beginning the introductions. "These are my friends, Marsha and Kimmi."

"Nice to meet you both," Meka said, admiring the beauty of the women. The sisters could pass for twins although they weren't. They were fair skinned with short haircuts and one was just a tad taller than the other. "This is going to be so fun. I love hanging out with my beautiful sistahs."

The sisters couldn't get a take on Meka just yet, but she kind of reminded them of Whitley from the sitcom *A Different World*.

Once again, the doorbell rang.

"That must be San," Persia said. "She's always the last to arrive." Persia ran off to let San in and rejoined Meka and the other women in the kitchen thereafter.

"Meka, this is my best friend, San," Persia said. "San, this is Meka."

San held out her hand to shake Meka's. Meka was standing there with her mouth damn near to the floor. San was a five-foot, eight-inch bombshell. She had straight hair that went down to the upper part of her back. You could tell she practically lived at the gym by the cut of her body. Her skin was flawless, makeup applied like a pro. And she was chocolate. Dark. Black as a bowling ball.

"You are soooo cute to be dark skinned," Meka said.

Silence fell upon everyone in the room. The shit was about to go down. And they hadn't even put the damn DVD in yet.

San looked Meka up and down several times. She took a deep breath and smiled.

"I'm not dark skinned. I'm black," San replied. "Which makes you what?"

Persia, Kimmi, and Marsha all snickered. That was just like San's style. Not to clown, but to come back with game. But Meka, not even really listening to the words that were coming out of San's mouth, continued on with her ignorant talk.

"Oh, people think I'm mixed with something all of the time," Meka said, completely flattered. "Some of them still don't believe me when I tell them that I'm African-American. I guess because I wasn't cursed with skin as dark as yours or coarse hair. But you are an exception. What do you do to get your hair so straight? Do you use one of those hot combs? It really works for you. I would have even been your friend in high school."

"Meka!" Persia said. "Have you lost your muthafuckin' mind?"

Meka had never heard such language fall from Persia's lips. She had always pictured Persia as this soft-spoken, light-complected, long-haired pretty girl. To Meka, Persia was acting like the dark-skinned nappy-headed girls with that black attitude that she kept away from in school.

"Excuse me?" Meka said to Persia.

"Who do you think you are to come here and insult my friend like that? Hell, you're insulting me."

"Persia! I can't believe this is you," Meka said, shocked.

"Don't let the light skin fool you," Persia said. "I do know how to take this to the street and if the street's too far, we can take it where we are."

"Obviously I made a big mistake accepting your invitation," Meka said, grabbing her purse and jacket.

"And obviously I made a big mistake by extending you an invitation, so why don't your take your color-struck ass and get the fuck up out of here? And just for the record, it was your husband's idea for me to invite you to hang out. Obviously he doesn't think you can make friends on your own and now I see why. Your being here by no means was my idea. So you can blame it on Reo!"

Meka stormed off with Persia close behind to slam the door behind her. Persia was beyond heated. It took everything in her not to grab Meka by the hair and beat her down, but it would have been hard getting a grip. After the damage Breezy had done, Meka's stylist had had to cut plenty of it off to get it back in good condition. Persia simply took a deep breath and walked back into the kitchen.

Her friends were standing there as if the entire day had been ruined. No one knew what to say to change the tone. Persia looked around the room and noticed the bottle of wine that Meka had brought. She ran over and grabbed it quickly, as well as the chicken breasts.

Persia ran back to the front door and couldn't get it opened quickly enough.

"Hey, Meka, you forgot something," Persia called. "Take your light-skinned liquor and your light-skinned appetizer and shove it up your light-skinned ass!" She threw the contents into Meka's hands.

The bottle hit the tire of Meka's pearl-colored Cadillac and shattered onto the car. Persia had been aiming for the sidewalk but her throw was a little long. The chicken landed on the front hood of the car. Scared for her life of this crazy deranged woman, Meka jumped into the car and drove off.

Persia and her friends stood in the doorway in hysterics.

"I hope I didn't mess up her light-skinned car." Persia laughed.

13

A PLACE FOR YOU

Klarke had just unpacked the last box of the very few boxes she had moved to her new place. Her new living room furniture had been delivered that same day and she was worn out from arranging everything. That's why she furnished her home one room at a time, with the bedroom being first, so that she wouldn't be overwhelmed all at once. But today it was official. The living room was the last of the last. She was fully moved into her home.

She had used her debit card to purchase the living room furniture, as she had done for her bedroom furniture as well as HJ's and Vaughn's room-slash-guest room. She had to buy linen for the kitchen, which she decorated in ivy with ivy-printed dishcloths, dish towels, burner covers, place mats, floor rug, and a white clock printed with ivy. She had to purchase two bathroom sets, one for the main bath and one for the master-bedroom private bath. She decorated the main bath in purple and her private bath in black and red to match her black-and-red satin comforter set she had in her bedroom.

Klarke's stomach ached thinking about how much money she had spent and still she had no job. She was afraid to even look at the balance of her bank account.

"I need a job," Klarke said to Breezy who was helping her put away the new dishes, pots, and pans she had purchased from Value City. She was just now getting around to doing all that. She had been spending most of her time job hunting. "They hiring where you work?"

"One almost-felon with a scandal is enough at my joint," Breezy said. "My boss be wanting to ask me so bad if I really had anything to do with the death of my father."

"You're kidding me," Jeva said, entering the kitchen with Maria. Today was the first day Klarke had the pleasure of meeting Maria. Jeva recruited Maria to help them add the final finishing touches to getting Klarke situated and christening her new place.

"Girl, he be dancing around words, too pussy to just come out and ask. But fuck it. During review or Christmas bonus time his punk ass always hooks a sistah up. I guess he scared I'm going to take him out too or something. I don't pay them white folks no mind."

Maria cleared her throat.

"Oh, my bad," Breezy said to Maria. "I keep forgetting you're white."

"Never mind me, I'm talking about Jeva. I mean how would you feel if we walked around using the words 'black folks'?"

"Where did you say you met this chick?" Breezy asked. It was obvious she was getting ready to tear into Maria by the tone she was using.

"Oh, don't worry about it," Jeva said to Maria, breaking up the fight before it started. "I don't pay that kind of stuff no mind."

"Well, *mi madre* taught me to always be proud of my heritage, each of them."

"Oh, are you mixed with something?" Klarke asked. She could tell that Maria was mixed with something because she had that exotic look about her, kind of like Jeva, just not as obvious with all the dye and makeup. She didn't want to ask her, though, because she remembered Jeva telling her how much she hated always being asked if she was mixed with something.

"Yes my mother is Cu—"

The loud doorbell cut off Maria, scaring the women. In unison they all screamed. They had no idea the doorbell was that loud.

"Girl, what do you have your doorbell set on?" Breezy asked. "One notch above loud as hell?"

"I'll get it," HJ said as he came running down the steps. "Finally, the pizza man is here."

"Let me get the money," Klarke said, exiting the kitchen to go find her purse.

"Hi," HJ said to the deliveryman as if he knew him.

"Hey, kid," the deliveryman said.

With money in hand Klarke came around the corner. Her heart was racing and her palms were sweaty. She knew that voice, but she never thought she'd ever hear it again. As Klarke walked up to the door her suspicions were correct. The voice did, in fact, belong to the man that she thought it did, her second ex-husband, Rawling.

"Well, well, well, if it isn't Miss Klarke," he said, smiling a huge grin. "What a surprise."

"I should say the same," Klarke said in a stale tone. She could not believe that this forty-year-old man was delivering pizzas. She hoped to God that it was his second job.

"Long time no see," Rawling said, trying to get sexy on her.

Right now Klarke didn't know if she wanted to spit on him, scratch his eyeballs out, or just slam the door in his face. But whatever she decided to do, she wasn't going to do it until after she got her two extra-large pizzas and two two-liters of Coke. Klarke took the Coke bottles that were sitting on top of the two pizza boxes. "HJ, grab the pizzas, honey, and take them into the kitchen."

HJ did as he was told. "Take care, little man," Rawling said as HJ walked away.

Klarke handed him two twenty-dollar bills and waited on her five dollars and ninety-eight cents change. Ordinarily she would have allowed the deliveryman to keep the change, but no way in hell was she going to give that bastard a tip.

"So how's life treating you? Obviously pretty well," he said, scoping out her new leather furniture. "I know you heard about that little incident with me and one of the students at the community college. I hope you didn't believe everything you heard. It wasn't what they made it sound like. I didn't know she was only seventeen. Yeah, I had to do my time, though. But it's all good baby, baby."

It was clear that Rawling was going to be the old man in the club trying to get a feel on the young girl's booties on the dance floor. This fool might as well have had a gold tooth, a brim with a feather, and goldfish swimming around in the heels of his shoes. He was a fucking mess and he could see that Klarke wasn't interested in anything that had gone on in his life. Her eyes were cutting him like a knife.

"I been working at this pizza joint for a minute now, my uncle owns it. Society isn't too quick to forgive a brotha, especially when he gotta report where he lives and the sex-offender flyers get plastered all over the neighborhood and thangs. Hard to get hired anywhere. But I'm maintaining. Hey, maybe one day I can stop by and perhaps . . ."

Before he could finish his spiel, Klarke attempted to close the door but he stopped it with his hand.

"Hold up, Miss Lady," he said smiling. "I can understand if you might not want to kick it with me and all, but a brotha can't even get a tip?"

Klarke thought about that one for a second before responding.

"You mean to tell me that you don't have any of that money left that Harris paid you?" Klarke asked.

If only Klarke could have bottled up that look of sheer shock on Rawling's face. He didn't even know how to respond. How could he respond? Nothing that man could have said was worth Klarke listening to. But obviously he didn't feel the same way as he opened his mouth to speak, maybe to perhaps explain himself or apologize even for taking a bribe to marry her. Before he could get a word out, though, Klarke slammed the door in his face. She stood looking at the closed door before bursting out laughing and heading into the kitchen with the Cokes in hand.

"What's so funny?" Breezy wanted to know as she devoured a slice of pep and cheese pizza.

Klarke couldn't stop laughing. She was laughing so hard that her eyes filled with tears.

"Ma, you so crazy," HJ said, exiting the kitchen with several slices of pizza and a paper cup full of soda.

"Share. We want to laugh too," Maria said.

"What's funny?" Jeva asked, laughing. By now everyone was laughing. Laughter was definitely contagious.

"Karma is what's funny," Klarke finally answered.

"Who's she?" Maria asked.

The women all stopped to look at her as if she was stupid.

"You'll never guess who just delivered the pizza," Klarke said.

"Who?" the women said in unison.

"Rawling!" Klarke started laughing again.

"You are shitting me?" Breezy said. "I thought he was an instructor at the community college."

"Well, seems as though Mr. I'm-too-sexy-for-my-shirt caught a case messing around with one of his underage students."

"No way," Jeva said as her jaws dropped.

"Um-hm, and from the sounds of it he had to do a little time for his crime," Klarke added.

"Serves the son of a bitch right," Breezy said, popping a pepperoni in her mouth.

"And I swear to God, y'all," Klarke laughed, "if that fool didn't remind me of Jerome-Jerome from the Martin Lawrence show."

"Who's Rawling?" Maria asked, confused at the matter.

"He's one of Klarke's ex-husbands," Jeva answered. "To make a long story short, Klarke's first husband paid him to rig a relationship and marry Klarke."

"Why?" Maria asked, on the edge of her seat.

"Harris felt as though he was paying too much money to Klarke in alimony so if he could get her married off then he wouldn't have to pay anymore," Jeva replied. "Rawling planned to stay married to Klarke long enough for Harris not to have to pay alimony, but not long enough where he would have to."

"That totally blows," Maria said, noticing Klarke's laughter turning to hurt. "You okay, *mami*?"

"*Si,*" Klarke said with a warm smile to Maria.

"Here, eat something," Maria said, handing Klarke a paper plate with two slices of pizza on it.

"Thank you," Klarke said, taking it. "Where did you say you found this girl again, Jeva? I like her."

Klarke bit into the pizza and it was as if everyone was watching her chew. Everyone noticed how bummed she was all of a sudden and didn't know exactly what to say to comfort her.

"Don't let that loser get you down," Jeva said. "He's a delivery boy now. Karma is funny."

"That's not it," Klarke said. "I'm not worried about him. I knew nothing good would come of his sorry ass."

"Then what's wrong?" Jeva said.

"God is a restorer," Klarke said.

"Huh?" Breezy said.

"You heard of Vickie Stringer?" Klarke asked.

"No," the women all replied.

"Well, she's an author," Klarke informed them. "I read a couple of her books while locked up. She has this saying that God is a restorer. He restored her life. So now I'm looking at myself. I've been restored. When I went to prison I lost everything, including my spirit. It was an awful time. But now, like the blink of an eye, I have it all back again."

"*Mami*, you should feel blessed," Maria said, throwing her pizza crust in the trash. "Not everyone gets a second chance."

"Oh, I feel blessed. There's no doubt about that. I know I'm blessed. But now, how am I supposed to maintain it all?"

"You're going to have to do what the rest of the world does," Breezy said. "Work and maintain."

"How easy was it for you to get a job again?" Klarke asked Breezy. "Will I still be looked at like a felon even though I was cleared? I mean you said yourself, Breezy, that your boss still tries to bust your ass and you only spent three days in jail for something you didn't do. I did four years."

"I didn't mean to make it sound easy," Breezy said. "It's going to take some time and yes, there is still going to be a stigma attached to you. But Klarke, you have always been able to do whatever you have set your mind to."

"Yeah," Jeva said in agreement. "I'm sure there's something out there waiting for you."

As if Klarke was having an epiphany she said, "Jeva, you're right. Something is out there waiting for me, my desk."

"Your desk?" Jeva said with a puzzled look on her face.

"Never mind," Klarke said with her mind churning ninety miles a minute. "Come on, ladies. Let's eat up. We worked hard today."

Klarke's attitude had quickly changed. The women could tell that something was brewing up in that brain of Klarke's. But what in the world was it?

"Mr. Kemble, there's someone here to see you," the receptionist spoke through the intercom. "She said to tell you that she's an old friend of yours."

The receptionist in the office of Kemble and Steiner, where Klarke used to work, sat waiting for a response.

"Well, will you ask this old friend if she has a name?" Mr. Kemble said.

Klarke signaled to the receptionist with her hand to give her the phone. The receptionist did so hesitantly.

"I'm only the number-one executive accounts representative this company has ever had," Klarke said.

"I'll be damned!" he shouted. "Have Miranda escort you to the conference room. I'll be there in a sec."

Klarke hung up the phone and instead of having Miranda, the receptionist, escort her to the conference room she went by herself. She had worked there for two and a half years. She knew exactly how to get to it. It was right around the corner from the reception desk.

Klarke walked the path to the conference room. Once she got

in there she walked around admiring the new furnishings. Some interior designing had been done since the last time she was in there.

Klarke walked around the conference room table touching each chair on wheels along the way. The conference room table was now a deep mahogany that had a glass slab over it to protect the wood from scratches. Klarke reminisced how she and Mr. Kemble, whom she calls by his first name, Evan, had sex once on the old conference room table. It was more of a shiny cherry wood. Thank goodness it didn't have a glass slab over it. Her ass cheeks would have left a print. Klarke couldn't help but giggle out loud at the thought of the encounter. Although it only lasted a couple of minutes, she'll remember it a lifetime. He was her first and only experience with a white man and boy did he shatter the myth.

"Klarke!" Evan said, surprised as he entered the conference room. "Is that really you?"

"It's really me." Klarke smiled, while checking out Evan. He had dyed his hair from blond to black. Perhaps it had started to gray. And he was sporting a spiked moussed do. He still had that California white boy complexion and those gorgeous ocean blue eyes.

"Wow, wee," Evan said as he walked over to Klarke, picked her up, and spun her around. "Klarke Taylor, Miss Class Act herself."

"Oh stop it. You're making me blush," Klarke said shyly. "Then again, don't stop." She didn't bother correcting Evan on her last name.

They both stood there admiring one another. Klarke never guessed that there would still be some sexual tension between them. She and Evan were old news. Yeah, they had performed the horizontal mambo a couple of times, but the relationship never went past that. Not that Evan didn't want it to. If Klarke had seriously considered dating Evan for real, they'd probably still be together today. But once she met Reo in the flesh, no other man had a chance in the world.

"You look good," Evan said as he sucked slowly on the Altoid he had in his mouth.

"You too," Klarke said. She hoped that Evan couldn't see her trembling as she thought about how he had eaten her out with an Altoid in his mouth and the tingling afteraffect it had on her throbbing clit.

"You cold?" Evan asked. "Looks like you caught a chill."

"No, I'm fine."

"I know you're fine. I was asking you how you felt, not looked."

"Well, yeah, thanks," Klarke said, in disbelief that that sorry-ass line had passed over from the brothas to the white boys.

"Come on, let's go to my office," Evan said, grabbing her hand. They could feel the electricity between them. Vibing off of the same sense, Evan released Klarke's hand. Thank goodness he did. If he hadn't dropped her hand she was liable to drop her panties.

Evan led Klarke to the elevator up to his high-rise office. The company was full of new faces and some old ones too. Klarke passed Renee's desk which was still in the same old cubicle with the same old nameplate hanging up. Klarke couldn't believe she was still there. Her work had always been mediocre. People at the job used to place bets on who she was fucking in order to keep her job. The odds were that she was fucking the daddy, Evan's father, the real man behind the name Kemble.

When Klarke got to Evan's office he pointed for her to sit down in the chair in front of his desk. He then walked around and sat down in his chair. Klarke couldn't help but notice the wedding picture of Evan and his wife on his desk.

"Aliyah, right?" Klarke asked as she remembered bumping into Evan and his then-fiancée in the mall right before she went to the prison. She remembered her face because she looked so much like Klarke.

"Huh?" Evan responded.

"Your wife. Her name is Aliyah, right?"

"Oh, yeah. That's my girl," Evan said, picking up the picture and smiling at it.

"You two got married. That's great. She was a beautiful bride."

"Thank you. She's a beautiful woman," Evan said, staring into Klarke's eyes almost as if he was speaking of her.

"That's good. You seem happy. I'm glad you're happy."

Changing the subject, Evan stated, "So, what brings you back to your old stomping grounds?"

"Well, actually, I came back to hold you to your words."

"And what words were those?"

"That once everything blew over, that my desk would be waiting for me. Unless you've been living under a rock, you know the whole story about everything. Needless to say, everything has blown over."

"Mr. Kemble," Renee said, knocking on Evan's open office door. Klarke sat in the chair facing Evan with her back to the door.

"Oh," Renee said. "I didn't realize you had a visitor. I can come back."

"Oh, it's okay," Evan said, walking from around his desk and over to Renee. "I was just talking to our newest employee. Come in and say hello."

As Renee walked over to shake hands with the woman in the chair her eyes filled with tears when she saw that it was Klarke.

"Guess who's back?" Klarke said as she hugged Renee tightly.

"Klarke! Oh, I'm so sorry, Klarke," Renee whispered in Klarke's ear as tears fell from her eyes and onto Klarke's shoulder, staining her white dress shirt. "I'm so sorry for all that you've had to go through. I admire you so much. If you ever need anything, I mean anything, don't you hesitate to ask."

"Thank you, Renee," Klarke said, grabbing a tissue off of Evan's desk and handing it to Renee.

"Renee," Evan said. "You'll be needing to order Klarke here a nameplate for her new cubicle."

"Make sure you put Klarke Laroque on it," Klarke said. "I haven't gone back to my maiden name."

"There's always going to be a place for you, Klarke," Evan said, rubbing his hand across her cheek. "Here at Kemble and Steiner and in my heart."

This time when he held her hand, he didn't let go.

14

THE INTERLUDE

Klarke, Breezy, and Jeva sat on the edge of Jeva's bed.

Klarke's knee was bouncing, Jeva was nibbling on her nails, and Breezy got up off of the bed and began to pace. Jeva stood up and joined Breezy in her pacing.

"Will you two stop it already?" Klarke shouted. "You're not making the wait any better."

"Oh, gosh, I'm sorry," an apologetic Jeva said, joining Klarke back on the bed. The girls were silent. Breezy continued pacing.

"Here, honey," Jeva said, patting a space in between her and Klarke for Breezy to come sit down.

"What is it with this honey mess?" Klarke finally asked. "Ever since I've been back home you two been acting funny. Honey, baby, hugging, and carrying on. I mean, what the fuck?"

Breezy stopped pacing and looked at Jeva. Jeva put her head down like a child caught with her hand in the cookie jar.

"See," Klarke said, pointing her finger. "See, that right there. That look between you two. Is there something you two aren't telling me?"

"No," Breezy said quickly, but not before Jeva could say yes.

"Well, what is it?" Klarke demanded to know.

"Do you really think it's the time for this?" Breezy said to Klarke.

"Hell, yeah, I do," Klarke responded. "Now what is it?"

"No," Jeva said quickly, but not before Breezy could say yes. At this point a frustrated Klarke got up off the bed and put her hand on her forehead.

"I can't take this Abbot and Costello act you two have going on," Klarke said.

"We kissed," Jeva confessed, looking up at Breezy as if she had just turned her best friend in to the police.

"Okay, keep going," Klarke demanded.

"French kissed," Jeva continued. "It was just for a few seconds."

"It was in the heat of the moment," Breezy jumped in nonchalantly. "Jeva was dealing with her breakup with Lance. I was dealing with losing my father. We were emotional. We were losing you. At that moment we felt alone."

"Oh, a *Boyz N the Hood* pity kiss?" Klarke said, shaking her head.

"Really, it was nothing," Breezy said, smacking her lips. "It was a *Silkwood* kiss."

"A *Silkwood* kiss?" Klarke asked with a puzzled face.

"It was nothing?" Jeva said, offended.

Ignoring Jeva, Breezy said to Klarke, "You know, like the kiss in the movie *Silkwood*. Cher kissed Meryl Streep and it was just that, a kiss. Nothing more came of it. You knew the two loved each other, but only as friends, and the kiss wasn't anything sexual. I mean, it didn't affect their friendship. It was something that just happened and they never talked about it again. They just went on, friends as usual. That's what Jeva and I decided to do. Besides, it's embarrassing to talk about. That's why we never did, until now, that is."

"Are you sure that nothing else just happened?" Klarke said, frowning.

"I mean maybe a touch here, a pat there, general caressing, but that was as far as things went. And it was just that one instance. That's why I ended up moving out of Jeva's house. There was a little sexual tension between us, I'll admit. But crossing that line and stepping into unknown boundaries wasn't worth ruining our friendship over. So if you're asking if we bumped coochies, hell no."

"And what's wrong with my coochie?" Jeva said as she stood up. "Not good enough to bump? I can't believe you just sat here and said that I meant nothing to you."

"I didn't say that you meant nothing. I said that the kiss meant nothing," Breezy said.

"Same thing," Jeva said.

"Is not," Breezy said, waving her hand in the air.

"Is too," Jeva insisted.

"Okay, you two done went from Abbot and Costello to Lucy and Desi Arnaz." Klarke interrupted the brewing argument. "I don't know why you two have been acting so funny, like I was going to think anything different about you. You could have told me this when it happened."

"It happened years ago," Jeva said as she began pacing. "Right before you went to jail or while you were in jail. I can't remember."

"So you mean to tell me that the kiss was so insignificant that you can't even remember it?" Breezy said, upset.

"I am not about to sit here and listen to you two argue over a lousy kiss," Klarke said, standing in between the two.

"It wasn't lousy!" both Breezy and Jeva shouted.

"Well, at least you two can agree on that," Klarke said. "Do you think the test is ready?"

"I had forgotten all about it," Jeva said.

"Let's all go look at it together," Breezy said.

The three women joined hands and headed toward the master-suite bathroom.

"Wait a minute," Klarke said, stopping the girls right before entering the bathroom. "No matter what the results of this test are, we're here for each other, right?"

Both Jeva and Breezy nodded.

"We're going to support one another no matter what changes occur in our lives, right?" Breezy asked.

Both Klarke and Jeva nodded.

"And we're going to support any decisions any of us might ever decide to make, right?" Jeva added.

Both Breezy and Klarke nodded.

The women once again headed into the bathroom.

"Wait," Klarke said, stopping them once again. "Let's say a prayer."

The women bowed their heads and Klarke led in prayer. "Dear Lord, thank you for being better to us than we have been to each other and ourselves. Heavenly Father, we ask you to bless us as we go forth for the results of this test and to bless us as we deal with the results no matter what they might be.

"Dear Lord, we say this prayer in the name of your son and our savior, Jesus Christ. Amen."

"Ready?" Jeva asked, still holding onto Klarke's and Breezy's hands.

"Ready," Klarke said with sigh.

"Ready," Breezy said, taking a deep breath.

The women headed straight to the sink where the pregnancy test sat. They looked down at the pink positive sign and embraced in a group hug as tears flowed down their faces.

"God knows what he's doing," Klarke said. "He doesn't make mistakes so the timing must be right."

But for some reason, the timing for a baby just didn't seem right.

15

THREE'S A CROWD

Breezy had just made it in from work to be greeted by yet another jailhouse letter from Guy. Receiving letters from him was starting to get worse than receiving bills.

"If this fool sends me one more fuckin' letter," Breezy said, dropping it into the wastebasket without even opening it. "One more and I swear for goodness I'm going to file harassment charges against him."

Breezy kicked off her shoes, then bent over to pick them up, catching one more glimpse of the letter.

"Oh, damn!" Breezy said, retrieving the letter from the wastebasket. Although her blood boiled when letters from Guy arrived at her doorstep, she was always slightly curious as to what he had to say.

Breezy ripped open the letter and read the same old mumbo

jumbo about how he was innocent and if only she'd just visit him once how he'd never bother her again. After reading the letter, once again she placed the letter back in the wastebasket. As Breezy headed to her bedroom to get comfy she thought about how paying Guy a visit just might be the trick to get him to stop sending her letters. She was confident that she could shut his ass down in person. So she decided that she needed to put closure to the Guy situation once and for all.

As Breezy sat in the waiting area of the jail she thought about getting up to walk away a thousand times. This was the same prison waiting room she had visited her father in so many times and now here she was visiting the man accused of murdering him. What the fuck could Guy possibly have to say? Why should she even listen?

I'm stupid for being here, Breezy thought to herself as she tapped her fingernails on the round mint-green table.

If she hadn't fucked with Guy, a married man, in the first place, then her father would be alive today and she wouldn't be here visiting the man accused of murdering him. She'd probably be sitting at home watching a game on the tube with her pops. She was sure he would have forgiven her for the secret she had kept from him for so many years. He was a forgiving man.

Her father had been like a best friend to her growing up. Breezy never gave a care about what anybody thought of her with the exception of him. She didn't even care what her own mother thought about her. Breezy loved her mother because she was her mother, but had never been as close to her as she had been with her father. When Breezy's mother divorced her father while he was in jail, Breezy pretty much cut her off completely. They called each other on birthdays sometimes, but Sunday dinner was out of the question.

There was a point when Breezy needed a place to stay, right after the death of her father when she had lost her job and was down and out. She had to literally beg her mother to allow her to stay with her and her new husband until she could get on her feet. Breezy would have rather gone to hell, but she didn't have a choice. Jeva saved her, though. She used some of her trust-fund money to get a new home. She had been living at a hotel because Lance had put her out. Jeva told Breezy that she could stay with her until she got herself together. Breezy would forever be grateful to Jeva for that.

Jeva was actually the one who convinced Breezy to tell her father the truth about Judge, how he really hadn't raped her. How her father believing for all those years that he had gunned down the man who had raped his daughter was a lie. It was hard for Breezy to accept that the death of her father was probably her karma for fucking around with another woman's husband. God wanted her to suffer even greater pain for her actions.

If Breezy hadn't believed in that karma bullshit before, she did now. She had gotten an abortion several years ago and one of the protesters warned her that bad karma would come to her for that act of abomination. That was back when she and Guy first started messing around. Guy insisted Breezy get an abortion. Keeping the other woman a secret from his wife was a feat in itself. Hiding a child from the affair was unthinkable. Guy was quick to give Breezy three times the amount of what the abortion actually cost. Keeping this in mind, a year after that Breezy faked a pregnancy to get four times the cost of an abortion from Guy. It was always in the back of her mind how God would punish her.

"Baby girl, you lookin' good," Guy said as he approached the table. He was wearing a sky blue jailhouse jumpsuit and a smile. He actually had his arms out as if he thought that Breezy would embrace him with a hug.

Breezy looked up with a solid look on her face. Arms wide

open and smiling from ear to ear was this big-ass, fine, buff, chocolate hunk of a man.

"Looks like jail has been good to you," Breezy said. "Too bad you had to come here for a makeover." She took a deep breath and said, "Sit down. I'm not here to reminisce so make this shit quick. I'm only here for closure and to keep you from mailing me anymore jailhouse goo-goo ga-ga."

"You still got that fly-ass mouth I see," Guy said, smiling. "That shit always did turn me on."

"Dude, you been locked up for almost five years," Breezy said. "A barnyard sheep would turn you on."

Guy began to laugh out loud, almost uncontrollably. Breezy stood.

"I don't have time for silliness," Breezy said.

"Hold on, baby girl," Guy said, grabbing Breezy's hand. "As badly as I want to see that ass walk away, I want you to stay and listen to what I have to say even more."

Guy gestured for Breezy to sit back down. She smacked her lips, sighed, and then planted her apple-shaped bottom back into the chair.

"I didn't do it, Breeze," Guy said sincerely. "I was set up. You know I would never do no shit like that. Murder? Come on now."

"You ain't saying nothing you haven't or couldn't have said in a letter, so why I am I here?"

"I haven't told you everything. There's some stuff I didn't want to put in a letter because I've got my attorney working on some things for me and these muthafuckas don't let nothing come in or out without putting their noses in it."

Guy leaned in and whispered. "Baby, my ex-wife set me up. She was going after you. She wasn't expecting your father to be there. He surprised her and so she killed him. She was at your apartment to kill you. When all was said and done, she didn't care who was dead as long as she had a body to pin on me. She had planned on setting me up for the murder regardless. She planted all that evidence to convict me and had the nerve to tip the police off with an anonymous call."

"If all that's the case, then why are you still locked up? Why isn't she here?" Breezy asked smugly.

"I'm working on it. I just hate being here knowing that you believe I'm the one who murdered your father. You know how much I cared for you, woman."

Guy's story sounded crazy enough to be true. It was only a matter of time before Guy's ex-wife got fed up with his cheating ass. Hell has no fury like a woman scorned. Breezy knew that feeling all to well. Breezy had always been pretty good at reading people, but Guy's story just seemed too far-fetched.

"You don't believe me, do you?" Guy said with a sigh. "We're having a hard time getting the DA to believe me too. But the DA doesn't know me, Breezy, and you do."

Breezy took in Guy's words and thought momentarily in silence. "Guy, you know what?" Breezy said, still not believing it herself what she was about to say. "Maybe what you are saying does have a ring of truth to it. I mean after five years, I'm sure you could have come up with a better story than that."

"I knew it. I knew you would, baby, once you heard what I had to say," Guy said excitedly. "Now I just need your help in getting the system to believe me."

"You're kidding, right?" Breezy said. "You think you 'bout to put me to work? Who the fuck do I look like, Nancy Drew? I'm not about to rehash the past and help defend you."

"But I didn't do it. I didn't do it!" Guy shouted angrily, slamming his fist down on the table.

Guy's reaction startled Breezy. She stood up to leave once again.

"Please, Breezy. She set me up. My ex-wife set me up for a crime I didn't commit."

"Is everything cool?" a husky security officer walked over and asked.

Breezy stood and thought for a minute. "Yeah, everything's cool."

The security officer gave Guy a dirty look, then walked away.

"See," Guy said. "See how these muthafukas are. They out to get me just like my wife. I swear to you, Breezy, on everything. I didn't kill your father. My wife did and she set me up and now I'm serving time for a crime I didn't commit. I know I cheated on her. I know I was wrong for that. But to ruin my life like this?"

Guy was desperate and out of breath. Breezy stood there watching him plead to her with his last breath before replying, "Perhaps you should consider yourself lucky. Your wife could have run you over three times with her Mercedes."

Breezy winked at Guy, then walked away, leaving him there to rot in jail. Now he would be out of her life forever and she could focus on moving on. That's probably the real reason why Breezy's night with Hydrant scared her so much. The last time she had been with him was when she was juggling her relationship with him and Guy. She never had to put 100 percent of her feelings into Hydrant alone. She always had Guy to fall back on if things went sour. It used to take two men to fulfill all of Breezy's needs. But all she needed in her life was just one man. Her and that one special man. She didn't need some third-wheel jailhouse pen pal confusing things. Three's a crowd.

"Hey," Breezy said into the phone. After her visit with Guy earlier that evening she couldn't wait to get home and attempt to patch things up with Hydrant. She had closed one chapter in her life and it was time to move forward with the next.

After taking a very long pause Hydrant responded, "Hey," in a very dry tone.

"You mad at me?" Breezy asked in an irresistible voice.

"Nah, ma. I don't get mad. But sometimes I get confused, so would you mind telling me what the fuck was up with that Cinderella move?"

"I got scared," Breezy admitted.

"Scared of what?"

"You. Me. Us."

"That's cool. But didn't I deserve a phone call? A note? A fuck-you or something?"

"Yes, you did. That's why I'm calling you now."

"But look how much time has gone by," Hydrant said, starting to reveal some of his anger.

"At least this time I'm calling." Breezy threw an angry tone right back at him.

"Hell, I could have run off to Vegas and gotten remarried by now with all the time you let lapse."

"But I'm calling," Breezy said, now in a more intimate tone. "I'm putting you before my pride."

"I thought you were trying to lose me again, girl."

"No. I don't want to ever lose you again. That's why I'm so scared."

Hydrant wasn't used to the vulnerable side of Breezy that he seemed to be talking to over the phone. Although he had never met her before, he knew she must have existed somewhere deep down inside.

"I ain't changed, ma. I'm the same ol' G, you know? You can holler at me about whatever."

"Okay, then let me just put it like this. I don't want to be fuck buddies, Hydrant."

"I can't tell. You the one who dipped on me after getting what you wanted."

"Don't even go there." Breezy laughed.

Hydrant joined in with a chuckle of his own, then got serious again. "I know you're scared, Bria. I'm scared too."

"You are?" Breezy was surprised to learn.

"Yeah. I mean, I have a baby girl now and the choices I make in life are choices for her too."

Why did he have to go and bring his little girl up? Breezy had almost forgotten about that factor.

"You still there?" Hydrant asked.

"Yeah," Breezy said in a hushed tone.

"Look, it's getting late," Hydrant said. "You wanna come over? Hold up, let me rephrase that. I want you to come over."

"Don't you have to go to work in a few hours?"

"Yeah. But I wanna hold you until the alarm goes off."

That line did it for Breezy. She packed a toiletry bag and headed straight to Hydrant's house.

Breezy could feel Hydrant's breath on the back of her neck. He had this light snore going on, but nothing that would keep her awake, if she could ever get to sleep, that is. Breezy was lying on her side, Hydrant was laying on his side too with his body pressed up against hers. His left arm was softly hanging over her waist. Breezy had an itch on the back of her thigh that she wanted to get, but she was afraid that if she moved, Hydrant would roll over and face the opposite direction. She didn't want that. What she wanted was to stay tightly snuggled up underneath him. Well what she really wanted was for his head to be buried in her pussy, tongue thrashing and her returning the favor to him thereafter. But she was trying to take into consideration all the celibacy talk Jeva had been feeding her. Stuff like it was never too late to become a virgin again.

Hydrant hadn't made any sexual advances toward Breezy, but that didn't keep Breezy from wanting to take him in his sleep. When she arrived at his home he escorted her straight to his bedroom where only the night-light was on. She had on pajamas under the long raincoat she wore to his house. The two simply climbed into bed. Hydrant checked the alarm on the clock to make sure it was on. He kissed Breezy on the forehead and thanked her for coming over.

That was a clear sign to Breezy that all he wanted to do was fuckin' cuddle. But every now and then Breezy would wiggle her bootie up against Hydrant's pipe, just hoping it would get hard. She needed a sign that would permit her to say the hell with that celibacy shit and climb his bones. But tonight didn't look like it was going to be the night.

That itch was still driving Breezy crazy. Finally she scratched it. Her movement woke Hydrant.

"What's up, ma?" he asked Breezy, leaning on his elbow to look down at her. "You all right? You need something? A glass of water or something?"

Yeah, I need something. Your dick inside of me, fucking the shit out of me. That's what I need, she wanted to say. "No, I'm fine."

Hydrant looked at the clock. He had three more hours of shuteye ahead of him. He kissed Breezy on the forehead and smiled. They repositioned themselves and within a minute Hydrant was back to snoring.

Breezy wanted so badly to just slip her hands in her panties and work magic with her fingers until cum gushed from her. That type of movement would wake him for sure, but Breezy didn't care. Her

Sunday brunch-turn-sexcapade with Hydrant reminded her of just how much she missed a good dick, not just dick, but a *good* dick. Since being with Hydrant, Breezy had gone through more batteries than the Energizer Bunny. She had even burned out her deluxe waterproof dildo. The shower was the best place to masturbate. The water beating against her skin only enhanced her climax.

Before Breezy knew it she had successfully managed to slide her hand down her panties without waking Hydrant. Slowly her fingers fondled her clit, getting her nice and wet. After only moments her fingers were inside of her full throttle.

"What you doing?" Hydrant raised his head and asked.

Scaring the shit out of Breezy, she screamed and yanked her hand out from her panties.

"Oh, my God! Hydrant, you scared me!"

Hydrant started laughing.

"Oh, you think it's funny that you scared me?" Breezy asked, almost angry.

"No, I think it's funny that I caught you with your hands down your pants," Hydrant said as he continued laughing.

Breezy sat up, embarrassed. What could she say to make the moment any less humiliating? Hydrant quickly took care of that. He grabbed the hand Breezy had used to masturbate with and began licking her fingers. Breezy melted.

"You don't ever have to do that shit with Hydrant laying here beside you, baby," he said while working his tongue up and down Breezy's fingers. "And if you do ever get the urge to just touch yourself, wake a nigga up so he can watch."

Hydrant grabbed Breezy's face and pulled her mouth into his. They tongue fucked for what seemed like forever. Then slowly Hydrant unbuttoned her pajama top and began caressing and sucking her titties.

"Damn, I love these big-ass coconuts," Hydrant said. Breezy could feel his steel beam hard against her side. She grabbed it through his boxers and massaged it with the palm of her hand.

"Put it between them," Breezy told Hydrant.

Breezy moved over to the middle of the bed and scooted down to the center. Hydrant followed suit after removing his boxers so that he was completely naked. He placed his perfectly cut physique on top of Breezy and slid up until he laid his pipe right on her chest, between her breasts. Breezy pressed her breasts together until they squeezed his dick.

After only a couple of strokes Breezy said, "Go get some baby oil or some Vaseline."

Hydrant got up and fumbled around on his dresser. He came back with a bottle of cocoa butter lotion and began squirting it on Breezy's breasts.

"That's cold." Breezy giggled. She began to run her fingers through the lotion. Hydrant threw the bottle down and smacked his dick back between Breezy's titties. He pumped up and down. Breezy squeezed tighter and tighter. Hydrant's moaning and his dick hitting her in the chin made her feel good. It made her feel good knowing that she was making him feel good.

"This is some old-school shit right here," Hydrant said as he looked down, using the glare of the night-light to watch his dick poke in and out from between Breezy's breasts.

"Fuck 'em baby. Fuck 'em," Breezy groaned. Breezy always did like titty fucking when she was younger, but she hated when little-dicked men wanted to do it. She liked a dick that hit her chin, not a dick she had to squeeze her titties around so tightly that it felt like her nipples were going to pop off just to hold the little fucker down in between them.

"Oh, shit," Hydrant said.

I know this nigga ain't about to cum already, Breezy thought. But no sooner than she thought it, Hydrant was squirting, giving her a pearl necklace, nut all over her neck and face.

Hydrant had been the only man Breezy had ever allowed to give her a pearl necklace. Guy had begged her to allow him to give her one, but she refused. For some reason his begging for it just made it seem degrading. Breezy never understood why men just didn't let a woman whip out her specialty on them. Why did they always have to ask for shit? Let a bitch suck your dick without asking or pulling her head down toward it. Men were hard creatures to grasp. But Hydrant, Breezy understood every inch of him.

Breezy took off her pajama shirt and used it to wipe her face. Hydrant wiped himself off with his boxers. Breezy scooted back up to the top of the bed and Hydrant quickly pulled her back to the center of the bed by her legs and buried his face in her pussy. Her juice was all over his face, even on his eyebrows. He knew how to eat pussy. He wasn't scared to get his face wet up in it.

Hydrant had Breezy twitching all over the place. She grabbed his hair like handlebars and pulled him hard into her pussy. She came in less than a minute. Hydrant wasn't no joke when it came to giving head. He didn't play around with the pussy. He took care of business.

"Did that feel good, baby?" Hydrant asked as he lay next to Breezy, giving her a minute to come down off of her high.

"That felt better than good," Breezy said, huffing and puffing. Cumin' that hard seemed like work. "Let me return the favor."

Breezy positioned herself between Hydrant's legs and went straight for his balls. She licked and sucked on them, then worked her way down to that spot in between Hydrant's ass and balls. He went fucking crazy, like some little bitch. That was the hot spot that most women made the mistake of ignoring.

Breezy paused and grabbed hold of the flat sheet. She used it to wipe Hydrant's private area off because she could still taste a little bit of the lotion. Then she went back to handling her business.

"I've missed you so much," Breezy said in between licks, sucks, and pops.

"I've missed you too," Hydrant replied. "You're the only one who knows how to do me right, girl."

Once Breezy finished setting it off by inhaling Hydrant's balls, she massaged them while sucking him like a vampire. Breezy could barely get her hand around his dick. It had to be the fattest dick in the world, hands down. He could put a house fire out if he pissed on it, as big as that dick was. Breezy sucked Hydrant with a smile on her face.

Before Breezy knew it, her pussy was dripping wet. She wasn't going to be satisfied until she felt Hydrant up inside of her. She climbed up on top of him and slid down his dick like a stripper on a pole.

"Work it, baby," Hydrant said as he watched Breezy bounce up and down. "Do that shit, ma."

"Oh, uh, oh, uh oooh," Breezy moaned on the edge of the cliff, ready to fall off.

"Let me hit that from the back," Hydrant whispered.

Breezy got up out of the bed. Hydrant got up and stood behind her. He bent her over the bed, inserted himself inside of her, and tore that ass up. His body thrashing against hers sounded like a pimp smacking around the bitch who didn't have his money. He thrusted in and out. Breezy was so wet Hydrant could have sworn that he felt her juices splashing on his dick.

Hydrant was using every muscle in his body as he damn near did squats trying to get deeper into Breezy. Her titties were jiggling and smacking against one another. Hydrant was a minute from bustin' a nut when Breezy turned it into thirty seconds by reaching her hand between her legs and grabbing Hydrant's balls.

"Baby, you know I always love when you do that," Hydrant said.

Breezy smiled. Hydrant spoke as if the two had never been apart. As if it was just yesterday she had let him give her a golden shower in the shower. Breezy felt like they had never been apart. She came off of that thought alone. Together they moaned and groaned in ecstasy, then collapsed on the bed. Remaining as such until the alarm went off two hours later.

The sound of the alarm made Breezy and Hydrant jump. Hydrant got up to turn the alarm off and headed straight to the shower.

"He's better than me," Breezy said to herself as she rolled back over, knowing she needed to get up, go home, and get ready for work herself.

Breezy heard the shower water start and decided to get up and join Hydrant. She got out of bed and turned on the light. She walked over to Hydrant's dresser and picked up her overnight bag that was sitting on the floor next to it. As Breezy bent over to get it she couldn't help but notice Hydrant's wallet sitting there on the dresser.

"Damn, damn, damn," she muttered. Why was she being tempted? Breezy couldn't resist picking up the black leather Perry Ellis wallet and going through it.

There were no phone numbers in it. No condoms, which confirmed that Hydrant was telling Breezy the truth when he said that he hadn't been with a woman since his ex-wife and hadn't planned on being with one until he found the right one. Breezy admired the handsome picture of Hydrant on his driver's license, which expired his birthday of that year.

Breezy was glad to see that Hydrant had some credit going on. He had two Capital One credit cards and a Huntington Bank debit card. The flicker of the American Express card made Breezy's pupils dilate. Hydrant had it going on. She smiled and closed the wallet up to set it back down on the dresser, but before she could a piece of paper fell out. She picked it up and opened it to find that it was a store receipt. Breezy noticed that it was from a jewelry store and was dated the day before. As Breezy read the details of the purchase she became infuriated.

"Son of a bitch," she said as she discovered that the purchase was for a bracelet personally engraved with the words I LOVE YOU SAMARI on it.

Immediately the vision of Hydrant fucking some other broad ran through Breezy's mind. The thought that she had just sucked his dick knowing he had probably fucked somebody else before she came over his house made her sick to her stomach.

Without a moment's more thought Breezy barged into the bathroom. She ripped the shower curtains back with the receipt in hand.

"If you love Samari so much, why isn't she here instead of me?" Breezy said in a complete rage.

"What? What are you talking about?" Hydrant said with soap all over his face. He tried to open his eyes but they started stinging.

"Fuck you, Hydrant. You talk a good game, but you still ain't no better than the next sorry-ass nigga."

"Breezy, what in the hell are you talking about?"

Breezy threw the receipt at Hydrant and he barely caught it. She stormed out of the bathroom, slamming the door. She managed to quickly slip her clothes, shoes, and raincoat on, grabbed her bag and headed toward the door. Just then Hydrant came out of the bathroom butt-naked, dripping wet.

"Damn it, Breezy!" he shouted. "Wait a fucking minute."

"I don't have a minute," Breezy said, admiring his delicious well-hung dick. "Maybe Samari does, but I don't. Who is she anyway, Hydrant? Let me guess. The ex-wife."

"She's my daughter," Hydrant said calmly. "Now, do you wanna pick your face up off the floor now or are you going to step over it on your way out?"

Breezy didn't know what to say. She was dead wrong and feeling like a complete idiot. She was so used to men being dawgs that she always looked for the worst in them. She realized at that moment that she had a lot of work to do on herself. She had to make a change if she was ever going to have a healthy relationship with Hydrant. Hydrant shouldn't have to pay for the sins of other men.

"You've never even bothered to ask me my daughter's name," Hydrant said with a hurt look in his eyes.

Breezy stood there ready to take her tongue-whipping like a woman.

"I know you, Breezy," Hydrant continued. "It's been a while, but I know you. You think I didn't read right through you when I mentioned to you that I had a daughter? I remember back in the day you telling me how you never wanted to settle down with a man who already had kids. Okay, so maybe that hasn't changed, but I was hoping it had. Baby girl, I know you are a Leo and you like to be the center of attention, but there is another woman in my life, my little mama. I love her deeply and no other woman can compete with the type of love I have for my daughter. But I'm hoping to grow to love you just as deeply in a different type of way if you'll let me."

Hydrant walked closer to Breezy. She watched the water droplets travel down Hydrant's hairy chest.

"You let me love you how I want to and no other woman will be able to compete with that type of love."

Hydrant placed a juicy kiss on Breezy's lips. "All right? Is that all right with you?"

Breezy nodded.

"You better get going before you're late for work and I can't have no broke-ass woman in my life. Just lock the bottom lock. I need to get dressed before I catch pneumonia."

Breezy smiled and said okay. But before walking out of the room she said, "I'll let you."

"Let me what?" Hydrant said.

"Love me." Breezy exited feeling like a natural woman.

Klarke, Jeva, and Breezy were piled up on Breezy's bed watching some videos of shows Jeva had recorded while Klarke was in jail. She loved Sunday night movies, Lifetime movies, USA movies and popular reality shows. She was one of those rare folks who still recorded absolutely everything even though reruns played almost back to back or you could eventually find them on DVD somewhere. She had let Klarke borrow a heap of them so that she could catch up on shows she missed while incarcerated. So far Klarke's favorites were the MTV *Real World Las Vegas* and the *Friends* episodes she had missed.

The women were supposed to be window-shopping but it was raining cats and dogs. One would have thought that the rain would have melted these women. They didn't care if the mall was an inside facility, and most women wouldn't either. It's something about the rain that keeps a person in the house.

"I can't believe she kissed her best friend," Klarke said, referring to a heterosexual female character on *Soul Food* who had just indulged in a French kiss with her lady lesbian friend.

"You want another slice of pizza?" Jeva said in a nervous tone to Breezy.

"Yes. Sounds good," Breezy said, taking two slices and putting them on her plate.

"Damn, girl," Klarke said. "You're eating like it's going out of style."

"You're the one who damn near ate an entire Genos pizza to yourself," Breezy said in her defense.

"Did not," Klarke laughed. "I only had five slices."

"And these are only my fifth and sixth," Breezy said.

"You've made my point for me," Klarke said.

"You're the one lookin' a little thick these days," Breezy said, squeezing Klarke's thigh.

Meanwhile Jeva rubbed her hand on her stomach.

"I only had three and they are not agreeing with me," Jeva said. She gagged, then jumped up and ran into the bathroom.

Klarke walked over to the closed bathroom door to ask if Jeva was okay, then went back over to the bed with Breezy.

"I went to see Guy," Breezy said, then took a bite of her pizza and returned to watching *Soul Food*.

"You did what?" Klarke sat up and asked. "Why in heaven's name would you go see the man who murdered your father?"

"I don't know. I just felt like I had to. For closure or some shit. I don't know," Breezy said, throwing her hands up. "He kept writing me. He wouldn't stop and I just had to go there and put an end to it all."

"Well, what did he say?"

"What every jailbird says, that he didn't do it."

"By the look on your face and the mere fact that you mentioned the visit out of the blue means that a part of you might believe him."

Breezy remained silent, still watching *Soul Food*. Klarke picked up the remote and turned the television off.

"Well, do you?" Klarke asked.

"I guess a little part of me does. He says his wife set him up."

"Is that possible?"

"Hell, anything's possible."

"So what are you going to do?" Klarke asked.

"What am I going to do? Stay black and die. That's what I'm going to do." Breezy snatched the remote from Klarke's hand and turned the television back on.

"But if he's innocent then he doesn't deserve to be there. After dealing with what I've dealt with, I could never let an innocent person rot away in jail without doing something."

"Well, what if he isn't so innocent?" Breezy asked.

"What if he is?" was Klarke's comeback. "I'm not saying to start an all-out crusade carrying a sign that says FREE GUY. I'm just saying that you can do something as simple as make a phone call to the prosecutor's office, the DA, the detectives, or something. That's all I'm saying."

Breezy looked at Klarke as if her words were making sense and getting through to her. She paused, then said, "Nah, let him rot."

Just then Jeva came out of the bathroom looking clammy.

"You okay, girl?" Breezy asked.

"Yes," Jeva answered with a cough. "I don't think Genos agrees with me today."

"You might be getting that bug that's going around," Klarke said.

"What's it called?" Jeva asked.

"Pregnancy."

Breezy had just lit the candles on the dinner table that was set for two. Hydrant was on his way over for dinner, and running late. Breezy had gone out and purchased this sexy-ass fire-red chemise that was trimmed in black lace. She was whole-thangin' it with the matching garters and red strappy stilettos with fur. The black lace choker was the finishing touch.

She wanted tonight to be extra special. There was something important she needed to tell Hydrant about their relationship. She had thought long and hard about what she wanted in life, and she came to the conclusion that it was a life with a good man. She wanted to settle down, get married, and have kids of her own.

Breezy had parted her bobbed hair and placed it in two low ponytails that went to her neck. She figured she'd add the youthful girly touch that tended to turn men on. The nicely cut porterhouse steaks were looking good on that George Foreman grill and she had picked out the two largest baking potatoes in the supermarket batch. She planned on topping them with lots of butter, cheddar cheese, sour cream, and bacon bits, not to mention the bottle of Moet she had chilling for Hydrant. She had had that bottle sitting on her kitchen bar for about a year strictly for show. She figured that hopefully tonight would be worth cracking it. This was going to be a night to remember indeed.

Dessert was going to be a blast. Breezy had literally planned on serving herself to Hydrant on a platter. She had poured swirls of chocolate all over a turkey platter her mother had given her two Christmases ago. She was her mother's only child and all she got was shit like turkey platters and Chia plants as gifts. If it's the thought that counts, the gifts she received from her mother pretty much summed up what she thought about her.

Why in the hell her mother bought her a turkey platter was beyond her. She was single with no kids. Her meals consisted of frozen entrees or fast food. Who knew that platter would ever come in handy?

Breezy planned on placing the chocolate-covered platter in front of Hydrant and then placing her naked ass right on top of it, legs cocked. That's when the whipped cream would come into play. She planned on squirting it all over her pussy, allowing that to be Hydrant's sweet buffet.

Just when Breezy had taken the baked potatoes out of the microwave and put them on the dinner plates the doorbell rang.

Breezy positioned her titties to make sure that as much cleavage as possible was showing. She peeked through the peephole and saw a handsome Hydrant on the other side.

Breezy flung opened the door, placed her hands on her hips and stood in the doorway with her legs spread apart. The look on Hydrant's face was one of shock. He bent down very quickly to cover his little girl's eyes with his hands.

"You should have at least called and told me that you were bringing her," Breezy whispered angrily as she slipped on a pair of jeans and put on a sweatshirt. When she saw Hydrant's little girl standing there at his pants leg, she immediately raced into her bedroom to change. Hydrant had gotten his daughter situated and then went to check on Breezy.

"I wanted to surprise you," Hydrant said. "I wanted my two favorite girls to meet each other."

"Well, I wanted to surprise you too, if you didn't notice. That's what a surprise is, me getting all dolled up for you. Hell, flowers, a bottle of perfume, a box of candy. Those are surprises. But a kid?"

"I'm sorry," Hydrant said, laughing.

"Oh, you think this shit is funny? Your daughter's first impression of me is my imitation of Lil' Kim!"

Hydrant continued laughing, but he could see that this was no laughing matter to Breezy as she started to cry. He had never seen her so emotional.

"Come on," Hydrant said. "It's okay."

"It's not okay," she said, wiping her tears. "I wanted tonight to be special."

"And it still will be. It's nothing to cry over, ma," Hydrant said, taking Breezy's hand and rubbing it. "You sure that's the only thing the matter?"

"Yes," Breezy said, brushing him away. "Let's just go in there with your daughter before she gets into something."

"Hold up," Hydrant said, grabbing Breezy by the arm, stopping her in her tracks. He didn't care for her tone one bit.

"Are you pissed because my little girl is here and ruined the sexy evening you had planned?" Hydrant asked. "Or are you pissed for the simple fact that my little girl is here period? Let me know. Because if three's a crowd, I can leave you here by your damn self."

Breezy remained silent. Hydrant sighed.

"Look, baby," Breezy said. "This is new to me, dating a man with a kid and all. A man that I can see a future with. I don't want to sound cold, but I don't want to be the mother to some other woman's child. I want to be the mother of our child."

"First of all, I don't want you to be a mother to my daughter," Hydrant said calmly, but very seriously. "She has a mother. And secondly, she's not another woman's child. She's my child, the man you can supposedly see a future with. How far into the future . . . well, that's up to you."

Breezy began to cry even harder. She knew she was being a complete bitch and she felt bad. But her hormones were starting to get the best of her.

"You're right, baby," Breezy said, walking over to Hydrant. "I'm sorry."

He patted his chest, signaling her to place her head on it. Forgiving Breezy for being Breezy had never been hard for Hydrant.

Breezy placed her head on Hydrant's chest and took in the scent of his Cool Water cologne. She loved how he smelled.

"Thank you for bringing your daughter here to meet me," Breezy said. "That must mean that you think I'm special. I know people don't let their kids just meet anybody. Thank you, Hydrant. This lets me know for certain that I'm a good woman."

"Modest, aren't we?" Hydrant said with a chuckle.

"I don't mean it like that. I know I'm a good woman because of you, Kristopher Long. I'm everything you make me. I'm a reflection of you, and you, baby, you are a damned good man. You always have been."

Hydrant nodded his head up and down and smiled.

"Okay, what do you want?"

"You," Breezy was quick to respond.

"You got me," Hydrant said, touching Breezy's cheek with his knuckles.

"I just don't want any misunderstandings," Breezy said, grabbing Hydrant's hand. "I don't want to kick it with you. I don't want to mess around with you."

"Well, what do you want to do?"

"I want to go together, be a couple."

"You wanna be my girlfriend?"

"No. I'm too old to run around calling myself somebody's girlfriend. I just want you to know . . . I just want to know that we are exclusive."

Hydrant couldn't help but smile. "Exclusive, huh?"

"That means, no fucking with other broads. No having female friends that you don't tell me about within the first six months of our relationship."

"Hello . . . Hold up," Hydrant said, cutting Breezy off. "I don't need rules to love you and respect you. All I need is this right here."

Hydrant pointed to his heart while looking into Breezy's eyes, which melted her completely.

"You had me at hello," Breezy said, mocking the *Jerry McGuire* movie.

Hydrant planted a long kiss on Breezy's lips.

"You looked good as hell in that getup. We'll have to use it another time," Hydrant said, smacking Breezy's ass. "You are right. You are a good woman. And you know what they say about every good woman. Behind her is a nigga like me watchin' dat ass."

Breezy blushed and giggled.

"And that ass was lookin' extra thick in that little negligée, ma. Just like I like it."

"Well, it's about to get thicker," Breezy said, looking down.

"Yeah, 'cause we 'bout to tear that food up," Hydrant said, rubbing his tummy.

"It's about to get thicker because I'm pregnant."

Hydrant stood there in silence, Breezy still staring down at the ground, fearful of Hydrant's reaction.

"What are we going to do?" Hydrant asked softly.

The fact that he used the word "we" instead of "you" caught Breezy's attention. That let her know that he saw them as a team, which meant that he would be there for her. She knew her decision not to terminate the pregnancy was the right one. She had gone to the clinic, alone, too ashamed to have Klarke or Jeva by her side for a second abortion. She had contemplated keeping the baby up until the last date that the abortion could be performed. She was at the clinic two hours being prepped before they called her name to perform the procedure. When the nurse called her name she stood up and walked right out of the door. All of the protesters who she had given the cold shoulder to when entering the building cheered when they saw her run out in tears shaking her head. It was a clear sign to them that she couldn't go through with it. They gave her God's blessings and she knew that she would need them.

"I know this is not a good time for you to be having another child," Breezy started.

"Don't use that as an excuse," Hydrant said. "Any time is a good time to bring a child into the world, so if that's one of the one hundred excuses you have as to why we shouldn't raise this child together then you better come on with the other ninety-nine. That one is played out!"

Breezy looked at Hydrant and was filled with emotion. "If you had let me finish, I was going to say that I know this is not a good time for you to be having another child, but you're about to be a daddy again."

Hydrant broke down in tears. He picked Breezy up and spun her around.

"Oh man," he said, excited. "Oh, man. This is crazy. I don't know what to do with myself. Damn, girl, how far are you?"

"Almost four months," Breezy said.

"What? Four months? When were you going to tell me? When you went into labor?"

"I didn't know what to do, Hydrant. I was scared. I mean, we just started trying to make this thing work again and to get pregnant that early in the game. It must have happened our first time together. That Sunday afternoon. I kept getting my period, but a woman knows her body."

"Oh, man," Hydrant kept saying. He walked over to Breezy and rubbed her belly.

"This is why I wanted tonight to be extra special. I wanted to tell you tonight."

"Well it is extra special, baby," Hydrant said, kissing Breezy on the forehead. "Now let's go so you and my daughter can have a proper introduction so that she knows who the mother of her new baby brother or sister is. Besides that, we need to eat that delicious-smelling celebration dinner. I'm starved."

"Cool," Breezy said. "But you have to give her a piece of your steak. I'm eating for two."

The two laughed and headed out of the room. Before exiting the room Breezy stopped Hydrant in his tracks to say, "Oh, shit! I hope you brought dessert."

16

SKELETONS IN THE CLOSET

When Meka walked through the door Reo was sitting on the couch, alone in the dark. Initially, when she had left Persia's girlfriend day from hell, she had planned on driving straight home and cussing Reo the fuck out. She couldn't believe he felt as though he had to go around soliciting friends for her. But after a conversation with her mother, whom she called on her cell phone to vent to, she had a change of heart. Her mother convinced her that Reo only did it because he cared about her. That he probably thought it would be nice for her to be friends with his best friend's wife. Meka hadn't looked at it that way and thought that her mother was probably right. Meka felt that Reo probably thought he was giving Meka a break away from the kids. So instead of going home to bicker, she decided to go release some of her stress by shopping, but not before taking her car to the car wash.

"Hi, honey," Meka said, whisking through the door with a Coach shopping bag in each hand. Reo was sitting on the living room couch alone, in the dark. The only light was from the bathroom that they always kept lit during the night. Meka turned the living room lamp on. "Why are you sitting here in the dark, honey? Oh, let me guess. You found out about all the drama at Persia's shindig. Can you believe her? She's lucky I even blessed their ghetto asses with my presence. But don't feel bad, honey. At first I blamed you, but after talking to my mother, she convinced me to look at the entire situation from another angle. But I was still pissed to say the least so you know what I do when I need to get my emotions intact. I shop."

Meka held up the shopping bags and smiled a huge grin. Reo sat frozen on the couch as if she wasn't saying a word.

"I went to the mall and then I just had to stop off at the Coach store. I've been jonesing for the signature reversible belt to go with the boots I have. And what do you know? I had to have the fishing hat and the new hobo too. And once I got to the register I couldn't dare walk out the store without the cute matching cell phone holder. It was to die for. Now that I'm home I'm going to get dinner started right away and try to forget about the entire ordeal I went through today."

Meka babbled on and on, finally realizing that her words were going right into one of Reo's ears and out of the other.

"Baby, is there something wrong?" Meka said, putting the bags down. "Where are the kids? I thought you were going to get them after you and Nate's game of chess."

"They're still at my mother's," Reo said in a dry tone.

"Ohhh, I see," Meka said as she walked over to the couch and started unbuttoning her starched white blouse. Meka sat down on the couch and puckered up to kiss Reo. Instead of kissing Reo, her lips hit some papers that Reo swished up in the air to block her.

"What's this?" Meka said, taking the papers out of Reo's hand.

"I should ask you," Reo said, rising up from the couch as Meka unfolded the papers and began to read them. Reo watched her facial reaction. She had been cold busted. Reo then began walking toward their bedroom.

"Where are you going? It's not what it seems. We need to talk about this," Meka said in a shamelessly guilty tone.

"There's nothing to talk about," Reo said as he continued walking. "And the question is not where I'm going. I'm simply headed in the bedroom to pack your shit. The question is, where are you going?"

Reo couldn't pack Meka's bag quickly enough. He wanted her out of his house and he wanted her out now! Fifteen minutes had passed before Meka joined Reo in the bedroom. Cool, calm, and collected, Meka appeared in the bedroom doorway as she watched Reo pull items from her drawers and stuff them into her travel bags.

"Darling, you're acting out of haste," Meka said as she walked over to the bed and sat next to the overnight bag. "I mean, you haven't even heard my side."

"Haste my ass!" Reo gritted between his teeth. "You told me there was no policy. When I told you that the detective investigating the murder of our child mentioned that you had taken a million-dollar life insurance policy out on our daughter you denied to me ever doing so. You said that he didn't know what he was talking about. You lied, Meka, and for the life of me I can't figure out why."

"I wanted to make sure that if we got back together that it was because of me and not my money."

"And now you're standing here lying to my face yet one more time," Reo said, slamming her Mary Kay makeup bag into her suitcase.

"I'm not lying," Meka said. "It's the truth."

"Bullshit! You and I both know that I'm worth way more than that on my own. You've seen my portfolio." Reo stopped and stared at Meka. "And now I've seen yours."

"The one day you bring in the mail my stupid investor decides to send me a cap on my investments from the distribution of the policy to my home address instead of my P.O. box," Meka said, rolling her eyes. "His ass is fired."

"Is that all you can think about right now? Firing your investor? You're acting like this is no big deal," Reo said, throwing his hands up.

"Because it isn't. Your imagination is just running wild. I mean what do you think? That I killed our baby because I had a lousy million-dollar insurance policy out on her?"

Reo paused and remained silent. His eyes said it all.

"Okay, now you're starting to scare me," Meka said in a more serious tone. "So there was a policy. Big deal!" Meka said in a nonchalant manner, shooing her hand in the air. "It just didn't seem important at the time when you asked me. I mean, I was mourning the death of my child."

"Our child, for whose funeral I paid," Reo said. He refused to be passive about the situation. "Besides, just a minute ago you said you didn't tell me because you wanted to make sure I didn't get back with you for the money."

"You're pissed because I didn't chip in on the casket?" Meka said, ignoring Reo's latter comment. "First thing Monday morning I'm going to take that money and deposit it into our joint account. That should cover my half of the funeral expenses and then some."

"Don't you dare!" Reo shouted. "Don't you dare make this out to be something so small. It's not about the money and you know it."

"Then what is it about?"

"Trust, damn it!" Reo said, angrily balling a fist. He had to take a deep breath and calm down. "It's about trusting one another and each other's motives. You lied about not having a million-dollar life insurance policy on our child and then you hid the money from me for how many years? What baffles me and worries me is why. Why did you do it? What do you have to hide?"

Meka searched desperately for the words she thought Reo might have wanted to hear.

"You know what? I don't give a fuck why. Besides that, I wouldn't believe a word that came out of your lying-ass mouth. I never will."

"You are seriously overreacting," Meka said, standing up, walking around to the opposite side of the bed where Reo was standing. "I don't understand why you're acting like this."

"What?" Reo said.

"It's almost as if you've been waiting for a reason to kick me out of your life. You're like a man who's cheating on his wife. He picks a fight so that he'll have a reason to storm off angry into the arms of the other woman." Meka sadly looked at Reo.

"I've been nothing but faithful to you," Reo said, pointing at Meka. "I'm an honest man. As hard as that may be sometimes, I've always been faithful and honest with you. I put up with bullshit from you that no other man in this world would put up with. Any other man would probably catch a case fucking around with your ass."

"I know. You've been a very good husband, Reo," Meka said, looking deeply into Reo's eyes. "I've tried to be nothing but a good wife to you in return," Meka said as tears started to form in her eyes. "I'll continue to be a good wife because I'm not going anywhere. You know you love me, Reo."

"You wanna bet?" Reo said, zipping the bag after stuffing a handful of panties into it. "Love ain't got shit to do with this. I'm not saying it's over forever. I'm just saying that you need to go right now. I need some time alone to get my head right. To see things clearer." Reo was so angry. He was angry because he couldn't make sense of the situation. This is the time when his father would have guided him. His father would have shed light on the matter. Damn, he was missing his pops. Reo fought back his emotions.

"I was hoping it didn't have to come to this," Meka said, pulling out an envelope of pictures that she had been hiding in her pocket. She threw the envelope down on the bed. Reo hesitated, but with curiosity getting the best of him he picked the envelope up and began looking at the pictures.

Reo's mouth dropped open. His heart almost stopped beating.

"What's the matter? Don't like the pictures?" Meka said, with a deliberately sad face. "And I thought you looked soooo cute standing in the hotel doorway with that hooker."

"These pictures were taken years ago," Reo said in a tone as if he could care less. But Meka could smell the fear and embarrassment rising up out of him like cheap cologne.

"There's no date on those pics," Meka said, shrugging her shoulders. "Besides that, fans don't care about dates. The proof is in the putting, or should I say pictures?"

"It's not what it looks like," Reo said, trying to pretend he wasn't sweating. "I met her at the bookstore I was signing at in New Orleans. I thought she was a fan. She offered to show me around the city. I had no idea she charged for her services."

Meka pretended to play a violin. "Poor Reo, got tricked by Tuesday the Trick. He didn't know he had to pay for her services, but yet there he is at the ATM machine with her waiting patiently for her fee."

Meka was referring to a picture of Reo at the ATM in the hotel lobby, with the call girl standing beside him. There immediately followed a picture of him handing her the money.

"Now while you're packing," Meka said matter of factly, "you might want to think about what a judge would think about this when we discuss custody of the children."

"What are you trying to say, Meka?" Reo asked, confused.

"I think you hear me loud and clear, Reo. The kids are mine," Meka said sternly. "I adopted Junior, remember? You spend so much time sucking up to fans across the country at book signings that no judge in his right mind would give you custody. I mean, sure you'll get visitation rights, but I'll probably get back into dentistry and start up my own practice somewhere like—well, I don't know—Atlanta maybe."

All of a sudden Reo's eyes narrowed as something else Meka had said struck him.

"You said Tuesday. How did you know that her name was Tuesday?"

Meka laughed. "No wonder Klarke—I mean *KAT*—knew she could con you with that little email scam of hers. You are just so damn gullible."

Reo's heart began to pound again.

"What did Tuesday tell you? That she was born in Atlanta but living in New Orleans? Yeah right. Her name is Tonya and the hoe is my second cousin on my dad's side of the family. She was on some actress-wannabee kick back then, so she didn't mind taking the gig. I had to pay her a grand though. I never thought in a million years you'd actually pay her the full fifteen hundred dollars she asked for. That bitch made twenty-five hundred dollars for fucking my man." Meka shook her head in disgrace.

Reo wanted to haul off and smack the shit out of her. But not even Meka would take him out of character.

"I wasn't your man at that time," Reo said, shrugging his shoulders.

"Oh, yes. That's true," Meka said, nodding her head. "Because I would have never done that to you if you were my man."

"Then why did you?" Reo asked, exasperated.

"You shitted on my pride," Meka said angrily. "That last night you and I were together before you got caught up with Klarke, we made love all night long. I allowed you to do things to me sexually that I would have never thought I'd let anyone do to me. And it felt good. It felt good because you were the man I wanted to spend the rest of my life with and what do you do after using my body for your sexual pleasures? You say 'thank you' and walk out the door. You wouldn't even spend the night with me. I just wanted you to hold me, but then you talked to me like I was some whore and then you slammed the door in my face and never called me again. Do you know how that made me feel?" Tears shimmered in her eyes. "And then to find out that I was pregnant with your child. My God. I was devastated. In the beginning I might have thought about using the baby as a pawn to get you back, but then I'd have to think about you wanting the baby and not me. That you'd try to take her from me. Those pictures were insurance that that wouldn't happen. I just ended up not having to use them." Meka looked up at Reo. "Until now, that is."

Reo shook his head, his hand on his forehead. He didn't know what the hell to think at this point.

"I hate that it all had to come down to this," Meka said. "I really do. I know it seems like I'm pulling your hoe card and all. But despite what you believe, I want to be your wife, Reo, living under one roof with you and our children. Sooner or later you would have to realize that I belong here."

Meka looked down at her Gucci traveling bags that Reo had

started packing for her. She believed that she had gotten through to him.

"Don't bother unpacking my things," Meka said, sure of her victory. "I'll do it myself. Dinner will be ready in about an hour. I'm making meat loaf."

Reo had just finished a book signing in Southfield, Michigan at Truth Bookstore. The bookstore was inside what Reo deemed to be the most ghettofabulous mall in America. To Reo's surprise, though, it turned out to be quite a successful signing.

Instead of going straight to his hotel room at the MGM Grand, Reo decided to play a couple hands of blackjack, where he easily lost five hundred dollars. Then he went to his hotel room to check his emails. He turned on his laptop and while it was loading he got a familiar knot in his stomach. That feeling hadn't been there in ages, but he remembered it all too well. Every time he turned on the computer now he got this weird feeling of excitement.

He was not only looking, but also hoping for that one email from KAT@myworld.biz. As his computer connected to the Internet, he thought about how good Klarke and he had been together. He had forced himself to put the memory in the back of his mind for the sake of his marriage. No matter how much Meka had hurt him in the past, two wrongs didn't make a right and that wasn't the type of man Reo was. That wasn't the type of man his father had raised him to be.

But after his big blowout with Meka, Reo was having a change of heart. He was devastated by the situation while Meka acted as if nothing had even occurred. It was unfortunate that he had to leave town on such a sour note with her. But he thought going on the road might be exactly what he needed, a chance to seriously think about his and Meka's marriage. But little did he expect that the fine memories of him and KAT would resurface.

Reo sat at his laptop reminiscing how when he and Klarke first met face to face he had arranged for her to meet him in Columbus. He made room reservations for her at the Double Tree hotel where he had a nice Jacuzzi bubble bath waiting for her. She was then supposed to meet him for dinner but instead he sent a limo driver to tell her that he wasn't going to be able to make it. The limo driver insisted that she utilize the dinner reservations anyway.

The driver drove Klarke to a nice downtown steak house where he then revealed his true identity to Klarke. It had been Reo all along. No man had ever gone to such lengths to surprise her and Reo had never gone to such lengths to woo a woman. It was truly romantic.

Reo closed his eyes and thought about how he loved the touch of Klarke and how he loved touching her. He asked himself a thousand times why he hadn't stood by Klarke's side. He should have known her well enough to see right through her false confession. Reo felt as though God was testing his faith in the vows he took and that he had failed miserably. Being married to Meka was turning into his punishment, not because Meka wasn't capable of loving, but because he was still in love with Klarke.

Reo finally got logged onto his AOL account and weeded through his fan mail. He then switched over to his personal email address where an email from Nate was waiting on him.

FROM: NateDawg2000@NateDawg.com
TO: RLQ812@Sunset.com
SUBJECT: Two hours

I tried to call your cell phone, but it was turned off. I figured you must still be at your signing or you did what I was thinking you might do.

You know Toledo is not even a full two hours from the Motor City. Try not to stray.

Holla back when you done playin' if you strayin'.

Peace

Reo laughed to himself then deleted the email. Prior to reading the email he had never thought about just how close in distance he was to KAT. Maybe that's why he was feeling a desire for her now more than ever. He had a mind to jump into his rental car and make his way to her, just to talk, of course. This might be the last time he was in a position to confront her and let her know how he truly felt. He wanted—no, he needed—so desperately to apologize to her for not standing by her side when she had needed him most. He knew he wasn't going to be able to sleep that night if he didn't go to her.

Reo followed the directions he had copied from Mapquest to get to Klarke's doorstep. He had gone online and found Klarke's address on www.zabasearch.com. It was a very popular people-search database. Thank goodness he wasn't some deranged stalking lunatic.

Reo parked his car at the curb directly in front of her place and noticed that the living room light was on. During the hour and a half drive, a small part of him hoped that no one would be home so that he wouldn't have to go through with it but could at least say that he tried.

Reo got out of the car and made his way up to the doorstep where he proceeded to ring the doorbell. After a few seconds, when there was no response, he rang it again. Still there was no response.

HJ was sitting in the living room watching television and Klarke was upstairs in the shower washing her hair. Unfortunately for Reo, Klarke had disabled the doorbell until she could work on getting the volume turned down.

After pushing the doorbell a third time, Reo gave up and walked away. The part of him that wanted to see Klarke again was devastated. Reo got back into his car, but before starting it, he saw a figure move across the living room window. It was HJ.

Reo got out of the car and walked back up the pathway and knocked on the door.

"Just a minute!" HJ yelled.

Trying to keep his eyes on the television and walking toward the door at the same time, HJ stumbled.

"Dang it," he said, catching his balance, then opening the door.

"Hello, HJ," Reo said, not knowing whether to smile or not. He didn't know how HJ would take to him after all of the time that had passed since they had last seen one another. "Do you remember me?"

HJ just stood there silently. He never thought he would see this man again. He had grown to care about him so much. They had been such a happy family once. HJ had actually grown to love Reo like a father. He had thought he'd always be in their lives. Feeling both angry and happy, HJ said, "Yes, Mr. Reo. I remember you."

"It's been a long time, son," Reo said.

"Don't call me son," HJ said. "I used to be your son, but not anymore. You left us. You went away. I never did anything to you and you left me."

Reo hadn't been expecting that. He never even thought how his and Klarke's split had affected her children's feelings toward him. When he had gotten back in Meka's arms again, he hadn't paid attention to anything he had left behind. Meka seemed to have occupied his every thought, not giving him time to think clearly about anything. But he couldn't blame her. He was a man.

It was his responsibility to make sure that he took care of his business as far as the kids were concerned. HJ didn't deserve to feel this way.

"I'm so sorry, HJ. I truly am," Reo said sadly. "You deserved so much more from me, you and your mother. That's why I'm here."

"How'd you find us?" HJ asked, still angry.

"The Internet," Reo replied.

"Figures," HJ said, blowing air through his lips. "You and Mom seem to have this thing for tracking each other down online, huh?"

Reo decided to ignore that one. "Is your mom around?"

"No," HJ said.

"Oh," Reo said, disappointed.

"But I'll tell her you came by." As HJ was closing the door Klarke came down the steps drying her hair with a towel.

"Was somebody at the door, HJ?" she asked.

"No, Mom," HJ said, quickly closing the door in Reo's face.

"Who was at the door?" Klarke moved HJ out of the way and opened the door. Reo had already headed down the walkway, but turned around when he heard the door open.

"Reo," Klarke said softly, the shock evident in her voice. Then her tone turned panicked. "What are you doing here? Is everything okay? Is it Junior? Oh, God. What's wrong?"

"Calm down, KAT. Nothing's wrong," Reo said, walking toward her. "Can we talk?"

Hearing Reo call her KAT sent chills down Klarke's spine. "Uh, yeah," Klarke said, waiting to hear what Reo had to say.

"Can we talk inside?" Reo said, nudging toward the door.

"Oh, pardon my manners," Klarke said, opening the door and letting him in. "HJ, go to your room please."

"Yes, Mom," he said, grabbing his box of Ho-Ho's. "What is it with the ex-husbands showing up on our doorstep?" he mumbled, then exited the living room.

Reo walked into the living room, then turned to face Klarke. "It's not surprising all the men in your life are racing to get back to you." He was looking dead in her eyes.

Klarke smiled and shook her head.

"It's not even like that," she said. "Have a seat. Would you like some coffee?"

"No, I won't be staying long," Reo said, sitting down on the couch.

You can stay as long as you like, is what Klarke wanted to say, but instead she sat down on the couch, and allowed Reo to tell her why he had come.

"I owe you an apology, KAT. I've been wanting to tell you this ever since you got out of prison. I just—facing you was just too hard. It is hard." Reo took a deep breath, then continued. "I wasn't there for you. I didn't stay by your side like I said I would in my vows. I knew what a good woman you were and yet I couldn't see the truth. I didn't bother to see the truth. I was weak, KAT. And I feel as though I've only grown weaker since. Now I know where my true strength lay."

Klarke put her head down. Reo's words melted her soul. At the same time, hearing his words gave her a sense of relief. Maybe now he could even go a step further and forgive her for the mess she made out of things as well.

"Reo, you don't have to do this. Considering everything that was going on, the games and the lies, all you could see was one person. A woman had manipulated and betrayed you into loving her. How could you trust anything I said or did?"

"Because I loved you and I knew better of you. I loved you before I ever knew you, KAT." Reo grabbed Klarke's hand and looked into her eyes.

Klarke closed her eyes. No one called her KAT except for Reo. She loved it. That was his pet name for her and she had been his pet. She wanted that whole thing back. But Reo now sat before her a married man. He was no longer an option.

"And I still love you," Reo said softly. "I just wanted you to know that even when you were in prison. Even when the world, including myself, thought you had murdered my baby. I still loved you. I was so angry at myself for still loving you."

"Is that why you married her?" Klarke couldn't help but ask, pulling her hand out of Reo's.

"She got pregnant and we decided that the best thing to do was to get married," Reo said.

"Cop-out," Klarke responded, shaking her head. "You don't marry someone you're not in love with."

"You were going to do it," Reo said defensively. "You didn't know that you would fall in love with me and yet you had planned on roping me in, this literary superstar, and marrying me."

Klarke put her head down in shame.

"But I'm not here to dwell on that," Reo said. "I'm sorry, KAT. That's all I came to say."

Reo stood up and closed his eyes. He couldn't bring himself to look at Klarke in the eye when he said good-bye.

"Good-bye, KAT," Reo said while walking to the door.

Tears filled Klarke's eyes as she watched him walk away. What she wouldn't do to just be able to stop him. She just wanted him to hold her one last time.

Don't leave, Reo. Don't leave me again, Klarke wanted to say, as her body called for Reo to caress her, but instead all she did was stand up and shout, "Kiss Junior for me, please."

Reo turned around. The sight of Klarke standing there killed him. Damn, he didn't want to look at her. She was all the woman, and so much more, that he had remembered. And on top of that, he was wise enough to know that her body was callin' him. He walked back over to her and embraced her. Holding her felt so damn good. It felt too damn good.

"Don't cry. Don't cry," Reo whispered as Klarke wept against his chest. "Don't cry," he whispered again into her ear. His lips barely touching her ear, but touching it just enough to give her chills. Reo kissed Klarke on the head. She looked up at him and before she knew it the two of them were locking tongues.

Reo grabbed Klarke by the back of the head and ran his fingers through her wet hair. With her arms around Reo's back, Klarke squeezed him. Her private lips were now just as wet. Before one thing could lead to another, Reo pulled himself away from Klarke. He didn't want now what he couldn't have forever.

Both stood out of breath. *What have I just done* was written all over Reo's face. No matter what, even though Meka wasn't the wife she should have been in Reo's heart, she was his wife in God's eyes. He walked out the door. Leaving Klarke standing there alone.

Reo felt like an addict walking away from his habit. The drug was right there in his face but he couldn't have it. This was a definite sign that he couldn't stop wanting his KAT cold-turkey. He needed rehab.

As Reo walked through his front door, the smell of Meka's meat loaf slapped him across his face. He almost gagged. Today he hated the scent of meat loaf, unlike the sweet smell of Klarke's citrus hair conditioner. Guilt swamped him. Who knew that that one kiss would make him feel so guilty? That's why he had fought the urge to contact Klarke. He knew that once he let her into his head, his heart, she would haunt him. Now he had this black cloud of guilt hanging over his head that he was sure would hinder his and Meka's relationship even more. He hoped that that one kiss wouldn't persuade him to decide one way or another on working on his relationship with Meka. He worried how she would feel about him kissing Klarke. He had never lied to or kept secrets from Meka. How could he start now?

Just then Meka walked out of the kitchen holding Junior's and Kimiya's hands. He shook off his thoughts of KAT and greeted his family with hugs and kisses. Being with her and loving another woman was going to be self-inflicted abuse. Reo didn't know how long he was going to be able to take it, being with one woman while being so in love with another.

It had been weeks since Reo had kissed Klarke. He had told Nate about it. He thought telling Nate would take the monkey off of his back, but every time he looked at Meka he felt a rush of guilt and he didn't know why. Here she had damn near blackmailed him to stay in the marriage. Not that he was sure that he would have divorced her. But here lately she had been attempting to prove herself. She even accompanied him to one of his book signings as his assistant. Meka had never been one to take on such a mediocre role. Even though she knew she was his wife, all the fans saw her as a flunky.

Meka even went as far as signing up for cooking classes so that she could learn to cook something other than meat loaf. All of a sudden she was a black June Cleaver. It was as if someone hit a switch that changed her personality. It was almost scary, like she was a Stepford wife. Reo was starting to realize more and more that Meka's love for him wasn't just love, but verging on obsession. An obsession of some fairy-tale lifestyle she saw the two of them living together.

Reo tried to enjoy the change, but every time he closed his

eyes he remembered that kiss with Klarke. Caught between a rock
and a hard place, what was an honest man to do? Reo decided he
needed to do what his heart was telling him to do, no matter what
the outcome might be.

Reo and Meka stood over their double bathroom sink brushing
their teeth before they went to bed. The turkey Meka had prepared for dinner—which was something she had learned in her
cooking class—had been particularly dry. Of course Meka pretended that it had been the best turkey on God's green earth. She
had invited Mrs. Laroque over for dinner to show off her meal.
Mrs. Laroque gave it a thumbs-up even though it took her three
glasses of lemonade to wash it down.

They both reached for the bottle of mouthwash at the same
time.

"Go ahead," Reo said. "Ladies first."

"Thank you," Meka said, grabbing the bottle.

Reo pulled two Dixie cups from the dispenser and handed
Meka one. She filled the cups then threw hers in her mouth like it
was a shot of Henney and began to swish it around.

"There's something I need to tell you," Reo said.

Meka stopped swishing for a minute to look at Reo. She spit.

"Speak up," she said, filling the cup with water to rinse her
mouth out.

"It's about when I was in Michigan," Reo said, looking Meka
dead in her eyes. She gave him a look letting him know to continue. "After my signing I drove over to Toledo."

Meka took a deep breath and tried to remain calm. She knew
what this little visit meant. He had gone to see Klarke. And just
that quickly she envisioned his strong hands caressing Klarke's
naked body as they had hot, sweaty sex. Reo thrusting in and out

of Klarke, Reo yelling in ecstasy as Klarke's nails ran down his back and he released himself inside of her. Reo tonguing her down as the two prepared for round two. Meka felt her eyes water.

"Did you see her?" she asked calmly.

Reo nodded.

"Did you fuck her?" Meka said, not beating around the bush.

"No," Reo said, lowering his head.

"But . . . ?" Meka said.

"But we kissed." Reo looked up at Meka. She seemed to be maintaining her composure so he continued. "I had only gone there to apologize to her for the way I handled the situation with the death of our baby. How as her husband, as a man, I should have seen her through things and not been so quick to walk away. It was something I felt I just had to do. I don't know what happened. Perhaps some old feelings got the best of me. I don't know. The next thing I knew I was kissing her. It's been driving me crazy. So I just felt that you needed to know this."

Meka took a sip of the water from the Dixie cup, swished it around her mouth, glaring at Reo the entire time. Swish, swish, swish. From left to right. She wanted to spit it in his face, but instead did it in the sink. She took a deep breath, then spoke.

"I don't blame you," Meka lied. "You're only a man. And I'm certain some old unresolved emotions got the best of you. But I am glad that you were able to see her one last time and get that issue off of your chest."

Reo stared at her in surprise. He would have almost rathered she spit on him, slapped him or something. Maybe deep down inside the only reason he was telling her was so that she would get mad and call it quits on their relationship. That would have made his decision-making process a hell of a lot easier. But Meka didn't get angry.

"But this proves why the trip I planned is necessary," Meka said.

"What trip?" Reo questioned.

"You don't think I've noticed how uptight you've been the past few weeks?" Meka said pleasantly, as if her husband hadn't just admitted an indiscretion. "Darling, I'm your wife. I've seen how stressed out you've been. So I took the liberty of planning us a nice long vacation. We're going away. I've taken care of all the details. I've let your agent and publicist know as well."

"I can't believe you did that without even checking with me," Reo said in a testy tone.

"That's because I knew getting you to go would be like pulling teeth. It's obvious that we need to get away. We need a fresh start. We need to get out of Ohio and go somewhere and rejuvenate. Start fresh on our relationship. It's just for a few months, not forever. We don't have to sell the house, we can rent it so that we have something to come back to."

"Wait a minute!" Reo said. "Hold up. That doesn't sound like a trip to me. It sounds like an escape, like we're fugitives or something."

"Reo it's only a matter of time before—" Meka said, stopping in the middle of her sentence.

"It's only a matter of time before what?" Reo asked.

"Before this starts to affect the children. Kids are smart, you know. Do you think they don't sense the tension between us? Reo, you and I have been together since high school. No matter what little spell you and Klarke shared, it can't compare to all of the years we've dedicated to one another. You didn't kiss Klarke because you wanted to. I think subconsciously you felt that you were paying me back in a sense. And, baby, that's not the type of marriage I want us to have."

Meka walked over to Reo and put her head on his chest.

"I love you," she said. "I know I have this crazy way of showing it, but I honestly love you, Reo."

Reo didn't know what to say. He should have been relieved that Meka didn't try to kill him for seeing Klarke, but he wasn't. He hadn't cared about her leaving him. Hell, he didn't even mind giving up half of his money and the house, just as long as he got his children. Reo couldn't help but question whether his feelings were based on one little kiss with Klarke. Had those few moments with Klarke made him see more clearly or had it blurred his vision?

"Tell me you love me," Meka said as she looked up at Reo.

Reo looked down at Meka and saw the young woman he had fallen in love with back at Brookhaven High School. She was sweet, beautiful, independent, and bossy, but loving. This was the woman he knew Meka to be. Maybe he had gone wrong somehow. Like Klarke, maybe he had not stood by her like he should have. Maybe he had been too quick to give up instead of just hanging in there. He had already severed his wedding vows one time and he didn't want to do it again. Meka just might have had the right idea. Maybe if he ran far enough, he would leave his feelings for Klarke behind. But he sure wouldn't be able to forget about her. Junior was a constant reminder of that.

Reo squeezed Meka tightly and said, "I love you too." Whether he truly meant it or whether his guilty heart was talking was yet to be determined. "Where are we going and when do we leave?"

17

TWO WEEKS' NOTICE

Klarke walked into work like a zombie. Her head wasn't right. Her heart wasn't right. She hadn't had a clear head since the night Reo walked out of her door and her life. It was such a major setback for her. It was clear that she wasn't anywhere near where she wanted to be in life. She had a son who suffered from nightmares, a daughter in jail, one ex-husband who couldn't face the fact that they would never be a couple again and another ex-husband who faced the fact very easily and had moved on to another woman.

Her personal life was starting to take its toll on her work life. With Vaughn being in jail and Reo making an appearance back in her life, she couldn't seem to stay focused.

She was grateful that Evan had kept his word when he told her that she would always have a place at Kemble and Steiner. His standing by his word had put an end to the bitter struggle of turning in resumes, filling out job applications, and going on countless interviews. But still her cup was half empty.

Months ago she had turned forty and had pretended to be sick with the flu so that Breezy and Jeva couldn't celebrate it. Klarke didn't see a reason to celebrate. Here she was, going on forty-one, and she wasn't any further along in life than she had been at thirty.

When Klarke got out of jail she had told herself that she wouldn't frown upon all of the things that she didn't have and be proud of all that she did have. That shit was easier said than done, for real.

Klarke walked through the office giving her usual morning hellos. She settled in at her desk, not even thinking about grabbing her morning cup of coffee. She was in a complete daze. It wasn't until the third time that Evan called her name that his voice even registered.

"Klarke!" Evan said for the third time.

"Oh. Yes," Klarke said in a startled tone. She looked up to see Evan standing over her.

"Good morning," Evan said, rolling an Altoid on the roof of his mouth with his tongue.

"Morning," Klarke said.

Evan paused, seeing that Klarke wasn't herself. He had noticed how distant and standoffish she had been the past couple of weeks, not to mention the errors here and there she had been making that were beginning to be quite costly for the company.

"Can I see you in my office?" Evan asked.

"Oh, if it's about that Green Day Publishing account, I took care of it," Klarke said. "My apologies again. I know it cost the company thousands to have to overnight that project."

"It's not the Green Day Publishing account," Evan said.

Klarke paused, trying to figure out what Evan wanted to discuss with her.

"Oh, is it Mrs. Wilkens and my not returning her call?" Klarke asked.

"Klarke, please," Evan said, closing his eyes. He dreaded having to do what he was about to do. "Can you just come into my office?"

Evan walked away. Klarke listened to the beat of her heart and started to worry. She grabbed a pen and notepad and headed into Evan's office.

"Close the door please," Evan said.

Klarke closed the door, then walked over to the chair in front of Evan's desk and sat down. He stared at her as she stared down at his desk. A hair was out of place. Evan had never seen a hair out of place on Klarke's head before. Not even if the wind blew. It was Friday and yet she had worn the same exact outfit that she had on Monday. The Klarke he knew would have never repeated an outfit in the same week, not even in the same month. It was evident that Klarke was not herself.

Klarke sat there listening to the silence that said everything. Her eyes began to water. She had been fucking up the last month or so and she knew it. Klarke had no idea how hard it would be to get her life back together and move on. Getting a place to stay, car, wardrobe, and job seemed easy compared to the impossible task of moving on. God had given her everything she needed to make a meal and yet she insisted on starving herself.

She knew that if any other employee had made the mistakes she had been making they would have been fired on the spot a long time ago. But Evan genuinely cared for her and that fact alone made it that much harder for him to have to let her go. Evan never dreamed of letting her go, from work or his heart. But he had to when it was clear that they would be nothing more than friends.

The day Evan rehired her, when he held her hand that first

time, it was electric. But this time, it was warm and friendly. As Evan held Klarke's hand, they looked into each other's eyes and an unspoken understanding that they would not make the mistake of mixing business with pleasure again passed between them. Besides, Evan couldn't afford to risk his marriage for the *what if* game. What if he and Klarke could be together? How much greener could the grass be? What if, just like before, after the two slept together, he liked her more than she liked him? It wasn't worth it.

Evan walked around his desk and over to Klarke. He kneeled down and looked up at her.

"Please don't cry," Evan said.

"I'm sorry," Klarke said as tears fell. "I know I've been screwing up something terrible. I just can't seem to get it together."

"Don't apologize," Evan said, taking hold of her hands. "It's my fault too. I threw you right back into work as if you had only had a weekend off. Klarke, you've been through a great deal. I shouldn't have expected you to just come back to work and pick up where you left off, with work or with me. I'm the one who's sorry."

"Am I fired?" Klarke said, cutting to the chase.

Evan looked down. He couldn't bring himself to say it.

"How about you just give me two weeks' notice?" Evan said. "And for old times' sake, how about I throw in some severance."

"You've always been a kind man," Klarke said, placing her hand on Evan's face. The warmth of her hand melted him like ice. He closed his eyes and took a deep breath. The last time, with Klarke's departure from Kemble and Steiner, although she was the one to quit, Evan still saw it within his heart to give her a severance package. It was good to know that he was still such a genuine man, as Klarke would damn sure need it. She would have to get back to the grind of finding a job. Man, had she fucked up!

Klarke looked down at Evan then immediately removed her hand and got up.

"Evan, I just want you to know that you'll always have a place in my heart," Klarke said sincerely. "All those nights in jail. I sat and thought about all of the things I should have done . . . all of the things I shouldn't have done."

"Was loving me one of the things you should have done?" Evan asked. He was never able to read Klarke well enough to know how she truly felt about him. Maybe not knowing had been a good thing. "Never mind. Sometimes not knowing is less painful."

"I guess I better go grab a box from the copy room and get to packing," Klarke said, clearing her throat.

"I'm going to miss you," Evan said. He knew this would be the last time he ever saw her again and his heart ached. At the same time he was relieved. He had been cheating on his wife mentally with Klarke. He remembered how good it felt being inside of her and he just wanted to relive that feeling one more time. Out of sight, out of mind is what he was now praying for with Klarke's departure.

"And I'm going to miss you too," Klarke said. She smiled then walked over to Evan and hugged him tight. "Your wife is so lucky," Klarke whispered in his ear. "She's got a damn good man. And if memory serves me correctly, you handle yours pretty well for a white boy."

Klarke pulled away and winked at Evan and proceeded to walk out of his office.

"Hey, Klarke," Evan called, stopping her in her tracks. "You're a class act."

"That's mighty white of you to say," Klarke joked, leaving his office and closing the door behind her. With her hand still on the doorknob, she pressed her back up against the door, closed her eyes, and cried.

Klarke was closing the door to a comfortable life and entering instability. She feared that same struggle she endured when she and Harris divorced. But what she feared most was falling back into that same black pit that landed her in her current situation.

Klarke let go of the doorknob and headed toward the copy room. Wiping her eyes clear, coming toward her she saw a familiar face.

"Hi. It's Klarke, right?" the tall slender woman said.

"Yes, Aliyah," Klarke said, extending her hand. It was Evan's wife, looking quite dazzling. She had come in her Sunday best, hoping that Klarke would see her, of course. She looked just like she did when Evan first introduced Klarke to her. Right before the trial of the baby's murder Klarke had run into Evan in the mall while she was with Jeva and Breezy. Klarke had always pictured some lovely blonde on Evan's arm. She had convinced herself that Evan only slept with her because he wanted to take care of his craving for chocolate, and that she had filled his appetite. But when she saw Aliyah on his arm in the mall that day, she knew that Evan had been real with her all along. That Klarke's color had nothing to do with any part of their relationship.

"It's good to see you," Aliyah said. "I've been meaning to get up here and welcome you back forever. Perhaps one day I can come and pick you up for lunch or something."

Aliyah was lying through her perfect white teeth. She got sick the day Evan told her that he had rehired Klarke. The green-eyed monster was definitely lurking.

"Perhaps not," Klarke said.

"Excuse me?" Aliyah said, only two inches from being in sistah mode.

"Oh, pardon me." Klarke laughed. "I didn't mean it like that. You see, today is my last day. I won't be working here anymore . . . ever."

"I'm sorry to hear that," Aliyah said, not realizing a grin was creeping onto her face.

"Do you want to try saying that one more time with a little more feeling?"

Aliyah put her head down in embarrassment, realizing that Klarke had just seen right through her.

"I'm sorry," Aliyah said kindly. "But now that you're leaving, I guess I can be honest with you. I hated when Evan came home and told me that you were coming back to work for him."

"Why?" Klarke asked, surprised.

"Why?" Aliyah repeated, her eyes wide. "Do you have any idea how high of a pedestal my husband has placed you on? That day I saw you in the mall I wanted to faint. I mean you can't deny that we could pass for sisters. Hell, even twins. I was so jealous. I felt that he picked me because I was the next best thing to you. I tried to wear my hair like you. I studied pictures of you from the company Christmas parties and I even tried to apply my makeup like you, flawless. Do you know that he even called me by your name a couple of times?"

Klarke was shocked. For one, she knew that Evan had a soft spot for her in his heart, but she never knew it was that deep. For two, she couldn't believe Aliyah was standing there telling her all of this.

"Yeah," Aliyah continued. "I thought I was going to lose Evan to the mere thought of you. He said that there was just something about you, that you had a spirit that just made people love you automatically and that you weren't easy to forget. He said you touched people's spirit. Just the thought of you made him want to be a good man to me. It took some convincing, but deep down inside I knew he loved me strong and in a weird twisted way I had you to thank for it. I can't sleep without him, eat, or think. I can hardly speak without him. I love my husband and trust him so much. But still, I was a little threatened by you."

"Well, as you can see, there was never anything to be threatened by," Klarke said.

"I believe that now. But it took some convincing when I found all those receipts from when he was putting fifty dollars a month on your books. That must have helped you out in there. Kept you from having to sell cigarettes." Aliyah chuckled.

Klarke was speechless. All along she thought that Harris was the one keeping her books straight. She couldn't believe her ears. She played it cool, though, responding, "Yes. I don't know what I would have done all those years. I can't thank him enough. As a matter of fact, would you please thank him for me one more time."

"Sure," Aliyah said.

"Please don't forget," Klarke pleaded.

"I won't."

"Well, I'm glad I ran into you today, Aliyah," Klarke said, grabbing her hand and patting it.

"Same here," Aliyah smiled. "You keep your head up, sistah."

Klarke nodded and proceeded to the copy room to grab a box to pack up her desk with her head held high.

Klarke was walking out of the prison building from a visit with Vaughn when she saw Harris walking up.

"Hey you," Klarke said to Harris.

"Hey yourself," he replied and immediately knew that something was wrong. He could tell Klarke had been crying. Her eyeliner was smeared. Normally she would have stopped off in the bathroom to fix it. But today she just said fuck it. "You okay?"

"Oh, yeah. Me, I'm fine," Klarke said, wiping her face.

Harris opened his arms to Klarke. She dropped her head, then buried her face in his chest.

"We're going to get through this, Klarke. We're going to get through this just fine." Harris patted Klarke on the back.

Klarke allowed herself to take in Harris's comforting touch, then slowly pulled herself away.

"Well, enjoy your visit with Vaughn," Klarke said. "By the way, where's HJ and Sissy? You didn't bring them with you?"

"No, I didn't want to get them out of school early again like I did last week," Harris said.

"Okay then," Klarke said. "I'm going to get going. Talk to you later." Klarke walked away and Harris went inside to visit with Vaughn.

Harris's visit had been draining for both him and Vaughn. Every time he saw her he couldn't help but feel guilty all over again. But he had to be strong for his little girl who seemed to be doing a hell of a lot better than he and Klarke put together.

As he exited the prison building and walked to his car he wanted to break. He had held back his tears in front of Vaughn because he wanted to be strong in front of her. He was a grown man. He didn't want his daughter to see him cry.

When he got into the car he put the key in the ignition and just sat there. All of a sudden he began beating his fist on the steering wheel. He beat it repeatedly until tears began running down his face. *How could she still love me?* Harris thought to himself. During his first visit to the prison with Vaughn, when she was tongue whipping him he felt that he had deserved it. But for her to now throw her arms around him and tell him how much she loved him seemed so undeserving.

He hadn't been there for her when she needed him most. He hadn't been there to take her to the park or watch her in school plays when he had the chance and now his time with her was dictated and chaperoned.

Harris's cell phone rang, interrupting his thoughts.

"Hello," Harris said after clearing his throat.

"I was going to meet her at the bus stop, Dad!" a frantic HJ shouted in Harris's ear. "The car didn't stop. The bus lights were blinking and the stop sign was up, but the car didn't stop. The car didn't stop. It hit her!"

"Calm down, damn it!" Harris shouted. "What car hit who?"

"Sissy," HJ continued frantically. "The ambulance is taking her."

Harris could hear a male adult voice in the background asking HJ for the phone.

"Hello, Mr. Bradshaw," the male voice said.

"Yes, please tell me what's going on."

"This is Officer Foster. Your daughter was hit by a car after she got off the school bus."

"How is she? Where is she?" Harris said in a panic.

"She's being taken to Toledo University Hospital."

"How is she?"

The officer paused. "Mr. Bradshaw, I really think you should get there as soon as possible.

Click.

Harris left his Lexus parked right outside of the hospital emergency-room door like it was a bike. Doors unlocked and all. As a matter of fact, his door didn't even close all the way as he jumped out of it and headed toward the entrance doors. No fancy car meant shit compared to the life of his child.

"My daughter was hit by a car and brought here," Harris said to the first nurse he saw.

"What's her name?" the nurse said as he led Harris over to the registration desk.

"Sissy . . . Sionne Bradshaw," Harris said. Once the cat was out of the bag and everyone knew that Harris was the father of Tionne's child, they immediately put Harris's name on the birth certificate and changed Sissy's last name to Bradshaw.

"She's in surgery," a female nurse intercepted. "Are you her father?"

"Yes, dear God, yes," Harris said in a desperate tone.

"Your daughter has lost a great deal of blood. We're going to need to take some of your blood and if you can call any other family members to come donate blood that would be great too."

"Sure," Harris agreed. "I can call my son to give blood also."

"That's good, Mr. Bradshaw," the nurse said in a calming manner. "That's real good, but first let's get you taken care of."

Harris pulled up his sleeve.

"Not right here, Mr. Bradshaw." The nurse giggled. "Follow me."

The nurse took Harris into a little room that she closed in with just a curtain. She took what seemed like enough blood to fill a gallon container.

"You just sit right here, Mr. Bradshaw, and rest up for a moment." The nurse smiled. "I'm going to bring you back some juice and a snack."

"My daughter," Harris said weakly, not having eaten all day.

"Everyone's doing their best." She smiled and that's the last thing Harris remembered before he passed out.

"Mr. Bradshaw, how are you feeling?" the kind nurse who had taken Harris's blood asked.

She was just a blur in his face as Harris came to. He had had such a long and draining day. He had missed both breakfast and lunch but hadn't thought about any of that before donating damn near a gallon of blood.

"What happened?" a groggy Harris asked.

"I didn't get that juice and snack to you soon enough. You got a little weak on us, but you're just fine now."

"My daughter, how is she? Did you give her my blood? Is she okay?"

"She's going to be fine. The doctors are finishing up and then they'll be right out to talk to you."

"So my blood helped?" Harris asked eagerly.

"Mr. Bradshaw," the nurse said, almost at a loss for words. "Never mind."

"No, please," Harris said worriedly. "Please continue."

"No," the nurse hesitated. "The doctor will be out to speak with you."

"Please!" a desperate Harris said.

The nurse paused, then spoke, "We weren't able to use your blood, but we did find some compatible matches."

"I—I don't understand," a confused Harris asked. "Do I have a different type than her?"

"Uh, yes you do."

Harris could sense that there was something else that the nurse simply wasn't telling him. "Is there something wrong?"

"Mr. Bradshaw, is Sionne your wife's child?" the nurse asked.

"What? What do you mean?"

"Is she your step-daughter?"

Harris had no idea what the nurse was getting at, but he didn't have time to figure it out, either. "What is it? Is there something you're trying to tell me?"

The nurse paused. "What I'm trying to say, Mr. Bradshaw," the nurse said, "is that there is no possible way that Sionne can be your child. You are not her biological father."

Harris sat by Sissy's bedside holding her hand. The doctor had just informed him that she was going to pull through. He was more than relieved.

He had just called HJ from the hospital pay phone. He heard Klarke in the background while they were talking. HJ had called her. She immediately raced over to pick him up so that they could go to the hospital together.

Harris contemplated whether or not he would tell Klarke the news about Sissy not really being his child. Perhaps that would change things between them. Klarke would see that he wasn't guilty of the ultimate marital crime, having a child outside of the marriage. That might make it easier for her to forgive him for committing adultery. They could try to start over.

As Harris sat there holding Sissy's hand, he heard Klarke and HJ coming. Harris looked down at Sissy, who was breathing through tubes. Her little chest was moving up and down. This was the child he had raised as his own. Ironically he thought about Heather, how he had denied her. Was this his karma?

Nonetheless, if Harris told Klarke, eventually others would find out. He had loved Sissy like his own blood. She had already lost a mother. How could she bear to lose a father? Besides that, Harris had already hurt one daughter and he didn't want to hurt another. For once he was putting someone else's heart before his own. At that moment he decided against ever telling a soul, which included Klarke. Even from her grave, Tionne had gotten the "W."

18

GUESS WHO'S COMING TO DINNER

"Thanks for inviting me over for dinner, Jeva," Maria said as she sat on Jeva's couch munching on a veggie tray Jeva had laid out. Heather was in her room playing with her Barbie dream house while Jeva was in the kitchen preparing dinner.

"It's no problem," Jeva said, standing in the kitchen doorway with a fork in her hand. "I know with going to school and being a teacher's aide you don't have a lot of time to eat right. I'm sure those kids drain you."

"Sometimes I don't know who's worse," Maria joked. "The kids or the professors. I wish I could just meet some rich guy and live off of an allowance that he gives me. You know, sitting around eating Bon Bons and watching *The Bold and the Beautiful* every day."

"I had that dream once too," Jeva said, now back in the kitchen putting the last touches on her green-bean casserole. "Then I woke up."

"Hey, sometimes dreams come true. My mother is living proof of that. At one time she was just a poor Hispanic girl over in Cuba and now look at her."

"Your mother's Cuban?" Jeva asked.

"Um-hm," Maria replied.

"You never told me that."

"You never asked."

"Well, I knew you were mixed with something, but I didn't bother to ask. I used to hate when people would look at me and before they even inquired about my name they wanted to know my nationality. I figured if you wanted me to know that you'd tell me."

"It's no big deal, so I'm telling you now," Maria said, going back to the original topic. "My father gives my mom a monthly allowance. I think it's something like one thousand or fifteen hundred dollars a month."

"See, that's what I'm talking about," Jeva yelled from the kitchen as she peeked at the baked chicken that was in the oven. "I like a man who knows that a woman needs taking care of and not one of them men that says, 'Baby, you have to tell me when you need something.'"

"Yeah, I'm not with that, begging a man for what he should know you need," Maria said, gnawing on a celery stick. "But you have to be smart enough to bank some of that money too."

"What do you mean?" Jeva asked. "You want some cranberry juice?"

"Yeah. Um-hm," Maria said with a mouth full of celery. "I'll take some juice."

"Okay. Now go ahead with what you were saying."

"Oh, yeah. See, my mom never spent the allowance my father

gave her. She saved every last penny for I don't know how many years. When she wanted to shop or something, she used the credit cards. Her allowance was separate from bill money. So she just passed off her expenses as bill money."

"That was smart," Jeva said, taking two glasses out of the cabinet. "But how did she explain all the extra cash to your father?"

"She opened her own bank account at a separate bank from where she and my father had their joint account. She hid that account from him for years until one day she accidentally paid the bills with the wrong checkbook. Checks bounced all over the place. My dad started getting phone calls about bills not being paid."

"But I thought she never spent a dime," Jeva said, pouring the cranberry juice. "She should have had plenty of money to cover the bills, shouldn't she?"

"That's the same thing I said," Maria responded. "But she had made a couple of excessive withdrawals, clearing out the account. My older sister, Geenie, thought that perhaps Mom ran off to the casinos, caught the gambling bug and blew it all. My brother, Anthony Jr., thought Mom was keeping the pool boy and spent it all on him. Anthony Jr. is a writer so we never take his theories to heart. But she definitely had something to hide because she used her mother's maiden name on the account, Dawson. That was another mistake. She signed her married name on the checks instead of Dawson."

All of a sudden Maria heard a loud crash. She jumped up and ran into the kitchen. "You okay?" Maria said in a panic. Jeva was just standing there with a frozen look on her face. The two glasses that had been filled with cranberry juice were splattered at Jeva's feet. "Jeva, talk to me. What's wrong?"

Jeva looked up at Maria with tears in her eyes. Hearing the name Dawson made Jeva feel as though a spell had been placed on her. Her mind was blank and she couldn't move. All she could do was think about that day in the park when she thought she was going to meet her birth parents. But instead of her mother and father showing up, some Oriental man showed up to meet with her instead.

The man's name was Mr. Christian and he showed up with an envelope full of cash and instructions regarding a trust that had been set up for her by her birth parents. He informed Jeva that her parents wanted nothing to do with her and that she should stop her attempts to seek them out. He then handed Jeva the envelope full of money. He told her that everything was hers to keep but there was one stipulation attached. He told her that if she continued seeking out her birth parents that she would have to pay back all of the money. Mr. Christian made it clear that her parents had a new life and didn't want anything to do with her. They were pretty much begging her to stop looking for them. Jeva chose the money. It wouldn't make having grown up without knowing her real parents any better, but it would make a better life for Heather.

Jeva tried to get Mr. Christian to tell her more about her parents in detail, but he was very standoffish, but she'd never forget his introduction, "I'm Mr. Christian, a representative of the Dawsons." That name stuck with Jeva ever since.

"Jeva, can you breathe? Are you diabetic? What's wrong?" Maria had approached Jeva and was shaking her by the arm. "Say something, damn it! You're scaring me."

Jeva looked up at Maria and softly spoke. "I think I'm your sister."

Maria had just finished helping Jeva clean up the broken glass and cranberry juice from off the kitchen floor. When Jeva first started hanging out with Maria she had contemplated just for a second Maria being her long lost sister, but chalked it off as being one of her fairy-tale hopes. If you took away the bleached hair, the two women looked uncannily similar. And the way Heather took to her added to her suspicions. Slowly, but surely, even Jeva herself had been feeling a strange connection with Maria. It was more than just feeling like she had known her all of her life, but as though it was meant for the two to meet in this lifetime.

One thing in particular had convinced Jeva that Maria could not have been her sister. She specifically recalled Mr. Christian saying that her biological parents had five other children in addition to her. When Jeva first met Maria in the gym she told her that she only had three brothers and sisters. There had to be a missing piece to the puzzle.

Jeva sat down at the kitchen table while Maria emptied the dustpan of the last bits of glass.

"Are you sure you are okay?" Maria asked Jeva. She had already asked her a thousand times while they had cleaned up the mess, but Jeva kept shaking her head no.

"No, I'm fine," Jeva said in a low tone.

"But you are not," Maria said, joining Jeva at the table. "I know you haven't known me that long, but you can talk to me, Jeva. Please, let's talk about this."

Jeva closed her eyes and took a deep breath.

"Maria, I know it sounds wild," Jeva said with her eyes still closed. "But I really think that I'm your sister."

A look of shock came over Maria's face. Jeva slowly opened her eyes to witness it. Maria stood up and began pacing the floor.

"But I don't understand," Maria said, agitated. "You are just some girl I met in a gym and now all of a sudden you think we are sisters? That's *loco* all right."

"I don't know if you are or not," Jeva said. "There are just a lot of coincidences."

"Like me bumping into you at the gym?" Maria said sarcastically. "I bet that type of thing happens all of the time."

"Actually it does," Jeva said seriously. "I've seen it on the *Montel Williams* show before."

Maria paused and looked at Jeva as though she had lost her mind. "You gotta stop watching so much television," she said.

"Maria, this is not a joke," Jeva said as she stood up and walked over to Maria. "Your mother's maiden name, that's the name my adoptive parents used."

"So what?" Maria said, refusing to jump on the bandwagon of Jeva's far-fetched theory. "I bet there are millions of people whose last name is Dawson."

"My mother is Cuban, and my father is white," Jeva said.

Maria began pacing again.

"Sisters, huh?" Maria asked. "What other so-called coincidences do you have? As a matter of fact, what facts do you have?"

Jeva didn't reply, she just sat back down at the table. She couldn't respond. One thing was bothering her. The fact that Maria only had three brothers and sisters. Perhaps Jeva had jumped the gun. Perhaps the devil was playing tricks on her. Everything appeared to be adding up, but at the same time not adding up. Jeva didn't know what to think at this point.

"You said you only have three other siblings, a brother and two sisters, right?"

"Yes," Maria answered. "Geenie, Anthony Jr., and Jennifer."

Jeva buried her hands in her face and shook her head.

"Our youngest brother, Marcus, died of kidney failure when he was only eight."

"So you had four brothers and sisters?" Jeva said, standing up. "There were five of you?"

"Yes," Maria said, "but like I said, my brother Marcus—"

"I know, I know. I heard you," Jeva said as she began to cry. "Maria, listen to me." Jeva walked over to her and put her hands on hers. "Your *madre* never mentioned having had a child, a daughter who would have been her eldest child?"

"No," Maria said. "Don't you think I would remember something like that? My parents would never. They would never give up one of their own. Never! *La famile* means everything to them."

Maria pushed Jeva's hands away, stood up, and exited the kitchen. Jeva followed her. Maria picked up her purse and jacket that were lying across the leather recliner.

"Where are you going?" Jeva asked.

"I think I should leave now," Maria said, putting on her jacket.

"Leave?" Jeva said, alarmed.

"You've got a problem and you need to face it!" Maria said, her voice raised in excitement. "I know being abandoned is a hard thing. But at some point in your life you are going to have to deal with it. You can't go around hoping that every stranger you meet is one of your long-lost family members."

"That hurts, Maria."

"I'm sorry, Jeva, but I have to go." Maria quickly walked to the door and unlocked it.

"I guess leaving runs in the family," Jeva said coldly.

Maria paused with her hand on the doorknob.

"What's going on?" Heather asked curiously as she came down the steps. "You two sound like you're fighting."

The two women stared at Heather.

Jeva walked over to Maria and spoke in a whisper. "Please help me, Maria. Just give me answers. That's all I'm asking. And if you won't do it for me, then do it for her."

Maria looked over at Heather, standing there staring back at them.

"You're not fighting, are you?" Heather asked sadly.

"No, *chiquita*," Maria said with a smile. "Everything *es mucho buenos*."

"Then why do you have your jacket on?" Heather asked. "I thought you were staying for dinner."

"Uh, I was," Maria stuttered. "But I forgot about a big exam I have tomorrow. I have to go home and study."

"Okay, well I hope you do good."

"Thank you, sweetie."

"*Adios*," Heather said as she headed back up the steps.

Jeva looked at Maria with a desperate look in her eyes. She waited for a response.

"We're having dinner at the house in a couple of weeks. I'll tell Mom to set an extra plate, that I'll be bringing a guest for dinner. Hopefully, you can get all the answers you'll need."

"Thank you, Maria. Thank you so much," Jeva said as tears rolled down her face. "I know you don't want to believe that your parents would keep a secret like this from you. Maybe this is all just a big coincidence."

"I'll call you with my flight information so that you can see if you can get on the same flight," Maria said with very little expression, still in shock from Jeva's accusations.

"You don't have to leave, you know," Jeva said. "There's plenty of food."

"I think I've lost my appetite," Maria said, trying to smile but failing miserably.

"Okay. I'll wait for you to call me with the flight information."

"I'll talk to you soon," Maria said, walking out of the door, but before leaving she stopped and said to Jeva, "Oh, and, Jeva. There is no such thing as a coincidence. Everything happens for a reason. Everything."

"So are you going to go?" Chauncy asked Jeva as they sat down on the park bench. They were at Hollingwood Park, the same park where Jeva had met Mr. Christian.

"Not knowing is what's killing me, Chauncy," Jeva said as she admired her medium-length acrylic nails. The little Chinese woman had done such a lovely job on them the day before. She had suggested a lovely deep burgundy, the color of a fine sweet wine. "The fact that my parents made me a thousandaire on a promise not to hunt them down was proof enough that they don't want to know me. If I go, I'll have to give back all of the money. Do you know how much I've spent already?"

Chauncy chuckled and grabbed Jeva's hand. "I just don't see how all the money in the world could take away wanting to know your biological parents after more than three decades of not even knowing their name," Chauncy said with sincerity and concern for Jeva's state of mind. "I know you and I have only been seeing each other for a few months, but you've talked about your adoption and biological parents more than anything. It's obvious that you haven't just taken the money and run. You still think about them every day, wondering if you made the right decision. That means you have a conscience. I love a woman with a conscience."

Jeva sighed.

"It's so hard, Chauncy," she said. "I don't know what to do. Everything in me wants to hop on that plane to Nevada with Maria. But I'm so scared. I'm scared that they might not be my family. I'm even more scared that they are."

"If I were you, which I'm not, I don't think I could not go," Chauncy said. He brought Jeva's hand to his lips and kissed it. "Whatever decision you make is the right one. The only thing you need to take into consideration is right now. Never mind about yesterday or tomorrow. I'm here for you."

Jeva looked up at Chauncy and smiled. He always tried to get all philosophical when he was trying to say something but didn't know how to say it.

"What in the hell are you trying to say?" Jeva asked.

"Hmm, let's see," Chauncy said as he put his elbow on his knee and his hand on his chin. "Fuck their money. I got cha back!"

Jeva smiled at Chauncy as her eyes welled up with tears.

"Did I say that right?" Chauncy asked with a proud grin.

"Yes," Jeva said. "You said it right. Everything about you is right."

"Then it looks like we better go shopping," Chauncy said as he stood up with Jeva's hand in his. "The weather is a little warmer in Nevada than it is here."

Jeva stood up and wiped the tears from her eyes before they could fall.

"Maybe you can pick out some Daisy Duke short shorts," Chauncy said, licking his lips. "You can give me my very own private show."

"Come on, silly," Jeva said, pulling Chauncy by both hands. "You are so special. It took all of these years for me to get the courage to step to you. I could kick myself for not doing it years ago."

"You had no control over when our souls would mate," Chauncy said. "Just be glad that they did."

"I could learn to love you, you know," Jeva said, kissing Chauncy on the lips.

"Does that mean I can hit that tonight?" Chauncy teased.

"Oh, so now you're this expert at talking slang?" Jeva asked.

"Everybody knows the language of love," Chauncy said as the two headed to the mall for their own private little peep show.

Klarke, Breezy, and Jeva had just finished their meal at the Cheesecake Factory and were looking over the dessert menu. The women knew the menu by heart, but always looked it over for GP.

"Is something on your mind?" Breezy asked Jeva, who hadn't said but two words since they walked into the restaurant.

"Actually there is." Jeva sighed. "Did you notice anything peculiar about Maria's father when you met him?"

Breezy puckered her lips and went deep in thought. "No, not really," she said.

"I meant, did you think that I maybe looked a little bit like him?" Jeva said, hoping for a yes.

"He was white," Breezy said. "The white in you probably resembled him because you all look alike anyway."

Jeva sighed. "This is not the time for jokes, Breezy."

"Who was joking?"

Klarke laughed under her breath. As far as she was concerned, these two might as well have hooked up and become a couple, because they sure did act like one.

"Anyway," Jeva said, rolling her eyes. "I know you guys are going to think that I am crazy, but I think that man was my father and that Maria is my sister."

"What?" both Breezy and Klarke shouted at the same time.

"Your father?" Klarke asked.

"Yes," Jeva said. "There's a strong possibility that Maria's father is my biological father." She paused, then told them about the incident when she invited Maria to her house for dinner. She told them how Maria offered to allow Jeva to accompany her to Nevada.

"I can't believe you're just now telling us," Klarke said, surprised that Jeva hadn't told them before now.

"I didn't know what I was going to do and just in case I chose to keep the money and let this thing go I didn't want you guys to think I was crazy," Jeva said.

"We are your girls," Breezy said compassionately, grabbing Jeva's hand.

"Yeah," Klarke said, grabbing her other one.

"We gon' always have your muthafuckin' back regardless. You hear me?" Breezy said, squeezing Jeva's hand.

She nodded.

"All right then," Breezy said, letting her go. "That's more like it."

"So are you going or what?" Klarke asked.

"I don't know. Maria only gave me two weeks' notice," Jeva said. "I have to cover an event for the Toledo newspaper that same weekend. I'd have to figure out what to do with Heather."

"Heather can stay with me," Klarke said. "HJ can keep her entertained and I'm sure Harris will allow Sissy to come play with her. And can't you call your friend Patty who used to cover for you all of the time at your old job to help you? Do you still know how to get in contact with her?"

Jeva thought about it for a minute. Even though Patty worked for Jeva's old boss, she had helped Jeva with some shoots since then. Jeva was sure if she explained the situation to Patty that she would help her out. Patty was always up for making a few extra ends.

"And I can go with you," Breezy said. "You need somebody there who can have your back. Anything can go down and you know your punk ass ain't 'bout it."

"Girl, you are as big as a house," Jeva said.

"I'm not due for two more months," Breezy said.

"But you look like you can drop any day now," Klarke added. "There's no way your doctor is going to let you travel."

"Don't worry," Jeva said to Breezy. "You'll be there in spirit."

"Can I offer you ladies dessert?" the waitress asked them.

"Oh yeah," Klarke and Jeva said at the same time.

"None for me," Breezy said.

The waiter took Klarke and Jeva's orders, then left the women to chat.

"What?" Klarke said.

"You're not having any cheesecake?" Jeva added.

"The thought of it is making me sick," Breezy said, rubbing her round belly. She was wearing a white, long-sleeved maternity blouse with ruffles around the neck. She looked absolutely adorable. "I haven't been able to keep anything down. I get all cramped up and then puke all over the place. I can't wait to drop this load so that things can get back to how they used to be."

"Get back to how they used to be," Jeva said sarcastically. "Yeah, right!"

"Tell me about it," Klarke added. "Getting up in the middle of the night warming a bottle or pulling a titty out. Changing diapers and burping. Breezy, I don't think that's how things used to be."

"Oh, God," Breezy said, sticking her tongue out as if she were gagging. "Now I'm even sicker. I wish it would come out as big as Hydrant's other daughter so that I don't have to worry about that stuff."

"So how are you and Hydrant's daughter getting along?" Klarke asked.

Breezy smiled. "Samari is an angel."

Klarke began looking around. "Hydrant's not here so you can tell me the truth."

"Seriously, she's a doll. I can't wait to have my own."

"That's wonderful, Breezy," Jeva said.

Klarke stared at her friend and almost wanted to cry. Breezy had always kept a hard shell around her emotions, hiding from her demons. To finally see the real, happy Breezy made Klarke teary-eyed with joy.

"What's wrong?" Breezy asked as tears flowed down Klarke's face.

"I'm so happy for you, Breezy. You have no idea. I'm so glad that somebody's dream is coming true. I mean Jeva may be only days away from finding her biological parents. She's well off, able to pursue her passion of photography. She's able to take wonderful care of Heather and Chauncy keeps a smile on her face. Then there's you. You're reunited with the man you never should have let get away in the first place and you're getting ready to have a beautiful baby. I just wish my shit was on point. Why is my shit so fucked up?"

For the first time, Breezy and Jeva were witnessing the pillar of their group crumble.

Breezy swallowed her own tears and said, "Uh-uh. There'll be no pity parties around here," Breezy said. "You're too strong for that."

"I'm not! I'm not!" Klarke shouted. "I'm tired of hearing that. 'Klarke, you're so strong.' Well even the strong get weak sometimes. Why does everyone expect me to be the last house standing after the world's worst earthquake? Why can't I take a break from being the strong one? Isn't it somebody else's turn? Who was the strong one while I was in jail? Huh?"

"It was still you, Klarke," Jeva said. "You made us strong with your strength even through those metal bars. Your letters. Your conversations. Klarke, you have such a divine spirit."

"I don't want to hear that bullshit," Klarke snapped. "I know you two stood by my side and looked out for me while I was locked up, but not once did either of you ask me if I really did it or not. Yet you claim to know me so well."

"That's not fair, Klarke," Jeva said defensively. "Who were we to question you?"

"My friends," Klarke said, hurt. "You were my friends and not once did either of you say, 'Klarke, did you do it?' 'Klarke, why did you do it?' That hurt. It hurt knowing that my best friends thought that I was capable of murder."

Breezy wanted to snap the fuck off, but for the first time in her life she thought before she spoke.

"Are you mad at us or are you mad at him?" Breezy asked softly. "Because I see you're hurting and I'm going to let you get off your fly-ass comments, but you need to start being honest with yourself. This isn't about us. This is about him, so don't use us to say what you should be saying to that nigga. Yeah, we're your girls, but we didn't stand before God and take vows with your ass, Reo did. You had that man in your living room where you could have told him exactly how you felt, but you let him walk out the door."

Klarke didn't respond. She knew Breezy had her pegged.

"Now I done worked up a goddamn appetite. Where in the hell is that waitress so I can get me a goddamn piece of cheese-cake!" Breezy yelled.

Klarke sat there looking at Breezy with the look of death in her eyes.

"If you weren't pregnant," Klarke said, balling her fist.

"If I weren't pregnant, what?" Breezy said, snapping her neck. "Bring it on, Cletus. Don't be scurred."

Klarke couldn't help but laugh.

"Damn it, I hate you," she said to Breezy, throwing her hands up in the air.

"And I love you too, Klarke Laroque," Breezy said, winking. "Now what are you going to do with yourself?"

Klarke paused and then said, "Y'all, I can still feel him. I can still smell him, and taste him." Again, Klarke started to cry.

Breezy took her friend into her arms and comforted her as she shook with tears. She hated seeing Klarke hold onto the dream of someday living happily ever after with Reo, a man who belonged to someone else now.

"And our baby, Breezy, our son!" Klarke cried. "I threw him away. I threw him away into that woman's arms. If I had known that's who he'd end up with, I swear I would have never done it. But it's too late."

"It's going to be okay," Breezy said, holding Klarke. That's all she could say to her over and over again. All she could do was allow her to cry on her shoulder for what seemed like an hour.

Deciding to have their desserts to go, the women got themselves together and exited into the mall. They walked halfway through the mall silently, not admiring anything in any of the stores.

"I'm so happy," Breezy said, breaking the silence. "For the first time in a long time I am completely happy and I'm having a hard time being happy about being happy because the godmothers of my baby aren't happy."

Then Breezy broke down like a big baby right in the middle of the mall. Her hormones were on the blink again.

"Honey, don't cry," Jeva said. "I'm happy. I'm just a little scared, that's all. No matter how my visit to Nevada turns out, I'm going to be okay. I have all the family I need right here."

When Jeva and Maria arrived at the Nevada airport there was a limo waiting for them at baggage claim. Maria's father had arranged it. He had wanted to pick them up himself but he had an important meeting that didn't let out until two hours after their flight was scheduled to land. The limo ride to Maria's parents' home seemed longer than the three-and-a-half-hour flight.

Jeva pretended to be asleep for most of the flight so that she didn't have to make conversation with Maria. She didn't want to discuss how the situation would develop. What questions Jeva would ask to trigger the subject matter or find the smoking gun she was looking for as proof that Maria's parents were in fact the same people who had given her up for adoption.

After about thirty minutes the limo turned into the private drive of a huge three-story home. It was white with red trim and had beautiful French doors with a silver frame. There were electric candles in each window, which added such an elegant touch. It had to be about a six-bedroom home. Maria was excited to be visiting home regardless of the underlying circumstances. Jeva felt like Little Orphan Annie pulling up in front of Daddy Warbucks's place.

She pictured her mother opening the door and greeting her with open arms. Jeva would announce her identity and without hesitation, her mother would come clean, apologize, and she would be accepted into the family. Then later, Daddy Warbucks would come home and decide to adopt her into their lives forever.

It was a pretty picture that Jeva was painting, but the first thing she wanted to ask them, if they did turn out to be her parents, was why.

The limo driver unloaded Jeva and Maria's bags. Jeva dug ten dollars out of her purse to tip him. In the meantime, the doors to the home were flung open and an older woman, two young women, and a young man came out of the house to greet Maria. Jeva assumed this was Maria's mother, sisters, and brother.

"Hola, mami," the older woman said, grabbing Maria by the face and kissing her on the lips.

"Hey, ma," Maria said, throwing her arms around her. As she hugged her she closed her eyes. She opened them, then looked over at Jeva. She began to hug her even tighter as her eyes became tearful.

"*Que pasa, mami?*" Maria's mother asked. "Why you cry?"

"I just missed home," Maria said, still looking over at Jeva. Maria's mother followed her eyes over to Jeva.

"Oh, this must be your *amigo* from Ohio," Maria's mother said, walking over to Jeva while the younger women and guy greeted Maria.

"Welcome," she said to Jeva as she hugged her. Jeva almost melted. She returned the hug. Jeva wondered if she could feel the same thing that she was feeling. Did this woman feel, deep in the pit of her stomach, that she had just thrown her arms around her daughter? Without a doubt, this woman was Jeva's mother. She could feel it. Now all she had to do was prove it.

For the next hour Jeva felt just like family as everyone sat around talking, laughing, and drinking. They were like the Waltons. They included Jeva in every conversation, asking her about her background, which gave her a golden opportunity to mention her adoption. She volunteered her age and the name of the adoption agency. Maria's mother never blinked until she mentioned the fact of how her biological parents sent a representative to deliver a cash-filled envelope to buy her out of their lives forever. Maria's brother and sisters went on and on about how much of a low-life they were to do that to Jeva. They tried to convince Jeva that she was better off without them. Both Jeva and Maria paid close attention to Maria's mother's erratic actions. At the same time they both looked at one another. They knew they were sisters. It was only a matter of time before everyone else would know it.

"I'm going to go check on dinner," Maria's mother said, standing up, a ploy to run away from the conversation. "Dad will be home soon."

"I'll help you," Jeva said, standing up, putting down the apple martini she had been sipping on.

"Oh, no," Maria's mother said, looking as if she had something to hide. "You stay here with the kids. I'm fine."

No way did she want to be alone with Jeva.

"I insist," Jeva said, not taking no for an answer.

"Well, if you insist," Maria's mother said with a fake smile.

Jeva looked over at Maria. This was the moment they had been waiting for.

"So Maria tells me you used to live in Toledo," Jeva said, entering the kitchen behind Maria's mother.

"*Si,*" Maria's mother said. "I'm making rotisserie chicken. Do you like chicken?"

Who in the hell doesn't like chicken? Jeva thought to herself. "Yes, ma'am," Jeva replied.

"So is that where you met your husband, in Toledo?" Jeva said.

"Um-hm," she replied, taking the chicken out of the oven.

"That's where my parents met each other," Jeva said.

"You know, you shouldn't be so hard on them," Maria's mother said. "They gave you fifty thousand dollars and a trust fund. I mean, think about all of the other kids who got put up for adoption whose biological parents could care less about seeing to it that they had a trust fund to live off of."

Both Jeva and Maria's mother froze. Maria's mother knew she had fucked up. Jeva told them how she was given an envelope with cash in it, but not once had she mentioned the exact amount that was in the envelope nor had she mentioned anything about the trust fund.

Maria's mother took a deep breath. She didn't know what to say next.

"Why?" Jeva asked. She had waited years to ask that question. "Why, Mom?"

"None of that matters," Maria's mother said, slipping oven mitts on her hands to pick up the chicken. "And don't call me Mom."

"Of course it matters," Jeva said with a puzzled look on her face. How could this woman be acting so nonchalant?

"Are you speaking for the both of you?" Jeva asked. "Or should I wait for your husband to come home and hear it from him?"

Maria's mother slammed the roaster with the chicken in it down on the counter.

"Don't you dare!" she said, grabbing Jeva by the arm. Jeva looked down at her arm. Even through the oven mitts, her mother's grip was powerful and painful. "You've been paid to keep quiet, goddamn it, and that's just what the hell you're gonna do. You got that? I gave up every red cent I had saved over the years to you and you didn't have a problem taking it."

Maria's family would be glad to know that their mother didn't have a gambling problem nor was she keeping a pool boy on the side. This explained what happened to the depletion of her nest egg, causing checks to bounce.

Jeva was petrified. The sweet and beautiful Cuban woman that once was, had just turned into a demon right before her very eyes.

"You got that?" she repeated.

Jeva was speechless and could only nod in the affirmative.

"You mustn't whisper one word and if you mention this to Maria, so help you God," she said in a threatening tone.

Just then Maria came through the door. "Daddy's home," she said, trying to wade in the thick fog of tension. "Is everything okay?"

"Yes, honey," her mother said, grabbing her by the face with the oven mitts and kissing her on the lips. "Let's eat!"

She grabbed the chicken and headed out of the kitchen and into the dining room. Jeva and Maria stood quietly.

"Well?" Maria asked.

Jeva didn't answer her. She swept past her and headed out of the kitchen. Maria sighed in relief. She was glad that her parents had more heart than the people Jeva accused them of being. But at the same time, she wouldn't have minded having Jeva as a sister, but she would settle on just being her friend.

Jeva pretended she wasn't feeling well and skipped dinner. Instead she laid down in the guest room. Actually, she didn't have to pretend. She was absolutely sick to her stomach. She had been crying so hard that she had a splitting headache.

It always seemed as though whenever Jeva's dreams were within reach, they were snatched away again.

Jeva sat up on the bed and she looked at herself in the mirror above the dresser. She didn't like what she was seeing. She was tired of other people determining the outcome of her life. It was time to put a stop to it once and for all.

She wiped her tears away and headed back downstairs. She was just in time for dessert.

"Jeva, you feeling better?" Maria asked when she saw Jeva enter the dining room.

"No," Jeva replied sharply. "But I will be once I get this off of my chest."

"Perhaps you need to take something," Maria's mother interrupted nervously. "There's something for everything in the upstairs bathroom medicine cabinet. Maybe you should head back up there and see what you can find."

Jeva walked over to her father and took a deep breath. "I'm sorry that you have to find out this way," she started. "If you want your money back, I swear to God if it's the last thing I do, I'll pay you back every penny."

"Jeva, honey. What are you talking about?" her father said, puzzled.

"I'm her," Jeva said, swallowing the knot in her throat.

"Don't do it," Maria's mother said angrily through her teeth.

"I'm your oldest daughter, Jeva Alicia Price," she said, swallowing the knot in her throat. "I'm the daughter you threw away thirty-four years ago."

Everyone at the table gasped with shock. Maria stared in disbelief.

"Honey, what is she talking about?" Mr. Fendell said to his wife.

"Not at the dinner table, sweetheart," she replied.

"Some girl is standing here telling me that she's my daughter and you say not now?" he said, appalled. "You're damn straight we're going to talk about it now."

"I'm your firstborn," Jeva said. "I'm the one you didn't keep. The one you put up for adoption. The one you paid to stay out of your lives."

"I have no idea what you're talking about," Maria's father said. Jeva could tell by the look on his face that he was absolutely clueless.

"Thirty-four years ago I wasn't even in Toledo," he said as he thought about it for a moment. "Wait a minute!"

He stood up from the table and stared off. "I was in Toledo, briefly. Honey, that's when we first met. I left for about a year and a half to go back to California with my parents. But I came back. You said that you had something to tell me, that same night I proposed to you. You never did tell me what that something was. Is this that something?"

Maria's mother closed her eyes to hold back the tears.

"Is it?" he yelled.

"Yes, but sweetheart, you have to understand," Maria's mother said, getting up from the table to go grab hold of her husband's arm. "I was so young. When you left and I found out I was pregnant, I had no idea you'd come back to me. Honestly. I knew how your parents felt about the little spic back in Ohio. We were from two very different backgrounds. You, the white boy from the right side of the tracks and I was this Cuban immigrant who they thought didn't even deserve citizenship in their country. I worked hard to fit in. Highlighted my hair. Paid a speech therapist an obscene amount of money to help me control my accent. Look at me now. I'm living the life that any blue-eyed, blond-haired American white woman would kill for. Now I can be myself. I can use my native tongue. But back then my pregnancy would have been frowned upon. They probably would have even ordered me to have an abortion, but I had the child, *papi*. I had our baby."

"I don't understand. We married and had five other beautiful children," he said, confused.

"How in the hell was I supposed to know you'd come back for me?" she cried. "You were a young man, independent, and worldly. When you left me I thought I would never see you again."

Maria and her brother and sisters sat in silence as the truth unfolded.

"What is this about paying money back?" Mr. Fendell demanded.

"She kept looking and looking for us," Maria's mother cried. "She would have ruined everything. Everything! Just like she's doing now."

"So you paid her hush money to keep quiet?" he asked.

"Every dime I had ever saved. I had to," she said, crying uncontrollably. "Please forgive me. Please."

Mr. Fendell put his hand on his forehead. He couldn't believe what he was hearing. "When did all of this happen?" he asked.

Mrs. Fendell had her hand over her mouth. She couldn't speak as she choked back tears. Jeva decided to respond. "About five years ago," she said. Jeva then looked at her mother and cut her eyes. "I guess that explains what those huge withdrawals were probably about. You should be relieved to find that it wasn't a gambling problem."

"Please forgive me," Mrs. Fendell begged her husband as she cried.

There was silence as everyone awaited his response.

"Honestly, I don't know if I can," he said as he pushed his wife's hands off of him and walked away. He stopped when he got to Jeva. She was staring down at the ground, tears slipping down her cheeks. He wanted to say something. Do something. But he couldn't. He was in too much shock so he simply walked out of the house, got into his car, and drove away.

Maria's brother and sisters gathered to comfort their mother. Maria sat at the table, still in shock. She couldn't even look up from her slice of lemon merengue pie.

Jeva knew it was time for her to go. She went back to the guest room to get her things that she hadn't even unpacked.

When Jeva came back downstairs all eyes were on her with the exception of Maria, who still couldn't look at her. She felt guilty for even bringing Jeva to their home.

"Can someone call me a cab to the airport?" Jeva asked. She didn't care if she had to sit at the airport on standby for a flight home all weekend. She was getting the hell out of there. She was going back to Toledo to her real family.

"I will," her brother, Anthony Jr., said. He proceeded to the den where the phone book was and called Jeva a cab.

"I'll wait outside," Jeva said and walked to the door. Still wanting to live the life of a fairy tale, Jeva hoped that someone would stop her. That someone would accept her for who she was. But no one said a word.

Jeva opened the door when she heard her mother call. "Wait a minute!"

Jeva closed her eyes and sighed. She smiled to herself, then she turned around to face her mother.

"When you were growing in my womb," Mrs. Fendell said sincerely, "I hated you. I thought God placed you inside my body to poison me, as a punishment for fornicating. I thought you were going to ruin my life, *chiquita*."

With a look as cold and biting as the coldest winter ever, Jeva's mother looked into her eyes and said, "And I was right."

Jeva's heart stopped beating.

"I knew I should have just aborted you," Jeva's mother snarled.

"*Mami!*" Maria said, aghast.

Jeva wondered if any of her siblings were going to come to her defense or if they felt the same way their mother did.

"It doesn't surprise me that Maria brought you home," she said bitterly. "Maria always did have a soft spot for strays."

"Enough!" Maria ordered, running to her mother's side.

This had been an absolute nightmare. Jeva wished that she had never known that these people even existed. Without saying a word, Jeva walked out the door with her bags in hand.

Jeva got only halfway down the walkway before she stopped, turned around, and knocked on the door. Then she just burst right through it before allowing anyone time to answer it.

Jeva's entrance was quite startling to say the least. The siblings had been comforting their mother while she recalled her weeping sob story.

"Are you crazy?" Jeva's mother yelled as she stormed over toward Jeva.

"You know something?" Jeva asked calmly, fighting back tears. She was not going to allow this woman to see her cry. "You don't know how bad I wanted to just haul off and slap you across your face. You said some ugly things, things a mother should never say to her child no matter what the circumstance."

Her mother just stood there with her lips puckered and a smug look on her face. She could have cared less about what Jeva was saying.

"But I didn't slap you. You are my mother and because of that I had to respect you regardless. My best friend, Breezy, wanted to come with me for support, but I told her that I would be fine. I thought that maybe perhaps I would need some time alone with my mother and father. One on one. You know, chat the night away, make up for lost time. I told Breezy that she would be here in spirit though." Jeva looked down momentarily then looked back up at her mother who had this *get to the point* look on her face. "Well, in the spirit of Breezy . . ."

Jeva pulled her hand back and then hauled off and slapped her mother across the face, knocking her to the ground. Then she turned and walked away with a smile.

It was perfect timing as the taxicab pulled up. Jeva threw her luggage in the backseat, jumped in, and ordered the driver to the airport. Despite having just slapped her mother, Jeva rode off with a clear head.

Jeva couldn't help but think about whether or not it would be possible for her to have a healthy relationship with her father and not her mother. Perhaps her mother would come around. Perhaps she wouldn't. Jeva refused to spend the rest of her life worrying about it. Life was too short.

She had finally met her biological parents. They now knew who she was and where to find her. Jeva decided to release, let go, and allow God to be in charge of the situation. Jeva wasn't going to be bitter or bear a grudge. The past was the past and she wasn't going to let it determine her future ever again. She had a beautiful daughter, two best friends, and a good man waiting for her back in Toledo. After decking her mother, she wasn't so sure about what would become of her relationship with Maria, but hopefully she'd have her there in Toledo wanting to form a sisterly relationship with her.

For so many years Jeva had begged God to help her find her biological parents. She now knew the meaning behind the saying "Be careful what you ask for. You just might get it."

19

IT'S A BOY

"Bria Williams, please," Jeva said out of breath to the nurse. "She's been in labor about four hours. Has she had the baby yet? Can I see her?"

Jeva stood there, a little antsy. She had just gotten off the plane from Nevada when she checked her cell phone messages. Klarke had left her a message telling her that Breezy had gone into early labor and was at the hospital. She was only a tad over seven months, but she was as big as a house, so there really wasn't that much worry as to whether the baby would be underweight.

The message Klarke had left on Jeva's cell phone was a few hours old. Jeva hoped she didn't miss all the action.

"She is here, but let me check and see what's going on with her. You might still be able to see her if she isn't in delivery." The nurse walked away and Jeva waited impatiently.

Jeva had lucked out and only had to wait at the airport for three hours before she could get a seat on a flight back to Toledo. It was perfect timing for her to be home just in time for the birth of Breezy's baby. Maria was right, there was no such thing as co-incidence.

"Klarke!" Jeva called as she saw her walking down the hall with a cup of ice chips in her hand.

"Jeva, you made it," Klarke said, walking up to her and em-bracing her. "I called Maria's phone too and left a message. I'm glad you got it. Breezy will be glad you're here. You're one more person she has to beat up on," Klarke said.

"Is she clownin'?" Jeva asked.

"You know she showin' out. Those poor nurses and doctors got a case on their hands with Bria Nicole Williams. And poor Hy-drant. She calls him every type of bastard in the book whenever a labor pain hits her."

Jeva laughed. "Where's Heather?"

"Oh, yeah, she's home with HJ and Sissy. They're fine," Klarke answered. "Come on. Let's go in, because they are going to kick us out when it's time for her to deliver."

Klarke led the way to Breezy's room. "By the way, how'd things go in Nevada? Were you there long enough to accomplish anything? Did you find out if they were your parents?"

"Yes, they were," Jeva said in an ordinary tone.

"Congratulations, Jeva," Klarke said, hugging her. Jeva didn't raise her arms to hug Klarke back, nor did she seem thrilled.

"Oh, no," Klarke said, sensing Jeva's emotions. "Didn't go how you always dreamed it would?"

"Hardly," Jeva sighed. She quickly briefed Klarke on a few de-tails up until they entered Breezy's room. She promised Klarke to fill her in on all of the disgusting details later.

"Hey, mama," Jeva said, walking over to Breezy and kissing her on her forehead.

"Jeva, you're back," Breezy said, getting teary-eyed. She was extremely emotional to say the least. "How did things go? You didn't have to come back early because of me. You waited a lifetime for a moment like that. Did you finally meet your real parents?"

"I did, Breezy, but it wasn't good."

"Oh, honey, I'm so sorrrrryyyy," Breezy said as a sharp labor pain hit. "Oh, God!"

Hydrant, who was sitting next to her, stood up and gave Breezy his hand to squeeze. "Come on, baby, you can do this. You can handle this. Breathe. Breathe. I know it hurts, but it's bearable."

"How the fuck do you know?" Breezy yelled at Hydrant. "When's the last time you were in labor?"

Hydrant ignored her sarcasm while Klarke and Jeva cracked up laughing. Eventually the pain eased up and Breezy went back to conversing with Jeva.

"So they were assholes?" Breezy asked Jeva.

"No. My father, who is the insurance commissioner of Nevada, was shocked more than anything. It turns out my mother never told him about the pregnancy. She gave me up for adoption all on her own. So to make a long story short, not only is my mother glad she gave me up for adoption, she wishes I were never born. She wishes she had aborted me."

"Oh, no, Jeva," Breezy said, rubbing her hand. "Were those her words to you?"

Jeva nodded yes and tried to fight back the tears.

"Oh, baby girl," Breezy said, pulling Jeva down to hug her. Klarke walked over and rubbed Jeva's back.

"It's a good thing I didn't go with you," Breezy said. "I know she's your mother and all, but I would have had to slap the shit out of her for coming at you like that."

"I know you would have," Jeva said, rising up and wiping her tears. "That's why I slapped her for you."

"You what?" Klarke shouted in disbelief.

"You didn't," Breezy said with a smile on her face.

"I did," Jeva said. "And now that I stand here and look back on it, the worst part about it is that I wish I had slapped her twice."

Breezy tried not to laugh, but couldn't help it. Her laughing was contagious, soon Klarke began laughing and so did Jeva. Hydrant was in serious mode. He was about to experience the birth of his child. He just watched the girls giggle like a pack of hyenas.

"Oooooh," Breezy shouted. "Dear God!"

Just then the doctor came in followed by the nurse. Breezy was leaned over in agony. The doctor proceeded to check her out.

"It's time," the doctor informed them. "Ladies, I'm going to have to ask you to wait in the waiting area now."

"Congratulations, Mommy," Klarke said, kissing Breezy on the forehead. "You too, Daddy," she said to Hydrant.

"You're going to do just fine," Jeva said, patting Breezy on the hand. "I love you."

"I love you too," Breezy said, with a scared look on her face.

"Love you, babe," Klarke said.

"I love you too," Breezy replied, trying to stay strong, but she was scared.

"Take care of our girl, Hydrant," Klarke said, winking at him.

Jeva couldn't help but cry as she exited the room. She could see the look of fear in her friend's eyes.

"She's going to be okay," Klarke said, comforting Jeva.

"Did you see that look on her face, Klarke? She's scared to death." Jeva wept.

"You and I both have given birth and we too had that same

look in our eyes. But when it was over we couldn't have been happier. Remember?" Jeva nodded and wiped her tears away. "Now let's go grab a soda and wait for our godchild to be born."

"Push, Breezy, push," Hydrant said as he stood next to Breezy, coaching her.

"What the hell does it look like I'm doing?" Breezy snapped. "Oh, God!"

"Come on now, Bria," Breezy's doctor said. "Just hang in there. The head is out. Just give me a big one. Just give me one big push."

No sooner had the doctor asked, she received. Breezy pushed out a big plop of poop right there on the delivery table. The doctors and nurses were used to this type of thing so it didn't freak them out. Breezy was in so much pain that she had no idea that she had just dumped a load.

"Uhhh, uhhhhh," Breezy grunted as she sat up, allowing her knees to touch her shoulders. "I knew this position would come in handy for something one day."

"Bria." The doctor laughed. "Come on now, one more big push."

"Hydrant," Breezy said as tears began to fall from her eyes.

"I'm here, ma. Just push." Hydrant could no longer fight back his tears. He hated that look of fear and pain in Breezy's eyes. At the same time, he was so excited to be becoming a daddy again.

Hydrant kissed Breezy on the forehead and wiped away her tears. He never thought he'd see the day when Bria Nicole Williams would be overcome by so much emotion. He loved this side of her. It was something he could get used to. He could see now that motherhood was going to definitely change her for the better.

"It's a boy!" the doctor shouted.

"Look at all of that hair," the nurse said.

"I thought you shaved me," Breezy said, still finding the strength to joke.

"It's a boy," Hydrant cried.

"Can I see him?" Breezy asked.

The nurse placed the baby on Breezy's chest. When Breezy looked down at the baby she suddenly forgot about the horrendous pain she had just gone through. As she stared down at her man-child she couldn't imagine life without him. Breezy wondered if this was how her father felt the first time that he looked at her.

"Isn't he beautiful?" Breezy said to Hydrant.

"Yeah, baby," Hydrant sniffled. "You did good, ma. You did real good."

The nurse lifted the baby off of Breezy's chest.

"Listen, ma," Hydrant said. "I've been thinking about something."

"What?" Breezy asked.

"You and I both know that you are a handful." Breezy giggled. "I don't know how any man in the world can live with your ass. But what I've come to realize is that I don't want you to be the woman I can live with."

Just then Hydrant pulled out a purple four-carat diamond marquis. He grabbed Breezy's hand. "I want you to be the woman that I can't live without. I know that ever since that day in the mall when we bumped into each other things have been moving ninety miles per hour. But I don't like taking shit slow. Not when there's something I want now. So, Ms. Bria Nicole Williams, will you do me the honor of being Mrs. Kristopher Lorenzo Long?"

Without even thinking twice about it, Breezy spread her fingers so that Hydrant could put the ring on her finger and said, "Hell yeah!"

Hydrant slipped the ring on Breezy's finger as the doctor and nurse began to clap.

"Congratulations. Now do you want to follow me over here so you can see the little guy's first bath, Daddy?" the nurse asked Hydrant.

"Yeah, yeah," Hydrant said with excitement.

"Yeah, you stay with our baby," Breezy said. "I ain't trying to have them mixing our baby up with some ugly baby. I can't raise no ugly kids, Hydrant."

"I got this, ma," Hydrant said, kissing Breezy on the forehead.

"But first, go tell my girls real quick that we got us a boy," Breezy said. "I know their nerves are done."

"Okay," Hydrant said. Before walking away he kissed Breezy on the forehead and said, "I love you."

"I love you right back," Breezy said as Hydrant exited the room.

Outside of the room Klarke, Jeva, and Hydrant's mother and sisters could hardly contain themselves from suspense. Just as soon as they saw Hydrant they pounced on him like Tigger.

"Well," Klarke said. "Is it a boy or a girl?"

"It's a boy," Hydrant said as his forehead wrinkled up. He was so proud and happy that he couldn't hold back the tears. His mother and sisters circled him with a group hug. Klarke and Jeva hugged one another.

"I gotta go see my son's first bath and then tail him wherever they take him in this hospital," Hydrant said. "Breezy's afraid they'll try to swap our cute kid with some poor family who had an ugly one."

"That sounds like our Breezy." Klarke laughed as Hydrant vanished back into the room.

Just then Maria came around the corner.

"Hey, Maria," Klarke said.

"Hi," Maria said in a soft tone.

Maria walked toward them, not knowing how Jeva would react to her and Jeva not knowing how Maria was going to act toward her. Maybe she was there to pay her back for the slap she had thrown across their mother's face.

A knife could have cut through the thickness of the silence. Then Maria finally spoke.

"I got Klarke's message that Breezy was in labor here," Maria said to Jeva. "I didn't want to miss the birth of the baby of one of my sister's best friends."

Maria smiled and held her hands out to Jeva. Jeva grabbed her hands then pulled her close to hug her.

"I'm sorry about me and—," Jeva said.

"No, no, no, *mami*," Maria said to her. "I'm sorry, Jeva. I should have never put you in that situation. I should have just been honest with you from the first day I met you."

Jeva pulled back from Maria. She was puzzled by Maria's words. "Honest about what?" Jeva asked sharply.

Maria stepped a couple of steps away from the others. Jeva followed. Maria took a deep breath and found the courage to explain her hidden agenda with befriending Jeva in the first place.

"Jeva, before you say anything just hear me out," Maria said, biting down on her bottom lip. "It wasn't a coincidence that I moved here to Toledo. It was even less of a coincidence that I just happened to be on that treadmill next to you in the gym the day we met."

"I don't understand," Jeva said, shaking her head.

"It was several years ago when I caught the tail end of a phone conversation my mother was having. The only words I remembered hearing were adoption, your name, and Toledo, Ohio. It was troubling, because that wasn't the first time I had heard your name. I swore that as a teenager I had heard my grandmother say your name in an argument she was having with mother. I had always been curious, but never asked questions. It had been eating away at me for years. Then one day I just decided to take matters into my own hands. I got online and went to www.reliablesearchrsc.info.com and paid them to locate you."

"And obviously they succeeded," Jeva said sarcastically. "Why, Maria? Why didn't you just come to me and be up front? Instead you listened to me go on and on about my adoption."

"I'm sorry, Jeva," Maria said as tears fell down her cheeks. "I wanted to say something, I just couldn't. I didn't want to think that the two people who raised me, the people who I thought were the greatest parents in the world and could do no wrong, would ever abandon their own child. Let alone pay her to stay away."

"And I understand that, Maria. Honestly I do," Jeva said sympathetically. "But you played with my emotions. You sat there and listened to me tell you about my adoption and how it affected me. Look how you treated me that day at my house when I mentioned to you that I might be your sister. You blew up. You got so angry with me."

"I know, Jeva. I was angry. I was angry at the idea of the truth."

"But isn't that what you came here for, the truth?" Jeva asked.

Maria paused and sighed. "Yes. The truth is what I came here for. But I guess I wasn't prepared to face it and anger was the only emotion that I could feel at that moment. Maybe it was misdirected anger, but I was angry at you for being born. I was angry that your existence destroyed the picture-perfect family that I had grown up being a part of. But then I realized that I was angry with the wrong person. I needed to be angry with them, Mom and Dad. I wanted to just call them on the phone and scream to them that I had found their buried lie. That I had uncovered the truth." Maria paused. "But I wanted to see the look on their faces."

Jeva thought for a moment. "So instead you chose to serve them their lie on a platter. You decided to deliver me in person," Jeva said between her teeth. "You used me, Maria. You took me home to them knowing the truth deep in your heart the entire time."

Maria buried her face in her hands. "I'm so sorry, Jeva. My God, I'm so sorry."

"So I bet it was just as shocking to you as it was to me to find out that your father never even knew I was born," Jeva said as she fought back tears of anger.

"Well, it explained why he never even blinked when I brought him to your house and introduced him to you. I was hoping that he would see you, hear your name, and take you into his arms and apologize for the mistake he and Mother made all those years ago. If nothing else, I was hoping he would at least just tell the truth. But instead he did nothing," Maria said, shaking her head.

Jeva took a deep breath as her eyes watered. She was hurt by the way Maria handled the situation, but she couldn't be 100 percent certain of how she might have handled it herself. Her head wanted to be angry with Maria, but her heart reminded her of how she had wasted so much of her life being bitter and angry. She had a choice to make, to either continue being bitter and angry or to be grateful to finally know the truth about her biological family.

Maria and Jeva stood there looking into one another's eyes. Maria was praying to herself that Jeva would somehow find a way to forgive her, if not today, someday. But she needed her forgiveness.

Jeva put her hand on Maria's shoulder. "We're not going to talk about any more of this right now. You and I are sisters and we have a lot of catching up to do. No matter how we came together, I believe it's a miracle that we did. Some people search a lifetime and never find each other." Jeva paused as she started to get choked up. "I'm just glad you're here."

"Thank you, Jeva," Maria said, hugging Jeva. "I'm glad I'm here too."

Maria and Jeva pulled apart and looked at one another. Each of them had mascara running down their faces. They both looked like Tammy Faye Bakker. They each started to laugh.

"By the way," Maria said, pulling two tissues out of her purse, handing one to Jeva. "Dad will be here next week. He's taking some vacation time from work so that he can get to know his daughter. His oldest daughter."

Maria and Jeva smiled, then hugged each other tightly.

Just then, nurses and doctors ran into Breezy's room in a flurry of activity.

"What's going on? What's going on?" Hydrant said, as two nurses forced him out of the room.

"There's another baby," the nurse said. "It was hiding behind the other baby. We never even heard its heartbeat."

"Another baby?" Hydrant said with excitement. "I need to go in there and help her push. Please. Why are you making me go?"

Hydrant attempted to go back into the delivery room but the nurse stopped him.

"I'm sorry, but you can't," the nurse said.

By this time everyone could see the distress on her face.

"I'm the father. I was just in there," Hydrant pleaded. "You just saw me in there."

"Please, sir," the nurse said. "The doctor will be out to let you know what's going on. Please, just wait here."

As the nurse hurried back into the delivery room another nurse holding the baby boy exited.

"Hydrant, you go check on Junior," his mother said, already naming the baby after Hydrant. "We'll keep tabs on this one."

"But, Breezy . . . I know she wants me in there," Hydrant said. "I'll never hear the end of it from her if I don't get back in there."

"Son, you heard what the nurse said," his mother replied. "Now go on and check on that baby son of yours. They probably done switched it with Rosemary's baby by now. Go on, son."

"All right," Hydrant said, staring down at the ring he had just proposed to Breezy with. The nurses had asked him to take it with him until they finished up with Breezy. "All right. I'm going to go check on our son." Hydrant placed the ring down in his pocket and walked to the nursery.

About fifteen minutes passed before the doctor exited the delivery room covered in blood. The doctor's expression didn't look good. Jeva immediately began to cry.

"Is she okay?" Klarke asked the doctor. "Is everything okay?" Klarke too couldn't control her tears. Something just didn't feel right.

"She's fine," the doctor said.

Everyone sighed in sync. A nurse exited the delivery room carrying a crying baby.

"Thank you, Jesus," Hydrant's mother declared. "Oh, thank you, Jesus."

"She's a healthy six-pound baby girl and she's just fine," the doctor said.

"That's wonderful," Klarke said. "But I was asking about Breezy," Klarke said. "How is she?"

Everything after that was in slow motion. The doctor's eyes welled up with tears and she put her head down. She couldn't even look them in the face. Just then a couple of nurses opened the door to exit. That's when Jeva saw Breezy's body lying on the delivery table completely covered in a sheet. Jeva lost it. She squealed and fell to her knees. No one knew what was going on. Maria and Hydrant's sisters ran to Jeva's side.

"I'm so sorry," the doctor said. "The bleeding, we couldn't stop it. She hemorrhaged."

"Well, make it stop," Hydrant's mother ordered.

"I'm so sorry," the doctor continued. "We couldn't save her. Bria is gone."

"How do I say good-bye . . . ," the choir members sang as everyone exited the funeral home to head to the gravesite where Breezy's burial was to take place.

The rain beat down on the tent that was over the gravesite as the presiding minister chanted, "Ashes to ashes, dust to dust . . ."

"No . . . no . . . no," Klarke wailed. She had been so strong up to this point. But as the minister chanted the Bible verse as Breezy's casket was lowered and handfuls of dirt thrown upon it, Klarke lost it. "My friend. She was my friend. No . . . no . . . I don't understand. I don't understand. Why? Why?"

The funeral director and staff could hardly contain Klarke.

"No more." Klarke looked up to the heavens and pleaded with God himself. "No more."

Once Klarke was calmed down and seated back into one of the chairs that sat in front of the casket, a single rose was given to the family and friends.

Breezy's mother fainted a total of ten times. She was like a vegetable. She was overcome more by guilt than by grief. She had been estranged from her daughter, never taking the time to fully make amends to their relationship and now it was too late.

"Come on, honey," one of the pallbearers said to Klarke. "You ready for me to take you to the car?"

"Yes," Klarke said. The man lifted Klarke to her feet and turned toward the limo. Klarke looked back at Breezy's grave. She closed her eyes and drew a cross on her chest. "I love you, Breezy."

Klarke, along with Jeva, Hydrant, his mother, and two of his sisters got into the limo. This was one of the hardest days of Klarke's life. Losing Breezy, her best friend of twelve years, was harder than the day she gave up her own life to the jail system.

It was the middle of the night and Klarke hadn't slept a wink. She couldn't sleep for crying. Damn, she missed Breezy.

"Ma," HJ said, entering Klarke's bedroom. Her weeping had awakened him. "Ma, you okay?"

"No, HJ," Klarke replied honestly.

HJ hated to see his mother in this condition. Tissues were all over the place and her body trembled as if the temperature was below zero. HJ walked over to his mother's bed and lay down next to her, caressing her in his arms as if she was the child.

"I know it hurts, Ma," HJ said as a tear fell from his eye. "I'm going to miss Aunt Breezy too. I talked to Vaughn earlier and she's not taking it too well. She wanted to talk to you, but I knew you needed to rest. I knew you were hurting."

"It does hurt, HJ. Oh God, it hurts. Why? Why, God? Why did you let me out of prison just for me to come back to so much pain? WHY?"

By now Klarke was yelling at the top of her lungs. HJ knew all he could do was hold her until she got through this. He knew exactly how she felt. He had cried many nights after she went away to prison and plenty more nights when he was estranged from his sister. HJ knew that there was nothing he could say or do to make his mother's pain go away. So he held her until they both fell off to sleep.

"Mama! Ma!" HJ yelled, abruptly awakening from his sleep.

"HJ, what's the matter? Are you having another one of your nightmares?" Klarke asked, wiping her eyes.

"I remember now! I remember!" HJ was sweating bullets. He jumped up out of the bed and began pacing. He had both a look of worry and a look of relief on his face.

"HJ, what are you talking about?" Klarke asked, puzzled.

"The woman in my dreams. That woman at the funeral, at Mr. Laroque's funeral. I remember everything about that night now, Ma. I remember everything. Vaughn didn't hurt Reo's baby, Ma, and I didn't either."

20

I WAS MADE FOR YOU

"I know it all sounds crazy, Detective Edwards," Klarke said. Klarke remembered Detective Edwards as being a heavyset man, but it appeared as though he had gained even a few more pounds over the years. "But you've got to look into this. You've got to do something."

Klarke sat at Detective Edwards's desk waiting on a response after telling him everything HJ had told her. He had been the lead detective during the investigation of the murder of Reo's baby. He was the only person Klarke could think of to turn to for help. How she saw it was that he was the only person in a position to do something.

"You know what, Ms. Taylor?" Detective Edwards said, while gnawing on the eraser of his number-two pencil.

"It's Ms. Laroque," Klarke corrected him.

"I'm beginning to believe that you're a prelude to bad news."

Detective Edwards's statement didn't surprise Klarke at all. When Detective Edwards was investigating the death of Breezy's father, Klarke was there. When he was investigating the death of the baby, Klarke was there. It was no secret that he didn't care for Klarke.

"I might have to agree with you, Detective," Klarke said.

"Why should I believe this far-fetched story about your son having nightmares of a woman? Then he sees this woman at a funeral and says she's the woman of his dreams."

"*In* his dreams," Klarke corrected him. "He said the woman *in* his dreams."

"Anyway." Detective Edwards sighed. "Then he has another nightmare, dream, or whatever and he sees her throw the baby in the swimming pool. He's afraid so he waits for the woman to leave. He then tries to save the baby, but he can't swim. Now this is the part where your daughter comes in, right?"

Klarke remained silent at the detective's downplay of her allegations against Meka.

The detective smiled, then continued. "Your daughter sees the baby floating and your son standing there with wet pajamas from his failed attempt to rescue the child. She automatically assumes that her little brother killed the baby and so to protect him, she says that she did it. Then you turn around, to protect your daughter, and say that you did it. Is that the story you want me to believe?"

Klarke just sat there looking stupid. Her story sounded even more ridiculous with Detective Edwards telling it.

"Now you can be honest with me, Ms. Taylor, I mean Laroque. Is this just some ploy to get your old sweetheart back? You know, get the wifey out of the picture so that you can take her place. Kind of like something on one of them Court TV shows."

It was clear to Klarke that Detective Edwards wasn't going to help her. He was making a complete mockery out of the entire situation. Klarke picked up her purse and stood up.

"Thank you for your time, Detective," Klarke said with her head held high. "You have a good fuckin' day."

Detective Edwards chuckled. "Now just wait a minute, Ms. Laroque. You're serious as a heart attack aren't you?"

Klarke stood trembling, trying to hold back the tears. Still trying to be strong when she needed to be down on her knees, begging, pleading, and crying for Detective Edwards to believe in her and help her.

"I suppose even if you were trying to get back in Reo's life with this story, you wouldn't be waiting until the last minute, seeing him and the missus and the kids are heading out in a couple of days," Detective Edwards said in a boasting manner.

"What, do you mean?" Klarke asked.

"Yeah," Detective Edwards said as he stood up, pulling his pants up by his belt loops. "Mr. Laroque and I chat a couple times a year, ever since I investigated the murder of his baby. He called me just last week to say good-bye, that they were going away for a few months or so. The Caribbean I think it was."

"Then you've got to help me," Klarke said, walking over to Detective Edwards and grabbing him by the suit jacket. "You've got to look into this now."

Detective Edwards looked down at Klarke's hands clinching his jacket, then looked at her with glared eyes.

"Oh, I'm sorry," Klarke said, releasing him.

"To be honest with you, I don't think I could get the *National Enquirer* to believe this story, let alone my superiors," Detective Edwards said.

Klarke was tired of him toying with her. She knew it had been useless coming there.

"That's why I'm going to help you." Detective Edwards smiled. He picked up the phone and summoned his partner, Sams, into his office. Within seconds Sams peeked his head into the office.

"What can I do you for?" Sams asked Detective Edwards.

"Sams, you remember the beautiful young lady right here don't you," Detective Edwards asked. "From the Laroque case." Klarke recalled Sams as being a rookie investigator back then.

"I believe I do," Sams said, entering the office to shake Klarke's hand.

"Well, the little lady here has brought something to my attention that's going to take some fast work and long hours."

Sams didn't look too thrilled. He had enough open cases he was working on without the added work.

"What is it and how much time do we have to solve the case?" Sams asked, rolling his eyes.

Detective Edwards chuckled and looked at Klarke, then back at Sams.

"Let me just put it this way. Sams, do you ever watch Court TV?"

Klarke had been watching the clock, pacing. The countdown was on. Here it was, the morning of the day Reo and Meka were scheduled to leave and God only knew when they would be returning. Klarke hadn't heard a thing from Detective Edwards. She had been calling his office and cell phone leaving message upon message with no word back from him thus far. Now she was beginning to think that those couple of days she had held onto the information that HJ had given her would make a crucial difference.

Klarke looked over at the telephone that just wouldn't seem to ring for the world and decided to keep up suit and make yet another call to Detective Edwards. Klarke picked up the phone and dialed the numbers. She placed the phone to her ear and waited to hear the ring, but she heard silence.

"Hello?" she said. "Hello?"

"Hello," a voice said. "Ms. Laroque?"

"Detective Edwards," Klarke said with relief.

"I dialed your number but didn't hear a ring," he said.

"I was calling you," Klarke said. "Please tell me something good."

"Well, I have good news," Detective Edwards said, in a not-so-excited tone.

"From the sound of your voice it must not be all that good," Klarke said.

"We went back to question some of your neighbors from your old neighborhood where the murder took place. Sams had discovered something in the files that warranted some further looking into. When we first investigated the situation at least two of your neighbors saw a white Neon parked a block away from the scene of the crime the night of the incident. No one had ever noticed the car before nor could they recall ever seeing it again afterward. They assumed someone had an overnight guest or something. Well, as you know Meka doesn't drive a white Neon."

Klarke was on pins and needles wishing that Detective Edwards would just get to the bottom line. She impatiently waited while he continued.

"But Sams and I contacted every rental car company at the Columbus International Airport and voila, bang. We found it. The day of the murder, literally hours before, Meka rented an economy car from Budget Rental Car. Do you want to take a guess at what type of car she received from their fleet?"

"A white Neon?" Klarke said as tears fell.

"You've got it."

"I knewed it! I knewed it!" As Breezy would say. "So has Meka been picked up?"

"We're working on it," Detective Edwards assured her. "It's just circumstantial evidence. We're going to keep looking though. It's too soon to make any arrest or anything at this stage."

"But you don't have time," Klarke said frantically. "They're leaving in a few hours, aren't they?"

Detective Edwards looked at his watch. He recalled Reo telling him that they had an early afternoon flight out. It was ten-thirty in the morning. Early afternoon was anywhere between twelve noon and two o'clock P.M. "Yes. I know. That's the not-so-good part. I know it seems like all of this is a day late and a dollar short, but we won't be able to press any charges against her on just that alone."

"That's bullshit, Detective," Klarke said. She knew he was only trying to help her so she calmed down and spoke in a calmer tone. "I'm sorry, Detective. I know you're going out on a limb for me with this case. But I know there's something you can do. There has to be. You can take her in for questioning or something. I've seen it on Court TV shows."

Detective Edwards took in a deep breath and then sighed. "As you know, Ms. Laroque, this is not Court TV. We can't wrap this case up in thirty minutes like they do on television. My hands are tied at this point. We're all the way here in Toledo and she's in Columbus. It's not like we can call her up and say, 'Mrs. Laroque, can you spend two hours driving to Toledo so that we can question you regarding the murder of your baby?'"

"Then go to her!" Klarke demanded. "Put in a call to the Columbus Police Department. I know they'll help you. They don't want to see a murderer walking the streets any more than we do."

"That's not how it works," Detective Edwards said. "You know just as well as I do that she'll refuse to volunteer to come in for questioning so we'll need a warrant. There's paperwork involved. I mean, maybe we could get a judge to issue a warrant, but that would take time. We're onto something and that's a good thing. I say we don't cause her any suspicion. We let them go away on their little trip and by the time they get back we'll hopefully have a pile of evidence against her and perhaps even be able to take something to the Grand Jury."

"No! No!" Klarke cried. "You're asking me to allow my daughter to sit in jail while that bitch walks freely on a beach with white sand. The sooner you handle this the sooner my innocent daughter will be out of jail."

"Have you even talked to your daughter about this?" Detective Edwards inquired.

Klarke paused. "No," she answered softly.

"I know you haven't. Because you still have doubts too."

"That's not true," Klarke tried to say in a convincing voice. But the detective wasn't buying it. Over the last couple of days Klarke hadn't shared the information HJ told her with Vaughn. Klarke wasn't 100 percent sure in her heart that what HJ was telling her wasn't just one of his nightmares.

"It's very true or why else wouldn't you get your daughter's side of the story? Have you ever talked to your daughter about this or are you afraid of what you might hear? Ms. Laroque, have you ever even asked your daughter if she really killed the baby and why? I mean, did anyone ever ask you that question while you rotted away in jail?"

"Fuck you!" Klarke said angrily. It was evident that Detective Edwards had struck a chord. Here Klarke had been so hurt by the way people were so quick to assume that she was capable of something so heinous that they never even bothered to ask her if she did it. Why were so many people afraid of the truth? Now Detective Edwards had brought it to Klarke's attention that she was one of those people too. She was more angry at the truth than she was at Detective Edwards for speaking the truth. "It's clear that you don't want to help me, Detective. So I'll just take it from here and handle this myself. I don't have to talk to my daughter. My heart is talking now and it's speaking the truth. She's innocent and I won't let my son go away with that murderer. What do you think she might do to him?"

"Don't you dare get involved with this investigation," Detective Edwards said. "Your interference would only mess things up."

"Mess what things up? From the sound of it you don't even have a plan. But you know what, Detective, I do."

"I'm warning you, Laroque. We'll call off this entire investigation if you get involved and you'll never find out the truth while your daughter sits in jail and rots. Just let us take care of this. When you came to my office with this far-fetched story I believed in you enough to look into it. Now you've been able to trust me this far. I promise you that you still can," Detective Edwards pleaded. But Klarke had already dropped the phone, grabbed her car keys, and headed out the door.

"Ma'am, you can't get through without a boarding pass," the security woman at the terminal entrance of the Columbus airport said.

"Look, you don't understand," Klarke said, trying to maintain her composure. "My son and my husb . . ."

Klarke had to catch those words from rolling off of her tongue as her eyes filled with tears. "Please," Klarke continued. "Someone can escort me. Walk with me. I don't want to do anybody any harm. I don't have any weapons, bombs, or anything. I'll strip butt-naked if you want me to. Just please, time is wasting. You have to let me through the gate."

Klarke could barely get her words out. Her heart was beating ninety miles per hour and she was damn near out of breath. On top of that her car was probably being towed. She had driven straight to Columbus International Airport in an attempt to stop Meka and more so, to stop Reo and her son from going with her. She had no idea what she was going to do or say when she confronted them, but she knew she couldn't sit back and let things happen. She had to make them happen.

In proving herself to the security guard that she meant her every word, Klarke began to pull her tank top over her head until a male security guard grabbed her arm and stopped her.

"That really won't be necessary, ma'am," the male security guard said, starting to feel sorry for her. "What are the names of the individuals you are looking for? Perhaps we can page them. Do you know their airline and flight number?"

"No, I don't. But they're going to the Caribbean. I don't know which airline or flight number. Please, please. Just help me," Klarke begged.

"Ma'am, you don't even know if they're departing through this particular gate," he said.

Klarke hadn't thought about all that. She just ran to the first gate she saw in a panic. Now she was standing there looking stupid and hopeless.

The security guard waited for a response from Klarke, but he could tell by the look on her face that she had hit a brick wall. He thought for a moment, then nodded to Klarke and said, "Follow me."

He led her to an airline ticket counter. By this time Klarke was in tears. The security guard handed her a tissue to wipe the mucus that was rolling out of her nose onto her lips.

The security guard asked the clerks behind the ticket counter to help her in any way that they could to find the people she was looking for. One of the younger female clerks asked Klarke a few questions like the passengers' names and destinations, then punched a few keys into the computer before replying, "They're not on our airline."

"Oh, God no," Klarke said, wanting to fall out.

"Just a minute," the clerk said. "We'll find them."

By this time Klarke had attracted attention. Everyone under the sun, including ticketed passengers, were trying to help. After an eternity the clerk returned to say to Klarke, "I've found the airline and flight."

Klarke suddenly was warmed by a ray of hope until the clerk continued, "But I'm sorry, ma'am. The individuals are already boarded and that plane has been cleared for takeoff."

Klarke put her head down and cried. She didn't care who watched her. She fell to her knees and cried. It felt as though the world was spinning and the hands of the clock were going around and around, leaving Klarke behind as time moved on. The clerk tried to comfort her, but when she placed her hand on Klarke's shoulder, Klarke pushed it away and just sat there crying. She was all alone. She needed Jeva there to tell her that everything was going to be okay. She needed Breezy there to kick ass so that she would have gotten through the damn gates in the first place. From Klarke's point of view she had failed. She had failed HJ, Vaughn, and Junior. She had failed Reo as well.

She should have put her morals and pride aside from the minute she got out of jail and told that man how she felt about him. She should have fought to get the courts to overturn her decision of giving up her rights as a mother to Junior. Their souls deserved to be together and she knew it. She knew that Reo knew it too, but yet she did nothing. Her pride forced her to do nothing and now things would never be the same. Sure he would be back in a few months, hopefully. But who was promised tomorrow?

Now too weak to even fight off caregivers, Klarke received the hand that patted her shoulder. She needed a comforting hand. Everything would be okay, she kept telling herself. Everything is going to be okay.

She thought about the words of the late great songstress, Aaliyah, "Dust yourself off and try again." That's exactly what Klarke planned on doing. The next few months would be so hard, but she would make it. Everything she should have done, she was going to do, God permit.

Klarke placed her hand upon the hand that sat on her shoulder. She got chills.

"Are you okay?" a voice asked in a Billy D. Williams–like manner.

The voice confirmed the feeling she had running through her body. When Klarke looked up, kneeled down beside her was Reo. She asked no questions. She got up, Reo rising with her, and threw her arms around him. She planted kisses all over his handsome face, and she cried.

Reo returned the affection, smiling and wiping away Klarke's tears. Klarke stared at him really hard, just to make certain that it was him. She touched his face. She smiled then hugged him again. That's when she saw Junior standing two feet from them holding his little sister's hand. Klarke began to cry even harder.

"Don't let this be a dream," Klarke said to herself. "Please don't let this be a dream."

"Oh, it's a dream all right," Reo said. "I plan to make it my business to see to it that the rest of your life is a dream come true."

Klarke had momentarily managed to calm herself down and stop crying, but the words Reo spoke only brought back the waterworks.

Reo signaled with his hand for Junior to come over with them. Junior let go of his little sister's hand and walked over to Klarke and Reo. Klarke kneeled down and looked into her son's eyes. She didn't say a word. She just cried and looked into his eyes.

Klarke looked up at Reo and said, "He has eyes like mine."

There wasn't a dry eye within view.

Like a page from a storybook, Junior put his little hand on Klarke's shoulder and said, "Don't cry, Mommy."

Klarke was beside herself. She looked up at Reo, surprised. She couldn't believe that he had just called her Mommy.

"He knows who you are," Reo said. "My father made sure of that."

"Um-hm," Junior confirmed. "Paw-paw showed me pictures of you."

Klarke grabbed Junior and smothered him with kisses. He began to laugh. She could breathe again. Nothing in the world was more soothing than the laughter of a child. As Klarke planted a kiss on Junior she looked over and saw his little sister standing shyly on the sidelines, giggling at her and Junior's kissing session.

"Hi," Klarke said to her. "I'm Klarke." She looked over at Junior then up at Reo and added, "I'm Junior's mommy. Who are you?"

"That's my little sister," Junior said.

Klarke held her hand out, but the shy little girl wouldn't grab it.

"It's okay," Junior said. He grabbed his little sister by the hand. She was still much too shy to show Klarke any affection, but she smiled at her.

Just then a dark cloud came over Klarke. She had just thought of something. She thought of Meka. Klarke stood up and looked at Reo with a weird look on her face.

"Where is she?" Klarke asked. "Where's Meka?"

Before Reo could answer, a loud ruckus caught everyone's attention.

"I'll have your badges, you car-wash cops," Meka yelled as she fought with the handcuffs that had her hands restrained behind her back. She looked up and saw what she didn't consider to be a Norman Rockwell painting. It was more of a nightmare. There stood her husband and her children with Klarke. She could have spit fire.

"You!" she said to Klarke. "I should have known you were behind this. Do you really think this little plan of yours is going to work?" Meka shouted at Klarke like a mad woman. "And let me guess, you've been planning this with her the whole time?" Meka said, turning her attention to Reo. "You've been playing the good husband, making me think that we were going to work things out and be together, while all along it's been nothing but one big act. You are such a little bitch, Reo. If you had any balls you would have stood up to me a long time ago and not played these stupid games. Did you really think society would give a fuck about an author who sleeps with prostitutes?"

Embarrassed slightly by the comment, Reo looked at Klarke and said, "I'll explain it to you later."

Of course Reo knew that society didn't care about what he did for his extracurricular activities, but that wasn't his concern. He worried more about what his children would think of him, or what a judge might think if he ever had to fight Meka for custody of his children.

"I won't let you two get away with this," Meka yelled as two officers began to lead her out of the airport. "My babies! My babies!" she said, looking down at her daughter and Junior.

Klarke couldn't resist this moment. She stepped forward and walked over to Meka.

"Don't worry about them. I'll take good care of them," Klarke said as she moved in closer to whisper in Meka's ear, "They can call me Mommy now."

"Bitch! Bitch!" Meka said as she went ballistic while the officers carried her out of the airport.

Klarke turned to face Reo when she was stopped by a man in a long black coat.

"You Klarke Taylor?" the man said. Klarke presumed he was a detective. He just had that look about him.

"No," Klarke replied. "I'm Klarke Laroque."

"Pardon me," the man said. "I have a call for you." He handed Klarke the cell phone that was in his hand.

"Hello," Klarke said with a puzzled look on her face.

"Thank goodness I know low people in high places," Detective Edwards said. "Or else we couldn't have pulled this off. But I trust I won't regret this."

"You won't, Detective Edwards," Klarke said as she began to choke on tears. "Thank you."

Klarke handed the phone back to the man in the long black coat. He smiled at Klarke, nodded at Reo, then walked away.

"I thought you were gone," Klarke said, walking back over to Reo and the children.

"I couldn't do it," Reo said. "I couldn't leave you, KAT. I always knew deep down in my heart that I was made for you and that you were made for me."

Just then Junior pulled on Reo's pant leg. "Daddy, does this mean we're not going to the beach?"

Reo laughed. "No. We'll go to the beach, just not today." Reo scooped Junior up in his arms and looked at him. Junior looked back at him with a smile on his face.

"So tell me. Now what do we do, son?"

Junior looked at his little sister, looked at Klarke, then looked at his father and replied, "We go live happily ever after."

Reo, Klarke, and Junior started laughing. Klarke picked up Reo's daughter who still wasn't terribly comfortable with her. She reached for her father and Reo took her out of Klarke's arms, but again she smiled at Klarke and buried her head in her daddy's chest.

This was a dream come true for Klarke. As the four of them walked out of the airport she didn't even concern herself with what her next step would be. All she knew was that she was going to spend the rest of her life with her soul mates, all of them.

EPILOGUE

———————————

———————————

———————————

The evidence against Meka was overwhelming, not to mention that the state had eye-witness testimony, HJ. This was what aided them in getting a warrant for her arrest in the first place. Her own mother even testified against her. Meka had tried to say that she had rented the white Neon to go on an out-of-town shopping spree because she didn't want to put the miles on her own car. She insisted that she had in fact gone shopping with her mother and had been with her the entire evening on the night the baby was murdered. But when Meka's mother was called to the stand and asked to raise her right hand and swear on a Bible to tell the truth, she was unable to lie, not even for her daughter. Needless to say, no plea bargains were given to Meka and the jury sentenced her to death for the murder of her own child.

As far as the money from the insurance policy . . . Well, Reo's publicist told him about some producer/rapper who was running a marathon to raise a million dollars for the New York City Public Schools. He gladly donated the proceeds from the insurance policy Meka had taken out for their deceased child to the cause.

Vaughn was released from jail. The state was going to try and pin Sister Beasley's death on her, but the coroner ruled that her death was caused by a 99 percent blockage in her artery. Soon after her release, she and her mother along with HJ, Reo, Junior, and Reo's and Meka's daughter relocated to a small mansion on a white beach in sunny California. With Vegas only a drive away, Reo and Klarke packed up their children in their black Lincoln Navigator and paid a visit to the wedding chapel at the Rio Hotel, which is the same place where they had gotten married the first time.

Jeva and Heather were able to make it to the wedding, seeing that they now resided in Nevada. Jeva and Maria had become inseparable. Jeva was able to form a wonderful bond with her father and her siblings. She and her mother weren't on the best of terms, but her mother was truly working on it. She still had some self-healing and self-forgiving to do before she could love Jeva the way a mother should. Fortunately for her, her husband and children forgave her for her betrayal and continued to support her as well as welcome Jeva into their family.

When the position for a general manager at the Cheesecake Factory in Caesar's Palace opened up, Chauncy relocated to Nevada to be with Jeva and Heather. They haven't gotten married yet, but they haven't slept together either. But when a man moves across the continent for a woman, wedding bells are definitely in the near future. It looked as though Heather would finally get a daddy again, one who loved her and would never walk out of her life.

Every Memorial Day, Klarke and Jeva pack up the kids and head back to Toledo to visit Breezy's grave. They sit at her gravesite with a portable stereo and play her favorite song, "Gypsy" by Stevie Nicks. They also spend time with the twins, Lil' Kris and Bria.

Hydrant ended up buying a bigger house and moving his mother in with him to help raise the children. Breezy's death was the hardest thing in the world for him to deal with. Every time he looked at their beautiful twins he saw their mother. Hydrant was content living the rest of his life with his mom and raising all three of his children. He never remarried.

Vaughn and HJ visited Harris throughout the year. Harris had finally moved on, realizing that he had no other choice but to let the hopes of someday getting back with Klarke go. He knew that he and Klarke only had one thing in common, their children. He saw it as a blessing that after all they had been through, they could still be friends and raise two beautiful, law-abiding children.

Harris never did remarry or even get a steady girlfriend, for that matter. He was happy though. He continued raising Sissy as if she were his biological daughter and continued working every day and paying bills. And every now and then he'd frequent a strip club or two. He'd rather pay to play than pay for her ass to stay. In Harris's eyes, the love of a woman could very well be the real root of all evil. So he settled for spending the rest of his days with the soul mate he had known all of his life, but was too blind to see . . . his damn self!

1. Which character do you most identify with in the book? Would you classify this character as a "good guy," somewhat of a "bad guy," or someone neutral who just happened to get caught up in someone else's problems?

2. Did Reo have an obligation toward his former step-children (Vaughn and HJ) once he divorced their mother? Do you agree with the saying that if a man marries a woman who already has children, once he divorces her then he divorces her children as well? Explain your position.

3. Do you think it was right for so many people to protect one another when it came to the death of Reo and Meka's baby? How should this situation have been handled initially?

4. Were you satisfied with the way the story ended? What unresolved issues would you have liked to see worked out, and in what way did you imagine these issues resolving?

5. When you consider the lives each of the characters led, did each one of them eventually get what they deserved? Were there any characters who you felt were dealt an unjust hand? Were there any characters who you felt were not held accountable for their actions?

6. Were there any twists or outcomes that you found to be too predictable? If so, what were they? Were there any that you didn't see coming at all?

7. Do you believe in soul mates after reading this book? Do you have a different outlook on what a soul mate is?

St. Martin's
Griffin

*For more reading group suggestions visit
www.stmartins.com/smp/rgg.html*